About the author

Christine Marion Fraser is one of Scotland's top selling authors with world-wide readership and translations into many foreign languages. Second youngest of a large family, she soon learned independence during childhood years spent in the post-war Govan district of Glasgow. At the age of ten she contracted a rare illness which landed her in a wheelchair and virtually ended her formal education. From early years, Christine had been an avid storyteller; now she began a lone apprenticeship in writing, but it wasn't till 1978 that *Rhanna*, the first novel in the popular series, was published. She went on to write seven more volumes about island life and is also the author of the successful *King's* saga, the *Noble* books, three volumes of autobiography and three romantic novels.

Christine Marion Fraser lives with her husband in an old Scottish manse on the shores of the Kyles of Bute, Argyllshire.

Praise for KINVARA and Christine Marion Fraser

'[*Kinvara*] is a story set in a small, remote Scottish community where the landscape is harsh, the coast is rugged and the inhabitants are colourful and memorable. . . . [A] lovely book and the author brings the people and the place of Kinvara alive' *Telegraph & Argus*

'A rollicking good read . . . Fraser is Scottish publishing's best-kept secret' Jackie McGlone, *The Scotsman*

'Christine Marion Fraser writes characters so real they almost leap out of the pages . . . you would swear she must have grown up with them' *Sun*

'Christine Marion Fraser weaves an intriguing story in which the characters are alive against a spellbinding background' *Yorkshire Herald*

Also by Christine Marion Fraser

Fiction

KINVARA
KINVARA WIVES

RHANNA
RHANNA AT WAR
CHILDREN OF RHANNA
RETURN TO RHANNA
SONG OF RHANNA
STORM OVER RHANNA
STRANGER ON RHANNA
A RHANNA MYSTERY

KING'S CROFT
KING'S ACRE
KING'S EXILE
KING'S CLOSE
KING'S FAREWELL

NOBLE BEGINNINGS
NOBLE DEEDS
NOBLE SEED

Non-fiction

BLUE ABOVE THE CHIMNEYS
ROSES ROUND THE DOOR
GREEN ARE MY MOUNTAINS

KINVARA SUMMER

Christine Marion Fraser

CORONET BOOKS
Hodder & Stoughton

First published in Great Britain in 2000 by Hodder & Stoughton
First published in paperback in 2001 by Hodder & Stoughton
A division of Hodder Headline

A Coronet Paperback

10 9 8 7 6 5 4 3 2 1

A CIP catalogue record for this title is available from the British Library

ISBN 0 340 76714 6

Typeset by Palimpsest Book Production Limited,
Polmont, Stirlingshire
Printed and bound in Great Britain by
Mackays of Chatham PLC, Chatham, Kent

Hodder & Stoughton
A division of Hodder Headline
338 Euston Road
London NW1 3BH

For our dear Ethy and George, so far away but never forgotten. Your visit to 'Rhanna' in 1999 made the years roll back as we remembered the yesterdays we had shared. Another 'wee chardonnay' is on the menu now. Slainte Mha and haste ye back! From Chris and Ken, Big Fig, and 'Rhanna of Rhanna'.

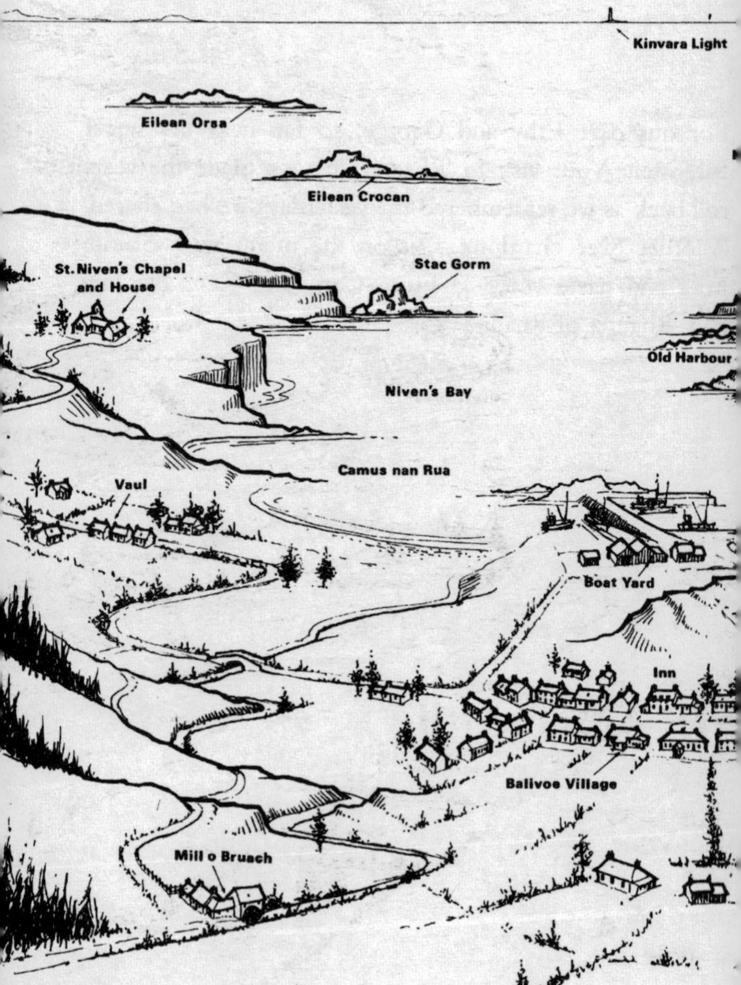

Kinvara Light

Eilean Orsa

Eilean Crocan

St. Niven's Chapel and House

Stac Gorm

Old Harbour

Niven's Bay

Camus nan Rua

Vaul

Boat Yard

Inn

Balivoe Village

Mill o Bruach

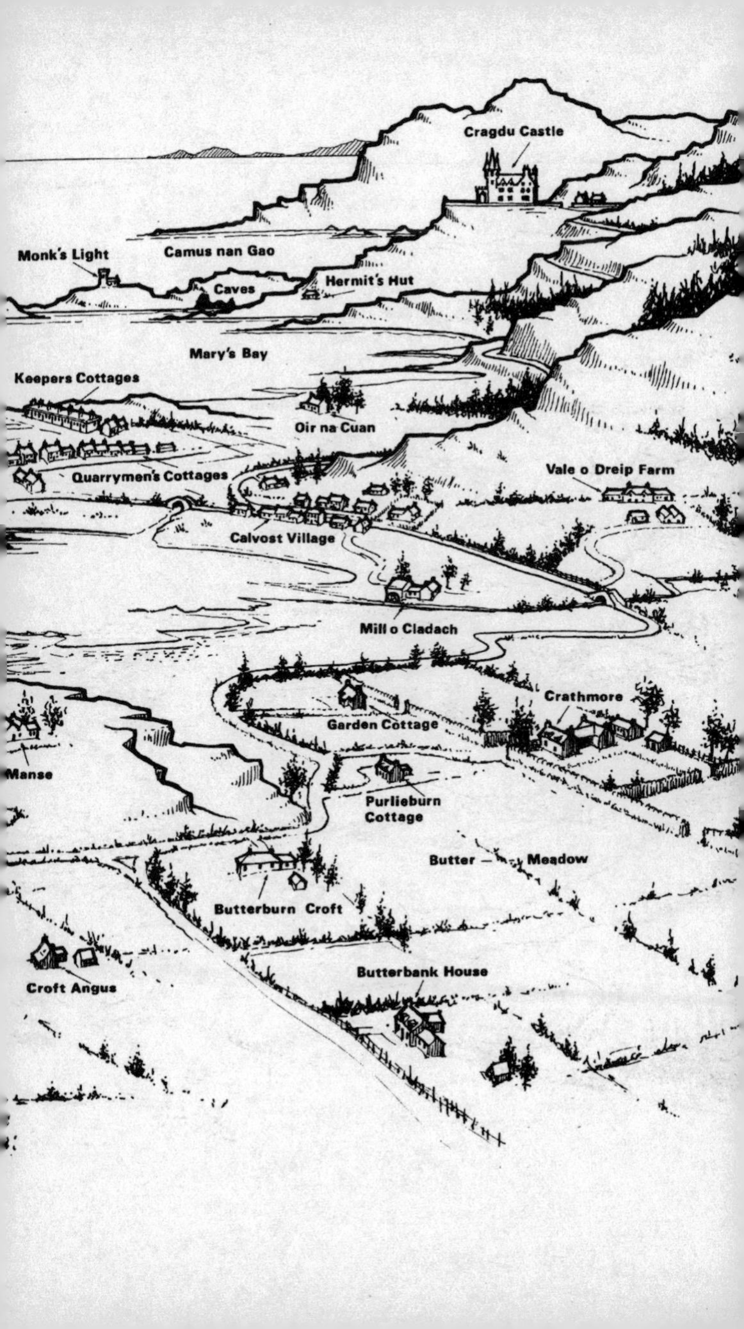
Cragdu Castle
Monk's Light
Camus nan Gao
Caves
Hermit's Hut
Mary's Bay
Keepers Cottages
Oir na Cuan
Quarrymen's Cottages
Vale o Dreip Farm
Calvost Village
Mill o Cladach
Crathmore
Garden Cottage
Manse
Purlieburn
Cottage
Butter — Meadow
Butterburn Croft
Butterbank House
Croft Angus

The Kinvara Peninsula

Late June 1931

Chapter One

Vaila knew all about the small islands that lay off the coast of Kinvara. From her bedroom window in No. 6 Keeper's Row she was able to see them quite plainly, especially lumpy little Stac Gorm, lying within the great curving cliffs of Niven's Bay, its sheltered shores much favoured by grey Atlantic seals in mild calm weather.

Further out to sea rose the basaltic structure of Eilean Crocan, pitted with caves, fringed by tiny white beaches that shimmered and sparkled on really blue summer days. Eilean Orsa was the most distant of all, long and low, wild and storm-lashed, golden and beckoning when its lichen-covered reefs were caught in the light of the setting sun.

Stac Gorm, being tidal, was more accessible than the others, and was a popular place for locals and visitors alike. The travelling people came for the whelk picking; fishermen dug in the wet sands for lug worms; young lovers wandered in the moonlight; toddlers splashed in the rock pools: schoolchildren played imaginative games in the cool dark caverns and were occasionally stranded when they forgot all about time and tides.

Vaila loved to go there whenever she could but liked

it even better when Rob Sutherland, her father, took her out in Charlie Campbell's boat to those other isles beyond Niven's Bay. If she closed her eyes she could imagine the cut of the bow through the waves, her father's black hair tossing in the wind, could almost hear his deep laugh ringing out as they drew nearer to Eilean Crocan.

And then the magic of his strong big hand in hers as they wandered over the beaches, gazing in wonder at the black mouths of the caves; watching the seabirds wheeling and dipping among the great rocky outcrops; stopping to picnic on the white sands of Monk's Cove where an Irish missionary had landed long ago before sailing over to mainland Kinvara.

Vaila drew very close to her father during these precious times alone with him. He seemed to open up and expand as he spoke to her in that nice easy way of his, his face growing animated when he told her about the myths and legends that surrounded the Kinvara coastline, his dark eyes often dreamy and faraway when he went on to talk of boyhood days and of the numerous small adventures he'd had whilst growing up.

And then she would ask about her mother, Morna Jean Sommero, never tiring of hearing him talk about the young woman he had loved from their first moment of meeting and how she had borne his little daughter in Shetland only to discover that he had met and married another woman in her absence.

'We hurt each other terribly,' he once said quietly to

Vaila. 'I never knew about you until it was too late. By then I had a wife and a son and though I loved you dearly I had to keep your identity a secret from the world.'

'But everybody knows about me now, Robbie, even Grampa Ramsay,' she had said pensively, the use of her father's Christian name coming easily to her lips since it was the one she had used from babyhood.

'Ay, even Grampa Ramsay, but it took the death o' your mother to make everyone come to their senses. What I did was wrong, grown-ups are supposed to be wise and sensible but I was neither. I argued with Morna and allowed her to slip through my fingers and I wasn't being fair marrying Hannah when I was so mixed up about everything. She was so good and understanding when your mother died and suggested that you come and live with us at Keeper's Row. Your Aunt Mirren wanted to bring you up in Shetland and if that had happened we might hardly have seen one another.'

'Oh, but it was a great love you had with my mother.' Vaila had sighed then, tears springing to her eyes at the romance and beauty of it all. 'When I grow up I want what you and my mother had and I'll never get married until I find it.'

'Ah, Vaila,' he had said wistfully. 'A love like that is a rare and wonderful thing between a man and a woman. Some people go through their whole lives and never ever find it. But you are the child of my heart, you were born of joy and tenderness, these qualities have been bred in you and surely one day you will meet someone who will share your feelings. Stay a wee lass for a while yet though. Childhood days are the best and you must enjoy them while you can.'

He had grown still and quiet after that and hadn't wanted to talk any more and young as she was she knew that he was thinking about the events of his past life and was reliving them in his memory.

A tear came to Vaila's eyes as she lay in her bed in her bright little room and thought about these lovely outings she and Robbie had shared and how lonely she often felt when his job took him away from her. He was deputy head keeper of the Kinvara Light, a lonely grey tower that rose stark out of the sea twelve miles south-west of Calvost.

On clear days the flashing of the great octagon could plainly be seen on the horizon, in bad weather it was almost obliterated by mist and rain that came sweeping in over the wild turmoil of the Atlantic ocean. That was when the foghorns began their mournful hooting, the lights in the signal tower started winking, and when Johnny Lonely the hermit scurried up to the headland to light his warning beacons on the point.

Vaila's thoughts turned to her mother. She had been just a tiny girl when Morna Jean had died, but pictures sometimes came to her and she remembered a pretty dark-haired lady who had talked to her about the seals and the other creatures that lived in the sea round Mary's Bay.

Vaila frowned and wished the memories of her mother weren't so hazy . . . yet the laughter was clear enough . . . and quite often she imagined that she could hear her mother's voice inside her head . . .

Getting up, she went to the window to prop her chin in her hands and gaze towards the beach and the bay and the little white house known as Oir na Cuan which meant Edge of the Ocean.

She had once lived there with her mother and sometimes she wished she lived there still, so near the sea and the rocks and all the little boats that sailed past Mary's Bay on their way round to the harbour. Several families had occupied the house over the years but none of them had stayed very long and it had lain empty for a while. Now another family were moving in, today in fact, and in a few days' time the Mill O' Cladach would also be occupied by a different set of people, the previous miller having left some months ago . . .

A movement from behind made Vaila look round. Essie was awake, not saying anything but just lying there on her pillows, contented and quiet, looking up at the ceiling as if she was seeing something that no one else could see in the fingers of sunlight dancing above her.

Vaila went over and sitting down on the bed she smiled at her little half-sister and gave her a hug. Four-year-old Essie was a passive dreamy child with big blue eyes and a tumble of silky flaxen hair framing her delicately featured small face. She was a beautiful child and Hannah often said she didn't know who her daughter took after as no one else in the family had hair that bright or eyes so strikingly blue.

'Come on, Essie, waken up properly.' Vaila pulled back the quilt and gathered her sister into her arms, 'Let's go and see Andy and play for a while before Hannah calls us. We'll take our things with us and get dressed in Andy's room.'

Chapter Two

Andy had wakened early and was having his 'thinking time'. He liked this quiet morning hour because it was then he could really concentrate on all the things that were in his head, especially the magic of words which he made up into little rhymes as he went along. His mind was like a fertile plain, filled with deep thoughts and emotions so vivid he felt he would sometimes burst with the frustration of not being able to give proper voice to his feelings.

Because he had been born with cerebral palsy, a lot of people who didn't know him thought he was mentally retarded and spoke to him as if he was still a baby. He longed to shout at people like that, to tell them that he wanted the same things as them, that he felt pain and hurt as much as any other human being who lived on the earth.

But he knew he would never be able to communicate in the normal way and had very quickly learned that the only way to make his life bearable was to absorb as much knowledge as possible, to observe the world around him and to revel in his ability to create stories and poems in his head. He couldn't explain to himself what it was that allowed him to do this, it was something that had been there from an early age, a force that was in the very spirit of him and which gave him great personal joy.

Yet these very gifts had eventually brought him to the edge of more despair, for what was the use of them if he couldn't express them or in some way write them down so that others could share them. He couldn't go to school like other children, he would never learn to read or write or do any of the things that other boys of his age did.

Then it had happened. The answer to his prayers. Coming to him in a most unexpected way just after his eighth birthday last March, in the form of Miss Catherine Dunbar who had not long taken over her new teaching post at the Balivoe village school.

Miss Catherine, as she quickly became known, had caused quite a stir of interest on her arrival. For one thing she was a woman and a very attractive one at that, with flashing green eyes, fiery red hair, and a curvaceous figure that drew admiring comments from the men and caused a few raised eyebrows among the womenfolk who didn't like the bold and proud way that Catherine carried herself.

'It isn't natural for a woman to be doing a man's job,' stated Tillie Murchison, who, with her younger sister, Tottie, ran the tiny draper's shop in Balivoe, the pair of them being known collectively as The Knicker Elastic Dears.

'She must be a clever lass,' Effie Maxwell, the district

nurse, said thoughtfully, 'to have gone through university to train as a teacher and to learn languages as she has.'

'That won't do her much good in a place like Kinvara.' Mattie MacPhee nodded. 'Can you imagine that Malky Law, for instance, trying to get the grasp o' a foreign language when he can't even speak English right.'

'She'll soon get fed up with it,' nodded Jessie MacDonald with conviction. 'The village school will just be a stopgap till something better comes along.'

'Oh, I don't know about that,' Mattie said slyly, looking pointedly at Jessie as she spoke. 'The menfolk are just falling over themselves to get at her and wi' her being such a good-looking lass she can have her pick o' the bunch and leave the dregs for those that are less fussy.'

Jessie, who had reached the age of forty-five and was as yet unmarried, much to her chagrin, treated Mattie to an almighty glower and flounced out of the shop with her nose in the air.

Sadly Effie shook her head. 'Now see what you've done. I myself have never hungered for a man but Jessie is desperate for one and has never been the same since Harriet Houston from Ayr went and netted Charlie Campbell of Butterburn Croft. Miss Dunbar is already causing trouble and her only five minutes in the place.'

'Och well, she's just a slip o' a lass yet,' Big Bette said comfortably. 'She'll soon learn no' to be brazen in a place like Kinvara. Jessie's right, a girl like that won't stick it for long, she'll never have Stuart MacCaskill's stamina nor his strictness and she'll need both if she's to survive some o' the cheeky wee upstarts she'll have in her classroom.'

But Big Bette and her cronies spoke too soon. Catherine Dunbar soon proved herself a match for any of the 'cheeky wee upstarts' who thought to take advantage of her newness and her femininity.

'A holy bloody terror!' was the opinion of seven-year-old Malky Law who had learned to curse before he could walk and who revelled in mischief of all sorts. Malky came from a large poor family living on the outskirts of Balivoe and in his anxiety to see the new teacher he had taken the trouble to slick his hair down with axle grease and had donned the one pair of shoes that the younger Laws shared whenever an occasion of merit arose.

Malky had gone to school with the sole intention of intimidating Miss Catherine and impressing his mates in the process. Instead she had intimidated him and had made him the laughing stock of the classroom when she had told him to blow his nose, stand up straight and not to speak with his mouth full.

'But, that's the way I always speak, Miss,' he had stuttered, growing more crimson by the second as titters of laughter arose from all sides.

Miss Catherine had stared at him and it really seemed to him in those fraught moments that sparks flew out of her green cat's eyes and bristles of fire shot out from her hair.

'Really, Malcolm?' she had intoned after eternity seemed to elapse. 'And here was me thinking you had come to school with breakfast still in your mouth. Oh well, don't worry.' She became brisk. 'I'll give you some speech exercises to take home with you and when you bring them back I want the pronunciation of them to be so perfect you'll be simply longing for us all to hear them.'

Malky could have died there and then. Everyone was sniggering, even his most devoted friends who normally thought he was wonderful and unquestioningly went along with everything he suggested in the way of adventure.

When class was finished for the day he looked at the paper she had handed him and gulped with dismay. He couldn't even spell the bloody words, let alone pronounce them and it was with a heavy heart that he wound his way homewards.

When next he had come face to face with the teacher she made him stand at the front of the class and read out the lines she had given him.

'No! No! Malcolm, you still have a whole boiled egg in your mouth!' she had scolded when he was only quarter way through. 'Mares and lairs! Blood and mud! Caught and fought! Repeat, repeat, over and over, and . . .'

At that point she had swung round to glare at the rest of the class who were in a state of considerable amusement at Malky's discomfiture . . . 'You can all do the same while Malcolm leads the way, like a song, with rhythm and feeling. Mares and lairs! Blood and mud! Caught and fought!'

The class began to chant. After a while the room rang with the jubilant sound of their combined voices. This was better than staid old lessons any day. Good old Malky. Trust him to cause a diversion in the middle of a working day . . . 'Mares and lairs! Blood and mud . . .'

A shock wave hit the classroom when Miss Catherine called a sudden halt to the enjoyment and, pouncing on Joan MacNulty in the second row, she ordered her to spell mares and lairs. Taken by suprise, Joan stuttered and stumbled and went to pieces. The boy next to her did the same. Up, down, they bobbed, as if they were on springs, and everyone gave a sigh of relief when the teacher at last rang her little handbell to signal that dinnertime had arrived to put an end to their agony – with the exception of Malky Law, who received his comeuppance at the hands of his mates behind the playshed and again when he went home with his jersey in tatters, his trousers scuffed and torn, and the sole of one precious shoe hanging from its upper.

Miss Catherine had arrived, and never again did any of her pupils think it was going to be plain sailing under her ruling. Nevertheless she taught well and thoroughly and was soon respected by children and parents alike.

'She calls a spade a spade.' Big Bette nodded approvingly, having gone by that adage all through her own life. 'The bairns will always know where they stand with her and realise if they try to take advantage she'll just give as good as she gets.'

Catherine had certainly been very plain-spoken when

she had called at No. 6 Keeper's Row to talk to Hannah about Andy. 'I have met him once or twice on my travels,' she had explained to Hannah when she was settled by the fire with a cup of tea, 'and he has told me how much he enjoys learning and looking at books.'

'He *told* you?'

'Ay, just that,' Catherine nodded pleasantly. 'I have a brother with cerebral palsy. He also has speech difficulties but I'm attuned to what he says. Colin has done very well for himself and has had books published on astrology – a subject he has been interested in all his life. I'm sure your son could make something of himself too – given the proper encouragement – and if you're agreeable I would like to come here whenever I can to teach him how to read and write.'

Hannah didn't reply to this. She had been bitterly disappointed by Andy's handicaps and hadn't credited him with any intelligence in his early days. Now she knew better. The passing years had proved his awareness of everything that went on around him. He glowed with a hunger for life, was always asking questions, never satisfied till he got the answers, throwing temper tantrums in his frustration at being unable to fully participate in the sort of activities that were beyond his physical capabilities.

Schooling for him was something that no one had ever mentioned, now here was this fresh-faced young woman, waiting for Hannah's reaction, drinking her tea in a very composed manner as she smiled at Essie who was sitting on the rug crooning to the rag doll in her arms.

'I see you like books yourself, Mrs Sutherland.' Catherine's eyes had fallen on the bookshelf above the dresser, crammed with literature of every description.

'Oh, yes,' Hannah's eyes lit up. 'I've always been a bit o' a bookworm and could never get enough reading when I was younger.'

'Then it's from you that Andy gets his love of words.' Catherine spoke softly though inwardly she was triumphant. She had hit on the right note, and while the going was good she went on, 'Just think what it would be like for your son to enter the world of books, to know the joys that you and me have always taken for granted. And you could help him to do that, Mrs Sutherland. How rewarding it would be for you, knowing that you have led Andy into a new and wonderful phase in his life.'

That did it for Hannah. It was her chance to make it up to her son for the years she had rejected and scorned him, and when the young teacher went away she felt so inspired that she retrieved one of her own books from the shelf and just sat staring at it as if she was seeing the words for the first time.

After that a whole new world opened up for Andy. He learned fast and was soon lost in the delight of his discoveries. With admirable patience his mother set time aside for him every evening and Catherine came as often as she could. Whenever Rob came home from lighthouse duty he was delighted with his son's progress and quietly pleased to see how much Hannah's attitude had changed towards the boy. Her struggle to believe in him had been long and hard but now she really seemed to be enjoying the challenge that Catherine Dunbar had set her.

Rob's appreciation of Catherine's generosity of spirit showed on his face every time she entered No. 6 Keeper's Row and in her turn Catherine began to look forward to going there and soon integrated herself into the family. Everyone was satisfied, not least Andy, who read and read and could never get enough of learning, and though his large shaky writing left a lot to be desired, at least he could do it, even if half the time he was the only one who understood it.

Andy's thinking time was rudely shattered. His sisters were piling into his room, Vaila laughing when she saw that Breck, a large cross-collie with a penchant for the finer things in life, had sneaked upstairs again and was sprawled on the bed, his big snuffly nose stuffed firmly into Andy's neck, his tail, with its feathery white tip, gently twitching when the girls appeared.

Breck had been Andy's constant companion since babyhood. They went everywhere together, the dog pulling his young master along in the wooden cart that Rob had made years ago. Referred to simply as 'Breck and the boy' they were a familiar sight in the neighbourhood. People came out of their houses to talk to them and to generally see that they came to no harm: if Hannah wanted anything from the village store she sent her son with a note to Big Bette MacGill who would come out of her shop to personally attend him; Jake Ferguson, the butcher, seldom failed to bring a bone out to Breck if his young master was inside for any length of time and all in all the dog and the boy had become a familiar and well-kent part of the landscape.

Hannah was well aware of how much her neighbours spoiled her son and his canine companion but that didn't mean to say she was going to bend the rules of the house for them or for anyone. Breck knew full well that his place was in his basket below stairs. If Hannah caught him on Andy's bed she would chase him downstairs with the kitchen broom and sometimes all round the house as well if she was in a mood to do so.

But the lure of a soft bed was irresistible to Breck and he knew how best to avoid a confrontation with both Hannah and her broom. He was quicker than she was, it was as simple as that. He could identify her footfalls a mile away, even when she thought she was being very cautious and stealthy. But she was light on her feet was Hannah and quite often she managed to get a good swipe at his rump before he could tuck it hastily away.

The girls posed no such threat however and not one eyelid did be bat when the door opened to admit them, Vaila to put a chair against the handle as soon as she was inside, her eyes sparkling as she said softly, 'Bouncy time.'

At her words, Andy grinned, Essie gave one of her delighted chuckles; soon all three children were jumping up and down on the bed, causing the springs to creak, the iron frame to rattle, disturbing Breck's repose to such an extent he clambered to the floor to groan and sigh and to eventually sink his head in his paws in a most dejected manner.

After a few minutes of this Vaila called a halt and began to help Andy to get washed and dressed and to finally don his calipers. She had been doing these small tasks for her small half-brother for some years now and they were quite at ease with one another as they talked and laughed, while Essie sat on the floor to pull on her clothes, taking her time about it, more concerned with decking Breck in her frock than she was about putting it on herself.

'Oh, Essie,' Vaila sighed, pushing her dark curls off her face. 'You should be ready by now, you know Hannah will be angry if we aren't down on time.' But Hannah was seldom angry with her perfect little daughter. When they all appeared late in the kitchen Essie only needed to run to her mother and smile up at her for the clock to be forgotten, Breck's transgressions ignored.

Andy and Vaila glanced at one another. That was one good thing about Essie. As long as she was on the scene Hannah seemed able to disregard the sort of small misdemeanours that would otherwise have earned a scolding.

Breck went into his corner and waited for his breakfast; Andy adjusted his calipers and settled himself at the table; Vaila went to help her stepmother dish the porridge, humming a little tune as she did so.

Tomorrow was her tenth birthday, Granma Rita had made her a cake, but she was saving it till her father came home next week. The thought of his return made Vaila's heart feel even lighter. The long summer holidays stretched ahead – and she just knew that they were somehow going to be special and more exciting than any that had gone before. She could feel it in her bones – the way old Bella of Appletree Cottage felt her 'rheumies' whenever there was going to be a change in the weather.

Chapter Three

Hannah looked at Vaila as the child sat eating her breakfast. Strange how quickly time had passed, tomorrow she would be ten, five years had come and gone since her mother had died so young and so suddenly. It had been such an unexpected tragedy, sadder still when it became apparent that she had suffered from a weak heart for years and hadn't told anyone – not even Rob.

Doctor MacAlistair had known of course, as had Mirren Sommero, who knew most things about her younger sister having brought her up in their home in Shetland after their parents had died in a boating accident.

Hannah went into a muse, thinking about Morna, how she had borne Rob's child in Shetland without his knowledge, never knowing that in his loneliness and despair he had gone and married himself to another woman . . . on the rebound . . .

Hannah sighed. Years had passed since that time yet still she felt unsure about her place in Rob's life. What a disappointment she must have been to him after someone as lovely and as alive as Morna. Hannah had never got over the feeling that she had let him down somehow, especially after the advent of Andy . . . her eye fell on Essie whose arrival she had dreaded after the terrible time she'd had at Andy's birth. But it had been a triumph from the start and she had never regretted it for one moment. Beautiful little Essie, with her fair tresses framing her flawless face, sunny natured from the day she was born, always laughing, so delighted with her own small world, perfectly happy and contented with everything and everyone in it . . . Thank God for that! She might easily have been born with some defect or other – especially after . . .

Hannah shuddered and didn't allow her thoughts to dwell further on Essie, instead she turned them towards Vaila who had been such a comfort from the day she entered No. 6 Keeper's Row, so good with Andy, always willing to help, as if sensing that her stepmother found it hard to cope with the day-to-day burdens imposed on her by the running of a household.

Vaila still cherished the memories of her own mother and clung to small reminders of her early days spent at Oir na Cuan, and while she respected the mother role that Hannah played in her life she had never attempted to call her anything else but by her Christian name. Hannah liked it that way. It was right somehow. Vaila was unmistakably her father's daughter, their love for one another was special and precious – and Hannah occasionally experienced a small twinge of resentment because she sometimes felt he made more of Vaila than he did of Essie . . .

Hannah's attention moved to Andy, feeding himself in a

most efficient manner, the son she had said would never be able to perform the most basic personal tasks now proving to be as good as anybody – clever too with his books and his learning . . .

A feeling of satisfaction filled Hannah's being. They were a real family now and next week when Rob came home it would be complete . . .

'Hannah, can I clear up now?'

Hannah came out of her reverie to see Vaila gazing at her rather anxiously.

'You seem in a terrible hurry this morning, Vaila.'

'Joss said he would meet us early because . . .'

'You want to go down to Oir na Cuan to see the new people moving in.' Hannah gave a knowing nod. 'On you go then, I'll clear up here and wash the dishes. Essie's gone out the back. Bring her in before you leave, she'll be needing her face and hands wiped.'

Essie was in the garden dismembering a butterfly. Sitting there in her white pinafore, surrounded by flowers and tall grasses, she looked the picture of fair innocence, especially when she glanced up at Vaila's approach and smiled in her beguiling way.

Vaila was horrified when she saw the torn butterfly in her small sister's hands. 'Essie!' she cried, 'why are you doing that?'

Essie was unperturbed. 'Bad butterfly, eating Essie's flowers.'

'No, Essie, butterflies don't eat the flowers, they just

drink the nectar and take the pollen away to make more flowers grow. Promise you won't do it again.'

But the child merely shook her head and went running off, swishing carelessly through the grass, humming a little tune as she went, her hair a bright beacon in the sunlight.

'Come back, Essie,' called Vaila. 'We're going down to the beach and you've to come with us.'

Essie paused and half turned as her big sister caught up with her. 'Only if you promise not to tell Mamma about the butterfly.'

'Alright, I promise, but only if you say you're sorry and will never do it again.'

Essie folded her hands behind her back and swayed from side to side. 'I'm sorry, Vaila, and I won't do it again.'

'Honest injun?'

'Honest injun.'

Vaila held out her hand. 'Come on, then, Hannah's waiting to wash your face.'

'Will she kiss me, Vaila?'

'I suppose so, she always does when you're out o' her sight for more than a few minutes.'

'I wish she wouldn't,' Essie murmured under her breath as she went with her sister into the house to receive her mother's tender administrations.

* * *

Joss was there as he had promised, waiting for the young Sutherlands outside No. 5 Keeper's Row. Joss was the only child that Janet and Jock Morgan could ever have and they had lavished their love on him from the moment he had drawn his first breath. Now he was a fine big lad in his eleventh year, obliging and kind and always ready to do anyone a good turn. He had said he would carry Andy over the shore to Oir na Cuan because the ground was too rough for the cart and soon they were all trekking down through the dunes, Andy on Joss's back, Vaila holding onto Essie's hand, Breck running along in front, delighting in the freedom.

'I can't stay long,' Joss told Vaila as they trudged along, 'I've taken a summer job at Croft Angus and said I would be there for eleven.'

'The Henderson Hens!' Vaila laughed, referring to Rona and Wilma Henderson, two large spinster sisters whose passion for keeping poultry had earned them their nickname. 'They don't normally want anyone but themselves poking around the croft.'

Joss shrugged. 'Ach well, they've got a lot o' work going this summer and I said I would help out. An extra bob or two will come in handy and I won't cause them any trouble . . .' He made a face. 'You know me, everybody's favourite, the girls at school fight for the chance to kiss me so I've started charging a halfpenny in case they take me for granted.'

'Big head!' Vaila jumped up and pulled his hair before running away from him, making Essie's little legs go like the dozen, causing Breck to bark and Andy to release one of his screeches as Joss took to his heels after Vaila. The teeth in Andy's head rattled, his skinny, frail body bounced up and down on Joss's shoulders, but he loved it and was sorry when they drew near Oir na Cuan and Joss unceremoniously dumped him in the sand and threw himself down nearby to catch his breath.

The laird's AEC lorry was parked outside the gate leading to the house and the man himself was just climbing into it but stopped when he saw the children. 'Just seeing the new folks in,' he explained in his unaffected way, his kilt lifting up in the breeze as he spoke. 'They needed a few extra bits and pieces for the house so I brought them along personally to make sure their first day would be comfortable.'

Captain Rory MacPherson was a striking figure in his clan kilt, lovat tweed jacket, and squashy tartan tammy, his hair swept dramatically to one side to hide the fact that he'd lost an ear in the war. 'As vain as a peacock' his wife fondly told him, to which he would just laugh and kiss her and tell her she wouldn't love him if he was any other way.

For all he was gentry he mixed well with people from every walk of life and was a respected and well-liked figure in the community. The children were quite at ease talking to him and when he finally took his leave of them they watched anxiously as the lorry made its slow and painful progress along the bumpy track and somehow managed to make it up through the dunes to the road.

The laird had told them that the new people went by the name of Lockhart and the children could see them moving about, popping in and out of the house, engrossed in the procedure of settling in, familiarising themselves with their surroundings.

'Let's go and offer to help,' Joss suggested. 'I haven't got all day and it's the quickest way for us to get a look at them.'

'Alright,' Vaila conceded. Joss picked Andy up once more and rather warily they opened the gate and made their way along the path, Essie holding her finger to her lips and chuckling.

'It's all right, I saw you outside the gate, watching.'

A young girl of eleven suddenly popped out of the bushes beside them, making them all jump. 'I'm Maida . . .'

'And I'm Mark, her twin.' A boy with brown curly hair and laughing eyes came out of the bushes behind his sister and stood grinning at the newcomers who were too taken aback to say anything.

'We knew people would be curious about us,' Maida sounded shy now that she was face to face with the youngsters who would be her neighbours. 'It's always the same in the country. We come from along Blair Atholl way and everyone there knows everyone else's business.'

'My dad's an estate manager,' Mark volunteered. 'Captain MacPherson's going in for pedigree Highland ponies and my dad is here to help him get started. We've to get a bigger house later but this cottage will have to do us for now.'

'I used to live at Oir na Cuan with my mother,' Vaila said, gazing over the beach to the little white house outlined against the shining blue waters of the bay. 'I sometimes wish I lived there still.'

They stood eyeing one another in silent appraisal. Maida was a pretty girl with golden tresses rippling down to her waist and eyes that were a deep blue in the smooth brown of her face. But she was at the skinny, leggy stage and she coloured when she tripped on a stone and glanced quickly at Joss to see if he had noticed.

Mark was gazing at Vaila as if expecting her to enlarge on what she had been saying but she was tongue-tied suddenly and was glad when Essie caused a diversion by suddenly breaking away to go toddling into the house, ignoring Vaila's shout for her to come back.

A minute or so later a woman came out of the house holding the little girl by the hand and smiling. 'What a lovely wee lass,' she enthused, 'I don't mind her coming in, she can visit here any time, in fact . . . why don't you all come in . . .'

Her eye fell on Andy astride Joss's young shoulders and a look of sympathy spread over her kindly face. 'Oh, yes, you must,' she insisted, 'I want to get to know you all and so will my husband.'

Joss hesitated but the others were looking at him, willing him to say yes, and so they followed Grace Lockhart into the house to meet Sandy Lockhart, her husband. Thereafter they drank milk and ate biscuits and made friends with a tortoiseshell cat called Primrose who had just emerged from a packing case and was staring big eyed at her new surroundings.

The house was fresh and airy with the windows and doors thrown wide. The newly painted white walls added to the sense of brightness, while the homely furniture and friendly pictures made it seem very welcoming. The youngsters soon relaxed and came out of their shells, even Andy who was at first too shy to make any sort of noise, simply because strangers were often surprised by the bigness of his voice.

Sandy Lockhart was able to put him at ease however, and even if he didn't understand a lot of what the boy said he was able to pick up on some of it, aided by his wife who seemed determined to make a good first impression on her young visitors.

A feeling of light and life came to Vaila as she gazed around her old home, the cosy hearth, the little nooks and crannies, the deeply recessed windows, the sills that were made to hold vases of wildflowers and trophies from the seashore. Here she had once lived with her mother, their voices had rung through the rooms, their footsteps had come and gone from the doors. Vaila drew in her breath . . . laughter sharp and sweet seemed to echo round the little house from those long-ago days and she felt sad and glad at the same time but couldn't say anything because it was only with her father that she could share her special thoughts and feelings . . .

'Vaila used to live here.' Mark's voice broke in on her musings and he was looking at her as if he knew what she was thinking.

'When I was just a tiny little girl,' Vaila said quickly, unwilling to go into detail at that moment.

'We have to be going.' Joss picked Andy up from his chair and hoisted him to his shoulders. They thanked the Lockharts for their hospitality and went off down the path to the track, each of them voicing their appreciation and liking of the new tenants of Oir na Cuan.

When they reached Keeper's Row, Joss went rushing away to Croft Angus, leaving the young Sutherlands to make their way indoors. They heard the voice of Hannah's mother before they saw her, and sure enough there she was in the kitchen, wearing one of Hannah's aprons as she stirred a savoury concoction on the stove.

Harriet Houston was a strong, domineering woman who had come to Kinvara some years ago after the death of her husband. Much to the amazement of the locals she had moved in with Charlie Campbell of Butterburn Croft, first as his housekeeper, then as his wife, a fact which Jessie MacDonald had never got over, having entertained high hopes of winning him for herself. To this day Jessie couldn't speak of Harriet without making some derogatory comment about her marital status, while the rest of the population thoroughly enjoyed discussing her also, albeit in a less demented and more tolerant fashion than Jessie.

Not that talk of any kind worried Harriet in the least. She wasn't the type to sit around moping and always kept herself busy, perhaps even more so when Charlie was out with the fishing smacks and she was left on her own for days at a time. She had come from farming stock and it wasn't long before she was raising cows and a few sheep and vying with Effie Maxwell to see which of them could breed the best pork and produce the fattest Christmas turkeys.

All in all, she had integrated well into the Kinvara ways and though there were those who remembered her as 'just an occasional visitor and a cheeky besom at that', she was now an accepted incomer who had somehow learned that her opinions weren't always the right ones, for all that she had a tongue in her head that could cut through steel.

The children liked her too, for despite her loud and bossy manner she had many good points, not least of them being her love of animals, her frankness and her wonderful talent for producing the most tempting dishes from the humblest of scraps.

Quite often she came along to No. 6 of the Row to make lunch for her grandchildren and Hannah had come to resign herself to these visits. Culinary prowess had never been one of her strong points. She was a 'good, plain cook' as she herself said and had no patience for unnecessary frills. Not like her sister-in-law, Maudie, whose 'flair wi' the flour' was legendary and who could face up to any challenge in the kitchen without batting an eyelid.

When Maudie and Harriet got together they allowed their imaginations to run riot as they pricked and patted and went mad with swirls of icing that somehow turned into gorgeous little embellishments on cakes and tarts. When Hannah tried this she only ever produced wobbly squiggles and shapeless mounds and after a while she gave up trying and left it to the experts.

The children loved it when either Maudie or Granma Harriet came to visit on any account and so they greeted the latter with enthusiasm and went to the sink to wash their hands without being told, anxious as they were to seat themselves at the table to partake of lunch and regale their elders with their morning's exploits.

Chapter Four

Vaila often thought how strange it was that she had so many half-blood relatives: Andy and Essie, her half-brother and -sister; Harriet, her stepgrandmother; Aidan her half-brother, born to her mother when she had married Robbie's brother Finlay to give her daughter the Sutherland name.

Vaila's future had hung in the balance after the death of her mother. Aidan had been alright, he had been accepted as one of the family and had gone to live with his father and grandparents at Vale O' Dreip, the big rambling farmhouse on the slopes of Blanket Hill. Aunt Mirren had wanted Vaila to live in Shetland with her but after all the secrets concerning Morna and Robbie had been revealed, their daughter had gone to Keeper's Row to be with her very own father.

It had been hard at first being separated from Aidan but now they were both quite happy in their different environments. He was the apple of Ramsay Sutherland's eye and Granma Rita had been delighted when he had come to live at the farm.

It was strange too that Finlay Sutherland had once been Vaila's stepfather but she had never taken to him nor he to her. Nowadays she called him Uncle Finlay and they got on quite well together now that they were no longer living in the same house. He had changed a lot from the Finlay she had once known and had never been happier or more contented. This was all due to Big Bette's niece, Maudie Munro, who had come to Kinvara for a holiday some years ago and had ended up as Finlay's wife.

Since then they had produced two bouncing children, 'as wild as the heather', to quote their Grampa Ramsay who grumbled and groaned about Maudie's sloppy ways and her 'boorach of a house' but who, nevertheless, enjoyed her company immensely and always found some excuse to drop in on her 'just to see how the bairns were faring'.

But despite his contentment, Finlay was still very much attached to his parents, especially his mother on whom he doted and relied upon for advice on numerous small day-to-day worries and problems.

'Once a namby pamby always a namby pamby,' Ramsay would mutter darkly but in Rita's eyes Finlay was a good son, sensitive and kind, a diligent worker, an excellent husband and father. If his own mother couldn't see fit to pamper him occasionally and lend a sympathetic ear then the world was indeed a sad place to be in.

Vaila sat at the table and looked at the cake Granma Rita had made to celebrate her tenth birthday. They were all here at Vale O' Dreip today, even Hannah, who had been so rejected by Ramsay Sutherland during her early years of marriage to Rob. But Hannah had done something to please him at last. She had presented him with a perfect granddaughter and if there was one thing that Ramsay approved of it was perfection in the human form, both mental and physical. It had taken him a long time to come to terms with Andy's disabilities; over the years his attitude had softened yet even so he was never entirely at ease in the boy's company.

The same applied to Vaila. He found it hard to be really comfortable in her presence; a fact that owed itself to the guilt he felt at having called her a bastard of unknown origin before making the discovery that she was Rob's daughter and a blood Sutherland after all. Five years had passed since then but it was still there, lurking in the back of his mind . . .

His cool, blue gaze fell on Vaila and a memory came to him – a young woman with spirit in her glance, fire on her tongue – standing up to him, letting him know what she thought of him. He had only met Morna Sommero once or twice but he would never forget her – and now her child had that same defiant look, brave and unafraid . . .

Ramsay caught Rita's eye on him, watching him as she always did . . . ever since that business over Catrina Simpson . . . he hadn't meant to touch the girl but she was so winsome and bonny and had always seemed to be asking for it . . . rape they had called it – when it had been all her fault.

And of course she had gone and gotten herself pregnant, saying it was his baby when it could have been anybody's. Even so, he'd had to pay for it, thanks to Colin Blair who had demanded silence money before he'd married Catrina to give the child a name. A handsome boy he was too, he'd glimpsed him a few times in the village . . . he'd be about five by now, another example of time passing . . .

Ramsay went into a muse, thinking about Catrina, how the sight of her could still turn his legs to jelly, especially when he remembered how she'd looked that night in the kitchen with the firelight playing on her bonny face, her breasts springing out from her frock, full and creamy white in his hands . . . sweat broke on his brow at the thought . . . if only she would agree to see him again he would make it worth her while. But when he had suggested this to her once she had made it quite plain that she wanted nothing more to do with him.

He went over the meeting in his mind, the surprise he'd felt at bumping into both her and her son out there in the village street for all the world to see. He had soon recovered his equilibrium however and had acknowledged her by courteously raising his hat and telling her quietly how well she looked, his attention then turning to Euan who stared boldly back at him. 'He's a fine boy, Catrina, a real credit to you.'

'Ay, that he is, Mr Sutherland,' Catrina had answered, a wary look creeping over her face.

'And so he should be, with all that sillar I fork out for his upkeep.'

Catrina's chin went up. 'And only right that you should do so considering the part you had in the affair.'

'Of course,' he had lowered his voice even further, 'I could make it a bit more if you would let me and only you and me need ever know.'

Her eyes had flashed then, darkly and dangerously. 'If you think I would ever let you lay one finger on me after what you did then you're even more stupid than I thought. Take care, Mr Sutherland, even servant girls have their pride and you'd best leave well alone if you know what's good for you.'

He had recoiled at the look of sheer hatred on her face and had gone hastily on his way, angry at himself for having let her see a chink in his armour. Oh, she had pride alright, too damned much for her own good – still, he had comforted himself, there were others who didn't have the same principles as Catrina. Rita didn't have eyes in the back of her head and there were those who would do anything for a bob or two . . .

'It's a lovely cake, Granma,' Vaila was saying, jumping up and giving Rita a hug. 'But I'll save it till Robbie comes home, then we can all have a bit.'

'Robbie,' Rita said musingly, 'do you often call your father by his Christian name?'

'Sometimes,' Vaila laughed, 'but usually only in my thoughts and when we're alone together.'

'Disrespectful,' Ramsay said with a frown. 'You have to respect your elders, Vaila.'

'Oh, I do,' Vaila's face took on an expression of studied innocence. 'But only if they earn it. My father will always have my respect but I called him Robbie when I was just a tiny little girl – before I knew I was a true blood Sutherland.'

Rita hurriedly put her hand to her mouth to stifle a snort of laughter, Finlay sniggered, Andy let out a screech, Hannah permitted herself a small smile.

The look on Ramsay's face was priceless. Opening his mouth to speak he thought better of it and shut it again, contenting himself by glowering at Vaila before turning away to fiddle with the broken shaft of a hay rake.

'You should get Willie Whiskers to do that,' Rita told him.

'He's far too pricey, I'll make a better job o' it myself. He's only cut out for shoeing horses, though even there he sometimes isn't as good as he ought to be.'

Rita saw what kind of mood he was in and was glad when Hannah steered the talk round to other things, saying how much Kinvara was changing with all the new people that were moving in. 'The place isn't the same as it once was,' she went on, 'familiar faces have gone, every time I come out my front door strangers are looking at me and of course I have to be neighbourly and try to put them at their ease.'

Rita had to hide a smile at this. When Hannah had come to Kinvara as Rob's wife she had despised everything and everyone and it had certainly been hard going for her to get herself accepted, mainly due to her own unfriendly attitude and her tendency to keep herself very much to herself. Now she was talking as if she was Mrs Nice Neighbour personified and Rita didn't dare look at Finlay in case it encouraged him to say something he shouldn't.

But Hannah was in an unusually chatty mood that afternoon and failed to notice the amusement on her mother-in-law's face as she went on, 'Now that Mungo MacGill is giving up his position as head keeper of the light it means he and Bette will move out of Keeper's Row . . . and . . .'

She paused and Rita filled in for her '. . . That Rob will step into Mungo's shoes.'

'Ay, I suppose so.' Hannah spoke slowly, something in her rebelling at the idea of her husband taking over from Mungo. She had always hoped that Rob would grow tired of his job and take up something on dry land with normal working hours like everybody else. She had never grown used to those long weary months he spent away from home and her voice was bleak when she said rather limply, 'More changes. Mungo and Bette were a bit much to take at times but better the devil you know, as the saying goes.'

'The Lockharts are nice,' Vaila enthused. 'We went to see them yesterday and made friends with them. They've got twins, Maida and Mark, and we've to go and visit them whenever we want.'

'I wonder what the new mill folk will be like,' Rita put in. 'I believe they're arriving tomorrow.'

'They go by the name of Bowman.' Ramsay had pricked up his ears. 'Quite a tidy little family from all accounts. Seems Joshua Bowman, the father, belongs to some remote religious sect. He won't find anything like that here, of course, and would be better off joining the Free Kirk. It should be interesting to see what he's made of.'

Ramsay rocked on his heels and looked thoughtful; Rita gave Hannah a meaningful look and went to make the tea; Essie grew tired of playing with her dolls and toddled over to her grampa to beguile him with her chatter; Andy was preoccupied with the somewhat tattered contents of a small bookcase reposing in a corner. In the lull, Vaila and Aidan seized the opportunity to run outside and stare at one another.

'Let's go and see the Bowmans moving in tomorrow,' Aidan suggested, his eyes flashing in his brown face.

'Alright,' agreed Vaila. 'I'll tell Joss and see if he can come.'

'That would be great. Come on, race you to the hayshed. Last there's a cissy!'

Vaila loved the chance to play with her small brother, but even as he and she ran about in the sunshine an odd sort of anticipation was mounting in her at the idea of meeting the new tenants of the Mill O' Cladach.

Chapter Five

The Henderson Hens had fallen under Joss's spell. They loved having him about the place, he worked willingly and well and showed great initiative in everything he did. His knowledge about poultry was limited but it wasn't long before he was tending the chickens, the geese, the ducks and the turkeys as if he had been doing it all his life and the sisters were soon drooling over him and telling one another how lucky they were to get him.

'Such a willing boy,' Rona beamed.

'A pleasure to have about the place,' Wilma agreed, her eyes shining behind her thick glasses.

'Never a cheeky word out of him.'

'A truly charming lad, the Morgans are indeed fortunate to have a son like that.'

Rona nodded vigorously, causing one thick iron-grey curl to fall over her left eye. 'The one and only child they could have but what a prize,' she sighed. 'I sometimes wish we could have been blessed in that way, Wilma. Oh, I know we've always been perfectly happy and contented as we are but one wonders – what it would have been like.'

'No use wishing for the moon,' Wilma said briskly,

wielding a rolling-pin with energy and in the process sending little clouds of flour into the air. 'It wasn't meant for us, Rona, as fine you know, so stop looking like a broody hen and set a place at table for Joss. He'll need a lot of feeding, lads of that age always do, and with him working so hard he'll need even more and I must have these scones ready for him coming in.'

Rona sneezed and went to do her sister's bidding. When Joss came in everything was ready and the sisters were waiting. To hide his astonishment at the lavish spread on the table he went to the sink to wash his hands before going back outside to re-fill the bucket from the pump.

He took a minute to compose himself. He had told Vaila he would meet her and the others at two o'clock. It was half past one now and it looked as if the Henderson Hens were intending to make a meal of it.

Joss smiled at his own absurdities. Wilma appeared at the door. 'Come, dear boy,' she called. 'We mustn't allow the soup to get cold.'

Joss gulped. Soup as well as all that other stuff. He was hungry but he wasn't exactly a horse and the sisters might be hurt if he didn't sample everything in sight.

The reality was worse than he had imagined. The sisters tucked in heartily and expected him to do the same. They certainly knew how to cook, the soup was delicious, the steak and kidney pie so good he had second helpings and sat back replete.

'That was great,' he said enthusiastically. His eye fell on

the clock. 'But I have to be going now, I said I would meet the Sutherlands at two and it's quarter past now.'

Wilma's face fell. 'Oh, but I baked these scones specially for you . . .' 'And I made the oatcakes,' Rona chimed in, gazing at him anxiously through her glasses.

The door went. Rona arose to open it and saw Aidan standing on the step. 'Please, Miss Henderson,' he said politely, 'we thought we would come for Joss.' Rona looked over his head to see the other young Sutherlands waiting a little way off, together with a boy and girl that Rona had never seen before. The Henderson Hens were nervous of children *en masse* and an expression of apprehension flitted over Rona's large-featured face.

Aidan saw the look and hastened to add, 'We also wanted to see the geese and the turkeys and Essie likes talking to the ducks. No one else in the place has ducks as friendly as yours.'

Ramsay was always proudly proclaiming that his grandson was a born diplomat and now it seemed that he was right. Rona's attitude underwent a complete change and she positively glowed. 'Of course, no harm in that, none at all, you may come inside, young man, and wait for Joss. Don't forget to wipe your feet on the mat, there's a good boy.'

She was about to close the door when something made her hesitate. The rest of the children were standing in a little group, shyly watching proceedings. Rona took a deep breath. 'You may all come in, yes, do, the dog as well, can't have him wandering about annoying the chickens.'

'But, he's attached to Andy's cart.' Vaila explained. 'And he never chases chickens – except when he's bored and has nothing better to do,' she amended hastily, a vision coming into her mind of Breck rounding up, not only the chickens, but the ducks and the turkeys as well.

'Unhitch him anyway, there's a dear. He might start barking and we don't want that sort of irritation, do we? It would only get the geese going and then the turkeys and where would we all be then?'

Andy was struggling out of the cart. Rona watched him for a moment or two then to everyone's complete surprise she lifted him up as if he were a feather, tucked him under one hefty arm, and bore him away into the house.

The children piled in after her. Wilma's brows rose as her kitchen was suddenly invaded by 'an army of young people' while the two Croft Angus dogs, Pebble and Rebel, slunk from under the table to sniff suspiciously at Breck. Then the tails began to wag. Breck and Rebel were brothers, having been fathered by Pebble some eight years ago when he had 'caught' one of Morna Sommero's young labrador bitches.

All three dogs were soon engaged in playful combat while the children stood in a row, hands folded behind their backs, respectful and silent, trying not to look too obviously at the sisters who were a fascinating pair with their big booming voices, their striped butcher's aprons and clumsy boots, and the habit they had of blinking at each other behind their glasses and saying, 'Isn't that right, dear?' when they had some point that needed to be confirmed.

Maida and Mark in particular were totally enthralled by everything the sisters said and did and the others looked at them anxiously when a snort of laughter escaped Maida's lips.

Essie was the only one to remain at ease and going over to the table she boldly helped herself to a jammy scone and proceeded to eat it with great enjoyment.

'What a dear little girl.' The sisters glanced at one another. 'Quite lacking in manners, of course,' Wilma went on, 'but she's very young yet and will no doubt improve as she gets older.'

'It will just go to waste anyway, Joss was unable to finish everything.' Rona sounded disappointed about this. 'No sense in keeping it so I'll just pop it into a paper bag and you can share it between you later.'

The children crowded to the door and filed out, murmuring their farewells, Maida clutching the bag of titbits, Joss glad to escape from what had become an awkward situation. At the last minute Vaila remembered Andy but she needn't have worried. Rona came out with him safely tucked under her arm, deposited him in the cart, and tied him in securely. 'There you are, all present and correct. Wilma and I will see you tomorrow then, Joss,' she added, turning to that young man with a beaming smile.

'Ay, eleven sharp, Miss Henderson,' he nodded and took to his heels after the others who were disappearing down the dusty track. Aidan however had waited for Joss to catch up. Joss was Aidan's hero. He tried to emulate everything the older boy did and secretly wished that he could attend the Catholic school in Vaul and go to St Niven's Chapel as Joss did. But he never voiced his thoughts to anybody and particularly not to Joss, knowing it would only bring trouble if Grampa Ramsay got to hear of it.

It wasn't so bad for the rest of the young Sutherlands, neither Rob nor Hannah had any religious prejudices whereas Ramsay was positively biased towards any faith other than his own. With all that in mind, Aidan never mentioned Joss Morgan's name in his grandfather's presence, nor indeed that of the young curate, Father Kelvin MacNeil, whom Aidan admired tremendously and whose company he enjoyed whenever their paths crossed.

As for Joss, he treated Aidan in the same way that he treated everyone else; with patience, kindness, and a tolerance that was admirable in a lad of his age. He was no angel however and never suffered fools gladly, always quick to speak up if anything annoyed him. But his great sense of humour and love of the ridiculous allowed him to see the funny side of life and people liked having him around, especially his young contemporaries who saw him as a bit of a dare-devil. When Joss set out to do something he seldom gave in till it was completed, much to the dismay of his mother whose heart was often in her mouth at some of the deeds he got up to.

But he never deliberately meant to worry her or anybody else and he would never have hurt Aidan by telling him he was a pest sometimes the way he followed along like a shadow and tried to copy everything that Joss did. In some ways it was gratifying to be held in such high esteem, though he knew Aidan would rather have died than let his feelings be known. With this in mind he dug his hands into his pockets and gave vent to a tuneless whistle as he neared the spot where Aidan was waiting. 'Come on,' Joss spoke gruffly. 'Why are you hanging about like that? You look like a lost fart with toothache.'

This appealed to Aidan. Joss had a marvellous store of nonsensical sayings and both boys were soon shrieking with mirth and holding each other up as they went to join the others.

Maida and Mark were acting the fool, mimicking the Henderson Hens with such comical accuracy that no one could resist joining in the fun. Amid bursts of laughter they reached the road, waving to Harriet who was working in the garden of Butterburn Croft. 'I want to visit Granma,' Essie stated and ran off without ado, sure of a welcome from the grandmother who had always spoiled her.

'Does she always do what she wants?' Mark asked, gazing after Essie's tiny figure.

'Essie's just Essie,' Vaila said simply. 'Everyone makes a fuss o' her because she's so bonny.'

'But, she's . . .' Mark didn't finish what he was about to say, Maida had poked him in the ribs to be quiet and he sulked a little because he wanted to be on his way and it looked as if they would have to stop and talk to Harriet who had come down to her gate to wait for them coming along. Essie was hanging onto her granny's skirts, chuckling in her merry little way and asking if she could stay for a while because her legs were tired.

Harriet patted the child's golden tresses, glad of the chance to pause from her labours. It was a calm, blue day with the sun beating down from a cloudless sky, the heady scents of the warm fields hung in the air while the sea beyond Camus nan Rua was a dazzling sheet of silvery light.

'It's on days like these I'm glad I came to live here,' Harriet said almost to herself. 'And of course to be near you, my wee lamb,' she added, smiling down at her granddaughter.

The wheels of Andy's cart were making squeaky noises as he came up to the gate. Harriet gritted her teeth. She was hot and sweaty and not in a mood to be patient with her grandson, for while she had long ago accepted his difficulties she often found herself being irritated by the length of time he took to get his words to come out.

'It's alright, Granma,' Vaila interpreted Harriet's mood. 'We only stopped because Essie wanted to see you.'

A smile touched Harriet's strong mouth. 'Well, aren't you the wise one, and you only just turned ten. Alright, on you go, I'll keep Essie here for her tea and bring her home afterwards.'

A delighted Essie put her chubby hand to her mouth and giggled in triumph, soon forgetting her companions as her granny bore her away into the house to ply her with home-made lemonade and biscuits.

'Just as well,' Mark said as they set off once more. 'She's too little to hike along with us.'

'She would only spoil things,' Maida agreed.

'And you're both too new to say what you think so just shut up,' Joss said mildly, but with a rebellious tightening of his mouth that Vaila knew well.

Maida coloured and gazed repentantly at Joss with her big blue eyes while Mark made a wry face and put his arm round Vaila's shoulders. 'Sorry I spoke about your sister. I should learn to keep my mouth shut. My mother's always telling me it's too big for my own good.'

There was something very open and honest about Mark that appealed to Vaila. She smiled at him, spirits were restored, and they were friends again when they stopped at the Brig O' Shee to hang over the parapet and throw stones into the foaming green water below.

'Can I join in or is it only for children?' Father Kelvin MacNeil's voice came from behind and as he dismounted from his bike a row of faces turned to acknowledge him with pleasure. In his early thirties, he looked little more than a boy himself with his tousled fair hair and laughing eyes. He was a great favourite with the children of Kinvara because he listened to them and respected their opinions and tried to be fair about everything, which didn't mean to say that he was afraid to use discipline when the need arose.

Having just returned from the Hebridean island of Barra from whence he had sprung, the children were especially pleased to welcome him back, plying him with questions about his holiday as he accepted a stone from Joss and hurled it into the river with a mighty swing of one long arm.

'Is it true there's a castle on Barra surrounded by water?' Aidan asked excitedly.

The priest nodded. 'Ay, indeed there is, Kismull Castle in Castlebay. A real fortress if ever there was one. Just the place to pour boiling oil on your enemies if they come too near with their boats.'

The boys loved that, they wanted to know more about Kismull Castle and their voices rang in the air as they walked with Father MacNeil along the road, taking turns to haul Andy along in his cart when the way became steep and Breck began to pant.

'I'm just going to visit your parents, Joss,' Father MacNeil said as they reached the Mill O' Cladach road end, 'and I hope to see you in chapel soon.'

Joss coloured. 'I've been busy, Father.'

'Never too busy for God. I know it's a bit far to walk to Vaul but you could always hitch a lift or get yourself a bike.'

Joss nodded eagerly. 'I'm saving up for one, I got myself a summer job at Croft Angus.'

'The Henderson sisters, eh?' The priest ignored the squeaks of mirth coming from Maida. 'An admirable pair of ladies, you'll be alright with them, Joss, eccentric they may be but their hearts are in the right place.'

'Ay, Father,' Joss said humbly, though his eyes were twinkling.

'Right then, I'll be getting along. Where are you off to, by the way?'

'The Mill O' Cladach, just to watch the mallards,' Vaila explained evasively.

Father MacNeil grinned. 'Pull the other one, people watching, more like. No harm in that, none at all, and just to prove it, I might stop on my way back and watch them too.'

He bent down to speak to Andy for a moment then with a cheery wave he was off, pedalling briskly along, his black coat flapping in the breeze, an assurance in the way he carried himself that made Aidan look lingeringly after him.

'Ask Grampa to get you a bike,' Vaila said as she followed his gaze.

But he shook his head. 'No, it isn't that, it's . . .'

'Are you coming or not?' Joss was losing patience. '*The Blythe Spirit*'s due in at the harbour later and I promised Mam I'd pick up some stuff for her.'

'Can we come?' Aidan hopped from one foot to the other as he waited for the answer.

'Maybe, but only if you stop jumping about like a grasshopper.'

'Great!' Mark grinned at Maida. They had only been in Kinvara for three days, yet already they felt at home here. The scenery was exciting and magnificent, the people were interesting, they had made friends with Joss Morgan and the Sutherlands, adventure and discoveries of all kinds loomed on the horizon and the Lockhart children just knew they were going to be happy here.

Chapter Six

The Mill O' Cladach was a peaceful spot, set in a gently undulating meadow filled with sweet smelling clover and scarlet poppies. This was where the seabirds gathered to preen themselves and where the song of the curlew mingled with the gurgle of the Cladach Burn as it meandered along between banks of rushes and swaying grasses. Here the wildfowl had their nests; mallards quacked and poked for food; swans with their cygnets glided gracefully in the pools where the river met the sea.

Yet despite its serenity there had always been life and movement here and an odd sort of silence had fallen when the previous mill family moved away and the huge wheel had stopped grinding. In the months that followed, Conrad O'Connar, the miller of Bruach, had professed delight at the extra business the move had brought him but he had enjoyed the friendly rivalry that had existed between the two mills and was inwardly glad that the Mill O' Cladach was to be tenanted once more.

A large cart, piled high with household necessities, was parked outside the mill house and the horse was still in his shafts, despite the fact that he was lathered in sweat and hanging his head dejectedly.

'My dad would have something to say about that,' Mark said disgustedly as he and his companions wandered past the house. 'He hates to see horses being ill-treated.'

At that moment a girl came out of the house to hesitate briefly at the door before coming down the path. She was a thin, bespectacled figure with a mass of raven hair, a stubborn chin and a determined mouth that made her look mature beyond her years.

But despite her unremarkable appearance there was a compelling aura about her and the children stared in fascination as, while she was ordinary enough in both face and form, she was dressed in rough sackcloth and was wearing an old-fashioned black hat that would have better suited Dolly Law of Balivoe who had worn the same head covering for as long as anyone could remember.

'Can I help you?' The girl was looking at them curiously, her voice even and cultured and bearing only a faint trace of English accent.

'We came to ask you that.' Joss found his tongue.

'I would like to know why you haven't rested your horse,' Mark said in his forthright manner. 'The poor brute's done in and you could at least unhitch him and put him in the shade.'

'It's none of your business what we do with our horse,' she returned coolly. 'I don't even know you or anything about you and I think you had better go away before my father comes out.'

Joss grinned. 'Aw, come on, no need to get het up over nothing. Mark's right, your horse should be unhitched after such a long journey. You ought to know all that, you look like a sensible girl.'

Anger flashed in the girl's eyes. 'He hasn't come all that far for a beast of burden, only from Achnasheen where we collected our things from the train. After that we stopped several times to rest both ourselves and the horse.'

'Did you stay at a post inn?' Maida spoke for the first time, not at all sure if she liked this newcomer with her arrogant face and somewhat haughty manner.

'No, of course not, there are far too many of us for that.' The girl looked surprised. 'Waste not, want not, why spend precious money at an inn when we had blankets and a perfectly good cart to sleep in.'

'Maybe the horse didn't sleep,' Mark persisted. 'And even if he did he's still come a long way and needs attention.'

'As a matter of fact I wanted to unhitch him but my father wouldn't let me. He said we first had to give thanks to the Lord for bringing us here safely. That's why we haven't unloaded the cart – and the horse's name is Jacob by the way – I called him that myself soon after we got him.'

She held out her hand. 'I'm Rebecca Bowman and I'll be twelve soon. I have two brothers younger than me, Caleb's eleven and Nathan nine, my mother is called

Miriam, my father, Joshua, we're a very united family and only mix with strangers if they show they are worthy enough. I shouldn't be out here speaking to you now but I saw you gaping at our personal belongings and thought I had better see what you wanted.'

She sounded unbearably polite, her voice was stilted and stiff, as if she was repeating parrot fashion things that had been instilled in her mind.

'We aren't strangers,' Vaila said with spirit. 'We've belonged in Kinvara all our lives. It's you who are strange and you'd better try and be a bit friendlier because everybody here knows everybody else and they don't like folks who are snooty.'

'Anyway,' Joss intervened hastily when he saw that Vaila's temper was getting the better of her, 'it's a mill you've come to, not a monastery. Once you've got this place up and running there will be comings and goings all day long so you'd better get used to it.'

'I suppose so.' Rebecca's voice was softer now. 'We had a tower-mill in England and that was busy enough but they were all people that we had known for years. Then my father decided he wanted to come to Scotland to run a water-mill and to spread the word. He's good at preaching and he's good at milling, I suppose you could say he knows everything.'

'Even how to save souls of ignorant natives like us.' Joss spoke sarcastically, then he relented when he saw that she was looking at him rather doubtfully. 'Forget it and let's be friends. I'm Joss Morgan, and I live up yonder in Keeper's Row.'

The others also introduced themselves, Rebecca smiled politely and there followed an awkward little silence. 'Look, there's Johnny Lonely,' Joss, glad of the diversion, pointed towards the shore. 'Now, there's a real hermit for you, he lives in a hut in Mary's Bay and likes to keep himself to himself but somehow knows everything about everybody. He does odd jobs when he's really hard up but mostly he fishes and baits rabbits and combs the beach for bits and pieces. When he's in the mood he tells great stories about shipwrecks and other disasters and if he takes to a person he does so in a big way and trusts them to be his friend.'

'He likes Andy,' Vaila smiled at her brother. 'They're both wanderers and meet up on their travels.'

Rebecca glanced at Andy, undecided whether to speak to him or not in case he couldn't understand. In the next moment she was left in no doubt about his capabilities. He had seen Johnny and was getting out of the cart. adjusting his calipers as he straightened, waving and shouting till Johnny looked up and waved back and began making his way up towards the mill.

'Johnny!' Andy yelled, as the top of the hermit's shaggy dark head appeared over a rise. The next minute he was making straight for Andy to lift him up and spin him round till the little boy was laughing with delight.

Then Johnny seemed to come back to earth with a start. Gently he lowered Andy to the ground and looked long and hard at Rebecca who was watching him intently. The two stared at one another till a movement from above distracted Johnny's attention. A woman had come out of the house to stand at the door and gaze about her in rather a lost fashion. She didn't seem to notice the children nor the man on the track below and not one of the children noticed her either because they were all too busy staring at Johnny who was behaving in an even odder fashion than usual.

Something strange had happened to him in the last few moments. His breathing was uneven as if he had been running; his hand was shaking as he drew it heavily across his mouth; his face had turned pale under its coating of grimy tan. He seemed to be struggling to compose himself.

'What goes round must come round.' His voice came out suddenly, harsh and clipped, making everyone jump. 'Ay, indeed, no one can play God and get away with it forever. Somehow I always knew it would happen, the de'il has a habit o' catching up with his own . . .'

At this point he looked deep into Rebecca's eyes. 'Take care lass, what's for you won't go by you – but you've got spirit, I can see it in you – just keep your head above water, only the weak will go under.'

With that he gave a curt nod and walked quickly away, leaving the children gaping after him. 'What a horrible man,' Rebecca said with a shiver. 'Who is he to tell me anything – and how can he begin to know anything about me?'

'Johnny knows things other people don't,' Aidan whispered in awe.

'Maybe it's his way o' saying welcome to the place,' Joss hazarded.

'But he never speaks to people he doesn't know.' Vaila felt eerie and strange at the recollection of the hermit's cryptic words. 'And he never gives anything away about himself – yet, he spoke as if he was giving us a hint about something – as if he knew who you were, Rebecca.'

Mark chuckled and made a face at Rebecca. 'Maybe he can read lips – or was hiding behind a bush when you were telling us your father was here to save our souls.'

'Don't joke about it,' Vaila said sharply. 'Johnny does give people the creeps by hiding and listening and jumping out at them, and there are those who really do believe he can read lips and sometimes minds as well.'

'Hallo there!' A well-known voice hailed them. Father MacNeil was coming along on his bike, wobbling a bit because the path was overgrown with tufts of grass. As he drew nearer he dismounted and, holding his hand out to Rebecca, he said warmly, 'Welcome to Kinvara, I'm Father MacNeil, parish priest of St Niven's chapel in Vaul. I came along to ask if there was anything I could do to help you settle in. You must have come a long way and I see you haven't yet managed to get your belongings into the house.'

But Rebecca refused to take his hand. Instead she jumped back from him as if she had been burnt. 'Please go away,' she faltered unsteadily, 'before my father comes out.'

Thus rebuffed, the priest also drew back. 'I see, I'm sorry if you feel that way.' The look on his face was one of hurt bewilderment. 'I'll get along then before I cause you more embarrassment.'

He nodded at Joss. 'I'll see you in chapel soon, Joss. Your mother has promised she'll send you along.' With that he mounted his bike and pedalled slowly and rather dejectedly away.

Aidan bunched his fists. 'You shouldn't have talked to him like that,' he told Rebecca. 'He's our friend and wouldn't harm anybody.'

But she wasn't listening, all her attention was focused on Joss. 'You, too,' she said in a horrified voice. 'I didn't know or I wouldn't . . .'

She halted. A tall man with a shock of black hair threaded through with grey had appeared on the doorstep. 'Rebecca!' he called in a deep booming voice. 'Inside this minute and help your mother make tea.' Then in the next breath he roared, 'Nathan! Caleb! Come outside and get this cart unloaded! And don't take all day!'

Two boys emerged and came scuttling down the path, the bigger being well built with an aggressive jaw and a sullen demeanour, the smaller, gentle and refined-looking and obviously nervous as he hurried to help his brother. Both wore roughly woven black jackets and wide-brimmed hats that looked uncomfortably warm as the sun beat down on them from above.

'The horse, Rebecca, what about the horse?' Mark said urgently.

She shook her head. 'He'll have to wait, I must go and help Mother.'

'It's alright, Rebecca, I have to find the kettle first.' Rebecca drew in a startled breath as a tall spare woman with a weary face and hair scraped back into a bun was suddenly there at her elbow.

'Where did you come from, Mother?' the girl asked raggedly. 'I didn't see you coming out of the house, I hate it when you spring out of nowhere like that.'

'I was just finding my way, Rebecca, I discovered a little door at the back leading onto the meadow and I came round to the front by an overgrown pathway.' The woman's voice was meek and quiet. 'Come dear, help me find the tea things, your father will be thirsty after all his efforts.'

Neither the boys nor their parents had acknowledged the Kinvara youngsters and Rebecca was giving every impression of having forgotten their existence.

'Miriam and Joshua,' Joss said musingly as they departed the scene.

'Caleb and Nathan,' Vaila added. 'They've all got biblical names – even the horse.'

'I've got a biblical name,' Joss pointed out.

'Me too,' Mark laughed.

'Not like theirs, Old Testament and old-fashioned.'

'That's because they belong to a strict religious order,'

Aidan said knowingly. 'Grampa told me all about it at bedtime last night. They don't have ordained ministers or churches and are very narrow and straight – and if they don't like Joss or Father MacNeil they won't like me either.'

Vaila smiled. 'What makes you think that?'

'Because Aidan was an Irish monk who went from the monastery at Iona to be a missionary in Northumbria and then he went to Lindisfarne to become its first bishop.'

'What's that got to do with you?' Mark said scathingly.

'Because Aidan was a saint – just like me – and Joshua Bowman won't like having another saint about the place when he thinks he's the only one.' A gleam of devilment shone in the little boy's eyes. 'So you'd better all be nice to me or I'll turn you into ugly warty frogs.'

'Wizards do that, not saints,' Maida said with a toss of her fair tresses.

Dolly Law passed by in her cart, puffing happily at her clay pipe, her hat pulled well down over her face to shade it from the sun. Joss choked on a spurt of laughter. 'Maybe she belongs to the same sect as the Bowmans. Dolly and Shug don't believe in churches either, they're a law unto themselves.'

'Like a lift?' Dolly had stopped a short distance away.

The children glanced at one another guiltily. 'It's alright, Dolly,' Joss told her, 'we haven't so far to go.'

'Aw, be a devil and hop on, I'd be glad o' the company.'

'What about Andy?'

'No bother.' Dolly climbed down, untethered Breck, and threw both him and Andy unceremoniously into the cart as if they were sacks of coal. Throwing Joss a rope she instructed him to tie Andy's cart to the tailboard.

Dolly grinned at Mark and Maida, showing two good teeth in an otherwise broken row. Her face was grimy, her hair lank and oily, her hands looked as if they hadn't been washed in weeks. She was expecting another baby in the autumn and her little tight pudding of a belly strained against the worn material of her grubby apron. But none of these mattered to the youngsters. Dolly was kind, she was happy and carefree, she did things that other people didn't and to hell with what anybody thought.

Joss and Mark opted to walk behind the cart since they considered it was too much for Sorry to pull all of them. But the others piled in and made themselves comfortable among the sacks of clean washing that Dolly was delivering to those houses that couldn't afford a laundry maid but still liked to pretend they were a cut above the rest by farming out their dirty clothes to various washerwomen in the area. Dolly did not mind collecting and delivering such items, just as long as she didn't 'get her hands soiled' as she put it, by doing such a menial task as laundering for anybody other than her own lot.

The women of Kinvara smiled at this; it was indeed a rare sight to see a line of Dolly's washing fluttering in the breeze. More usually it was a pair of Shug's drawers looking lonely and sorry for themselves as they hung suspended by one peg for weeks, or a grey vest or two belonging to the children whenever they were lucky enough to have a vest they could call their own. Dolly's answer to supplies of fresh clothing was simple. When the need arose she went round the doors collecting 'rags for charity' and then she would go home to her family to share the loot and drink a toast to the philosopher who had maintained that charity began at home.

Everyone knew of course what Dolly did with their cast-offs but nobody minded, it was as good a way as any to ensure a certain amount of well-being for the Law children since they had their pride even if their parents didn't and woe betide any youngster who pointed the finger at them.

Dolly began to sing as they went through Calvost village. Big Bette was standing outside her shop, massive arms folded over her billowing bosoms, tongue in full flow as she enjoyed a gossip with Long John Jeannie, the doctor's wife, named so because she was always 'mending the arse' of her husband's combinations.

The children waved, Dolly waved, Bette and Jeannie nodded acknowledgement, the little procession trundled merrily on its way, Sorry trotting in her sedate fashion, Andy's cart bumping along at the rear. 'I'll say that for Dolly,' Jeannie nodded. 'She's always been good with bairns.'

'Ay, and just as well,' Big Bette returned, her double

chins becoming more pronounced as she bent her head and lowered the tone of her voice. 'With her having another one in the oven she must indeed have a liking for wee ones – among other things,' she added meaningfully.

'Shug would have had a hand in that too,' Jeannie said mildly, not wishing to be drawn into a discussion about the Laws' marital adventures. She looked pointedly at Bette. 'But then, he isn't the only one in Kinvara to enjoy his bit pleasures, as I'm sure you'll agree, Bette.'

Bette reddened slightly. Trust Jeannie MacAlistair to bring the talk round to a personal level. Her lips folded. 'I hope you're no' implying anything about me and my Mungo, Jeannie. Him and me are not like the Laws. His duties as head keeper o' the light means we are separated for months on end and it is only natural that we should feel the need o' some comfort when we get together again.'

She snorted and pushed up one pendulous breast in a defiant gesture. 'Besides, we have always been able to control ourselves in that respect, it is an easy enough matter to jump off at the junction instead o' going the whole way. The Laws don't care about that side o' it, they just go on till the steam is coming out their ears and to hell with the cost! It doesn't seem to matter that their bairns have to go barefooted to school just as long as they get their beer and their baccy and whatever else takes their fancy.'

Jeannie remained unperturbed by this outburst. 'Now, now, calm down, Bette. I myself have never hankered after children and am perfectly happy with just me and Alistair though that doesn't mean to say I haven't wondered what it would have been like to have had a family. The Laws have too much, you have enough to satisfy you, I have none and there might come a day when I will sit back and think how nice it would be to have a daughter or son to take care o' me. But it is the way o' things, you and Mungo jump off at the junction as you put it, Dolly and Shug go the whole road, when the going gets rough and you end up in the surgery, Alistair is there to mend your ails and set you on your way again. We're all here for a purpose, Dolly Law and her family are no exception, and you have to admit they brighten the place up with their wit and their wiles.'

Bette grudgingly conceded to the wisdom of Jeannie's words and might have let the subject rest had not Effie breezed up at that moment, her mobile face displaying her interest as she tried to pick up on the conversation concerning the Laws.

As the doctor's wife, Jeannie prided herself on her discretion. 'Ay, you're right enough, Effie, we were talking about the Laws and just saying how lucky Dolly is, having a midwife like yourself to deliver her bairnies.' The smile she gave Effie was beguilingly sweet as she went on, 'She isn't getting any younger and it must be good for her to feel she's in such safe hands.'

'No, indeed, she isn't getting any younger,' Effie agreed. 'But when the Lord created rabbits he created Dolly and she will go on having them till either she or Shug drops.'

Jeannie raised her brows. 'Rabbits?' she queried, deliberately misunderstanding.

'Ooh well, you know what I mean,' Effie said cheerfully. 'There will always be rabbits and there will always be Laws.'

'And there will always be nurses who are the souls of diplomacy when it comes to their patients.'

'Of course,' Effie returned rather stiffly, 'my patients have always been able to trust me and can tell me anything – knowing it will never go beyond my own two lips.'

'Of course,' said Jeannie, then in the same breath she added, 'Flour, that's what I came for and what I mean to have. The doctor likes his bread home-made and if I don't get back soon there will be none for his tea.'

The women disappeared inside the shop and when Connie, housekeeper to the manse, came in at their backs, the subject of the Laws was forgotten in favour of little snippets of talk regarding the minister and his family.

[illegible]

[illegible] understanding.

[illegible]

[illegible]

And [illegible]

[illegible] until [illegible]

[illegible] the [illegible] did [illegible] and [illegible]

[illegible] the [illegible]

[illegible] hope [illegible]

[illegible] and wants

[illegible] the [illegible]

[illegible] Dhupa [illegible]

Chapter Seven

A surprise awaited Andy when he got home. Catherine Dunbar, the schoolteacher, was there and with her she had brought a typewriter. At first no one noticed it in the general buzz of movement and talk, which was more pronounced than usual because Harriet was also there and with her she had brought Essie who had decided that she didn't want to stay at Butterburn Croft for her tea after all, but wished to have it in her own house instead.

For quite several minutes Harriet's loud voice dominated the scene as she glowingly recounted the things that Essie had said, the small adventures they had both shared whilst feeding the animals and picking flowers which the little girl now clamoured to put in a vase 'before they died of thirst'.

The rest of the young Sutherlands had no hope of recounting any of their own exploits of the afternoon, not while Essie was holding the floor with her wiles and wants and the winning smiles she was throwing in the young teacher's direction.

And then Catherine Dunbar made a very strange

remark, one that caused both Hannah and Harriet to raise their brows and look askance at the visitor.

'You are indeed a very bright girl, Essie,' Catherine murmured sweetly, 'but when you come to school next year you will have a more critical audience to contend with and will need to learn that others want to shine too.'

'What an odd thing to say to the bairn.' Harriet was immediately on the defensive. 'As if she could understand what that means.'

'She will,' Catherine said softly, the green of her eyes very pronounced as she faced up to the matriarchal Harriet. 'At least, I hope she does for her own sake. Children can be cruel, Mrs Campbell, and I only want what's best for Essie when she leaves the nest and has to face the wider world.'

There might have followed a clash of personalities had not Andy suddenly spotted the typewriter sitting on the table. He had seen such a thing once before, when his father had taken him to visit the Reverend Thomas MacIntosh at the manse and they had been invited into that good man's study for tea and a chat.

The minister had not failed to notice Andy's interest in the machine and he had shown him how it worked, explaining that he used it to type up his sermons when he was in a hurry.

Ever since then, Andy had dreamed of one day owning a typewriter of his own and now here it was; a big solid brute of a thing, just asking for someone to use it, and he was so excited he let out a screech that drowned out all else and made everyone turn to stare at him in amazement.

'Yes, it's for you, Andy,' Catherine nodded, her delight at his reaction making her eyes sparkle. In the excitement of the moment she forgot the difficulties she'd experienced in getting such a heavy piece of equipment to Keeper's Row intact. Her only mode of transport was her bicycle, and there had been not a soul in sight when she'd staggered out of the schoolhouse with the typewriter in her arms. Then Dokie Joe MacPhee, husband of Mattie, had come clattering along with a wheelbarrow and into it he had deposited Catherine's burden, stoically lugging it along the road and being a great help till one of the wheels had collapsed under the barrow and for the rest of the way she and Dokie had carried the machine to its destination.

When she had thanked him for his trouble he had given her a reproachful look. 'You only had to ask someone, lassie,' he had chided gently. 'We all help one another in these parts. If we didn't we might as well be dead in a place like Kinvara and the sooner you learn that the better.'

Now, seeing Andy's face, Catherine knew it had been worth all the trouble, and she was further rewarded when she told him that the machine was his to keep, having been replaced by a more up-to-date model which now reposed in her study for the furtherance of her teacherly duties.

Stumbling and falling in his haste to get to the table, the little boy half fell into a kitchen chair to simply stare at his new possession in awe. 'Try it, Andy,' Catherine encouraged him. 'I've brought some paper to start you off, fit a sheet in, like this – adjust it – and just tap away. Write your own name, anything you feel like doing.'

The rest of the family crowded round as Andy's trembling fingers came down like sledgehammers on the keys. Hannah shook her head but for once managed to keep her doubts to herself. No one else spoke, tension, heavy and thick, settled like a blanket over the room. Andy tried again but his hands were like bunches of bananas on the keys, clumsy and uncontrolled.

'Take your time, Andy,' Vaila said quietly, as she placed a steadying hand on her brother's bony shoulders. Andy made another useless attempt and a yelp of sheer frustration escaped from him.

'Me try,' Essie clamoured, reaching over and touching the machine with her chubby fingers. 'No, Essie, this is Andy's typewriter,' Catherine said firmly. 'He's going to learn to write on it and no one else is to touch it in case they break it.'

Over her head the eyes of Hannah and Harriet met in a look that spoke volumes. The young teacher was indeed taking over! Who was she to tell anybody what they should do outside of the classroom? And besides, she didn't know Andy as well as she thought, his muscle control was as unpredictable as his temper tantrums and she would never get him to write one letter on that *thing*, never mind his own name.

But Catherine Dunbar had patience as well as determination, and taking one of Andy's fingers in her own she made him tap down sharply on the keys. The letter 'A' appeared, followed by 'n' and in seconds the little boy was able to see his own name on the paper. Bubbles of excitement frothed down his chin. In his eagerness to try for himself he pushed Catherine's hand away and almost angrily he attacked the machine.

'He's done it!' Vaila gave a shout of triumph and grabbing Essie she waltzed her round the room before rushing back to hug her little brother and laugh with him over his latest achievement.

Hannah looked at Catherine. 'What can I say but thank you for trying so hard with him.'

'Ay,' Harriet confirmed gruffly, 'it's no wonder the bairns in your classroom are finding out there's more than just fresh air between their lugs.'

Andy was indicating that he wanted his new treasure installed in his bedroom and when Harriet and Hannah carried it up between them he clumped along at their back and that was the last anybody saw of him till teatime.

Harriet made a large pot of tea and brought it to the table along with a batch of fresh scones straight from her own girdle. Everyone gathered round to eat and drink while Vaila regaled them with a vivid account of the afternoon's visit to the Mill O' Cladach.

'Three children,' mused Catherine. 'We will no doubt be seeing them in school after the holidays – together with the Lockhart two. I can see I'm going to be kept busier than ever, helping them to settle in, getting them used to my way of teaching.'

'No doubt you'll manage that quite nicely,' Harriet commented drily.

'No doubt,' Catherine agreed calmly and lowered her head to hide her smiles. It felt good to get the better of Harriet who was always holding the floor about something and thinking she knew better than anyone else when it came to matters concerning children.

In the little lull that followed, the only sound to be heard was that of Andy's typewriter clattering away busily upstairs. Absently Catherine sipped her tea and nibbled her scone and wondered what Rob would have to say when he came home from lighthouse duty and beheld his son's new acquisition for the first time.

That night, sitting round the dinner table, Rebecca bowed her head, closed her eyes, put her hands together, and placed the tips of her fingers to her mouth. Caleb, Nathan, and Miriam did the same. Joshua Bowman began to speak, starting by asking the Lord to bless them in the new life they had chosen in Kinvara, going on to hope that the future would be happy and fruitful for them all and asking that strength be given them to face all of life's eventualities and that their devotion in serving the Master would grow even stronger with the passing of time.

Miriam carefully eased one cramped buttock a fraction and hoped the potatoes weren't burning; Caleb thought about his empty stomach and wished his father would finish his monologue so that they could get on with the meal; Nathan wriggled in his seat and licked his lips nervously because he hadn't emptied his bladder before being called to table and desperately prayed he could hold on for another few minutes; Rebecca was remembering the meeting she'd had with Joss and the others and a little smile hovered at the corners of her mouth as she thought about some of the things they had said to one another.

There had been a quality of frankness about the conversation that had appealed to her – though Joss was just a bit too outspoken for her liking. And he was Catholic! He went to a Catholic school and attended a Catholic church and her father would never allow her to speak to him again if he ever found out. Her mouth tightened defiantly. She wouldn't tell him. Not yet anyway. He would find out sooner or later but for now he needn't know and she might get to meet Joss again.

'Rebecca.' Joshua's voice cut into her thoughts like broken glass and she opened her eyes. 'It is your turn to say Grace – and this time speak up so that we can all hear what you have to say. Every word clear and precise, as if you really mean what you say.'

'Clear and precise, Father.' Before Rebecca closed her eyes for the second time she glimpsed Nathan's tortured face and knew that his weak bladder was letting him down again. She could smell the potatoes burning yet her mother sat there, ramrod straight and unmoving, never indicating by one word or gesture the concern she might be feeling for the ruination of the meagre meal that would be their last till breakfast.

Caleb's jaw was jutting worse than ever, one day he would say something, one day . . . every fibre in Rebecca urged her to hurry through Grace but she knew better and forced herself to speak slowly and deliberately while the soup grew cold in its dish on the table, the potatoes charred themselves on the stove, and Nathan gave up trying to control his bladder and wet his trousers with a feeling of relief mixed with deepest shame and self-loathing.

If he could be more like Caleb and Rebecca everything would be fine. They were able to stand up for themselves and allow their feelings to show whenever they were upset or angry. He had never been able to do that, instead he blubbed like a baby when he thought no one was looking and seemed to be afraid and unhappy all the time. If it wasn't for Rebecca he would die altogether. She was strong and bold and covered up for him whenever she could.

'Nathan, you aren't listening.' Joshua's eyes were blazing their wrath upon his youngest son. 'Stop fidgeting or you'll do without food and go to your bed on an empty stomach.'

'Yes, Father,' Nathan returned humbly. Rebecca's knee nudged his under the table and suddenly he felt better. She had finished saying Grace in that cool, collected manner that always brought him a certain measure of comfort and security and he knew she would make it alright for him because she was Rebecca and she was unafraid.

Chapter Eight

The laird was visiting Ramsay at Vale O' Dreip with the intention of discussing a business matter. The Master of Crathmor, however, being a true Highland gentleman and an easygoing one at that, was never a body to hurry anything, believing that the social graces should take precedence above all else and that one should first have a neighbourly chat and a dram or two, before getting down to more serious affairs.

Thus it was that he sat at Rita's kitchen table, homely and at ease, his kilt fanned out over the seat in case it should get creased, great hairy knees spread wide simply because his splendid girth allowed for no other pose – and anyway, only cissies sat with their legs together in case something should fall out that might be offensive. The laird didn't care what fell out as long as it wasn't the loose change in his sporran or the Skian Dhu that nestled against one stout calf inside his stocking.

In one hand the laird clutched a glass of Ramsay's best malt whisky, in the other was a piece of Rita's freshly baked apple tart, deliciously warm and fragrant from the oven.

Captain Rory MacPherson was sublimely happy sitting there in Vale O' Dreip's farmhouse kitchen with its comfortable big armchairs, its brasses and family photographs and wag-at-the-wa' clock, the two brown and white 'wally dugs' sitting sentinel on either side of the ever-burning black-leaded range. It was a cosy peaceful room to be in and the favourite one in the house, the parlour being reserved only for lesser known visitors and the meetings that Ramsay occasionally held for senior members of the Free Kirk.

In summer, however, the kitchen could be uncomfortably hot and today the windows were thrown wide to catch the breezes that blew against the muslin curtains and made them billow lazily about.

Sheba, the laird's haughty and unpredictable Siamese cat who went with him almost everywhere, was taking her ease on the sill, swatting a fly with a sluggish paw, keeping one slanted blue eye on the farm dogs slinking around in the yard over near the sheep pens. Sheba did not have a good relationship with dogs of any kind, with the exception of the Crathmor spaniels which she tolerated because she had to, and Andy's dog, Breck, who had sorted her out very thoroughly when he was just a pup, thus earning her respect for ever more.

The remainder of Kinvara's canine population were creatures that had to be kept very firmly in their lowly place and normally Sheba would have had a go at the Vale O' Dreip sheepdogs. But today it was too warm even for her exotic tastes and she was quite content reclining on the sill, tormenting the fly without actually killing it and looking very graceful and beautiful as she did so.

Meanwhile, her master was gradually coming round to the main reason for his visit, a request to graze and exercise his ponies in a portion of Ramsay's abundant acres. The laird was going in for his new venture in a big way, for as well as pedigree ponies he was also hoping to invest in a small herd of prize Highland cattle and his enthusiasm was boundless. But as the lands of Crathmor had shrunk considerably since the war he simply didn't have the space he needed to expand his breeds and his herds and his tongue was most persuasive as he explained all this to his host.

He paused to take a large swig of whisky before going on to say warmly, 'Emily's been wonderfully supportive. She and the kiddies are down at the paddocks every day, helping with the beasts, fetching and carrying, lifting and laying. We have stable boys, of course, and Sandy Lockhart is a bit of an all-rounder as well as being an excellent pony man. I couldn't have asked for better in that respect and all in all I'm feeling quite pleased with myself these days.'

He cocked an eye at Ramsay. 'Well, what do you say, old chap? I know you make full use of your land but there must be a bit you can spare . . .' He chuckled. 'Seems odd that, me coming cap in hand to Vale O' Dreip when I used to own the damned place. The war undoubtedly changed my circumstances but that's life, one has to bend to the inevitable and no point in complaining.'

Ramsay liked Captain Rory, they had always got on well together and conducted themselves amiably in both social and business affairs. It was also in Ramsay's best interests to keep on the laird's right side and he therefore granted that gentleman the desired grazing permission, the financial side of it being arranged in a barter system that was acceptable to each of them.

They shook hands on it and the laird was making preparations to depart when a rumble of cart wheels, accompanied by loud shouting, made Sheba leap down from the window in fright while Ramsay and his visitor rushed to the door to see what all the fuss was about. A horse and cart were ascending the steep track at a terrific pace, the animal straining and pulling with all his might while the driver whipped him unmercifully.

The farm dogs went crazy. Barking, howling, snarling, they pelted down the road to lunge at the horse's head and nip at his flying heels. The man yelled at them, the girl at his side let out a muffled scream, all hell was let loose in a place that had been drowsily calm and peaceful only moments before.

The farm-hands came running, Linky Black Jack and Ryan Du leading the way, Softy Law bringing up the rear, waving a hefty stick and an expression on his face that belied his nickname. They roared, Ramsay roared, but the dogs paid no heed and were further incensed when the errant whip inflicted stinging lashes of pain on their bodies that made them howl all the louder.

The horse went mad altogether. Flecks of foam flew from his mouth, his eyes rolled wildly. Whinnying and champing he careered into the yard to rear up and kick out in terror, his hooves clattering down on the bonnet of the laird's AEC lorry parked at the farmhouse door.

The master of Crathmor had several modes of transport at his disposal but more than any other he loved his ex-war department lorry and kept it in pristine condition. Emily laughingly complained that he cared more about the AEC than he did for her but on this occasion it wasn't the dents on the bonnet of his precious motor that brought a rush of fiery colour to his face and caused his eyes to nearly pop out of their sockets with rage.

Ryan Du and Softy Law had seized the horse's bridle and between them were managing to calm him down but the only thing the laird could see in those blind moments of fury was the black bearded face of the man with the whip in his hand.

'Declare yourself, you heathen!' Captain Rory shouted. 'As the Lord is my judge, and before I'm very much older, I want to know the name o' the de'il driving this chariot o' cruelty and destruction.'

The man looked down his nose at this. 'If it's anything to you, I'm Joshua Bowman, the new miller of Cladach, and I'd like to know what gives an old goat like you the right to speak to me as if I were dirt.'

With a snarl of unbridled rage the laird reached up to grab Joshua by the throat and pull him down off the cart, 'You *are* dirt, Bowman!' he ground out, spraying Joshua's face with tiny particles of spit as he spoke. 'And for your further information I am Captain Rory MacPherson, master of Crathmor and landlord of much that I survey, including the Mill O' Cladach and its policies, and if I had met you before granting you tenancy of the place I can assure you this incident today would never have happened and all would be as it was before your arrival tainted the very air the rest o' us breathe.'

A tense-faced Joshua whipped his hat from his head and made his apologies, while everyone else stood around watching as the little drama unfolded, with the exception of Rita who was helping an ashen-faced Rebecca out of the cart and placing a motherly arm round the girl's trembling shoulders.

'It's alright.' Rebecca hated herself for having shown weakness in front of everybody. 'It was just the bumping of the cart that made me feel a bit sick.'

'And little wonder.' Rita, sensing the girl's aversion to anything bordering on sympathy, chose her words carefully. 'I feel the same way when my husband is in a hurry and goes helter-skelter down that terrible track of ours. A cup o' tea will soon make you feel better.'

But the laird wasn't finished with Joshua yet. Fingering the heavy ornate buckle of the leather belt that circled his generous middle he told the other man, 'If I ever see you ill-treating that animal again I'll horsewhip *you* and that isn't a promise, Bowman, it's a threat.'

Joshua licked his dry lips. 'It won't happen again. I only did it because he's a lazy brute and I'm sorry now that I got him without knowing his nature. The deal was done by post and the first we saw of him was at Achnasheen station. Perhaps in time he will improve.'

'Only if you do, Bowman. He's a bonny beast and will give good if he gets it in return – as do all creatures – be they animal or human.'

Joshua's lids came down over his strange glittering eyes. He'd had just about enough of his new landlord for one day but somehow he managed to keep his voice even as he said, 'I'm sorry about the damage to your vehicle, I'll have it fixed of course, it should be an easy enough matter to knock the dents out and if I can't do it myself a good blacksmith and a heavy hammer should suffice.'

The laird froze. 'My own man will see to it,' he imparted tersely. 'The AEC isn't just any old lorry you know, it's ex-war department, it's special and it deserves special treatment. But don't worry, Bowman, I'll send you the bill. In that way your conscience will be salved and we will all be the happier.'

Humility of any kind went against the grain of Joshua Bowman. In the space of just a few minutes he had bowed and scraped more to this man than to any other and it was all he could do to make a curt acquiescence before turning away to extend his hand to Ramsay. 'I've been hearing about you as a man of great spiritual inclinations and I was coming over today to make myself known to you. I can only hope that what happened just now won't colour your judgement of me since I earnestly wish us to be good neighbours as well as bedfellows in Christ.'

Ramsay took an immediate and instinctive dislike to the new miller of Cladach and felt uncomfortable at being singled out like this in front of the laird. It was as if he and Joshua already knew one another and were close enough to share some sort of mutual conspiracy. Something in Ramsay rebelled at the label this stranger was putting upon him. Bedfellows in Christ indeed! What an unfortunate turn of phrase for anybody to use. Only a person with a keen sense of his own importance would say such a thing and Ramsay vowed there and then to have as little to do with the man as possible.

The laird, looking red and annoyed, was not for making any sort of conciliatory gesture towards his latest mill tenant and after extracting a comb from the depths of his sporran to smooth his ruffled locks he bundled Sheba into the AEC and made a rather noisy exit down the farm road.

'He's a hard man,' Joshua commented shortly.

'He's a fair man.' Ramsay leapt to the defence of his friend. 'Anybody will tell you that. You haven't been here long enough to know his character and should never judge on a first impression.'

Ramsay pulled himself up at this point. That was exactly

what he had done with Joshua Bowman. The man certainly had asked for it, but hard though Ramsay was, he felt he had reacted too hastily in this instance and, forcing himself to speak politely, he went on to invite the newcomer into the house.

'Though mind,' he quickly added, 'I'm very busy just now and only set aside an hour or so to discuss a business matter with Captain MacPherson.'

'Have I missed something?' Finlay, who had gone off with Aidan and Vaila to the hayfields after lunch, came up with them at that moment, his blue eyes flashing a little because he could see that his father was upset and Finlay enjoyed that since Ramsay was so good at upsetting everyone else.

'Ay, fortunately for you,' Ramsay replied drily, leading the way into the house without enlarging on the subject. Aidan, curiosity getting the better of him, followed the adults inside but Vaila hung back to look at Rebecca who, though still pale and shaken, had no desire to be shut up indoors on a blue day like this.

'I think we should have a talk.' Vaila threw the other girl one of her radiant smiles. 'And I know a good place where we can go for a bit o' privacy.'

Rebecca hesitated, but only for a moment. Accepting Vaila's proffered hand she allowed herself to be led along. Ever since coming to Kinvara just a few days ago she had been aware of a strange sense of elation growing inside her. She could put no name to the feeling but only knew that it was there, making her feel so lighthearted that she cared not where she was going just as long as it afforded her the sort of hiding place she had so longed for throughout her life.

Chapter Nine

'The *latrine!*' A round-eyed Rebecca stared at the sturdy little stone structure built over a fast-rushing stream some distance from the house. It was painted a subtle shade of green and was discreetly hidden from view by the overhanging fronds of silver birch trees and a bank of flowers planted by Rita to 'perfume the air'.

'We call it the wee hoosie,' Vaila explained with a giggle.

'I know what it is,' Rebecca said scathingly. 'We've got one at the mill but when you said a secret place I imagined somewhere much nicer than this.'

'It is nice, the nicest wee hoosie in Calvost next to ours at Keeper's Row. Father put a map of Kinvara on the back of our door and it's fine to sit there and pinpoint all the places that you know. Wee hoosies are great places to get away from everyone and I often go to ours just to think and dream and escape from the house when it gets too crowded.'

'I know what you mean.' Rebecca spoke with feeling. 'A place can be crowded with just a few people in it, all telling you what to do and talking at once.'

The door of the wee hoosie creaked on its hinges as Vaila pushed it open, disturbing a tiny mouse, which scuttled into a corner, and allowing an angry bluebottle to zoom out into the sunshine. Rebecca however was too taken up with the interior of the building to notice anything else and she just stood in the middle of the flagged floor, gazing around her in fascination, her glance going from the vase of fresh pine sprigs on the windowsill to the white-painted walls embellished with a large calendar and a print of a cow in a daisyfield contentedly chewing the cud.

'My Granma Rita put these in here,' Vaila laughed. 'She says if anyone has to be enthroned for a long time the calendar will remind them what day of the week it is and if they aren't in too long they can thank the cow for giving them porridge.'

Rebecca looked startled. 'Porridge?'

'Ay, you know, milk – porridge – one gives it, the other makes you go, so between them they have a big hand in keeping us regular and healthy.'

'Is that why there's a double seater?' Rebecca pointed to the companionably placed twin lids set into a wooden plank. 'In case the porridge works too well and has everybody running at once!'

The girls sat down, one on each seat, and were silent for a moment. Outside, the sun was beating down, the work of the farm went on as usual, but in here it was cool and quiet and it didn't take Rebecca long to decide that it was a good place to hide in after all.

She began to relax and started swinging her legs, Vaila followed suit. Keeping their voices low they began talking. 'I'm sorry about all that stuff I said the other day.' Rebecca looked down at her feet as she spoke. 'It was horribly unfriendly and I didn't mean half of it. I do that when I meet new people for the first time but it's just a front. I lied when I said we had been in the same place for years. I tell fibs all the time to make things seem better than they are. We move around quite a lot, I suppose we're a bit like gypsies really. I can never remember having a real home like other people.'

She took a deep breath. 'I don't know why exactly but it's got something to do with my father. He's never been very well liked, wherever we go people turn against him, nasty things begin to happen, and then we have to move on again. My mother won't speak of it but then, she never speaks much anyway and does everything my father tells her to do. She's Scottish, from the borders, and I think she's always wanted to come back to Scotland but we're no sooner here than my father annoys our landlord and the nastiness starts all over again.'

She went on to tell Vaila about the traumatic encounter they'd had with the owner of the Cladach mill, her eyes flashing when she described the laird's handling of her father and his threat to horsewhip him should the need ever arise.

'He really meant it too and he hinted that he would use his own belt to do it.' Rebecca, quite carried away at this point, spoke gloatingly. 'I've never seen such a wild-looking man as that new landlord of ours. His eyes were popping out of his head and he looked as if he would really have liked to kill my father.'

'The laird wouldn't kill anybody,' Vaila said stoutly. 'He's far too kind for that.'

'I'm not so sure, he certainly went at my father like a terrier goes for a rat.' She sighed. 'I often wish I had a nicer father, one that I could talk to and who would listen to me as a father should a daughter.'

'I've got a father like that and he's coming home tomorrow.'

'Really?' Rebecca eyed Vaila enviously. 'You really are glad about it, aren't you?'

'Of course I'm glad. He's the deputy head keeper o' the Kinvara Light and is away for months at a time. When he comes back we become a whole family again and everybody feels better.'

'That must be nice.' Rebecca sounded wistful. 'It wasn't always like that, though,' Vaila hastened to add, talking too fast in her anxiety to make the other girl feel better. 'I was once a bastard, you know, before my mother married my Uncle Finlay to give me the Sutherland name. Now my mother's dead and I live with my stepmother, Hannah, and Robbie, my real father. It's all quite complicated but makes sense if you stop long enough to work it out.'

'Really?' Rebecca's eyes were sparkling now. 'I'm a bastard too, at least I was till my father properly married my mother. They don't know that I know all this. I found out by accident when I was searching through some papers and found their marriage certificate, dated a year after I was born.'

Vaila stared. 'That must have been terrible for you, to find out like that.'

'Not exactly, I was quite intrigued by the whole idea, and of course it's something I can always keep up my sleeve as a sort of trump card should the need ever arise.'

Vaila began to feel that she had revealed too much about her private affairs and in an effort to mend this she said off-handedly, 'My father never meant to hurt anybody by what he did. My mother was the love o' his life and he would have married her if he hadn't already been married to Hannah.'

Rebecca's eyes flashed. 'I suppose you think you're a better bastard than me!'

'No I don't! That's a silly thing to say.'

They looked at one another and burst out laughing. 'I can't remember when I've had such fun.' Rebecca put a finger under her glasses to wipe her eyes. 'It's so good to have another girl to talk to. Brothers are alright but they can be difficult and my parents never listen to any of us. No doubt you just talk and talk when your father comes home . . .'

She glanced sideways at Vaila. 'I suppose that boy, Joss, must feel that way too, you know, the one with the fair hair and blue eyes and too much to say for himself. Have you known him a long time?'

'All my life. We grew up next door to each other and have always been good friends.'

'You must have lots of friends, I've never had any, not a real one anyway.'

'I'll be your friend if you like.'

Rebecca's eyes went misty. 'I would like that – even better,' her face took on a look of animation, 'let's pretend we're sisters. I had a sister but she died before I was born and I've often wondered what she was like. I've always wanted a sister even more than a friend and now I can have the two rolled into one – that's if you don't already have a sister,' she added hastily.

'I've got Essie, she's my half-sister, but she's only four, so I wouldn't really mind having an older sister as well. I've also got two younger half-brothers, me and Aidan had the same mother but he had a different father. Andy's got the same father but a different mother. I've got lots of other half-relatives as well. It's a long story and sounds a bit confusing but I'll tell you about it some day.'

'Andy's the one who makes funny faces, isn't he, the one in the cart? I was afraid to speak to him in case he didn't understand.'

'Andy understands everything!' Vaila flashed back hotly, her green eyes sparking with indignation. 'He's got cerebral palsy and can't talk or walk very well but he knows more than you or me ever will and one day he will prove it to everybody!'

'Alright, don't get so worked up. I've never come across

anybody like him before and didn't know what to expect.' She gazed pleadingly at Vaila. 'You will still be my sister, won't you? In spite of what I said about your brother?'

'Alright,' Vaila replied grudgingly, 'Only don't talk like that about Andy again. It hurts him when people think he's daft and all the time he's better than anybody.'

'That's settled then.' Rebecca, afraid that Vaila might change her mind, raced quickly on. 'We really could be sisters because we've both been bastards and we've both got dark hair although you're much prettier than me since you don't have to wear glasses. You've also got a wicked temper like mine, I saw a bit of it the other day and knew you had spirit. My brother Caleb's got a temper but he stoppers it up and explodes every now and then. Nathan's different, he's never been good at standing up for himself and I know he's unhappy because I hear him crying sometimes when he thinks no one is listening. I try to help him but it isn't always easy and our mother never speaks up for any of us but just acts as if she doesn't know what's going on round about her.'

The flood gates had opened for Rebecca, it was as if she was letting go of everything she had bottled up for so long, pouring out her heart as she sat there on the toilet seat in Vale O' Dreip's wee hoosie, Vaila listening and feeling a sympathy growing in her for someone as lonely as Rebecca.

'It will be different when you come to school after the holidays,' Vaila said when she could at last get a word in. 'You'll make lots of friends and so will your brothers.'

'No, it won't be like that, we've hardly ever been to school, we've all got to do our share of work in the mill and in between times our mother gives us lessons and our father makes us pray all the time. We have to get down on our knees and give thanks for everything and are only allowed out when every last chore is done and every prayer has been said for that particular part of the day. Even then we can't go anywhere that isn't approved of and must be back at a certain time according to the rules of the house.'

'Is that why you wear that hat and that frock? Is it a sort of uniform?'

'Of course not, silly, it's just that we mustn't be vain about ourselves and girls in particular have to cover their bodies in raiments of a sober and uncomely nature.'

She was sounding like a parrot again but in the next minute she gave a little giggle. 'I wonder why there are two.'

'Two what?'

'Toilet seats. Surely no one would want to do *that* with someone else in beside them.'

'We're doing it.'

'No we aren't, we're just sitting here talking.' They looked at one another and Rebecca's eyes gleamed. 'Let's.'

'Umm, I don't know, I don't really need.'

'Oh, come on, don't be a spoilsport, I'm dying to go.

It must be the sound of all that running water under us.'

'Oh, alright, I suppose there's no harm in it.'

They lifted the lids. Beneath them the stream churned and foamed and made their stomachs turn over. 'What if there's someone down there looking up,' Rebecca hazarded.

'Maybe Johnny Lonely searching for brown trout,' Vaila answered readily. The comical tone of her voice made Rebecca clutch her middle and soon they were both shrieking and rolling about.

'Now I really do have to go,' Rebecca said at last and before another second passed they sat down and with one accord gave full rein to the demands of nature and were quite delighted with themselves afterwards.

'There.' Rebecca arranged the rough material of her dress sedately round her ankles. 'Now we're real friends as well as earth sisters and won't ever be shy of one another again.'

The door creaked, Rita's surprised face appeared in the aperture. 'This is where you are! I've been looking for you everywhere.'

The girls clapped their hands to their mouths and ran off, and not even the sight of Joshua impatiently waiting beside the cart with a thunderous expression on his face could quell the new-found sense of happiness that his daughter had discovered that afternoon in Vale O' Dreip's wee hoosie.

Chapter Ten

There was a great feeling of anticipation at No. 6 Keeper's Row. Rob was at last coming home after an absence of three months and the family had been up at the crack of dawn, getting in each other's way, Essie positioning herself at the window to watch for the relief boat coming round the point, even though the time for its arrival was an hour away yet. Essie didn't mind. She was quite happy to sit on the padded window-seat and play with her dolls, looking like one herself in her ribbons and bows and little pink frock trimmed with pearly buttons and waterfall frills.

'Will Dadda bring me back a new doll?' she asked her mother for the umpteenth time and Hannah patiently explained for the umpteenth time that there were no shops out there on the black reefs that surrounded the lighthouse and they would all have to be content with just Rob himself.

'I want a new doll,' Essie persisted, pouting a little and tugging irritably at the ribbon that held her silken hair back from her face.

'You'll get one for your birthday when it comes,' Hannah promised as she bent down to plant a kiss on the child's peachy cheek. But Essie pouted worse than ever and struggled out of her mother's embrace. Vaila and Andy looked at one another because their little sister was spoiling the day with her sulks and never earning even a rebuke from the woman whose level of tolerance was normally limited.

'Go outside with Vaila and Andy for a while.' A very slight shadow of impatience crossed Hannah's face. 'It's too nice a day for you all to be stuck indoors – and take the brute with you,' she added, referring to Breck, who she had never really tolerated in the house, maintaining that his place ought to be in one of the sheds, since he was 'forever trailing in dirt on his great hairy paws'.

She made to help Essie down off the sill but the child squirmed out of her grasp and went stomping out of the house to throw her doll into a muddy puddle. 'Mamma's bad,' she stated baldly and, as if to prove her point, she placed the heel of one shoe on top of the doll's face and ground it into the mud.

Vaila and Andy looked at her in surprise since she was normally a placid, small being who seldom allowed anything to ruffle her feathers. But a new Essie had emerged that day and both Vaila and Andy experienced a faint twinge of unease as they heard the vehemence of her words and saw rebellion twisting her flawless features.

'Mamma isn't bad,' Vaila said with a frown. 'You're the one who's bad, Essie, ruining the day for the rest o' us and doing that to your doll. Pick it up this minute and I'll take it in and wash it before Mamma sees it.'

Essie, however, was having none of that, and further mutiny was declared when she lowered her brows, stuck her thumb in her mouth, and began swaying from side to side, all the while watching her big sister in a manner that dared retaliation.

'Right.' Vaila had had enough. Taking the child firmly by the hand she yanked her over to the puddle and was about to make her pick up the doll when Hannah appeared at the door to stare at the scene in amazement.

'Vaila! Why on earth are you treating your sister like that? Let her go this minute and behave yourself!'

Vaila opened her mouth to speak, just as Essie burst into tears and sobbed, 'Vaila threw Essie's dolly in a puddle! She's bad! Bad to Essie!'

The two older children, horrified by this, could only gape at the red-faced Essie but Hannah had enough to say for everybody. 'Into the house and up to your room this minute. Vaila! How could you do that to your little sister? And you old enough to know better. Wait till your father hears about this. He might feel differently about his blue-eyed girl when he finds out what she gets up to when his back is turned.'

Without a word Vaila ran into the house and up the stairs to throw herself on her bed and cry her eyes out while down below Andy was doing his best to defend her.

But he couldn't get the words to come out, and the

harder he tried the more tongue-tied he became, till Hannah lost patience with him and took Essie into the kitchen to soothe her with offerings of milk and biscuits.

'There, there, my wee lamb,' she crooned into the child's ear. 'No one will hurt you while I'm here, you know Mamma loves you and will look after you always.'

Essie remained perfectly still on her mother's knee and Hannah never saw the look of sufferance on her daughter's face as she endured the cuddles and the kisses and let the words of comfort wash over her. Because Essie wasn't really listening, she was thinking about Dadda and what he might bring her if he didn't bring her a dolly. And she might get a new one of these anyway when he saw the state her old one was in and how no amount of washing would restore it back to its original self.

Essie hugged herself and got down off her mother's lap. With an angelic smile she went out of the kitchen and climbed the stairs to Vaila's room where she clambered onto the bed, put her chubby arms around her sister's troubled shoulders, and said she was sorry.

Unable to resist the beguiling tone of the little girl's voice, Vaila sat up and dried her tears. 'Promise you won't tell lies like that again, Essie.'

'I promise, Vaila.'

'Honest injun?'

'Honest injun.'

Vaila got off the bed and picking Essie up she carried her downstairs and said to Hannah, 'It's alright now,

Hannah, I'll get Essie's doll and wash it and then we can all get ready to go and meet the boat when it comes in.'

'Ay,' Hannah nodded, glad to rid herself of the niggle of guilt that had been pricking her conscience since her hasty words to her stepdaughter. 'And I think it would be better not to mention this to your father after all, Vaila. He's been away a long time and we want his homecoming to be a happy one. I shouldn't have shouted at you – but you understand about Essie, don't you? She's very young yet, no more than a baby, and we all have to protect her as much as we can.'

'Ay, Hannah, I understand,' Vaila agreed, even though she didn't and was still smarting from the unfairness that had been meted out to her.

'The boat's coming!' Andy had found his voice and spoke loudly and clearly. He had climbed into his cart in readiness, Breck was standing by waiting to be hitched up, all enmity was forgotten in the excitement of the moment.

'Dadda! Dadda!' Essie clapped her hands with glee and rushed outside while Hannah tidied her hair in the mirror above the sink and applied a dab of powder to her cheeks. She knew she looked older than her thirty-five years, her brown hair was sprinkled with grey, her sallow skin seldom looked anything else but dull, no matter what she did to make it look better. Her one redeeming feature was her amber brown eyes, and today they were shining back at her from the mirror because soon she would see her man again and the responsibilities that she often found so hard to bear would be halved. Rob was such a rock of a man, so able to stand up to any crises that arose, possessed of a strength of mind that she knew would never be hers . . .

But enough of that! This was no time to be morbid. Turning away from the mirror she went outside with the intention of seeing to Andy, only to find that Vaila had already secured him safely in his seat and had hitched Breck up to the cart. Another spasm of guilt seized Hannah. She shouldn't have been so hard on her stepdaughter, it had been such a small matter really. It was natural for children to argue with one another and Essie could be trying at times. 'You're a good lass, Vaila,' she said quietly, placing her hand on the child's curly head. 'I don't know what I'd do without you sometimes.'

'I like doing things for Andy.' Vaila sounded a bit distant and Hannah sighed. 'It isn't just Andy, it's everything, to me you're like my own daughter and I couldn't have asked for better.'

By now, all the families who lived in Keeper's Row had spied the boat coming in and were emerging from their houses to make their way down to the harbour.

'I see you've beaten me to it for once.' Janet Morgan came over to Hannah, her face alight because she missed her husband dreadfully when he was away and could hardly contain her delight at his imminent return. Janet was twenty-eight and young for her years, blonde and blue-eyed and so slightly made it seemed impossible that she was the mother of a strapping boy like Joss. But Janet had married Big Jock Morgan when she was just seventeen and had very quickly become pregnant. She and Jock had been overjoyed when a son was born to them and would have had 'an army of bairns' by now had not the doctor told them that Joss was to be the one and only.

By way of compensation Janet had fostered a number of children over the years, the most fondly remembered of these being little Bonny Barr who had come to Janet from the nearby Fountainwell Orphanage. But Bonny had gone back to her natural mother after a while and though more children had followed, Janet hadn't been able to bear the pain of parting with them and had decided against taking any more for the forseeable future.

Joss was therefore a treasured child but for all that he had never been mollycoddled. His parents had encouraged independence in him and were proud of the way he was able to make decisions for himself and of how well he could handle the world around him.

At Janet's words, Hannah nodded, pleased enough to see her young neighbour, though there were times when she felt irritated by Janet's bubbling enthusiasm for the most trivial incidents, especially those concerning her son. On this occasion, however, Hannah felt just as buoyant as Janet and was able to say enthusiastically, 'The bairns have been awake since first light, waiting for the boat coming. It seems so long since Rob went away and no doubt you feel the same about Jock.'

'Ay, indeed.' Janet patted Breck and took Essie's dimpled little hand when that young lady held it out with the sweetest of smiles on her rosy lips. 'Joss went off ages ago.' Janet went on, 'He likes to watch the puffers coming in and of course, rain or shine, he never misses the boat bringing his father home.'

'My dadda's coming home.' Essie stated firmly.

'Ay, he is that, and he'll be surprised when he sees how big you've grown since he went away.' Janet was entranced by Hannah's tiny daughter, a wonder in her that anyone as awkward and as plain as Hannah could have produced a child as beautiful as Essie. Janet had often thought it was as well that her neighbour had been blessed in such a way, she had been so miserable after Andy's birth, blaming Rob for the boy's defects, taking her feelings out on the people around her. All that was in the past however, she had settled well in the community she had once shunned. She was a good neighbour and a reliable friend and had plenty to smile about when she spoke about her daughter and was even quite proud of Andy in her own peculiar way.

'He's bringing me a dolly,' Essie continued with conviction, gazing at her mother as if anticipating an argument. Janet glanced from mother to daughter and wondered at the rebellion in Essie's tones. She was always such a sunny little creature but lately Janet had noticed fresh quirks in her nature, a sulkiness when she was reprimanded, an unwillingness to do anything she was told.

'Spoiled rotten,' was the opinion of Janet's cousin,

Kathy, who once or twice had given Essie's chubby fingers a light smack when she had dipped them defiantly into the lapbag that Kathy always carried to hold her precious knitting. 'Thinks she can get away with anything and of course, wi' a mother like Hannah and a grandma like Harriet, she does. Children need discipline. When my own lot were small I just yanked down their pants and gave them a good walloping and no harm did it do them. Oh, ay, a firm hand brings out the respect in them – just like puppydogs when they pee all over the floor and chew things up – purl two knit two together, wrap wool round the needles every sixth stitch, next row.'

Janet had laughed at Cousin Kathy's simple philosophies but somewhere at the back of her mind she knew the truth of the words and had tried to exert a bit of firmness over Essie when she was helping herself to sweeties from the jar on the shelf and wandering boldly into rooms that were out of bounds to visitors, no matter how small. Then, there was the business of the missing trinkets from the dressing table in Janet's room. Nothing of value really, and she could easily have mislaid them, no reason to make a fuss, none at all, and Essie had pleaded innocence when she had been asked, her lower lip trembling the way it did when she was getting ready to cry.

Janet had shrugged the matter off. The things would turn up when she was least expecting them, such a trivial incident anyway . . . even so she wondered about it and caught herself watching Essie's movements whenever she was in visiting – which was often as the child loved nothing better than to visit No. 5 of the Row . . .

'Oh!' At Essie's words Vaila's hand flew to her mouth. 'I just remembered something!' she cried and went running back to the house to pluck her sister's doll from its muddy grave. Into the house she flew with it to throw it into the sink with the intention of washing it later. She wasn't going to miss the relief boat coming in, not for Essie or for anybody else and she shut the door behind her with a snap and raced to catch up with the others.

Chapter Eleven

Half the village it seemed was at the harbour, some to collect household goods from the small coaster that was tied up at the pier; others to fill barrows and carts with coal from the puffer known as *The Blythe Spirit*. Children fished or pottered about in boats while old men, for whom it had become a ritual to sit on the pink stone walls and watch the world go by, puffed at their pipes and made sage observations about the activities of the people around them.

Big Bette was there that day for two reasons, one to supervise the unloading of a new bed from the coaster, the other to see her husband off on his final stint of duty on the Kinvara Light.

She seemed however to be more interested in the bed than she was in Mungo, and she stood there on the pier, waving her massive arms about as she bawled out orders to the man operating the ship's derrick while her three children scurried to her bidding, including her eldest son Joe who some said would never leave her apron strings though he was now a muscular young man of nineteen.

Quite a few of the villagers were also interested in

Bette's new bed and the comments flew as various hessian-wrapped bundles descended into the back of Shug Law's cart, Mungo having borrowed both it and its owner for the occasion. Sorry snickered in her shafts as the ancient cart sagged on its rusty springs and Shug hastened to pacify her with a nosebag filled with oats.

'Would you look at the size o' that mattress,' Mattie MacPhee commented in shocked tones as the item in question came into view, swinging unsteadily on the end of the hook and losing much of its wrappings in the process.

'It's big enough for four elephants lying tail to tail and still enough room for a little one.'

'Och, that's a bitty strong,' Dokie Joe mildly chided his wife. 'You have to be realistic as well as fair, Mattie.'

'Three elephants then,' Mattie amended grudgingly.

'And what would they be doing with three elephants in a bed?' Cathie MacPhee said laughingly.

'Well, knowing Mungo, he would find a use for the spare one,' Annie MacDuff put in, fiddling with a hair curler that she had omitted to remove when she was getting ready to accompany her husband to the harbour.

'The spare elephant?' Cathie looked startled.

'Och, no, the spare whatever. I'm sure Mungo wouldn't mind having a go at anybody who was foolish enough to get in beside him.'

'Wheesht, woman,' Jimmy 'Song' MacDuff said in a

theatrical voice. 'You're talking about one o' our senior kirk elders and a fine upstanding citizen o' the parish.'

Annie ignored him. 'I hear tell that Bette is going to store the bed in her shed till she and Mungo move out o' the Row. I'm sure I don't know why they want a new bed anyway. The old one looked perfectly good to me when I went to see Bette thon time she was laid up with a sprained ankle.'

'It will be the springs,' Catrina Blair said meaningfully. 'Bette and Mungo aren't exactly built like wood nymphs and we all know the sort o' things they get up to whenever they get the chance. It's a wonder to me they managed to limit their family to just three when they're so fond o' climbing under the sheets together.'

'Ay, not like yourself, Catrina, with just the one,' Mattie said, her gaze travelling to little Euan playing about nearby. 'You and Colin have been very subdued on that score and here was me thinking you would have had an army o' bairns by now. Colin was such a ready wee chap in the old days. It seems a shame – when he would have made such a good father too.'

She allowed her words to trail off and Catrina's cheeks flamed. It was as if the nosy besom knew that Euan wasn't Colin's son! Was it becoming so obvious? And if Mattie had guessed was she the only one? Or was it something that people whispered about among themselves as their memories took them back to the days of the young and carefree Catrina – the girl she had been before Ramsay Sutherland had robbed her of her youth and freedom.

Catrina drew in her breath. She had never forgiven Ramsay Sutherland for what he had done to her, never, for he had not only violated her body but her mind as well. Almost six years had passed since that dreadful night but the memory of it was so strong it sometimes seemed that it had happened just yesterday. And the cheek of him! Actually suggesting she and he should get together again that time she had met him in the street. Offering to pay her if she agreed to see him, as if money was the answer to everything. Oh, she would get even with him somehow! One day he would be sorry he had ever laid his lecherous hands on her . . .

She glanced at her son, she couldn't help but notice that he was beginning to display certain mannerisms that reminded her of Ramsay, the way his eyes flashed when he was angry, the arrogant expression that occasionally flitted over his face. God help her! She had never taken to him, had never been able to reach out to him in the way a mother should. Colin had suffered too, she knew how selfless he'd been, marrying her to give her child his name but more and more as the years passed she was unable to respond to him and hated herself when she saw how unhappy he often looked, how eagerly he tried to please her and make her love him . . .

'You aye did have a mite too much to say for yourself,

Mattie MacPhee.' Connie, the eldest of the Simpson girls, flew to her sister's defence, 'Colin *is* a good father in case you haven't noticed.'

Catrina had recovered and nodded in agreement. 'Ay, and who are you to judge anyway? If we were all like you there would indeed be a population explosion. You have enough bairns to start a Sunday school and enough cheek to have another if notion and age permits.'

'Well!' Mattie's rosy face took on an even rosier glow. 'Marriage has certainly changed you, Catrina, and it hasn't done you much good either, Connie. Maybe you should change places for a bit and see what happens. In the old days the Simpson sisters were renowned for their sense o' adventure and it would be a pity to let anything stand in your way now.'

The sisters glared at her and would have had more to say on the subject had not Cousin Kathy said thoughtfully, 'I was after hearing some talk that Mungo might be opening a gent's barber's shop in the village and I was wondering if there's any truth in it.'

'Ach, it will just be a rumour,' snorted Annie. 'Where would he learn to cut hair, I'd like to know. The man's never done anything else in his life but light lamps in yonder lighthouse.'

'It seems he learned it in the war.' Dolly Law paused to stuff a few shreds of tobacco into her clay pipe with a nicotine-stained finger before going on, 'He was in the Merchant Navy at the time and told Shug that he was such a dab hand wi' the shears the men used to give him their rations o' rum to do their hair.'

'Never!' Mattie burst out laughing. 'He'll never make a go of it. None o' the men would pay good sillar for a haircut when they can get it done for nothing. I just put a bowl over Dokie Joe's dome and snip, snip, the job's done in minutes. He goes about for a few days looking like a monk but it soon grows in and I've never heard him complaining.'

'He wouldn't dare,' Catrina said with a sniff. Mattie looked at her, Catrina looked back, unable to keep a straight face, then broke into infectious giggles, and tempers were restored as the women aired their various opinions regarding the affairs of Mungo and his wife.

'The relief boat's coming!' The cry went up and with its utterance the scene instantly changed. Groups of chattering people broke up, women and children surged forward to shade their eyes and watch the boat gliding over a sea that was calm and blue and void of violence of any sort.

As the boat came into the harbour Bette grabbed hold of her husband's hand and despite the fact that he was a big burly man with 'hands on him like meat cleavers' as Bette herself had often said, he winced as her plump fingers crushed his. 'Your last time at the light, Mungo.' She strove to sound glad about this, even as she mentally wondered how she would cope, having him under her feet all day. 'You'll be back home in a blink and then we'll have to see about opening up that little business you and me spoke about earlier.'

Mungo didn't look too enthusiastic about this. He wanted space to think about his future before coming to any hasty decisions. He was looking forward to devoting more of his time to a few of his favourite hobbies but Bette, as if reading his mind, said briskly, 'You'll have plenty of opportunity to have a wee think about everything in the next few months and while you're doing that I'll be keeping an eye open for suitable premises. There's a nice wee place next to the Chandlery in Smiddy Lane. It's just a storeroom really but I spoke to Jack Harkness about renting it and he seemed only too glad o' the chance to make a few bob.'

Her round dimpled face beamed into Mungo's. 'Och, don't look so worried, it will all come out right in the end, and just think how nice it will be for us to be exchanging all the gossip and talk when we put our feet up at the end o' a working day.'

She dropped a kiss on his cheek and ordered fourteen-year-old Babs to do likewise. Babs, big, busty, and buxom, got the operation over with quickly, too taken up with ogling a young fisherlad to pay much attention to anything else.

The boys solemnly shook their father's hand and said how much they would miss him. 'You be good, you lot,' Mungo said gruffly, a twinge of emotion touching his florid face. 'See and look after your mother and don't be getting into any mischief.'

'Ay, Da, we'll be good.' All three youngsters spoke the words in chorus, so used to uttering the same farewell year after year that none of them, not even Joe, felt they were too old for such simplistic promises.

'And I'll look after the new bed,' Bette hissed into her husband's ear. 'It will be fine and cosy in the shed and once it's settled into its new home we will have a grand time to ourselves trying it out for size.'

Mungo's ears reddened a little and he glanced round quickly to see if anyone was listening. Satisfying himself as to the contrary he dared to tweak Bette's meaty bottom and say in a breathy whisper, 'You do that, lass – and see and keep your hand on your halfpenny till I come back.'

Bette cackled her gleeful appreciation of this, Mungo moved away to join the rest of the relief crew standing on the cobbled edge of the pier, anxious to be on their way now that all the goodbyes had been said. It was always like this at the last moments of parting, the womenfolk and children putting a brave face on it, only too aware that the occasion was traumatic enough without tears adding to the feeling of gloom.

Annie MacDuff ran forward to enclose her husband in a last fond embrace. The curler that had been clasped in her hand somehow got entangled in the hair at the nape of his neck and in the laughter that accompanied his frantic efforts to remove it sorrows were forgotten and the mood was lightened for everyone.

Chapter Twelve

The returning keepers were descending on their families. Janet and Joss pounced on Big Morgan, sometimes known as Morgan the Magnificent because of his marvellous physique and bearing and his splendid blond beard and flowing hair tied back from his face with a little black band.

'Dadda! Dadda!' Essie had spied her father and began jumping up and down with excitement. Rob dropped his bag on the cobbles and came rushing over to embrace his family, standing back to gaze at them, the joy of the moment bringing a glow to his ruggedly handsome features.

'You've grown,' he laughed, tousling Andy's dark head, smiling at Vaila, lifting Essie into his strong brown arms and kissing her nose. 'Even Breck.'

'Not me too, I hope,' Hannah said, taking him seriously.

He put his arm round her waist. 'Well, maybe in all the right places,' he returned teasingly.

'Rob.' She coloured and moved away from him and he found himself wishing that she would forget what other people might be thinking and let herself go just once in a while.

'Robbie.' Vaila's hand curled into his as she murmured his name. The sun was glinting on the midnight black of her hair, her green eyes were sparkling as she gazed up at him and with a catch of his breath he saw that she was growing more like her mother with every passing day. And the sense of fun that had been in Morna was rapidly developing in her daughter. She was droll and mischievous and could make quaint remarks with such a straight face that very often it seemed that she wasn't being funny at all. But he who loved her best knew her best and this usage of his Christian name was a special little intimacy between them, a signal to one another that they knew about things that other people didn't.

Only Morna had ever called him Robbie, now he and his daughter shared that secret bond, one that had known its beginnings before she had even discovered that he was her father. Long ago and wonderful days, of laughter, of sunshine, of Morna, filling his heart and his soul with delight and sweet fulfilment that could never be surpassed. He had never forgotten how it had been with them and knew that he never would. His first and only love . . . so far it sometimes seemed, yet often so near it was as if he had said goodbye to her only yesterday, especially when he gazed towards that little white house standing down there at the edge of the ocean. Oir na Cuan. Where it had all begun, where it had finished . . .

'Rob! How nice to see you again.' Catherine Dunbar was suddenly there, smiling up at him, eyes flashing, skin aglow, her hair a bright beacon in the sunlight. Impulsively she reached up and planted a kiss on his cheek, much to his surprise and to Hannah's dismay. The impudence of the girl! Who was she to take such liberties with another woman's husband? In broad daylight too for all the world to see. And her a teacher of young children who ought to be setting some good examples. Hannah glowered long and hard at Catherine but that young lady, quite unperturbed, smiled at Andy and said she would call in to see him soon, before turning away to watch the various activities going on at the pier.

Hannah was right on one count. All the immediate world had seen Catherine's action, and Mattie MacPhee, with her keen appetite for gossip, was only too ready to pick up on this latest juicy morsel. 'Well, well, would you look at that now,' she murmured cryptically, 'our very own squeaky clean teacher behaving in the manner o' a Jezebel.'

'Ay, and our very own Hannah from Ayr looking none too pleased about it,' Jessie MacDonald put in avidly. 'Kinvara is going to the dogs these days, strangers butting their way in, pinching our menfolk from under our noses, changing a way o' life that has worked well for centuries.'

Mattie grinned into Jessie's tight-lipped countenance. 'Would I be right in thinking you're still hankering after Charlie Campbell of Butterburn Croft? Him that married Harriet Houston from Ayr who came here as a stranger and stayed to become a Kinvara wife? Ay, me, Jessie, you've got it bad right enough but all that is history now, new things are happening all the time, and it looks to me as if Miss Catherine Dunbar has more than the alphabet on her mind if that glint in her eye is anything to go by.'

'Yes, indeed,' Maisie Whiskers, wife of Willie the blacksmith, nodded sagely. 'Hannah from Ayr had better look to her laurels. I saw the way she avoided her man when he tried to give her a bit squeeze just now – and him just back after all these months away. She's a cold fish is that one and would do well to try to please him more when there's many a warm-blooded woman would give an eye tooth for a few minutes alone wi' the likes o' Rob Sutherland.'

'Ay, well, there's one thing for sure, you won't be one o' them.' Maudie Sutherland, puffing and huffing in her efforts to collect some supplies from *The Blythe Spirit* before it upped anchor, was in time to hear the tail end of Maisie's remarks. Hoisting her chubby two-year-old son onto the generous platform of her bosom, holding onto the hand of her lively three-year-old daughter, she treated the blacksmith's wife to an unusually belligerent glare. 'That kind o' talk won't get you anywhere, Maisie Whiskers,' she went on, her rosy, good-natured face taking on a stern expression. 'I won't have anybody talking about my brother-in-law behind his back and that goes for my sister-in-law too. As for eye teeth . . .' Mischief deepening her dimples she gazed long and hard at Maisie's rather sunken mouth and shook her head sadly, 'Only a memory, Maisie, only a memory.'

With that she took herself off, leaving a flabbergasted

Maisie to gape after her and stutter, 'What did she mean by that, I'd like to know, and her hardly five minutes in the place. And the affront! Addressing me by my nickname straight to my face! Oh, I know well enough what folks call me behind my back but coming straight out with it like that is the height o' bad manners. Mind you,' she sniffed and put her nose in the air, 'what else can you expect from these city folk? No breeding, no reserve, yet somehow they worm their way in and take over before you can blink. That young woman is getting too big for her boots since she went and wed herself to Finlay Sutherland and I for one will think twice before passing the time o' day with her again.'

'Strangers,' Jessie reiterated with utmost satisfaction. 'Next thing we know the gentry will be marrying commoners and there will be no order left at all then, none at all.'

'Ach, you're away behind the times, Jessie,' Mattie said forcibly. 'When The MacKernon picked that American lass to be his wife he was marrying out o' his class as you put it. It isn't so unusual for that kind o' thing to happen.'

'Ay, but she's from New England and she's rich,' Jessie went on doggedly. 'People like her are gentry in their own way, even if they don't have titles. Besides, she speaks posh for an American, so in a way they're evenly matched.'

'He married her for her money and she married him for his title,' Maisie said flatly. 'It's as simple as that. Gentry folks bend the rules when it suits them and it did The MacKernon more good than harm when he went and wed himself to her ladyship.'

The gossips were enjoying themselves. The harbour was an agreeable place to be that sunlit summer's day with all its comings and goings and so many people to observe and wonder about. Then something happened that distracted everybody's attention. Sorry had just reached the end of the pier with her load when without warning she collapsed in her shafts and sank down to the ground, eyes rolling, flanks heaving, nostrils distended, flecks of foam gathering on her lips. A shuddering breath shook her, a low moan issued from her throat, she lifted her head for one brief moment before sinking back to lie perfectly still and quiet on the cobbles.

'Come on, lass.' Shug bent down and grabbed her reins. 'This is no time to be playing games. Get up, we've got work to do!'

But there was to be no more awakening for Sorry. By the time her owners realised this fact a crowd had gathered and the comments began.

'You had no business allowing such a poor sick beast to carry such loads,' said one bystander.

'Ay, she was far too old for all the heavy work you made her do,' voiced another. 'No wonder the poor cratur' just went and died on you.'

'Ach, she was aye like that,' Shug hastened to defend himself. 'Even when she was quite young she had that bedraggled look about her. That was why we called her

Sorry, the name just suited her. But she was happy enough wi' us, we treated her like a bairn, she had everything any horse could ever want, right down to a sup o' my own ale when she was thirsty and a blanket from my very own bed in the worst nights o' winter.'

Dolly was too stunned to say anything. She just stood there staring down at her horse, her clay pipe hanging from her mouth, her face crumpling as she began to take in the full import of what had happened. 'My poor old friend,' she eventually whispered, tears marking a grimy course down her cheeks. 'What are we to do without you, I'd like to know? You were aye there when you were needed and though you grumbled and groaned you served us right well and I'm going to miss you sorely.'

'Ay,' Shug's voice had taken on a husky note. 'She even knew her own way to the inn and back and many's the night she took me home without so much as a tug o' the reins to guide her along.'

It was too much for Dolly. Falling on her knees she put her arms round the mare's neck and simply bawled with grief.

'Here, what about my bed!' Big Bette had arrived on the scene and wasted no time on sentiment. 'How are we to get it home, I'd like to know?'

'Is that all you can think about at a moment like this?' The villagers had changed face, the sight of Dolly clinging to her dead horse bringing a lump to even the most hardened throat. 'The poor beast has drawn her last and here you are worrying about that jumbo-sized bed o' yours.'

'The size o' my bed is *my* business.' Bette returned grimly. 'I paid good sillar for the use o' your horse and cart, Shug Law, and if you can't deliver the goods then I want my money back before I'm very much older.'

Shug and Dolly glowered at her long and hard, everyone else did the same and muttered to one another about her hard-heartedness. The problem of getting both Sorry and her load off the pier seemed insurmountable until help arrived from a most unexpected quarter. Joshua Bowman had seen the commotion as he was driving past the pier and now he came to offer his help, being very mannerly and courteous and removing his hat at the sight of the dead horse as if in a sign of respect.

Within minutes he had organised help. Several pairs of strong hands went to his aid as he unhitched his own cart and replaced it with that of the Laws. He then persuaded a local farmer to bring down his Clydesdale horse and some suitable farm implements so that Sorry could be transported back to her home and the 'decent burial' that her owners wanted her to have.

'Here, he's no' such a bad soul,' Maisie Whiskers observed. 'All that talk about him being the de'il in disguise and here he is behaving like an angel.'

'Ay, it's as well no' to believe all you hear,' Jessie agreed solicitously. 'All that business about him ill-using his horse and having words wi' the laird might just be a lot o' exaggeration. Captain Rory can be a devil himself betimes and might just have felt like putting the new miller in his place. The man looks genuinely upset about Sorry and certainly seems anxious to please.'

'Never judge by first good impressions,' Dokie Joe intoned meaningfully. 'I myself saw him using his whip too harshly on that poor beast o' his and I for one am no' taken in by him. The laird must have had good reason to have lost his rag with Joshua Bowman. I've worked to Captain Rory for a long time now and know him better than most. He would never chastise anybody just for the hell o' it and while he might be an old rogue at times he's aye been fair and honest in his dealings wi' his fellow humans.'

'Ay, ay, you're right enough there, Dokie.' Mattie agreed with her husband though there was a twinkle in her eye as she went on, 'Except when he's plotting against The MacKernon and pinching his timber – like thon time he made you and your pals cut down dozens of trees then took all the credit for handing them out to the bairns at Christmas.'

'Ach well, that was different,' Dokie Joe reddened at the memory of himself and a few other stalwarts humping the trees round the village in an effort to atone to the laird for having been caught stealing them – only to discover later that they belonged to The MacKernon who had been tucked away safely in America when the incident had taken place. 'That was just Captain Rory's idea of a joke, he's basically an honourable and sociable man, one who is normally only too ready to welcome strangers into the place and make them feel at home.'

Joshua Bowman was ready to go. He beckoned to Bette who sailed over very regally and graciously allowed him to help her climb into the seat beside him. 'Keeper's Row, isn't it?' he asked pleasantly. Bette nodded, he took up the reins and allowed Jacob to set off at a sedate pace, giving him the chance to get the feel of the heavy burden at his back.

Bette waved rather haughtily as she sailed past her cronies and Mattie's nostrils flared. 'Hmph, if anyone's a hypocrite she is! Only this morning she was decrying Joshua Bowman and saying what a monster he was, now look at her, all honey and fat smiles, doing and saying anything just for the sake of getting that bed o' hers safely up the road.'

'Never mind her, look at the teacher.' Maisie indicated the spot where Catherine stood, gazing after Rob and his family as they made their way homewards. 'Moonstruck, that's what she is, as possessed as any lovesick lass could be. If she could follow Rob home she would do so in a minute and if Hannah wasny there she might even climb into bed wi' him given half a chance.'

'Oh, here, that's a bit too much,' Dokie Joe protested. 'You women are the limit when you get going and it's time I went home. Come on, Mattie, the bairns will be waiting for their tea and you've done enough blethering for one day.'

'Well, of all the nerve, just like a man to complain after

listening and enjoying it all! And why can't you make the tea for a change? You're as able as I am and they're your bairns as well as mine.'

They went off arguing. The roar of an engine split the air and a very up-to-date MG sports car went flashing past. Jessie looked at Maisie.

'These motor cars are taking over the place. Before you know it they'll be everywhere, the roads will be that congested we'll all be killed just crossing the street to go our messages.'

'Ay,' Maisie mournfully agreed. 'My Willie will be out o'a job then, no smiddy to run, no horses to shoe, just motor cars fleeing about and the air reeking wi' fumes and noise.'

Commiserating with one another they went off, the harbour was quiet and deserted again, except for Dolly and Shug waiting for someone to come and help them take Sorry's pitiful remains home to their last resting place.

Chapter Thirteen

One of the first things Rob noticed when he got home was Essie's muddy doll lying in the sink. 'I see we have a casualty here,' he laughed, 'a case of into the washtub and out on the line to dry.'

'It fell in a puddle,' Hannah said by way of explanation.

'I want a new dolly,' Essie said firmly. 'Wee Fay's got lots of them in The Dunny window. Can I get a new one, Dadda?'

'That one will be fine when she's had a good bath. You only got her a couple o' months ago on your birthday, Essie.'

Essie put her chin on her chest and pouted. Rob gazed at her for a moment or two then he turned away and dug into his bag. 'Look, maybe this will make up for your doll. I made it specially for you, a little jewel case to store your beads and baubles in.'

But Essie refused to take the box and went stomping out to the back garden without a word to anybody. Rob frowned and shook his head but he was too glad to be home to allow such a small incident to spoil his homecoming and digging once more into his bag he produced a wooden pencil case for Andy and two more little boxes, one each for Vaila and Hannah, encrusted with tiny shells and colourful pebbles.

'Oh, Rob, you're so good with your hands,' Hannah said. 'I know you like making things but didn't think you had the patience for fiddly bits and pieces like these.'

'I haven't, but I had to fill the hours somehow and once I got started I couldn't stop. I even made one for my mother and for Maudie too.' He laughed. 'Big Bette had better look to her laurels, she isn't the only one in Keeper's Row who can make things from bits of wood.'

Vaila and Andy were exclaiming in delight over their gifts, the tiny shells so tastefully arranged, the pebbles gleaming like jewels against their varnished background. Vaila could picture her father as he worked, surrounded by darkness, the light from a lantern illuminating the contours of his face. Reaching up she kissed his rugged cheek. 'Thank you, Robbie,' she whispered softly before going off upstairs to the quietness of her room, where she opened a drawer and took out several small items of jewellery.

There was quite a collection of bangles and beads given to her over the years but the most treasured of these was an exquisite mermaid brooch carved out of polished wood. Her father had made the brooch for her mother and had given it to her one Christmas long ago when Vaila had been just a babe in arms. On that same night he had hung a silver pendant in the shape of a tiny lighthouse round his infant daughter's neck, long before she had ever known that he was her real father.

When she was older he had told her about that night and the love that had surrounded all three of them on their last precious Christmas together. Then he had given her the mermaid brooch, telling her that it was hers to keep for always, a reminder of the mother who had cherished her and whose memory was linked indelibly with the simple little ornament that he had crafted with such loving care.

Now it was in her safekeeping and as she placed it in her new box she vowed afresh to look after it always and never ever let it out of her sight, especially when she wore it to church on her best Sunday coat. Grampa Ramsay didn't like people to wear embellishments of any sort on the Sabbath, he had said it wasn't seemly to draw attention to oneself in such a fashion and that Hannah should know better than to allow her children to decorate themselves like little heathens for Sunday worship.

Vaila knew he was only angry with Hannah because she had never shown any inclination to take herself and her family to the kirk of his faith. Hannah, in fact, wasn't keen on churches of any kind and only went on sufferance to please her mother who wasn't all that keen on churches either, but felt it was the right thing to do in an isolated place like Kinvara where everyone ought to pull their weight in all matters pertaining to community spirit.

'If everyone thought like you, Hannah, the whole

structure of rural society would crumble about our ears,' Harriet regularly lectured her daughter.

Rubbish! Hannah silently opined but gave in to her mother's philosophies, firstly because it was the easiest way to get peace, secondly because she secretly enjoyed people-watching and never ceased to be astonished at the metamorphosis that seemed to seize her neighbours the minute they plumped their backsides onto the hard wooden pews in the kirk and gazed towards the Reverend Thomas MacIntosh in the pulpit as if he was salvation personified.

Vaila smiled to herself as she thought about some of the things Hannah had to say on her return from church. She could be very funny when she liked, in a droll sort of way, and made everybody laugh when she entertained them with her opinions over Sunday lunch, if she was in a mood to do so.

'What you doing?'

Vaila jumped and spun round to see Essie standing in the doorway with her thumb in her mouth.

'I'm putting my things into my new box, the one Father gave me. Why didn't you want yours, Essie? Our father made it specially for you.'

'I want a new dolly,' Essie persisted stubbornly.

'Well, you can't have one. Your old one will be fine once it's washed and hung out on the line to dry. When it is I'll help you to comb its hair and make it all pretty again.'

Essie digested this for a few moments, sulking a little

as she swayed from side to side and stared at the floor with her thumb still in her mouth. After a while, when she saw that Vaila wasn't going to coax her into a better mood, she came over and gazed down at the array of treasures lying on the bed. Her chubby hand came out to pick up the silver lighthouse pendant and she let it dangle beteen her fingers, her eyes big and blue as she watched the shine and gleam of it.

'That's my special necklace,' Vaila said proudly. She picked up the mermaid brooch. 'And this is my special brooch. It belonged to my mother and now it belongs to me.'

'Tell me about your Mamma.' Essie climbed onto the bed, curled herself up, and gazed at her sister expectantly. She knew all about Vaila having had a different mother from her whilst sharing the same father but had never quite grasped the intricacies involved in such a relationship. She was therefore fascinated by Vaila's stories of Oir na Cuan and the life she had once lived there with Morna Jean Sommero.

Vaila liked any excuse to talk about her mother and getting into bed she snuggled down with her small sister and began to speak of her early childhood, drawing on memory for some of it, mostly recounting the things her father had told her as she grew older.

Essie had heard the story several times before but was quite content to hear it all again, her eyes dreamy, her expression passive, as she listened without one single interruption. And all the while she held the silver lighthouse necklace firmly in her chubby grasp and from time to time held it up so that she could watch it gleaming in the light from the window.

Andy was desperately trying to tell his father about the typewriter given to him by Catherine Dunbar and nothing would do but that he and Rob should go upstairs together to view the machine that could keep the little boy occupied for hours on end. Breck went with them, after assessing that Hannah's broom was propped safely in its usual corner and that she herself was too busy at the stove to notice him sneaking away on the heels of his young master.

Rob looked at the typewriter sitting on a table by the window, surrounded by a litter of papers and scribbles and books lent to Andy by Catherine. Andy, red-faced with excitement, sat down and demonstrated his growing skills on the machine, watched by his father who felt a lump rising in his throat. The years slipped away, he remembered again a tiny scrap of life emerging into the world, frail and helpless, seemingly without aptitudes of any kind.

A child whose difficulties had forced him to seek strength and solace from his own small inner world. A world that must often have been frighteningly lonely, the searching, the struggling, the anger he must have felt when those around him had failed to understand the things he had tried to convey.

Now this, the moment that Rob had waited for, this boy of his proving to himself, to everybody, that he could do it. By God he could do it! And he would go on doing it till he had convinced everybody, not least himself, that he was as good, or better, than anybody.

Rob laughed. Andy laughed. A hyena-like screech that made Breck's ears swivel nervously backwards and forwards as he glanced at the door in case Hannah might be coming with her broom.

The surprises weren't over with yet. Andy opened a drawer in the table and from it he produced a piece of paper which he tremblingly gave to his father. 'For you,' he said, the words tumbling over one another. 'A poem I wrote for you.'

Slowly Rob read it aloud, his voice soft yet strong in the stillness of the room.

My Father

Light that shines on lonely skies,
Over yonder where he lies,
I know that he is watching me,
Far away and o'er the sea.

June dawn on my window pane,
Tells me he'll be home again,
Over waves that dip and soar.
He'll be coming back once more.

And now he's here and all is fine,
Warm brown hands touching mine,
Summer days long and bright
Stretching to the endless light.

Moonlight on the rocky shore,
Beckoning him to go once more,
Waning days, darkening night,
Goodbye Father, I'll be alright.

Something strange and sore tore at Rob's heart as he finished reading the last verse. He had always known that his long absences from home were a trial to his family but had thought them to be an accepted part of life at Keeper's Row. Now it came home to him forcibly that this wasn't the case. Andy's poem had just proved how much he missed his father and longed for his return. And what a way he had of putting his feelings into words, words that revealed a sensitivity that went far beyond his years.

'Andy,' he ruffled the boy's dark head, 'I'm going to keep this for always and read it over and over. It's good, it's damned good, I can't tell you how much it means to me.'

'Stories too, Father,' Andy nodded, 'lots and lots of them.'

Rob ran his hand over the scratched surface of the table where his son must have sat, hour after hour, creating his stories and verses. 'I'm going to make you a desk, Andy, one where you can sit in comfort with enough drawers to keep your things in and a bookcase for you to store everything within reach.'

Andy's dark eyes were shining. Triumphantly he typed the word 'Hurrah!' and returned the carriage with a zest that made it loudly ring.

God bless Catherine Dunbar, Rob thought, as he took Andy's hand and led him downstairs, followed by Breck who was most relieved to see that Hannah was still at the stove and appeared not to have noticed his absence from the room.

But he was wrong. 'I know you were upstairs,' she said, turning a flushed face to look at the dog who went humbly to his corner and tried to look as if he hadn't left it all day. 'I hope you weren't up on the bed, Breck Sutherland, wi' your fleas and your hairs and your great feet trailing dust all over the sheets.'

Breck hung his head and looked terribly ashamed. Hannah's lips twitched, she said nothing more, but shooed the dog outside because she said he was getting under her feet and only then did she take a morsel of biscuit from her pocket and push it into his waiting jaws.

Breck knew that her bark was worse than her bite, it had become a game with them now, one that he and she understood and enjoyed immensely – except of course when she was really being mad at something or somebody and took her feelings out on him with the business end of that hated kitchen broom.

* * *

That night they had Vaila's birthday cake for supper and as they were sitting round the fire enjoying the rich fruity slabs Rob told his daughter he would take her shopping one day soon to get her the present of her choice.

'Me too,' Essie cried immediately.

'It isn't your birthday, Essie,' Rob said reasonably. 'Besides, you got a box.'

'Don't want it.'

His jaw tightened. 'Persistence should have been your middle name, my girl. But if you really don't want it we'll just have to give it to another little girl, one who will appreciate it better.'

'No, mine.' Essie hastily got up from the table and went to retrieve the box from the chair where she had thrown it. Holding it to her chest she bore it away upstairs to her bedroom. Hannah looked at Rob and there was a strange expression in her eyes. 'You were a bit hard on her, she's only four years old, after all. Surely it wouldn't break the bank to buy her a new doll.'

'It isn't the money, Hannah,' he returned evenly. 'It's the principle. Essie will have to learn that she can't have everything she wants just by snapping those tiny fingers of hers.'

'The principle! At her age! You can't mean that. She's just a baby yet.'

'A baby who is growing up fast and changing by the minute. I see a difference in her, Hannah. She's developing into a little madam who wants her own way all the time and it's up to us both to discourage that.'

Hannah opened her mouth to argue further, when she saw Vaila watching her and was suddenly reminded about the incident that had taken place earlier in the day, concerning Essie's tantrums and the blame that had subsequently been laid on Vaila's shoulders.

Hannah felt uncomfortable under the scrutiny of Vaila's green and steady gaze and got up hastily to fetch more tea from the pot while Rob lit his pipe and settled back in his chair.

Vaila went on cutting and wrapping the remainder of her cake to give to Granma Rita and Grampa Ramsay and of course she mustn't forget Aidan or Maudie and Uncle Finlay nor her cousins and aunties. Joss and his parents had to have some too and perhaps she ought to save a bit for Miss Catherine who had been so good to Andy – not forgetting Aunt Mirren who was far away in Shetland but who was so regular at sending cards and parcels at Christmas and on birthdays.

She sighed and wondered if there would be enough to go round. Perhaps she shouldn't have eaten such a big piece herself when there were so many people to think about. She glanced up and saw her father watching Hannah with a troubled look in his eyes. She hoped they weren't going to argue about Essie all the time and this just the start of his leave. She wanted it to be good and happy with everybody enjoying themselves but somehow it never was like that when grown-ups got together and began disagreeing.

She sighed again and her father took his pipe from his mouth to say laughingly, 'You sound like a dog who has lost his bone. Stop worrying about the cake. I only ate half o' mine and you can have the rest for your little parcels. If you cut it up into fingers it will go round better and everyone can have a taste.'

She took the plate that he slid towards her. Their eyes met and they smiled and all at once everything seemed better. She was glad that he was home because when he was, all the usual day-to-day problems were halved and the house was brighter somehow.

She began humming a tune under her breath as she became absorbed in her task, never knowing of the anger simmering in Hannah's breast or the unease that was in Rob's.

Chapter Fourteen

When Hannah had awakened on the day of Rob's arrival she had hugged herself at the thought of having him home after being separated from him for so long. She had tried to imagine what they might say to each other when they were at last alone and had savoured the sweetness of her thoughts all through the hours of waiting for the relief boat to arrive.

But when he and she went to bed that night, certain little events of the day were niggling away in Hannah's head and she knew she wouldn't rest till she had brought them out into the open. For a start there was the incident concerning Catherine Dunbar and the disregard she had shown for Hannah's feelings when she had brazenly kissed Rob at the harbour for everyone to see and snigger at. True, it had just been a quick peck on the cheek, but even so, young unmarried women didn't go around doing that to married men, not in Kinvara anyway, except perhaps at funerals and weddings and even at the odd ceilidh when too much drink might be blamed for the abandonment of everyday conventions.

Then there was his unyielding treatment of Essie and

all that talk about principles being involved when all the time he was just acting plain stubborn in refusing a baby like that a new toy to keep her happy.

And she was such a contented little soul, one who demanded nothing more from her father than just a few indulgences now and then. He was quick enough to spoil Vaila. Oh, ay, his blue-eyed girl could ask for anything she wanted and get it without too much argument – if any.

Hannah stared at the window. It was a perfect summer's evening, bright and clear, the sea was the colour of pewter lightening to turquoise and gold where it touched the horizon. The small islands beyond Niven's Bay had darkened to purple and seemed to be floating on the calm reaches of the ethereal looking ocean. Through the years, Hannah had come to love the views from her window and often found solace in them when Rob was away on lighthouse duty.

She raised herself up on one elbow. Even from this distance she could see the great cracks and crannies in the cliffs of Vaul as plain as day; the smoke rising from the chimneys of the little hamlet itself; the dark spire of St Niven's Chapel piercing up against its darker backdrop of sturdy sycamores. Looking at the chapel reminded her of something she had heard about the new owners of the Mill O' Cladach. It seemed that Father Kelvin MacNeil had been rebuffed by Rebecca Bowman because of what he stood for and her just a skelf of a girl who probably knew nothing about religion except what her father had told her.

A strange man, Joshua Bowman, Hannah mused, with

that wild thatch of iron-grey hair and those odd glittering eyes of his staring right through you making you shiver. And his daughter wasn't much better. Hannah had only met her once when Vaila had brought her to the house on some pretext. She had been watchful and quiet and had given Hannah the creeps with her unnatural politeness and the habit she had of looking at you as if you weren't there or were appearing to her as a being from another planet who was expected to converse by telepathy alone – just like her father.

She wore those funny little glasses, of course, which might have had something to do with it, and she was young and new in an unfamiliar environment and Hannah knew only too well how that felt. Hannah had encountered Miriam only briefly as yet and had glimpsed the two boys from afar but from all she had heard they were a strange bunch and the less one had to do with them the better.

'I'd watch that one,' Hannah had told her stepdaughter when Rebecca had departed. 'She'll cause trouble someday, though who could blame her with a father like Joshua Bowman.'

But Vaila seemed to have taken a great liking to the girl and had gone huffily silent at her stepmother's words, later declaring somewhat rudely that they were all strange when it came to the bit and one should never pass judgement until they knew the circumstances better. Take Johnny Lonely, for instance, wasn't he the most unusual man anyone could meet, yet hadn't he touched them all in some way with his mystery and his independence of spirit, not forgetting the knack he had of worming his way into everyone's lives whether they liked it or not and in many instances lending a helping hand.

Take Johnny Lonely indeed! Wise words from such a young lass. Hannah herself had reason to be grateful to the hermit for various kind deeds, though to this day he often frightened the life out of her with that habit he had of creeping out of nowhere when a body was least expecting it.

And wasn't that him down there? A mere black speck on the beach. Combing the wrack for driftwood and anything else he could find to kindle those fires of his. He had been stranger than ever of late but in a different way from the usual. She had chanced upon him one day quite recently and instead of disappearing from view he had remained where he was, staring broodingly out to sea as if gripped by some dark and terrible thoughts.

She had heard about his reaction to his first sighting of the Bowmans, especially Miriam. Joss had told Janet and Janet had told Hannah and already quite a little enigma had sprung up as to the reason for the hermit's surprise at seeing Miriam – an insignificant creature if ever there was one and not the sort to instil any sort of curiosity in anybody's breast . . .

The bed sagged as Rob got in and Hannah gave a start. So absorbed had she been in her ponderings and wonderings about other people's affairs her thoughts had been diverted from all the small domestic worries that existed at No. 6 of the Row. The nearness of Rob beside her brought it all flooding back, yet in those moments it was very difficult to concentrate on anything that existed outside the intimate sphere of the bedroom.

It had been so long since they had lain together like this. There had been so many cold and lonely nights without him, just herself, alone with her thoughts, often so afraid of the emptiness she had risen to make cocoa in the kitchen and had sat with it by the stove, Breck's head on her lap, comforting her with his undermanding presence.

She had come to love him over the years, that big loyal hairy brute, who knew and respected every move she made, every thought in her head, who looked at her with eyes that were filled with humour and understanding and a wit that matched her own when it came to acting out certain little aspects of household routine. The broom, for instance, he hated that, yet he knew to expect it as part and parcel of everyday life should he break the rules once too often. It was a game they both played, a ritual that was as familiar as his bed, his bowl, his walks outside with Andy in his cart . . .

She could feel the warmth of Rob's body next to her own. He had just bathed in the zinc tub in the kitchen and she could smell the freshness of him, sweet and warm and very, very dear. She sensed the stirring of his limbs as he moved closer to her and her heart missed a beat.

'Hannah,' he murmured, 'it's so good to be home. I'd

forgotten what it was like to lie with you in the silence. I can still hear the roar of the ocean in my head, the pounding of the waves on the rocks, the surge of the wind around the tower. On the nights I couldn't sleep I would get up and look towards Kinvara and picture you going about the house, tending to the stove, making the supper, thinking maybe of your man out there on the light as you sat by the fire when the bairns were in bed.'

'Did you really do that, Rob? Really and truly. Think about me and wonder how I was getting on?'

'Of course I did. All the time.'

His hand slid round her waist and he was drawing her in close to him, nearer to that beating, living, pulsing heat that she knew would soon engulf her. His hand came up to her breasts, his light yet expert touch made her tingle all over. She felt herself melting, moving towards him, her body and soul crying out for the love of this man, his vigour, his passion. She wanted the awakening that only he could evoke in her, her darling Rob, the only man she had ever wanted or needed, the only one who had ever been in her life.

But she hadn't been the only woman in his. There had been others before her, women who had fallen at his feet, those who still hankered after him and wondered why he had married her. There had been Morna Jean, the love of his life – and now there was Catherine Dunbar, obviously sweet on him, showing her feelings in public, letting him see how she felt by her actions. Women like that were dangerous to have around.

She had to ask, had to know, about him and Catherine. She couldn't let a thing like that pass without knowing if some past incident between them had encouraged her to behave as she had. Her voice came out, harder than she had intended, and even as she spoke she knew she had picked the wrong moment to give rein to her doubts and fears. The lovely feelings of intimacy that had been theirs just seconds before melted away and a chilly void seemed to spring up between them.

She felt him tensing, he grew suddenly colder and his voice was harsh when he replied. 'Of course there's nothing between us. She's just been kind to Andy, that's all. It's only common decency to be grateful to someone who's as generous as she is.'

'And that's all that matters to you, isn't it? Anyone who shows the least bit of interest in your son has to be fawned over and indulged. Oh, don't think I haven't noticed the way you look at other women, especially when they're new and interesting and attractive. Perhaps Catherine Dunbar had ulterior motives when she came here pretending concern over Andy's welfare.'

'Hannah, I'm not listening to this, you're making things up in your mind, attaching all sorts of evils to everyday gestures and words.'

'Her kissing you wasn't an everyday gesture. She's far too forward for my liking, pass remarkable too, she made some cheeky comments about Essie last time she was here, implying that she was cossetted and spoiled.'

'You do make far too much of Essie.' He was a million miles away now, cool, distant, detached.

'And you don't make enough o' her,' she snapped back. 'Always it's Vaila and Andy. Why do you give them everything?'

'Because they ask for nothing.'

'Oh, is that so? Well, you don't know them as well as you think you do. What do you suppose goes on when you're away? Who feeds them and clothes them and tends to their every need at all hours o' the day and night.'

'Oh, come on, Hannah, they were both out o' nappies long ago. Why don't you just admit you've got more time for Essie than for anybody else. You're so wrapped up in her she's become an obsession with you.'

'Maybe that's because I've always had to be father and mother to her. She's only a baby still and with you away so much she needs more of my attention than the other two. You just can't see it my way because you always see only one side o' the picture, the loving dadda, the good provider, coming home to his doting wife and children and expecting to be met every time with open arms and unquestioning devotion.'

'Doting wife! That's rich! I get more affection from that dog down there in the kitchen than I've ever had from you and don't blame me if I'm forced to seek my comforts elsewhere. You've asked for it. Hannah, none o' this is my doing, you make things up in your mind until you're so mixed up you can't tell what's real and what isn't any more.'

'And whose fault is that! I've never betrayed you but it was an easy enough matter for you to turn your back on me when Morna was alive. You went to her like a dog to a bone, never caring about me or what I was feeling, thinking I was too daft to know what was going on in front o' my very own eyes!'

She had struck a wound that was still raw and sore and she could have bitten her tongue out. But there was no turning back now, words had been spoken that night that could never be erased and when Rob's voice came it cut through her like a shard of steel, sharp, icy, remote.

'So that's it, festering away all these years, out in the open at last. Well, I'm glad, because you're right, I still love Morna and I always will. I could have loved you too if you had let me, but there's something in you that won't allow you to get too close to anybody – not even your husband. You'll have to learn to open up your heart and your mind, Hannah, and become a real human being. Till then I want nothing of you unless you have something real to give to me.'

The bed creaked again, only this time he was getting out of it. She heard him gathering up his clothes, the door opened and softly closed, and she knew he had gone to the small, dark boxroom at the end of the landing.

Hannah lay quite still on her back, making no move of any kind. Her throat was tight with unshed tears. She wanted to turn the clock back but it was too late for that now and far too soon for apologies of any kind.

She looked towards the window. A young moon was rising above the honey gold of the sea, a sliver of light in the midnight blue of the sky. A lucky moon, the old folks said, one for lovers to wish on when the future was bright and all things that were good and new loomed on the horizon.

Love was old now, old and dead. The bed was emptier than it had ever been before Rob's return. She put up her hand to touch her face and was surprised to find that she was crying.

Kinvara

July 1931

Chapter Fifteen

It was the day of Sorry's funeral. The neighbours of Shug and Dolly Law thought it was going a bit far to use a grand term like that for the burial of an animal, no matter how well loved it had been. But the Laws, especially the younger ones, thought it was only right and fitting that Sorry should have a proper send off. There was nothing the people of Kinvara liked better than the excuse for a party, but only those who did not consider it tasteless to take part in an equestrian interment had been invited to attend the funeral, the mourners consisting mainly of Shug's mates and their spouses.

Shug had laid in a good supply of Knobby Sinclair's best beer for the event and a few of the good lady wives had made cakes and sandwiches for the 'wee purvey' to follow. Dolly had even made an attempt to clean the house for the occasion though in the end it was her daughter, Mary, who took the duster from her mother's hands and went over the streaks and marks that had been missed.

'Ay, ay, it's a sad day indeed for us all,' Shug declared, taking a generous swig of whisky from his glass and wiping away a trickle of dusty tears from his face. His grief was all the keener because Dolly had told him only that very morning that he would now have to get himself a more permanent job to pay for the new bairn that was on the way and for the horse they would have to get to replace Sorry.

'I myself never thought anything like this was going to happen for a number o' years yet,' he went on. 'That poor beast o' ours had the best o' loving care and attention and nobody was more surprised than me when she just went and died on us out there at the harbour for everyone to see.'

'Ach, well, it was quick,' Dokie Joe comforted solicitously. 'In the end she never knew what was happening and didn't have to suffer the indignity of being put to the knacker's yard when she was past it.'

'I would never have put my bonny beast to the knacker's yard!' Dolly wailed, throwing a belligerent glare in Dokie Joe's direction. 'She was part o' the family was Sorry and I treated her like one o' my own bairns. We will never get another one like her, she knew us better than we knew ourselves and liked the same things we did.' Her eyes filled up with tears. 'Oh, I could just die wi' sorrow when I think how she enjoyed a drop of beer mixed wi' her oats and a wee sup of ale now and then.'

'Maybe that's what killed her,' Willie Whiskers dared to suggest. 'I've been looking after horses all my life and I think I know what's good for them. Beer is a man's drink, water is for horses, the two were never meant to be mixed.'

'We never mixed her drinks,' Shug defended himself. 'She got them independently o' one another and I'll thank you, Willie, no' to make hasty judgements on family matters that don't concern you.'

A large hole had been staked out and dug for Sorry in the Laws' sizeable back yard. Shug had managed to excuse himself from taking part in this task, wriggling out of it by saying he didn't want to aggravate his bad back with all the stooping and bending involved. The younger Laws rallied round, so used by now to having a father whose state of health had always been doubtful they hardly needed reminding of it when manual labour was the order of the day.

But the Law boys were not their father's sons for nothing. To a man they were wise in the ways of the world and knew only too well how to appeal to the sentiment in human nature. Armed with nothing more than silver tongues and the wiles that had been instilled in them since infancy, they were adept at soft-talking even the most hard-headed of beings into bending to their will.

Children were easy prey. They had all loved Sorry and remembered her with affection; each of them had benefited at some time in their lives by a ride in the cart she had so willingly pulled or hitched alongside on their bicycles when their legs were tired from pedalling.

Ay, they would miss her. Yes, it seemed only right that they should return some of the kindnesses she had bestowed on them. They would get their reward in the knowing that they had helped in some measure to see her into her last resting place with the dignity she deserved.

So it was that a fair number of the neighbourhood youngsters had been persuaded into helping with the digging of Sorry's grave, an honour bestowed on only a chosen few. A labour of love to be carried out willingly and respectfully, no matter how tough the task, how hard the going.

All of this, tempered by the lure of the 'wee purvey' afterwards, soon saw the job completed, aided by Carrots Law acting as gaffer and Softy Law doing his overseer, being very thorough about his inspection of the work when the last boy had crawled out of the opening and the last spade had been thrown down.

Getting Sorry into the hole was not such a simple matter. The local farmers had rallied round with an assortment of slings and pulleys. Everyone sweated and groaned as they heaved and hauled the mare to her last destination inch by painful inch. But her stiffened limbs would not allow for easy entry into the ground. For a time she lay across it like a bridge, while Dolly, her nerves stretched tight with anxiety, sucked and blew on her clay pipe and the younger Laws stood around with their hands in their holey pockets, wishing it was all over with so that they could partake of the feast awaiting them on a trestle table laid out on the scruffy patch of grass that Dolly grandly referred to as 'the back lawn'.

But at last Sorry was safely interred and Shug conducted

a short but flowery ceremony that made every other man there squirm with embarrassment. While he was speaking Dolly went over and threw the mare's threadbare nose-bag into the grave along with a few old horseshoes to 'bring her luck on her last journey'.

'Ach, that's just being silly,' Willie Whiskers protested, 'I could have melted those down to make a new pair. All this sentiment over an old nag doesn't seem right and proper when there's many a human body goes to their rest without a soul to mourn them.'

Dolly withered him with a look. She watched as the hole was filled in, the last sod stamped over. 'We'll plant tatties in this spot,' she decided with swimming eyes. 'We're bound to get a good crop. Sorry will give back what she got when she was alive.'

'Ay,' Softy Law nodded, 'it will make a change from pushing up the daisies.'

'You'll never get anybody to dig the ground, Ma,' Carrots said with a meaningful look at his father.

Dolly's nostrils flared. 'Oh, ay, we'll see about that. I didn't raise five strapping lads for nothing! It's high time you all began pulling your weight after all the comfort and care I've given you over the years.'

The Law boys might have had something to say about that, but further argument was drowned out by the sound of the pipes as Dokie Joe, somewhat red about the ears and feeling ridiculous, hoisted them up and began blowing into the mouthpiece. He had agreed to a short performance only to pacify Dolly and not because he felt that it was right and proper in any way to pay homage to a humble old horse who had always looked half dead in life anyway and was probably glad to get out of it for a while.

Dokie knew his mates would tease and torment him for many a long day to come and all he wanted was to get the whole thing over with, so that he could get a 'good swallock' of the beer that had been promised to him afterwards.

He didn't bargain for the mercurial quirks of human nature. It was a haunting strain that he played and the effect on the gathering was electrifying, When the last note had been released it seemed to linger in the soft air of summer and there wasn't a dry eye to be seen, even those unsentimental beings like Willie and Moggie John MacPhee succumbing to their emotions at the very last minute.

'Ach, but that was beautiful just, Dokie Joe.' Dolly's grimy hanky was out, her face looked like a wet washing board from all the tears that had coursed down it that day. 'If Mattie was here I'm sure she would have enjoyed it too but then, it isn't everybody who has the sensitivity to appreciate the fact that animals have souls too and go to heaven just the same as any other body.'

Dokie Joe looked ashamed. He had shared his wife's sentiments regarding the Laws and their 'sensation seeking nonsense'. He had even shared her laughter when she had declared mischieviously, 'They are just being foolish and flogging a dead horse into the bargain if they expect any sane person to go to an affair like that.'

She had not laughed when her husband had told her somewhat sheepishly that he had promised to play the pipes for the event. 'You are only going for the beer, you daft bodach!' she had raged and she might have been right at that since his thoughts had been mainly for the drink and the ceilidhing that he knew would follow the formalities of the day.

Now, as if to atone for his sins, he went on to play more tunes on his pipes, and by popular demand he went right on playing, only stopping when he had run out of steam and just had to have a glass of beer which he downed in a few noisy gulps. After that, Willie Whiskers took up where Dokie Joe had left off and before long a good-going ceilidh was in full swing out there in the Laws' back yard.

Drawn by the music, more people arrived, among them Donald of Balivoe, who, casting aside past grievances against the Laws, brought with him peace offerings of two roast chickens to add to the feast and a bottle of best malt he'd been saving for years and wanted to taste before he went the same way as Sorry.

'She was indeed a long-suffering beast and never seemed happy,' he intoned in his deep voice as he made himself as comfortable as he could on a decidedly uncomfortable bench. 'If she had lived any longer she would just have endured more years o' hardship, so it's maybe just as well she went as quick as she did.'

Remarks like these did not fall agreeably upon the ears of Dolly and Shug and further war might have been declared between the two factions had not Dokie Joe raised his glass heavenwards to make a toast. 'Here's to Sorry, she served her masters right well while she was here on earth and long may she rest in pieces.'

'To Sorry.' The cry echoed round the yard.

'Here, whatever do you mean by that?' Dolly rounded on Dokie Joe. 'Rest in pieces indeed!'

'Ach, don't foul your breeks, lass,' Shug said in placating tones. 'We couldn't get her into the hole the way she was so we just had to bend wee bits o' her when you weren't looking.'

'Bend wee bits o' her?' Dolly was aghast. 'How could you do that to Sorry, the pain must have been terrible.'

'Ach no, she never felt a thing, I can assure you. Here, drink some o' this and you'll feel better. Donald didn't bring it along for it to sit on ceremony on a table, did you now, Donald?'

So saying he seized his wife's glass and poured in a good measure of Donald's best malt whisky, an action which made that gentleman grab hold of his own bottle in order to serve himself a stiff dram before it disappeared down the thirsty throats of the known drinkers in his midst.

By this time the atmosphere was decidedly mellow as everyone partook of the drams and the pints, the cakes and the sandwiches. Afternoon moved into evening, the air was like soft wine, imbued as it was with the scents of bluebells from the surrounding woodlands: buttercups and clover from the meadows; all mixed up with the sweetness of the earth and the tang of the sea.

The younger Laws had prepared a fire of driftwood and pine kindlings. A pile of logs lay in readiness. Malky Law put a match to the paper and in minutes a warm glow diffused the chill of evening. The old men gathered round it to smoke their pipes and tell their tales of bygone days when all the world had moved at a slower pace than now: boys and girls made eyes at one another and retired to the shadows to kiss and cuddle; somebody produced a mouth organ, songs were sung, verses recited.

It was the perfect end to a perfect day for most people but for Dolly it had somehow fallen flat. Sorry was gone. She might have seemed a poor creature to some but she had been a good, loyal, obedient servant to the Law family as a whole and her demise spelled doom for their future well-being. What would they do without her to carry their loads? How were they going to deliver washing to the gentry? Collect goods and fuel from the puffers? Fetch and carry for the folk from the big houses? They wouldn't even be able to make an honest bob or two from the hire of their cart and their horse. Sorry was gone. She would never come back – and they'd had to mutilate her poor old bones in order to get her into her grave!

And the new bairn was coming. Another mouth to feed. Another worry to contend with. Rags to dress it in, no shoes of any kind to put on its feet when it started school – if it was lucky enough ever to start school. The lack of shoes for her family had always nagged at Dolly. There were never enough of them to go round the Law household, despite the fact that some of the older ones were working. It all went on food – a bit of baccy too – and a pint or two at the inn. What was the world coming to if she had to feel guilty about enjoying some of life's pleasures? She wasn't getting any younger. In fact, she had felt tired and done this good whilie back and the loss of Sorry was the final straw.

It wasn't in Dolly's make-up to really worry about the future, she had always accepted life as it came, but tonight she was worrying, tonight she was depressed. The songs and the laughter around her only served to make her feel worse. This wasn't an occasion for merriment, they should all be in mourning like her. Wait till she got a hold of that Shug for daring to enjoy himself. He had never taken anything seriously in the whole of his life and it was high time he woke up to his responsibilities.

Dolly sighed. She gazed morosely into the fire, feeling very sorry for herself indeed. The tears pricked her lids, and before she knew what was happening she was crying softly into her beer and not caring very much about anything.

Chapter Sixteen

Into this motley gathering came the man himself, none other than Captain Rory MacPherson of Crathmor, hair and whiskers slicked to obedience, kilt swishing about his fine hairy knees as he came up through the gate and into the Law's back yard, his Siamese cat, Sheba, at his side, her own whiskers brisking out stiffly as she tested the air for the one scent that never failed to drive her to distraction.

It was there alright. Dog with a capital D. All around her in fact, slinking away into dark corners the minute she appeared, her reputation as pooch-hater personified being legendary among the canine population of Kinvara. Sheba had dogs of her own at home, a new puppy had just been introduced to the fold, causing great interest and excitement to the existing members of the family, both animal and human.

Sheba knew she had to put up with this small, irritating newcomer. Its winning baby wiles and the habit it had of attracting all the attention was a source of great annoyance to her but she had to knuckle down and accept it into her abode since there had always been dogs at Crathmor. As far as she was concerned the bigger ones were merely another part of the furniture and given time the latest addition would become just as useless as its elders.

So she suffered it, contenting herself by giving it an occasional cuff on the ear when she thought no one was looking and bullying it into submisssion if it dared to take liberties with any part of her anatomy.

There was no need for such tolerance outside the home however, anything that moved on four legs and smelled of dog was there to be teased and tormented and given a good hiding should the opportunity arise.

Sheba was therefore greatly delighted to be there by her master's side that evening of his visit to the Outlaws as they were known. One brindled bundle had not noticed her arrival, peacefully asleep as he was by the embers of the fire, filled to the brim with ill-gotten gains from the table and also slightly tipsy through drinking dregs of beer from every discarded glass he could find.

Sheba's fangs flashed, claws unsheathed she pounced, the dog woke howling from his slumbers. Bewildered and disorientated, his bloodshot stare was unable to immediately focus, but he felt the pain alright, digging into him relentlessly, making him draw back his lips in a ferocious snarl.

Rags was a fairly recent acquisition of Ferrets MacGlone, a country-wise itinerant who roamed the hills and glens with his ferrets in search of pests of all descriptions, hired by the local farmers who didn't mind parting with a bob or two for his services. Ferrets MacGlone also used terriers in his quest for rodents and rabbits. His old Jack Russell had recently expired and Rags had taken its place, bought from a roving band of gypsies for just sixpence, his pedigree doubtful but his rat-catching abilities being sworn on oath by every gypsy present at the time of the sale.

There was one thing the gypsies hadn't told Ferrets, that being the dog's aversion to cats, the main reason they had got rid of him in the first place. Ferrets had soon found this out for himself and had resigned himself to the sight of his dog taking off at high speed at the least sniff of anything faintly feline. Ferrets wasn't sure if the dog was unable to distinguish the difference between a rat and a cat but whichever way, the fact remained that Rags greatly relished chasing the creatures and, up until now, that was about all he had ever done with them.

So far he had remained the conquerer and was used to the sight of a cornered cat hissing at him from the safety of a wall or a tree. Never before had one dared to attack him, until tonight, when he could smell Cat with a capital C, right there on top of him, yowling and growling, using its claws and its fangs to great effect.

Rags wasted no time in retaliating. With a snarl of sheer rage he was up on his feet, shaking Sheba off so that she landed in an undignified heap on the ground. And that was where she remained for fully thirty seconds, because Rags had simply collapsed on top of her, pinning her down, using his paws and his teeth to petrify her into complete and utter silence.

It was the second time in Sheba's life that a dog had gained the upper hand. Breck Sutherland had been the first, sorting her out very thoroughly indeed whilst no more than a pup and earning her respect in the process.

Rags was even more masterful than Breck had been and Sheba lay perfectly still, shaken to the core, all the confidence knocked out of her in those few fraught moments.

'Here, lad, that's enough o' that, let the bugger go this minute before you kill her!' Ferrets MacGlone bore down on his dog, the laird bore down on his cat. He was having no more of her antics tonight. He was here on business and had no intention of being further distracted by the anti-social behaviour of his feline companion. Grabbing her by the scruff of her neck he stuffed her inside his jacket to button her in tight, knowing that she would soon settle down in the familiar warm confines.

The arrival of the laird had brought one or two worthies to their unsteady feet in a gesture of courtesy, a few of the more sober ones asking themselves what had prompted him to arrive at the tail end of Sorry's funeral, unless of course he had heard about the drams and the beer and wanted to sample some for himself.

Dokie Joe, who worked at Crathmor, was particularly deferential as he put down his glass, wiped the froth from his chin, and invited the newcomer to take his ease on a nearby log.

'No, I won't just now, thanking you just the same,

MacPhee, it's Shug and Dolly I've come to see . . .' His eyes raked the flushed faces round the fire, finally coming to rest on a lop-sided Dolly with her hat askew and her pipe turned upside-down to stop the rain getting in, though the said rain was purely a figment of her inebriated imagination, brought about by her own helpless tears and the splashes from a pail of water someone was pouring round the edges of the fire to keep it within safe confines.

At the sound of their names being spoken, Shug popped out from a bush where he had been relieving himself and Dolly somehow managed to rise to her feet. Without further ado the laird took each of them by an arm to propel them out through the gate and round to the front of the house where a neat little chestnut mare was tied to a railing, blowing gently down her nose as she waited, her ears pricking forward as the laird came towards her, followed by Shug and Dolly and the unsteady remainder of the funeral guests, some of them having departed when the beer and the whisky had shown signs of drying up.

'Well, what do you think of her?' The laird cocked an eye at the parent Laws. 'Not bad, eh?'

'Ay, a bonny wee mare, right enough,' Shug agreed with some reserve, glancing rather suspiciously at the laird who was well known for his habit of springing suprises of a rather uncommon nature on his fellow men.

'She's a fine beast,' Willie Whiskers said admiringly. 'As dainty as a daisy but strong looking for all that.'

'Och, but she is beautiful, just.' Dolly had fallen immediately in love with the shy little creature and went over to rub her forelock and blow gently into her nostrils. In return, the mare batted her long lashes, gave a little snicker of approval, and nuzzled Dolly's hand with her velvety nose, further captivating that lady who had forgotten her tears in the novelty of the moment.

'Well, she's yours if you want her.' The laird delivered his bombshell with great aplomb. 'She isn't a full pedigree but she's a good willing animal for all that. I heard about Sorry, of course, and for the last few days I've been mulling certain matters over in my mind. In the end I talked things over with Emily and she agreed with me that another horse was the only way to fill the gap left by Sorry's sad departure from this earthly coil.'

'Ours!' Dolly and Shug spoke in unison, everyone else gaped at the laird, one or two of the more cynical among them wondering just what he was up to this time.

'Ay, you heard right,' he grinned, rubbing his hands together in a typically enthusiastic fashion. 'I know how hard it's going to be for you now that your means of transport has been brought to a halt . . .' At this juncture he glanced at Dolly's hard little lump of a belly. 'One more on the way, a new mouth to feed, not to mention all the other expenses that go with it.'

'What's the catch?' Shug had been dying to ask that, the words came out, naked and unadorned, all caution thrown to the winds as a deadly premonition gripped him.

Thoroughly enjoying himself by now, the laird stretched the suspense out further by spending a few more seconds stroking his luxuriant whiskers and looking thoughtful, a little habit of his when he was getting ready to make some important pronouncement. 'Well, the truth is, Shug,' he said at last, 'I'm looking for another stable man, an extra pair o' hands to lighten the load as it were, business expanding and all that, never enough labour to get everything moving fast enough. You take on the job to pay for the horse, with an extra bob or two on the side if you throw in a little bit of overtime. In that way we'll all be happy and you'll have the added satisfaction of knowing you've paid back every penny you owe. Sweat and tears, Shug, sweat and tears, nothing ventured, nothing gained. It's a good adage to go by and one I hope you will appreciate when you've had a chance to think about it.'

At this, Shug choked so hard he had to be thumped on the back by several of his cronies. When he at last caught his breath he was too traumatised to make speech of any kind and could only watch wordlessly as his delighted wife rushed over to throw her arms round the Captain's neck in a flurry of gratitude. 'God bless you, Captain MacPherson, sir,' she said huskily, 'you have given me the answer to my prayers. I'll never forget your goodness and your kindness. I'm just that happy I could burst, that I could.'

Fresh tears were coursing down her face, this time brought about by sheer gladness. Planting a tobacco-tainted kiss on the laird's cheek she then turned her attention on the mare to stroke her and kiss her and to laugh like a hyena when the animal puckered its lips to kiss her wetly back.

'Oh, she's perfect, just perfect!' Dolly went into raptures. 'I love her already. I wonder if Sorry's old straw hat will fit her. No, it will have to be something grander. Maybe a felt one like mine wi' a flower in the brim. I'll call her Dancer because she looks as if she could just fly away wi' those dainty little feets she has on her.'

'It's a horse, not a bloody ballerina!' Shug had found his voice, he spoke scathingly, he felt trapped, that clever old bugger had landed him in it with a vengeance. Everybody, including his cronies, was crowing, fawning over the horse, shaking hands with the laird, as if he had done something wonderful and should be congratulated.

The master of Crathmor was not finished with the head of the Law household, yet, however. 'There are one or two conditions I have to make clear to you, Shug. Firstly, I'll expect the best from you. If, after a trial period I feel you aren't pulling your weight, the animal comes back to me. Secondly, I want you to get your shed fixed up so that she can have proper sleeping quarters in the winter. I myself will pop in personally from time to time to make sure she's being treated properly. A few months of hard work should suffice, you'll have paid for the mare by then. If all's to my satisfaction we'll see about keeping you in work on a more permanent basis – meantime, the mare is yours to love and to cherish.'

'Ay,' Willie Whiskers added his piece, 'she looks as if

she was cut out for finer things, a beast like that will no' take kindly to any old makeshift hut – no' like poor old Sorry who didn't know anything better.'

Dolly was really going off Willie by now, he had made enough derogatory comments about Sorry for one day without adding any more and she was about to give him a mouthful when her husband's fears about his future finally erupted into flabbergasted protest. 'A few months! With all due respect I'll be dead by then. Captain MacPherson! My back will just no' stand the strain. Nobody knows what I have to suffer in the course o' my day-to-day living and it's just no' fair to put this sort of onus upon me.'

'Do you want the horse, Shug?'

'Ay, of course I want the horse, but we could pay for it in other ways.'

'What other ways, Shug?'

'Well, I'm no' too sure about that yet, given time I'll think o' something, I've aye been good at dreaming up ways to make ends meet.'

'Quite,' the laird commented drily.

Dolly's eye was pinned on her husband, like a determined sheepdog she kept it there, never allowing it to drop or waver once. He knew when he was beaten. His shoulders sagged. His head dropped onto his chest.

'A few months, Shug,' the laird repeated.

'A few months,' Shug mumbled.

The master of Crathmor grinned. 'Right, that's settled. I'll need a lift home, but first I'll have that dram you offered me, MacPhee. I had a thirsty ride over here and feel in need of refreshment.'

The remaining funeral guests followed the Captain round to the Laws' back yard. There he was placed on the rickety bench and his glass personally filled by Donald of Balivoe who had hidden his bottle in the recesses of his jacket when it had shown serious signs of depletion.

'Bottoms up.' The laird held aloft his glass. 'Here's to Dolly and Shug. Today has been sad for them but tomorrow is another day and a new beginning. I'm sure no one will disagree with me on that score.'

No one did disagree. The glasses were raised. The party started all over again, thanks to the honoured guest from the big house who had brought along a few of his own bottles to ensure goodwill amongst his fellow men.

Chapter Seventeen

In the small hours of morning everyone took their leave of the Laws, Dokie Joe and Willie between them delivering the laird home to Emily who had waited up as she always did when he was out on one of his nocturnal wanders. Emily didn't mind, she never went further than a mild lecture on his latekeeping, thereafter settling herself down to listen to his colourful accounts of his adventures. Tonight she was particularly interested in what he had to say concerning his visit to the Laws and she made herself comfortable on the couch beside him, the dogs at her feet, an unusually subdued Sheba on her lap, a pot of tea and biscuits at her elbow, as her husband regaled her with his accounts of the evening.

Willie's wife, Maisie, wasn't quite as understanding as Emily. She grumbled and moaned at her husband from the minute he got into bed beside her with his 'drunken breath, his beery whiskers, and his great big sodden cold feet'.

'It's all the fault o' that brother o' yours,' she scolded, taking a line that Willie knew well and which he mouthed word for word as he lay with his face to the wall in resigned silence. 'Him and that wee runt, Shug Law, have got you by the lugs and just lead you astray at every turn. It would give me the greatest o' pleasure to take the three o' you and knock your silly skulls together, that it would. Dokie Joe was never the same after your sister dropped him on his head as a bairn and I'm beginning to think she must have done the same to you for you're as daft as any spring chicken when it comes to drink and wild parties.'

Willie allowed his wife to rant and rave and talk herself blue in the face. Long before she was finished he was sound asleep on his pillows, his lips puffing gently beneath his dazzling array of red whiskers, a little smile on his face as he dreamt the dreams of a man who worked hard and played hard and who had somehow managed to do it all happily despite having a wife who could suck grown men in like a vacuum and spit them out in small pieces when she was done with them.

The said brother wasn't having such a good time of it either. Dokie Joe had no excuses at all for having stayed away so long after swearing to Mattie 'only one tune on the pipes'. She was not at all amused at his late homecoming and 'a breath on him like a stag's backside'. He felt himself fortunate indeed that she didn't take his bagpipes and hit him over the head with them but contented herself instead by giving him a complete résumé of her night spent with her brood of children, one of whom had been sick all over the dog, 'no' to mention wee Norrie who had fallen in a burn and cut his legs and his trousers to ribbons'.

Dokie Joe lay inert in a chair. He listened and felt guilty because he had a conscience of sorts. He allowed Mattie to have full throttle before he took a hip flask and a rather crushed box from his pocket.

'I saved you some cake and sandwiches, lass,' he croaked in what breath he had left after playing the pipes and singing himself hoarse all night. 'A wee snifter too. The laird brought plenty along with him and when no one was looking I poured some into my flask.'

Mattie was somewhat appeased. 'The laird?' she queried, her appetite for gossip making her eyes gleam with interest. 'And what would he be doing visiting The Outlaws, I'd like to know?'

Her husband was only too ready to supply her with the required information. He talked, she heard him out, eating her sandwiches and supping her whisky as she did so, wee Norrie's torn trousers forgotten in the complete and utter enjoyment of the moment.

A golden dawn was breaking over the sea when Dolly and Shug at last got to bed. 'My, but it was a grand day altogether,' Dolly told her husband with a hugely contented sigh as she pulled a tattered patchwork quilt around her thin shoulders so that she could have a last puff of her pipe in comfort. 'Except for my poor, dear Sorry, of course,' she added hastily, a small twinge of guilt seizing her as she realised she hadn't given much thought to her old mare in all the excitement that had followed her burial.

'Ay, grand indeed.' Shug's tones were decidedly flat. 'Except when that rogue o' a laird turned up.'

'But he gave us a new horse, Shug,' Dolly pointed out, unable to keep a note of glee from her voice.

'Ay, wi' a life sentence attached. The price is too high, we would have been better getting a hand-cart.'

'A hand-cart!' Dolly hooted. 'And who would have pulled it, I'd like to know? Me wi' my belly, you wi' your back. A fine pair we would have made, dragging a heavy cart all over the place. Oh, no, Dancer came at the right time for us. I was at my wit's end wondering how we were going to manage without Sorry and there the Captain came, like a knight in shining armour, complete wi' his trusty steed. She is a lovely able wee beast and I just know she'll be happy wi' us.'

'A knight in shining armour!' Shug spluttered. 'More like a de'il in disguise if you ask me. I think he is just getting rid o' the dregs o' his stable now that he's gone in for pedigree ponies. Anybody wi' half an eye can see that. He's a fly old bugger and I'm the one who's going to suffer for it. How am I going to survive, I'd like to know, me wi' my back and all the other aches and pains I have to put up with?'

'You'll think o' something, you wouldn't be Shug Law if

you didn't,' Dolly said calmly as she lay back on her pillows. She smiled to herself as she remembered the laird's visit. Oh, but he was a bonny, kind man right enough, always in the right place at the right time. Where human nature was concerned he seemed to have a knack for digging deep down, getting to the root of problems, sorting them out in his own particular way.

Local opinions about this were many and varied. 'Ay, he's good at pulling teeth,' Donald of Balivoe had said often enough.

'A wily old fox wi' a nose for profit,' Dokie Joe maintained.

'A master at using the misfortunes of others to satisfy his own ends,' Jessie MacDonald had sniffed sourly after the master of Crathmor had paid twopence for a pair of her 'wally dugs' at a local rummage sale only to sell them years later at a greatly inflated price.

Dolly herself had often bemoaned his supposed meanness but tonight she put such uncharitable thoughts to the back of her mind. On this occasion the laird's ulterior motives had been to her advantage. He'd really sorted Shug out this time, achieving in minutes what she'd tried to do in years. She gave a little chortle of satisfaction. You're a saint among men, Captain Rory MacPherson, she thought. God bless you and keep you and long may you come to the rescue of damsels in distress like myself.

Shug was slithering down in bed, groaning about his back as he did so, saying that he really ought to have Doctor

MacAlistair come and examine him if only he could afford to pay the medical expenses involved.

'Oh, go suck a lemon,' Dolly told him rudely as she placed her pipe on the chair beside the bed and gave one last look at the brightening sky outside. Another day, a new beginning. Ay, it was that alright, new and bright and beautiful. Lying down she pulled her share of the patchwork quilt around her and closed her eyes. She was asleep in minutes, all her worries forgotten as she dreamed about a little horse called Dancer who transported her to realms of fantasy on wings of pure gossamer, strengthened by strands of spun glass made out of whisky bottles from the laird's very own cellars.

Word of Captain Rory's visit to the Laws flashed round Kinvara like lightning. 'The new horse will just go the same way as Sorry,' was the gloomy prophecy. 'Surely the laird must be growing soft in the head to give a good beast like that to the likes o' the Outlaws.'

'Oh, he knows fine what he's doing,' Willie said with the air of one who knew what he was talking about. 'I was there, I heard, I saw. He'll get his pound o' flesh out o' Shug or his name's no' Captain Rory MacPherson. Somehow he made that lazy bugger promise to work at last and I for one take my hat off to any man who can do that.'

'Ay, that's right,' Dokie Joe confirmed sagely. 'Shug won't be able to wriggle out o' it this time. The laird has witnesses to prove that he was acting fair and square and Dolly looked as if she might just kill Shug if he dares to try and back out o' this one.'

'Fair and square!' Jessie snorted. 'That man was never fair in his life. I just can't get over how he cheated me out of my own property and sold it again for a fortune.'

'He never cheated you,' Mattie said cuttingly. 'You put that pair of plaster ornaments into the sale yourself because you wanted rid o' them. The laird deserved any profit he made and should have got a pat on the back as well for actually persuading someone else to buy junk like that.'

'Junk! You've a cheek to talk. Your own house is full o' the stuff! It must be bad when that tink last week turned away from your door empty-handed when you showed him the rags you had to offer.'

A good going argument might have ensued had not Dokie Joe hastily taken his wife's arm to pull her away from the scene of battle, leaving everyone else to shake their heads in some disappointment, since it was always enjoyable when the formidable Jessie and the mighty Mattie pitched headlong into 'a battle o' the tongues' as Donald of Balivoe so aptly put it.

'Hmph, it's alright for some,' Hannah snorted as she poured water into the teapot while her sister-in-law, Maudie, mixed pancakes at the table, aided and abetted by Vaila who loved it when she got the chance to help her auntie with the baking.

'Fancy Shug Law getting a new horse in return for his services at Crathmor,' Hannah went on. 'He'll sit in a corner smoking and drinking himself silly and leave all the work to someone else.'

'Ach well, the Outlaws haven't got much to their name,' Maudie told her sister-in-law indulgently. 'It was a shame when their old horse turned her toes heavenwards and Shug at least has a proper job now, which in itself is something of a miracle. He's going round like a martyr, telling everyone he's only doing it for Dolly's sake and will likely end up an invalid for the rest o' his days.'

'It would serve him right,' Hannah returned snappishly. 'Shug Law is a lazy good for nothing who has never done an honest day's work in his life. Dolly's no better, the two o' them are well suited, beer and baccy, that's all they care about, that and breeding bairns as fast as they can make them. With their luck they could easily end up having shares in the laird's business. I wouldn't put anything past a pair like that.'

Maudie raised her eyebrows meaningfully at Vaila. Hannah wasn't in a very good mood these days. She was irritable, short-tempered and moody. She and Janet had already fallen out over some triviality and Catherine Dunbar, the schoolteacher, had been sent packing from the house only yesterday with a lame excuse and a few sharp words.

Vaila knew that her father wasn't sleeping in the same room as her stepmother any more. That first night of his homecoming she had heard them arguing as she lay in bed. After a while their door had opened and his footsteps had gone on up the landing to the tiny boxroom at the top. And that was where he had slept ever since, looking tired and drawn when he appeared at breakfast, Hannah not much better, neither of them finding very much to say to one another beyond a few necessary words of communication.

At first, Vaila had felt angry about this. Trust grown-ups to spoil things! It had all been so good during those first precious hours of her father's return, then, almost as she had predicted, everything had turned sour and nothing was the same any more.

As the days had gone on her anger had evaporated, to be replaced by a sense of exasperation. She had thought it was going to be a wonderful summer, spent with her adored father. True, there had been some lovely times during the haymaking. She had loved it despite all the hard work, working close to her father, seeing his strong body glistening with the sweat of his labours. All of them helping one another out there in the fields: men, women, children, the carts rumbling along the country lanes in the gloaming, the fragrance of the cut meadows hanging thick and sweet in the air, dances and ceilidhs in big cobwebby barns afterwards when camaraderie had been the order of the day and everyone had danced till the wee sma' hours.

Now there was a breathing space and she had imagined there might be some special outings with her father, instead of which he was taking himself off on solitary wanders, as if he hadn't had enough solitude during his long absences from home. Feelings of rebellion had gradually seeped into her being. If he could behave like that then so too could she. There were plenty of places she could go without him, lots of people she could go with. She had been seeing quite a bit of Rebecca Bowman lately, Joss too when he wasn't busy at Croft Angus, and Mark and Maida Lockhart were always ready to join in any activities in the offing. It was going to be a good summer and it was going to begin right now, today in fact, starting with a call to old Gabby the Clockmaker who was always pleased when small visitors turned up on his doorstep. Rebecca was longing to visit the old man and had arranged to meet Vaila near the Struan Bridge around three o'clock . . .

Vaila's musings were sharply interrupted at that point. The pancake mix had been transferred to the griddle, Maudie was at the stove presiding over it, her rosy round face flushed and warm, her plump, fluffy, feather bolster of a bosom heaving a little from her exertions as it was stuffy in the kitchen and the door had been left open to let in some air.

Everyone was preoccupied in what they were doing, no one had noticed the absence from the room of Maudie's children, two-year-old Kyle, and three-year-old Morven, both little minxes who needed constant watching. An ear-piercing yell came suddenly from outside. Maudie cried 'Bugger it!' and vacated the room, Hannah and Vaila did the same, all matters of domesticity forgotten in the urgency of the moment.

Only two young Sutherlands were out there in the sunlight, namely Andy and Essie, eyes round and wondering as they gazed towards the gorse bushes at the bottom of the garden. From these, the top of Morven's distinctive red head was to be seen, of Kyle there was no sign, only the sound of his high-pitched screams, echoing and re-echoing, as if from some deep hidden chamber below ground.

'The well!' Hannah gasped.

'Oh, dear God!' Maudie cried, lifting up her skirts as she spoke and making for the bushes at top speed. Morven was there alright, gazing down into the deep, dank recesses of the well, her small brother's heels held suspended in her dimpled grasp, a satisfied smile on her face as he hung there, not daring to make movement of any kind.

Maudie pounced, one small shoe came off in her hand, but he was soon safe, sobbing in her arms, laying all the blame for his experiences firmly at his sister's door.

'He hit me,' Morven stated baldly, 'so I put him in the well to pay him back.'

The other children were awed and not a little enthralled by this bold admission, not so Maudie. 'You wee bitch!' she cried, giving her daughter a hefty swipe on her sparsely covered bottom. 'If I ever catch you doing anything like this again . . .'

She paused, she sniffed, 'The pancakes!' she yelled and, as one, everyone raced back to the house only to find a few charred remains on the griddle and a terrible smell of burning in the room.

'Oh!' Maudie's good-natured face crumpled. She looked pale suddenly. Hannah went to get her a 'wee taste of brandy' to revive her, along with a cup of tea which had been keeping warm on the hob.

Half an hour later the situation was well in hand. Morven and Kyle were both ensconced in high chairs and strapped in firmly, Breck was enjoying 'the lickings' of the pancake mix in his corner, a fresh batch of pancakes reposed on the table, everyone was tucking in, including Maudie who had recovered from her fright and was piling jam as well as butter on top of the steaming morsels.

She and Hannah were talking amiably about the day-to-day running of a home and of the numerous small crises that could arise. After initial misgivings about having Maudie in the family, Hannah's opinions had swung in that young lady's favour and she had quickly formed a rapport with her good-natured sister-in-law. Maudie had the ability to smooth ruffled feathers and while Hannah would never, ever, have discussed problems of a personal nature with any member of the family she, nevertheless, felt soothed by Maudie's ready sympathies regarding all manner of minor incidents.

Chapter Eighteen

With her aunt and stepmother so engrossed in conversation Vaila saw her chance to escape. 'Please, can I go out for a while with Andy and Essie?' she asked hurriedly. 'It's a lovely day and I thought I might take a few pancakes along to old Gabby.'

'Ay, on you go,' Hannah nodded. 'Take Essie's hand if you have to cross the road and don't be late back, that man would talk the hind legs off a donkey and has no sense o' time – even if he is a clockmaker.'

Vaila wasted not a moment longer. Grabbing a handful of pancakes she wrapped them in greaseproof paper before rushing outside to collect Andy and Essie and harness Breck up to his cart, watched rather enviously by Kyle and Morven who were still tied securely into their respective high chairs.

'She's such a good wee lass,' Maudie commented as the children departed. 'A mind o' her own like her father but a bairn that can be trusted to do as she's told just the same.'

'Ay, she can that,' Hannah agreed lightly, even as she wondered just what was in her stepdaughter's mind these days. The child most certainly knew about the row that had taken place between her parents and Hannah had seen a watchful look in her eyes whenever they were all in the same room together – as if she was waiting for the next move on the board – hoping perhaps for some sign to signify that all was well and that everything would go back to normal again.

Hannah bit her lip. If only it was that easy. If only she hadn't opened her mouth and said things that would have been better left unsaid. Rob was a million miles away from her now and as the days passed it was becoming more and more difficult to reach him. Where did he go when he took himself out of the house, she wondered? Oh, she knew he went to visit his parents at Vale O' Dreip and Maudie had said that he sometimes popped in to see her and Finlay at River Cottage on the Sutherland estate. But surely that couldn't be all. What did he do the rest of the time? Who was he seeing?

He had told her quite plainly he would find his comforts elsewhere if not in the marriage bed. A man like that needed a woman. He would be hungry for one, desperate to find his pleasures after all those weeks away at the lighthouse . . .

And she had sent Catherine packing from the house only yesterday. He wouldn't like that when he got to hear about it, he wouldn't like it at all. Perhaps he was with the girl right this very minute, giving and receiving all the comfort he could ever want.

Dear God, there she was doing it again! Speculating.

Thinking the worst. He had plenty of places to go, people to visit, favours to return to those who had helped him out recently when extra hands had been needed on his little patch of croftland. He and Charlie Campbell were great friends and often went out fishing in Charlie's boat. He knew everybody in Kinvara for heaven's sake! He belonged here and everybody loved him, everybody . . .

There came a thump and a scream. Maudie had just unstrapped Kyle from his high chair and in his anxiety to get down he had slithered out of her grasp to land on the floor with painful results. In sympathy with her brother Morven too started screaming and in the mêlée that followed Hannah forgot her own troubles in her efforts to alleviate those of her sister-in-law.

The bluebells were knee high in the woods. Essie just had to go there to pick a bunch to give to old Gabby. After that she wanted to make a daisy chain to hang round her neck and without ado flopped down on the warm verge to pull at the wildflowers with her chubby fingers.

It wasn't a day to hurry or worry. The waters of the Kinvara coastline were azure blue, merging into a heat-hazed sky where gulls soared in the thermals and seals popped their heads out of the calm shallows in the bay. The fields were ablaze with scarlet poppies, the meadows golden with buttercups, stretching off into the wide summer yonder where larks sang from soaring heights and lapwings uttered their haunting notes.

The children were content to stop for a while: Vaila to make sense of Essie's carelessly picked blooms; Andy to climb out of his cart to join them in their pursuits; Breck to grab the chance of a snooze in the sun, while all around the bees droned and the burns chuckled down from the hills.

Bedecked in daisy chains they set off again, their steps taking them in the direction of Calvost village. Essie was in a jubilant mood, skipping along with her flowers in her hand, humming a little tune as she went. She loved any excuse that took her to see the old clockmaker and, as his house wasn't so far away, she had occasionally gone there by herself, unbeknown to her mother. Hannah was accustomed to her small daughter spending long hours in the garden and imagined her always to be safe there when she wasn't in the house. But Essie had little ploys of her own and slipped away from Keeper's Row whenever she saw her chance, sometimes visiting old Gabby, at others going to see Grace Lockhart at Oir na Cuan, who was always so generous with her time and patience whenever Essie's fair head bobbed into view.

All things considered, Essie was more independent than anyone could have guessed, and it annoyed her greatly when her mother still insisted on treating her like a baby. Four years old was getting on; next year she would be going to school like her big sister, then she would be leaving the house every day and could go to see old Gabby whenever she wanted.

Her chin went up. Refusing to take Vaila's hand she

darted suddenly onto the road when she saw Catherine Dunbar on the other side, just as the roar of an engine split the drowsing quiet of the countryside. There was a shout and a screech of brakes and the little red MG sports car that had been so conspicuous in the village of late came skidding to a halt just inches away from the little girl.

Catherine Dunbar came running, the driver of the car was climbing out, confusion reigned for several minutes as everyone fussed over Essie and ascertained for themselves that she wasn't in any way harmed by her experience. The driver of the MG sat down suddenly on the edge of the kerb. Pulling off his helmet and goggles he mopped his brow with the back of his sleeve and uttered a heartfelt, 'Phew! That was close! Thank God she's all right! She just ran out from the pavement before I knew what was happening.'

Catherine was staring at the young man, recognition dawning in her green eyes. 'Max MacKernon!' she gasped. 'What are you doing here?'

He was on his feet instantly, taking her hands in his, forgetting his fright as he gazed at her and laughed. 'I *live* here.'

'You live here! Oh, I know you told me you lived in a Scottish castle on the west coast but you didn't say exactly where.'

'I did, but you were always too busy to listen properly.'

'To tell the truth,' she blushed at this point, 'I thought you were making it up. You were always just so nice and ordinary I couldn't believe that you were really and actually one of the gentry.'

'Only by an accident of fate. My Boston-born mother married Lord MacKernon of Cragdu and Bob's your uncle! My stepfather adopted me and I came to be known in these parts as MacKernon the younger – though I've been away for so long I think everyone here's forgotten my existence. My job in my father's business keeps me busy, I'm also something of a plane enthusiast and do a bit of weekend flying at Renfrew aerodrome. Now I'm home for a spell and enjoying every minute.'

'Well, you've certainly been raising some eyebrows recently in that car. No one knew who you were, but the tongues were wagging just the same, "from the town", "daft and dangerous", "we'll all waken up one morning and find we've been killed crossing the road". Stuff like that. I saw you myself, racing past, but couldn't make you out for all the mufflers and helmets, not forgetting the goggles.'

'And you, Catherine? What about you? Are you on holiday in these parts?'

'No, I live and work here, in Balivoe school, but I am on holiday for the summer, enjoying the peace and quiet and the feeling that nothing ever changes in Kinvara – until today.'

They stared at one another all over again, amazed at the circumstances that had brought them together. She had said goodbye to Max Gilbert MacKernon at a graduation party in Glasgow university, she to start her teaching career, he to become a junior executive in his father's engineering company in England. She had never connected him with the elusive Lord and Lady MacKernon of Cragdu Castle, people she had heard about but had never yet met.

'We have a lot to catch up on.' He was eyeing her hopefully. 'How about coming for a spin with me sometime? Give us a chance to get to know one another all over again.'

'I don't think that would be a good idea,' she laughed. 'Not yet anyway. I'm the schoolteacher, remember? I have to set a good example and I doubt I'd do that haring around the countryside at a hundred miles an hour. Besides, you're gentry, I'm just middle of the road, never the twain shall meet, according to the class rules. Kinvara wouldn't forgive me if I broke them.'

'To hell with the rules! My mother never went by them and neither have I. Anyway, I'm not letting you go that easily. I'll pop into the schoolhouse sometime and you can give me tea. A very respectable pastime in these parts. How about it?'

'Alright,' she agreed with a laugh. 'Only, don't be too conspicuous when you arrive on my doorstep, that car draws attention for miles around.'

'I'll come on my horse. Nobody gives horses a second glance, and don't worry, I know what talk is in a place like this so I'll be very discreet and tether my steed at your back door where no one can see him and put two and two together.'

Highly delighted with himself he went off, after first making sure that Essie had not suffered any after-effects from the scare she had received.

Catherine too turned her attention to the children. 'Do you want me to come home with you? Just to make sure that you get there safely?'

Before anyone could speak Essie shook her head vigorously. 'No go home, go to see Gabby and take him bluebells.'

Catherine glanced at the wilting posy in the child's hand. 'Alright, but you had better hurry up before your flowers die – and make sure this time you don't go running over any roads without looking first.'

Andy conveyed that he would very much like to wring his little sister's neck while Vaila, anxious that she might be late for Rebecca, grabbed hold of the child's hand and gave it a little tug. 'I'll make sure,' she said firmly and Catherine nodded before going off herself – a bemused smile lifting the corners of her mouth as she re-crossed the road to resume her travels and go over in her mind her unexpected encounter with the young MacKernon of Cragdu Castle.

Meeting him had uplifted her spirits. She had been feeling somewhat dejected since Hannah had decanted her from No. 6 Keeper's Row, yet in some ways she hadn't been surprised by the rebuff, knowing in her heart that she might have done the same in Hannah's shoes.

Catherine's brow furrowed. Had she shown so plainly how much she cared for another woman's husband? How just the sight of Rob made her want to reach out and touch him and let him know how much he meant to her? It had been there, from the beginning, that small yearning, growing in intensity, till now her heart ached with longing whenever she saw him, a pain made all the greater in the knowing that he belonged to someone else and could never be hers.

Her thoughts returned to Max MacKernon. He had been such good fun during their college days together. With her it had never been anything more than friendship but with him it had been something else, something that she hadn't wanted to recognise in those days of learning and striving and chasing after ambition . . .

A movement on the shore caught her eye and she saw the figure of a man, way down there on the edge of the silvery sands, walking slowly along, head downbent, hands dug deep into his pockets, something lonely and lost about the way he was carrying himself.

Her heart accelerated. 'Rob,' she whispered, and without hesitation she went plunging down through the dunes to go flying over the beach, her feet as light as air, a singing in her heart that was like the echo of some sweet melody, familiar, yet unknown to her until now.

'Rob,' she said again, as she drew nearer. 'I thought it was you I saw. I hope you don't mind me breaking in on you like this.'

He looked up, his ruggedly handsome face taking on a slightly startled expression, as if he had torn himself away from some far and distant place and couldn't quite connect again with his surroundings.

'Catherine,' he acknowledged. 'I'm sorry, I didn't hear you coming.'

'I know, you were deep in thought, but I just had to come down to see you.'

Impulsively she spread her arms and threw back her head. 'Oh, it's such a lovely day, I feel like singing and dancing and laughing all at the same time and I would too if my feet didn't keep sinking into the sand like great big heavy millstones.'

Rob very much liked the look of Catherine that day. She was the picture of summer with her sparkling eyes and sun-flushed face, her hair a fiery halo round her neat little head, the flimsy material of her dress adhering to the contours of her slim waist and shapely breasts.

'Can I walk with you?' she asked, taking a few paces forward and looking back at him expectantly.

He hesitated. There was danger here, he thought. If he and she were seen together the tongues would wag, Hannah would get to hear about it, and the rift that had sprung between them would grow deeper, more impenetrable than ever.

Catherine had taken off her shoes, the wet sand was squeezing up between her toes, leaving behind tiny pools as she lifted her feet. He was reminded suddenly of childhood days, warm sand, sunlit seas, himself and Finlay splashing barefoot in the waves, carefree, abandoned.

'Alright,' he agreed with a lifting of his heart. 'Though I warn you, I might not have very much to say, I have a lot on my mind these days.'

'I'll be as quiet as a mouse,' she promised blithely and proceeded to chatter 'like a budgie wi' the runs' to quote Minnie MacTaggart who had looked after Father MacNeil's lively feathered pet whilst he was away on holiday and who had not yet recovered from the experience of 'so much meaningless noise'.

Catherine spoke about anything that came into her head, telling Rob about her meeting with the Sutherland children earlier and about Essie's scrape with danger, assuring him that nothing drastic had happened and that the little girl had learned a harsh lesson concerning road safety.

She didn't say anything about her banishment from his house, feeling that he would have said something about it if he had known. She also didn't mention Max. As yet she wanted to keep that part of her life private. It wasn't as if it would come to anything anyway. For the moment Rob was all that mattered, all that she cared about.

He was enjoying himself with her. She could see it in the way his eyes were crinkling as he listened to her nonsense, the relaxing of his demeanour, the way his laugh rang out when she tripped and fell in a rock pool and he had to help her struggle to her feet.

His hand lingered in hers, she could feel its warmth pulsing into her, then suddenly he drew it away as if it had been burned. 'Damn and blast!' he cursed, inclining his head towards a distant spur of rock. 'Johnny Lonely, skulking about watching us. Bugger the man! He's always springing up where he isn't wanted.'

'Johnny won't say anything, I've learned that much in the short time I've been here. See all, say nothing, seems to be his motto. Besides, we weren't doing anything, nothing that could give any reason for talk. You were only helping me to get up. Surely that isn't such a crime?'

'You don't know this place as much as you think you do,' was his grim answer. 'You only have to be seen walking with a woman in these parts for the gossip to start.'

The spell between them was broken, nothing she could say would recapture the magic of their moments together. Sitting down on a rock she dried her feet with the hem of her dress and pulled on her shoes, not looking up at him as he stood there above her, gazing silently down.

'Catherine,' he murmured at last, 'Thank you for talking to me today, you were like a tonic. I feel the better for having met you.'

Standing up, she looked straight into his eyes. 'I'll be here for you whenever you want me, Rob,' she imparted in a calm controlled voice. 'Every evening, over yonder, I go for a walk.' With a slight nod of her head she indicated the distant shoreline. 'I know a quiet place beyond the schoolhouse, one that not even Johnny Lonely visits, a tiny cove with white sands and small dry caves never reached by the tide.'

Briefly she touched his arm and then continued her

way along the beach, her retreating steps making deep impressions in the wet sand, as if she was leaving a trail for him to follow should he ever feel the need for her company in that tiny secluded cove beyond the schoolhouse.

Chapter Nineteen

A much subdued Essie seemed quite happy to take Vaila's hand as they went on their way, pausing only to wave to a supremely contented looking Dolly Law sailing past in her cart, Dancer in her traces, stepping out briskly, as if she too was enjoying the freedom of the road on that sunlit summer's day.

Rebecca was waiting at the Struan Bridge as arranged, hopping restlessly from one foot to the other and looking uncomfortably warm in her rough sackcloth dress and heavy hat. 'What kept you?' she demanded as soon as Vaila came running up. 'I've been waiting here for ages, eaten alive by midges and horseflies *and* I got stung by those nettles over there! I itch all over and I'm also horribly hot and thirsty.'

Privately Vaila thought that Rebecca's thick black stockings might have had a lot to do with her irritable legs and was about to say so when she thought better of it. Instead she explained about Essie's little mishap and went on to offer her friend a pancake from the greaseproof bag by way of appeasement.

'Why did you have to bring her anyway?' Rebecca said

peevishly, biting into her pancake without really tasting it and throwing the youngest member of the party a look of annoyance. 'She's much too little to take anywhere. If it had been me I'd have marched her straight home and put her to bed without another thought.'

Essie lowered her brows and scowled at the older girl. 'Go see Gabby,' she stated for the umpteenth time since leaving the house. 'Take him flowers.'

'Oh, alright, let's go if we're going. I can't stay away too long. I'm supposed to be doing my chores and would be too if Caleb hadn't said he would cover up for me till I got back.'

So saying she took off, her long legs carrying her ahead of the others till Vaila was forced to shout at her to wait till they had all caught up. 'I'm fed up waiting,' Rebecca returned rebelliously. 'I've been waiting half the afternoon all because your silly little sister tried to kill herself on the road.'

'She isn't silly and she didn't try to kill herself.' Vaila's own temper was hotting up for battle. 'She just made a mistake, that's all, and if you don't snap out o' your bad mood I'm not going into Gabby's with you – and that's final.'

Rebecca saw that her sulks were cutting no ice with Vaila and she drew in her horns immediately. 'Come on.' Putting her arm round her friend's shoulder she gave her a little shake. 'I'm sorry I was so nasty, don't take it to heart. I only got angry because my time is so precious and I just wanted to enjoy every minute of today.'

Andy was growing impatient with all three girls, the two older ones shouting at one another, Essie seizing the opportunity to wander away again to pick more flowers.

'Gerron, Breck!' he yelled in his gruff voice and the dog took off so vigorously that the others were forced to run to keep up, Rebecca laughing despite herself at the sight of Essie's sturdy little legs fairly stomping along.

Old Gabriel Cochrane lived in a small thatched dwelling set well back from the road at the edge of Calvost village. Surrounded by a rustic fence. the tiny garden ablaze with marigolds and lupins, the chimney pots rising up crookedly out of the thatch, bees and butterflies droning in and out of the flower spikes, it seemed a magical place forgotten by trouble and time.

Fixed to the tumbledown gate was a large round disc with Clockwork Cottage painted on it in bold letters. The very name had sent shivers of delight through generations of Kinvara children and now it was Rebecca's turn to be entranced as she stared at nooks and crannies stuffed with garden ornaments and watched the antics of the wild birds as they splashed happily in a shady, lily-strewn pool.

Unable to wait a moment longer, Essie went marching boldly up to the front door to rap the gargoyle knocker while Andy clambered out of his cart in readiness and the girls stood by expectantly. Old Gabby's appearance was as spectacular as his house and garden. He was a tall, arresting figure with a nut brown face, bushy brows, and a long white beard that flowed luxuriantly down over his sark. On his head he wore a tweed deerstalker hat almost entirely covered by fishing flies of every description though he'd never done a day's fishing in his life. 'They just look nice' was his answer to anybody who asked, 'and besides, they come in handy when I'm making my clocks and need a hook for the fiddly bits.'

Gabby wasn't really all that old; at thirty-eight he'd done his bit in the Great War and 'could do it all over again if need be', but to later breeds of Kinvara youngsters he was simply old Gabby and he didn't mind the title in the least. As he stood there on his step he seemed to fill every inch of doorspace and might have been a formidable figure had it not been for the wide grin splitting his face and his words of welcome. He ushered his young visitors inside, not forgetting Breck who was treated to a bowl of ice cold water from the well and a large tasty bone straight from the soup pot simmering on the stove, after Gabby had scraped off some of the meatier chunks for his own dinner plate.

Vaila handed over her rather depleted offering of pancakes which was very gratefully received indeed while Essie, not to be outdone, held up her bunches of flowers, now drooping their heads and looking very sorry for themselves. But Gabby was delighted with them and went to put them in water, while Essie chattered to him and told him about her brush with 'a nasty big motor car' on the way to his house. After that he made more of a fuss of her than ever, sympathising with her in his deep gruff voice and calling her his 'poor wee brave lamb'.

But he didn't forget the others and went to fetch creamy milk from the cool larder at the back of the house, bringing it back to the kitchen along with his own home-baked scones spread with bramble jam he had made himself in the big jelly pan hanging on a hook behind the door.

He made sure that Rebecca didn't feel left out in any way, talking to her in his nice, slow unhurried voice and plying her with little snippets of information regarding his own distinctive lifestyle. When he dropped a dollop of jam onto his beard he made no apology of any kind but simply mopped it up with one large hooked finger and inserted it into his mouth with serious intent, thereafter rising up from his chair to rinse his beard in a pail of water sitting on the slats under the sink.

Rebecca was fascinated. Her dark eyes sparkling she emitted a little giggle and Gabby laughed too. In fact they all laughed. It was that kind of house, bright and filled with atmosphere, cluttered with all sorts of knick-knacks. Cupboards bursting at the seams with gaily coloured dishes; tapestry stools placed cosily near the hearth; the inglenook at the fire stacked with tartan rugs, patchwork cushions, and piles of books; the floor littered with old newspapers and trays filled to the brim with tiny screws and clock innards. In amongst the debris three cats napped contentedly in patches of sunlight filtering in through the windows, adding to the homeliness of the scene.

'My wife, God rest her, made the house nice when she was alive,' Gabby explained with a rueful smile. 'She wouldn't like the mess of it now but if I don't have my things to hand I forget where I've put them so I just tend to leave them where they are.'

'It doesn't matter,' Rebecca said with a strange expression on her face. 'It must be lovely to be that free, to not mind about anything, never to care what other people think, not to have everything bare and spartan and exactly in its place. One day I'd like to have a house where I can do what I want and be me when I want.'

Gabby understood this, he nodded in agreement and pulled at his beard for a few thoughtful moments. 'You will, lass, you will,' he said eventually. 'But no one can ever do exactly what they want all of the time. Take me, for instance, if I had my way I'd spend my days in my garden, my nights with my books, the rest o' my spare hours playing my fiddle. If making my clocks were only a hobby I'd probably feel the same way about them, but they're my bread and butter, and while I take a pride in doing them I would rather be playing my fiddle – if you see what I mean, lass.'

Rebecca nodded. 'Yes, I see what you mean, but at least you don't have to pray to the Lord for everything that is given to you, no matter how small.'

'I give thanks, lass, I give thanks, safe in my bed at

night when there is no one around to hear my mutterings and I can give full vent to my feelings.'

'Want to see the clocks.' Andy was growing impatient again, Rebecca talking in that serious way of hers, Essie doing everything she could to gain attention, Vaila, like him, wanting only to leave the table in order to sample the rest of the delights that Clockwork Cottage had to offer.

Gabby gave them a tour of the house. Every room had clocks in them. Big ones, small ones, chiming ones sitting on mantelshelves, a grandmother and a grandfather standing sentinel in a tiny hallway, wag-at-the-wa's all over the place, a perky little cuckoo that suddenly rushed out from a dark corner to make everyone jump, several large tavern clocks waiting for their faces to be cleaned and re-numbered.

Gabby had commandeered a portion of the parlour as his workroom. The better off people in the district provided him with much of his business and in this room their various timepieces waited to be mended, cleaned, and generally overhauled.

But there was more to Gabby than just making and mending clocks and watches. In his spare time he also made toys, not just any old toys but the kind that worked; clockwork soldiers, music boxes, clowns that danced, tiny dolls with moving limbs. In pride of place was a working model of a steam engine and a paddle steamer with a funnel that puffed out smoke.

The young Sutherlands had seen it all before but were

always eager to see it again, Andy gazing in delight at the soldiers, Vaila clapping her hands at the antics of the clowns, Essie pestering Gabby to hold one of the little dolls, Rebecca not saying anything but taking everything in just the same, a sparkle of interest showing in her dark eyes when Gabby started up the steam engine for the benefit of his young visitors.

'Nathan would like that,' she said softly. 'He loves anything to do with trains and wants to work with them when he grows up. He's my brother, the youngest, and the only times I've ever seen him get excited about anything is when he's sitting on an embankment watching a steam train clattering by.'

'Bring him along, then,' Gabby invited, in his generous way. 'Just come in and have a look, even when I'm out the door is always open.'

Rebecca thanked him and solemnly shook his hand. It was time to go but Essie insisted on doing a little dance for Gabby before she went, her small body swaying to the tune she was humming, her rosy lips parted into a cherubic smile as she held her dimpled arms above her head and pirouetted round before making a wobbly curtsy as a finale to her display.

Gabby nodded his approval of the impromptu entertainment but he was anxious to get on with his work now and made a move towards the door.

'More?' Essie was unwilling to relinquish the limelight, she gazed expectantly at Gabby who shook his head and said he had promised to mend a chiming clock for Mrs Prudence Taylor-Young of Bougon Villa who was growing impatient to have the job done.

Essie pouted. She made no move to go. 'Come on.' Vaila grabbed her small sister's arm and bulldozed her to the door. 'Gabby's had enough o' you for one day,' she told the little girl as soon as the door of Clockwork Cottage had closed behind them.

'She's just a little show-off,' Rebecca stated laconically while Essie made one last defiant gesture as she daringly pulled a handful of marigolds from Gabby's garden to 'take home to Mamma'.

'She's torn all the heads off,' Rebecca said in disgust. 'Why does she get her own way all the time without being punished? If it was *my* father he would shut her in a room till she learned some manners and even then she might have to go without supper for a few nights to make her really sorry.'

Vaila said nothing to this. She was very glad she didn't have a father like Joshua Bowman with all his rules and regulations and she hoped Rebecca wasn't going to get all morbid on the subject.

But Rebecca's temper had been restored by her meeting with Gabby and she didn't dwell any further on Essie or her father. Taking Vaila's arm she said thoughtfully, 'I wish there were more like Gabby in the world. He's a very kind and happy person and I enjoyed meeting him. Kinvara certainly has its share of characters. Take that

Johnny Lonely, for instance, he's one of the most peculiar wretches I've yet encountered. He watches people as if his life depended on it. I've seen him hovering about near the mill spying on us and once he actually had the cheek to look in the windows, though I was the only one to see him doing it.'

She was silent for a moment before going on slowly. 'Yet, despite his oddness, I have to admit, there is something fascinating and interesting about him, that wild look of his, his elusiveness. I suppose I must be attracted by his air of mystery. There is no doubting he *is* different – just like old Gabby, only he's the complete opposite of Johnny, open and honest and willing to let you into his life.'

Kangaroo Kathy, named so because she always carried her knitting materials in a lap bag tied round her middle, was sitting on a bench in the sun placed strategically on a grassy knoll that afforded a perfect view of the sea, knitting needles clacking busily, counting stitches under her breath and not looking up as the children passed by and chorused a greeting.

'Ay, ay, a fine day indeed,' Kathy returned absently, 'but it's hot, hot, and already I've dropped two stitches because my fingers are all thumbs wi' the sweat dropping off them. Knit one purl one, och bother and bugger it! The damt wool's got caught on a safety pin and I've just dropped another stitch through blethering to you lot.'

'That's another one,' Rebecca observed as they left Kathy and her knitting behind. 'An individual I mean, daft as they come but likeable for all that and I love the way she weaves everyday talk into her needles as she goes along.'

'You should be there when she and Janet from next door get together,' Vaila laughed. 'They're cousins and Kathy drives Janet crazy with her knitting and her tales of her island upbringing. She was born in the Hebrides and though she speaks English she thinks in the Gaelic. My stepmother, Hannah, is afraid to be in the same room as her because she can never quite understand Kathy's way of talking.'

'Sounds like fun,' Rebecca said, thinking to herself how much she was coming to like living in Kinvara. There was a quaintness about it that she had never encountered before. The inhabitants were a mix of friendliness and dourness. She had already discovered how critical they could be towards one another, how suspicious they were about strangers, but in the main they were homely and tolerant and unlike any people she had ever met before.

Then there was Vaila. Making her feel part of the place, including her into any activity within her means, putting up with her strangeness, her lack of social graces, even displaying a certain amount of patience towards her in spite of that awful temper of hers. Rebecca's eyes sparkled . . . a temper that matched her own for quickness, one that she understood and could forgive since it belonged to a girl who was good natured in every other respect.

'Go home now.' Essie was growing tired. Her face was flushed and hot looking and her small legs were finding it hard going keeping up with those of her older companions. To her enormous surprise Rebecca suddenly bent to pick her up. 'There, I'll take you as far as the bridge, but stay still or I might drop you and only you will be to blame for that.'

Essie stayed perfectly still. She was too flabbergasted to move or to utter one word. Rebecca had been disapproving of her all afternoon, she had been superior and elderly and had taken every opportunity to indicate that this particular young Sutherland was nothing but a little nuisance who ought to have been left at home where she belonged. Now, here she was, sailing along like a princess, her wilted posy of marigolds brushing their golden pollen all over Rebecca's dark hair, her slackened feet drumming a tattoo against Rebecca's mobile thighs, the breath from her mouth moistening Rebecca's ear, her sticky fingers adhering to the nape of Rebecca's neck because she had to hold on somehow or she might be dropped and no way was she going to precipitate a catastrophe of such dire proportions.

The expression on Essie's face was priceless. Neither Andy nor Vaila had seen their small sister so obedient of late and as they marched along they glanced at one another with meaning. They didn't dare laugh or speak however, one untoward sound could mean the undoing of Essie, the spell that now gripped her could be broken, sending her plummeting to the ground in a flurry of knickers, bows and frills, not forgetting the marigolds she had so boldly and carelessly plucked from old Gabby's garden.

Chapter Twenty

Father MacNeil was coming along on his bike, wobbling into the side of the road when he saw the children on the pavement. 'A fine day,' he greeted as he came to a halt alongside them. 'Much too warm for cycling so I'm glad of any excuse to stop for a while.'

In truth, the priest, in common with everyone else in Kinvara, was consumed with curiosity about the Bowmans and their unorthodox lifestyle and wanted to know more about them. He was also still smarting from the rebuff Rebecca had given him during their first meeting and now saw his chance to try and make some headway with her. Naturally outgoing and friendly, he found it hard to understand anybody who could display ill feelings towards their fellow men, especially someone of Rebecca's tender years who should, in his book, be without prejudice of any kind.

In the last week or two he had discovered a bit more about Joshua Bowman and his narrow religious outlook and had begun to realise why Rebecca and her brothers were so stifled. With this in mind he threw her a sympathetic smile as he dismounted from his bike and propped it carefully against the bole of a nearby tree.

The Sutherland youngsters were truly pleased to see him as he was a great favourite with all of them. Rebecca however made no response whatsoever. Unwrapping Essie's arms from her neck she placed her hastily on the ground and was about to turn away when she seemed all at once to change her mind. 'How do you do, sir?' she acknowledged, politely extending her hand which he gripped warmly, never knowing that Rebecca's about face had been caused by a sudden sighting of her father in his trap high up on the hill road above Vale O' Dreip. She knew that he couldn't possibly see her from that distance but the very idea of him being in the vicinity had fired a spark of rebellion in her mind. Why shouldn't she speak to a priest if she wanted to? He was a nice man, one who had never shown anything else but friendliness towards her, who was looking at her now in a rather boyishly anxious fashion as he waited for armistice to be properly declared – like a puppy dog awaiting approval from its master's hand!

The ridiculous comparison caused a bubble of mirth to rise in Rebecca's throat. The stern lines of her young face relaxed. Father MacNeil noticed the softening and he relaxed too. 'I'm sorry I was rude to you the other day,' Rebecca found herself saying. 'It was wrong of me but I was strange and new here and it all got rather on top of me.'

She sounded so unbearably polite that Vaila felt herself cringing with embarrassment but it didn't last, the priest soon saw to that. Some lighthearted remark was made and before long they were all chattering away, Rebecca herself volunteering an account of the visit to Gabby's house and how much she had enjoyed it.

When the priest at last took his leave Rebecca's face was aglow. 'He *is* a nice man,' she stated, almost defensively. 'And I don't see why I shouldn't talk to him if I want – despite what Father might think.'

'But, he isn't here,' Vaila pointed out.

'No,' Rebecca's eyes roved up to the spot where she had last seen her father. 'Not exactly where we are, just nearby, but I felt, in here . . .' she placed her hand on her forehead, 'that in some ways he was standing right next to me and I was doing something to get back at him at last.'

'Is that why you spoke to Father MacNeil, just to get back at your father?'

'At first it was, then it wasn't, I forgot all about my father after a while and just talked for the sake of it.'

They had arrived back at the Struan Bridge. The moment had come for Rebecca to go home, the very thought of which robbed her face of the animation that had lit it for the past hour or two. 'I don't know when I'll see you again,' she told Vaila regretfully. 'It was bad enough getting here today and wouldn't have been possible but for Caleb. I'll try and think of some excuse to get away again if you've got anything planned. Mother doesn't seem to know where we are or where she is half the time but

Father's got eyes in his head like a hawk and sees everything that we do.'

She stood looking at her friend and her lip trembled just a little bit. 'It was wonderful today, the freedom, seeing you, meeting Gabby.'

With a sudden rush of movement she enclosed Vaila in a hasty embrace. 'Earth sisters,' she whispered, her breath warm against Vaila's ear, then she was gone, cutting down to the river and taking a short cut over the fields, hoping all the while that her father might not be home yet, that her absence would have gone unnoticed.

Vaila watched the tiny dot that was her friend running across the meadows, disappearing and reappearing according to the nature of the terrain. Something poignant seized Vaila. She felt bereft. She grappled with her feelings, trying in her young mind to understand the complexities of her friend's character. She had known Rebecca only a short while yet already felt attuned to her. There was a quality about the girl that was very likeable and appealing. Oh, she could be trying when she wanted to be, stubborn, unyielding, snooty, but when she allowed herself to relax she was another person entirely and she could be really amusing when she liked.

But there was more to Rebecca than just that. Beneath the cool exterior passions churned: there was a heart that throbbed with warmth: an inner strength that showed itself in many unexpected ways. Vaila felt that she had only just glimpsed a small part of the real Rebecca and she was eager to know more.

'Earth sisters,' she murmured to herself and liked the sound of the words, words that were different, new, exciting.

'Dadda!' Essie's voice rang out. Vaila turned to see her father coming along behind, his steps quickening as he saw his little family meandering on in front. In seconds he had lifted Essie onto his strong shoulders, was holding his hand out to Vaila, patting Breck, ruffling Andy's hair.

Andy forgot the small niggles of disappointment he had been feeling over his father's failure to start making the promised desk and bookcase. Vaila cast aside her doubts regarding his allegiance to his family's well-being.

He seemed happier somehow, the bounce was back in his step. He was tall, strong and handsome and he wanted to know what they had been doing that day, how Essie was faring after the fright she had received earlier.

'How did you know about that, Father?' Vaila asked in puzzlement. 'Were you there? Did you see?' She didn't call him Robbie. That was reserved for their private times together, except when she was carried away by some notable event and couldn't stop herself saying it. Also it wasn't the moment for levity, she had to let him see that she too could be aloof when she wanted to be.

Her question caught him unawares. For a moment he didn't answer then he said lightly, 'Let's say a little bird told me. Nothing happens in Kinvara without somebody somewhere finding out about it.'

She hated it when he spoke like this, as if she was a baby who had to be humoured, evading the issue, trying to pull the wool over her eyes. 'No, Father, that's cheating and you know it!' she cried hotly. 'Why can't you say what really happened?'

'Och, come on, now, don't take it so seriously.' He knew instantly that he couldn't get off so lightly where his eldest daughter was concerned. 'I met your teacher, that's all. She was concerned about Essie but wanted to assure me that no harm had been done.'

He threw Vaila an apologetic grin. 'How would you all like to go out in Charlie's boat tonight? Get away from the midges. I had a word with him earlier and he said that if we met him at the harbour after tea he would have the boat waiting.'

It was the salve that everyone needed. Andy let out a whoop of joy, Essie clapped her hands, Vaila held onto Rob's hand and felt that at last the summer was about to begin in earnest and everything would go back to being normal again.

They arrived home with sparkling eyes, buoyant and eager, but the minute they got indoors everything changed again. Hannah had not enjoyed her afternoon. The tiff she'd had with Janet had been preying on her conscience and as soon as Maudie had departed she had gone next door to try and make amends with her neighbour. Janet however was in a strange frame of mind. Her sunny personality usually allowed her to easily forgive the contrariness in others and normally she would have brushed Hannah's apologies aside and taken the blame for the disagreement on her own shoulders.

Today was not one of those days. She heard Hannah out in silence, her head turned away a little, not quite meeting the other woman's eyes as she spoke.

'I just thought I ought to come and say sorry for the mood I was in the other day.' Hannah began assertively since she didn't want Janet to think that she was being entirely humble. 'Nothing at all to do with you, Janet. Since Rob came back certain things have got on top o' me and I suppose I had to take my feelings out on someone, you were just there, that was all, nothing personal, and I – I hope you'll see it that way,' she ended rather lamely as she began to sense Janet's lack of response.

'Well, to tell the truth, 'Janet jumped up and began punching cushions into shape with a vigour that was not in keeping with her usual placid self, 'I'm glad you came in because there's something I've been meaning to talk to you about.'

She did look up then, straight into Hannah's eyes as she went on rather unwillingly, 'It's to do with Essie. At first I thought it was all a mistake, that it couldn't possibly be true, now I feel it *is* true because I've searched and searched and haven't been able to come up with any answers and knew you would have to find out sooner or later.'

Hannah had begun tensing as soon as Essie's name was mentioned. She took a deep breath. 'Janet, you're not making sense, in fact I would go as far as to say you're rambling. What has Essie got to do with anything, I'd like to know?'

It was then that Janet told her neighbour about the trinkets that had gone missing from her bedroom, her voice low as she told of her fruitless search for them, her subsequent descision not to say anything about the incident till she was completely and utterly sure that the things hadn't been mislaid or had fallen into some out of the way crevice.

'It isn't that they were of any real worth,' Janet said with a shake of her head. 'Except for a ring Jock gave me that had sentimental value. It's just the fact that they have somehow disappeared and I can't think of anybody else who could have taken them. Essie has a habit o' wandering into places in the house that she shouldn't. She takes sweeties and biscuits without as much as a by your leave or any sort of thank you.'

'How do you know it was Essie?' Hannah's voice was high and ragged. 'Did you ask her? Did you give her a chance to deny it?'

'Of course I asked and of course she said no. Oh, I hate all this! I love Essie and would do anything for her! But she has to learn the difference between right and wrong, she is a good child going to waste, and if you don't start doing something now, Hannah, it will soon be too late.'

'Going to waste!' Hannah yelped incredulously. 'How can you say that? The child has a nature as sweet as a flower, everybody loves Essie, everybody. To accuse her o' such an evil action is beyond my belief. What about that precious son o' yours? He isn't such a saint when all's said and done. He might have sold the things to make money. He's very fond o' money is your Joss and would do anything to get it. Anybody who works for the Henderson pair must be hard up indeed and in my opinion it would be in your own interests to look nearer home for your answers instead o' trying to lay the blame at someone's else's door!'

By now both women were white-faced and shaken, the point of no return had been reached. Without a word Janet got up and went to the door to open it, Hannah went out, the door slammed behind her with an almighty wallop, the birds were singing and the sun was shining but for Janet and Hannah it might as well have been darkest night without a glimmer of light showing anywhere.

Hannah was therefore in a very confused state of mind when Rob came in with the children and the atmosphere at the tea table was somewhat strained as she went over in her head the things that Janet had said about Essie, the things *she* had to say to her husband afterwards concerning the matter.

'I'm taking the bairns out in Charlie's boat,' Rob told her when the table had been cleared and the dishes washed and put away.

'Ay,' she said gruffly, 'but there's something I have to say to you first, something which would be better said with just the two o' us here.'

With that she sent the children upstairs to play for a while, all of them protesting at the order since they were anxious to be out and away to the blue, blue sea beckoning to them from the windows.

'Do as your mother tells you,' Rob said quietly, imagining to himself that a showdown was coming with regard to the row he had had with his wife on the first night of his homecoming. In many ways he was glad that this might be the case as the strain of living in such a tense atmosphere was beginning to tell on him. It would be so good to clear the air, get it all out into the open, to get on with their lives again. He could forget all about Catherine and the temptations he'd felt earlier when he'd been in her vibrant company.

When Hannah began to talk about Essie he couldn't quite take it in at first. This wasn't what he had expected; the low flat tone of Hannah's voice when she began recounting to him what Janet had said, the later turbulence of Hannah's words when she hotly defended her small daughter's honour and declared Janet to be no more than a trouble-maker, as if she was desperately trying to convince herself of that fact and was hoping to hear him agreeing with her.

'Get Essie down and we'll ask her,' he said baldly when she had at last finished speaking. 'You know it's the only way to deal with all this and the sooner it's over with the better.'

'Ay, no doubt you're right, though what good it will do when I already know the answer is another matter entirely.'

Going to the foot of the stairs she shouted her daughter's name. Essie came down, her face all rosy and fresh from a recent wash, her ribbons tied neatly into her shining tumble of golden curls, pearly teeth showing as she went to her father to wrap her arms around his legs and gaze up at him in her beguiling fashion.

He was having none of that however. Sitting her down on a stool in front of him he explained to her about Janet's missing trinkets and asked her outright if she had taken them.

'No, Dadda.' Vehemently Essie shook her head as she protested her innocence, her eyes big and blue as she gazed at him, her little rosebud of a mouth beginning to quiver ever so slightly at the unmoving note in his voice. 'Janet's bad to say that. I never took anything, I never!'

'There, that's quite enough for me!' Hannah enclosed her daughter in her arms and crooned soothingly into her ear. 'Mamma's here, my wee lamb, I knew you wouldn't do anything wicked like that. I'll look after you, I won't let anybody hurt you.'

Vaila and Andy arrived downstairs at that point, risking

a scolding for disobedience so eager were they to be on their way. Essie wriggled out of her mother's grasp and went to get her coat. The others were chattering, making up for lost time, telling Hannah about their adventures of the afternoon, picking bluebells in the woods; seeing Dolly Law with her new horse; the visit to Gabby.

Only then did Essie's near miss with Max MacKernon's MG sports car come to light; the arrival of Catherine Dunbar on the scene: Andy's eyes gleaming as he tried to describe the vehicle; Vaila carried away with enthusiasm when she spoke of her teacher and how good she had been with Essie.

Then somehow it came out, how their father had come to hear of the incident through a chance encounter with Catherine. One thing leading to another, Andy asking quite plainly when she would be allowed back to the house because he missed her and wanted to show her the poem he had written about his father.

'Allowed back?' Rob repeated his son's words, gazing at Hannah as he did so. 'I wasn't aware that she had ever been sent away.'

Everyone looked at Hannah then, she reddened and shook her head. 'It was between her and me, just a few words, that was all, I didn't expect her to just up and go and make a big drama out of it. Oh . . . I've had enough for one day. I'm going for a walk. I have to get out o' the house for a while, perhaps some fresh air will help to clear my head.'

Throwing her shawl over her shoulders she let herself out, leaving her husband to stare after her, a muscle working in his jaw as he did so. It was back to square one, no, worse than that, there were more tensions in the air than ever and more and more people were being drawn into the pit. Janet no doubt feeling cast out and unhappy about that business over Essie, Catherine implicated because of an impulsive kiss and one uncalculated encounter on the seashore . . .

He drew himself up at this juncture. Had it been so innocuous? Or had she deliberately set out to look for him in order to hypnotise him with her gaiety, her exuberance, her undoubted feminine appeal? These things she had hinted at as she was leaving, letting him know of her availability should he ever feel the urge to seek her out. That hadn't been so artless, the very opposite in fact . . .

There, he was at it now! Allowing his imagination to run riot, being suspicious, seeing wrong in everyday words and deeds . . .

The children were ready to go, he hoisted Andy up onto his shoulders and took a hand each of Essie and Vaila. Breck barked and frisked at their heels as they set off, revelling in the freedom, delighted to be unfettered for once and able to stop and sniff at every bush and tree on the way down to that big, wide expanse of clear, cool water.

Chapter Twenty-one

Charlie was waiting at the harbour as promised, a well-built, good-looking man in his mid-fifties with strong, dark Celtic colouring and deep blue 'seaman's eyes' that had set many a heart fluttering in the days of his youth when he had roamed the oceans of the world in the Merchant Navy.

Charlie's voice was husky and 'sensual' according to Jessie MacDonald when she had once dared to utter that tantalising word to describe the way he spoke. The only trouble was, she had inadvertently said it in front of Mattie MacPhee who seemed always to take a fiendish pleasure in teasing and tormenting the life out of Jessie whenever Charlie's name was mentioned.

On that particular occasion, Jessie left herself wide open to attack as Mattie reminded her gleefully she would never get the chance to enjoy the full benefit of Charlie's silken tones now that he had gone and hitched himself to Harriet Houston from Ayr.

'If he is like that in ordinary day-to-day speech, just think what he would be like in the bedroom, Jessie,' Mattie went on gloatingly, 'dripping honey all over the place, pouring itself into Harriet's lugs, coaxing her into doing things that you have likely never even dreamed of.'

'And what makes you think I have led such a sheltered life?' Jessie had blustered. 'Don't forget, I once left Kinvara for two years to nurse an old aunt in Edinburgh, how do you know what I got up to when I was away? That city is a den o' iniquity for all its posh exterior and I myself could not help but see the seamy side of life there. I learned a few things I can tell you, and as well as all that, I had my admirers, Mattie MacPhee, oh, ay, more than I can count on my two hands and a few more besides.'

'Och, you're as innocent as a babe in arms, Jessie, anyone can see that just by looking at you. No, no, it would take more than a puckle years in Edinburgh to make you change the ways o' a lifetime. Charlie's been at it a long time, his days at sea turned him into a very experienced sort o' man. I heard tell he had a lass in every port and these foreign wimmen are able to do things to menfolk that would make your hair stand on end. I myself saw pictures in a book once that made my eyes pop out their sockets but I didn't dare show them to Dokie Joe in case he got ideas in his head and me wi' enough bairns already to fill a Sunday school – as Catrina Blair herself brazenly told me.'

'Ay, that you have,' Jessie had returned sourly, 'surely nothing to boast about in these days o' war and want.'

That made Mattie prickle slightly. 'The war was over a long time ago, in case you haven't noticed, and my bairns will never want for anything as long as there's breath in me to do my bit up at the castle.'

More on her mettle than ever she went on. 'There will be no fear of Harriet getting herself pregnant at her age, she can let Charlie do anything he wants with her and he will be having a fine time to himself teaching her all there is to know about sexual adventure. Can you imagine it, Jessie, the sort o' things he has to say to her, the sweet nothings in her ear as she lies there tingling all over wi' anticipation, waiting for that one moment that has surely been the undoing o' women since time began . . .'

Jessie could take no more then, treating her tormentor to an almighty glower she flounced away, vowing to herself that never, never again, would she give that awful woman any more opportunities to tease her like that. It was wicked! Wicked! Jessie went home and thought about Charlie. He should never have allowed himself to be seduced by Harriet Houston from Ayr. It was wrong, wrong of him when there were so many deserving women of his own kind right here in Kinvara. It would serve him right if his marriage turned sour on him and if – *when* – it did she would be waiting right here to give him the shoulder that he would sorely need to cry on.

Charlie, however, was not the type of man to need anybody's shoulder to cry on, far less that of Jessie MacDonald who had never given him a moment's peace during the years of his bachelor status. Charlie was a man of great self-sufficiency who had always liked his freedom and still did. And he couldn't have chosen a more suitable woman than Harriet to be his wife since she liked her freedom also and didn't mind the hours he spent in his pursuits as she had so many of her own to fill her days.

Charlie's job with the fishing smacks could take him away for long spells at a time but Harriet wasn't perturbed by this. She had the work of the croft to keep her occupied: the land; the animals; the running of the home; her family living nearby; her grandchildren keeping her busy, especially Essie, who had such a firm hold on her grandmother's affections she only needed to snap a tiny finger to get her own way in whatever circumstances. And that was the one bone of contention that could occasionally spring up between Harriet and her husband. He maintained that she allowed the child too much of her own way. She told him he was being unreasonable in his attitude just because the little girl loved coming to Butterburn Croft as often as she could to see her granma.

For the sake of peace Charlie seldom allowed the argument to go beyond that point. Never having had a family of his own he told himself he was being selfish in trying to deny his wife her small indulgences since they couldn't possibly harm anyone. And anyway, he loved the children too, and took great delight joining with them in their youthful pleasures and pastimes. He had been only too willing to accede to Rob's request to take his boat out that evening and now he manoeuvred it alongside one of several little landing stages set within a shallow basin outwith the harbour. There he tied up his boat and ascended the half-submerged steps onto the cobbles above, not in the least minding a few minutes' wait, enjoying the bustle of the small craft in the bay, keeping a weather eye on a bank of cloud that had drifted in overland to settle itself on the sullen peaks of Cragdu.

Otherwise, it was a perfect summer's evening, warm and rather sultry, conditions that were just right for the midges that were beginning to swarm even here at the water's edge, making him breathe a sigh of relief when at last Rob hove into view, Breck running along in front to dive straight into the water and swim around with a comical expression of joy on his hairy face.

Soon everyone was safely settled in the commodious clinker dinghy that was Charlie's pride and joy. He was comfortably off was Charlie, having saved a fair little nest egg during his years at sea, but he was a canny man by nature and never spent money just for the sake of it. The boat was his one real indulgence and other than taking her out on the water he liked nothing better than to just tinker about in her, tarring her underside, painting and mending her and generally keeping her in pristine condition.

He had named her *Angel* because when he was out in her he felt as if the waves were transporting him along on wings of time and tide. This, combined with a sense of autonomy that he had seldom found in the more sedate modes of locomotion on dry land, made him welcome any opportunity to be out in her, the great sky above him, the hills and the cliffs all around him, the tang of the sea in his nostrils.

A soaking Breck was the last aboard but as soon as he was hauled over the side to land on the planks in an undignified heap Charlie untied *Angel* and they were off, rowing out of the harbour and round into Mary's Bay, where it was so calm there was no need to use the little petrol inboard motor. Charlie and Rob took turns rowing but soon shipped the oars to allow *Angel* to just bob about on the glassy waves.

Charlie, Vaila and Rob soon had their fishing lines out, but Andy was quite happy just to sit there and stare back at the land he thought he knew so well but didn't know at all when seen from this angle. He was beside himself with wonder as he sat on a cushion in the bow. It was a particular novelty for him to be afloat like this as, when he was younger, it had been considered unsafe for him to be taken out in a small craft owing to the difficulties he'd had balancing himself on anything more unstable than his cart. But he was stronger now, more able to control his limbs, more capable of doing lots of things he couldn't do a year or so ago.

Oh, wait till he got home to write about this! The seabirds wheeling and dipping all around him; jellyfish floating by in weird and silent motion; shoals of little fishes darting along; reefs and rocks and strands of seaweed down there in that secret sandy world beneath *Angel*'s keel.

And beyond all that, the expanse of shining water, the sparkling clean sands of the bay; the great cave-pitted cliffs of Kinvara Point; the stark turrets of Cragdu Castle; tiny white houses dotting the landscape; the encircling hills all around, going back, back, into shaded mists and lonely corries and distant other peaks that he hadn't known existed till now, this moment of new discoveries and different worlds opening up to him.

Rob saw the little boy's glowing face and was content. He had done right to bring his son out here tonight. It was an experience that was long overdue and would do him nothing but good. Rob himself felt the better for it. No wonder Charlie loved his boat and enjoyed his times out with the fishing smacks. There was something about the open water, not like the lighthouse where visions of it were limited to crashing waves, heaving seas, violent storms and mists that could blanket out the world for days. And it was static, once there you had to stay there till you were taken back to another static world of little white shells and people caught up in trivial worries and webs of emotion that could be all-ensnaring . . .

Hannah should have come with them. Out here on the glistening waves everything seemed somehow to fall into a better perspective. The world beyond was smaller, strangely unreal, giving out the illusion of tranquillity when all the time turbulence and unrest lurked inside every man-made brick . . .

He hadn't asked Hannah to come! He felt suddenly guilty about that. But she hadn't given him the chance, had just gone banging away out of the house with all those thoughts churning around in her head. God alone knew what she must be thinking about himself and Catherine right this very minute. There was nothing in it, nothing, yet it must have sounded to her as if it had all been contrived, that he and the teacher had planned their little trysts in the hope that nobody would ever get to know about them. Them! He had only met her the once – and it wasn't his fault that she had taken it into her head to kiss him at the harbour on the day he arrived home.

That kiss! What a fuss about nothing! Anybody would think she had seduced him right there and then for everyone to see. That was the trouble, of course. Everyone had seen the girl's impulsive gesture. Hannah most of all, and in her eyes he might as well have committed adultery out there in the open so annoyed had she been over the incident.

And it had preyed on her mind to such an extent she had chased Catherine from the house because of it. What exactly had made her do that? Didn't she trust him to be alone with the girl under his own roof? As if he had ever thought about Catherine in any light other than that of a good family friend.

All that had changed now, an issue had been made,

a situation had developed; whether he liked it or not his mind had been opened to other concepts about himself and Catherine. In spite of himself his vision of her had been altered – or had the layers of self-deception merely been peeled away to let him see how he had felt about her all along? He faced the truth then. He had to admit to himself that he had walked a very thin line that afternoon whilst in her presence. She had tempted him with her smile, her body, her veiled invitation to join her in some heavenly sounding place of privacy and peace – a place not even frequented by Johnny Lonely on his solitary wanders . . .

More danger, lurking behind every corner, ready to jump out on him when he was least expecting it . . . He gave himself a shake. He wouldn't think about it, not now, out here on the breast of the sea, the boat like a cradle, lulling him into a state of tranquillity, casting its spell over everyone: Andy so engrossed in his thoughts; Breck sitting proudly up at the bow; Essie cooried into Vaila, her doll on her lap, gazing in dreamy fascination at the seals popping their shiny heads out of the water.

Charlie guessed what Rob was thinking. 'It isn't always like this of course, tonight is the exception, meanness and roughness is what she usually doles out – she can blow up stink without much warning, as fine you know yourself.' He grinned. 'Whatever her mood she's my sort o' girl and to tell the truth I like it better when there's a little bit of excitement involved.'

He glanced upwards. 'There's a change coming, we'd better get back before the clouds open.'

'Ay,' Rob was reluctant to abandon *Angel*'s peaceful floating haven, he would have liked to have stayed much longer, looking at that other world beyond the bay, feeling remote from it, not wanting to belong to it in his present state of mind. But Charlie was right, the rain was coming, reality had returned, and with it came all the usual responsibilities, the main one being to get the children back on dry land before the overcast skies grew any heavier.

Hannah shaded her eyes and looked out to sea. Ay, there it was, Charlie's boat, bobbing gently on the waves, a good place to be now that the threat of rain was bringing out the midges. She wasn't particularly fond of boats herself though she might have gone out on a calm night like this given half a chance – but she hadn't been given any sort of chance – left out as usual, nobody caring what she was feeling or thinking, least of all Rob. Then she remembered, she hadn't given him the opportunity to ask her to go anywhere but had gone rushing out of the house in a flurry of temper and tears.

And small wonder! With all she had to think about. That business about Catherine Dunbar. Him meeting her as he had. She had been right about that all along, those solitary wanders of his taking him to places and people he didn't want anybody to know about. He might have got away with it too if it hadn't come out by accident, because there was one thing for sure, he would never have mentioned it and she would never have been any the wiser.

Of course, that didn't mean to say that that was the end of it. He could very easily go on seeing Catherine if he wished. Rob was quite capable of doing anything he wanted, when he wanted, and where a man and a woman of such obvious passions were concerned it wouldn't take much fuel to light the fires that were smouldering between them.

Oh! Hannah put her hands to her face. Fear and doubt invaded her being. She felt that all of it was her fault, that it had started that night of Rob's homecoming when she had said things to him that ought never to have been said. Yet, it was more than that, much more, she could feel it in her bones, something that had been there between them for years, hidden away, simmering under the surface, waiting to burst out like a festering sore.

She knew the answer to that even before she thought it. Morna Jean. Always it had been Morna Jean, that first love of his, that only love, there in life, still there after death, a girl he couldn't forget nor ever would. He had admitted as much on the night of the argument, proving to her that the allegiance of his heart was not for her but for a girl who still haunted him years after her passing.

Hannah dashed away a tear. She was just second best and she knew she always would be. No matter how hard she tried, whatever she did, she would never be good enough, never, and the one thing she thought she had done right seemed to be turning sour on her.

Essie. A child of great beauty, the little daughter she cherished and clung to with such devotion because in worshipping the perfection in Essie she could forget the imperfections in herself . . .

Hannah drew in her breath. She felt crushed and helpless. Everything was getting on top of her, first Rob, then the row with Janet, Essie under a cloud, a blemish being put upon that brave little character of hers . . .

Hannah hated herself but she had to know, had to discover for herself if Essie was telling the truth or not. Shading her eyes she gazed once more towards Mary's Bay. The boat was returning to shore but there was still time to do what she had to do. The rain was getting heavier. Drawing her shawl closer around her shoulders she hurried back to the house and ran upstairs to the room Essie shared with Vaila. A row of Essie's dolls stared at Hannah from the pillows of Essie's bed, their painted faces seeming to leer at her accusingly as she stood there hesitating, her fingers to her lips, guilt tearing her in two at the very idea of violating her small daughter's privacy.

She didn't have much time yet still she stood there, gazing at the little bed, the touches of sweet and innocent childhood, the ribbons hanging on the rail and the set of doll's brushes and combs on the bedside dresser; the miniature clothes that Essie played with for hours because she liked nothing better than dressing up her dollies and doing their hair, her tongue sticking out in concentration as she patted and brushed and muttered to them under her breath.

Hannah's eye fell on the jewel box that Rob had made for Essie, so rejected by her at first but now held in quite high esteem if Essie's use of it was anything to go by. She had proudly told her father that she had moved her 'most special' things into it and from now on was going to keep it only for her 'real treasures'. Hannah decided that this was the most obvious place to look for the missing trinkets and her hand shook slightly as she opened the box and rummaged about inside. But there was nothing, just the usual bits and pieces that any child might gather along with some colourful pebbles from the seashore.

A search through the dresser revealed nothing either. That left the bed itself and in a sudden flurry of decision Hannah removed the dolls one by one and threw back the quilt and pillows. All that came to light was a crumpled handkerchief with Essie's initial on it, a toffee paper and a lollipop stick. She had been eating sweets in bed and that was forbidden! Oh, but what was that compared to the other wrong of which she had been accused! Any child would do the same given half a chance and it was probably that greedy minx Babs MacGill who had given her the stuff in the first place!

Hannah let go her breath, never realising till then that she had been holding it so tightly. Relief washed over her like a tide. The little sweetheart. They had all been wrong about her. She was as pure as the driven snow and when Rob came home she wouldn't be slow to tell him so. Janet too, she had been much too quick to blame Essie for such underhand deeds and Hannah vowed there and then that it would be a long time before she allowed her daughter over that particular doorstep again – if ever.

Chapter Twenty-two

From the minute Charlie brought *Angel* into the anchorage basin a blight seemed to cast a shroud over everyone. At first it was normal enough. Mark and Maida Lockhart were pottering about on the strip of sand skirting the harbour wall, delighting in their surroundings, not minding the drizzle, collecting shells and other marine objects, pausing to watch an old man expertly gutting his catch of fish straight into the water. The offal was immediately pounced upon by the scavenging gulls that were never far away when an easy meal was in the offing.

Grace Lockhart was there too, picking her way along the tide line in the wake of her son and daughter, collecting the small pieces of driftwood which were such a welcome source of extra fuel for many of the villagers.

But as soon as the Lockhart twins spied Vaila they abandoned their pursuits and came scampering along a sandy sheep path, shouting out their greetings, running straight up to her to each take one of her arms and ply her with breathless questions.

'Where have you been?' Mark said bluntly, gazing quizzically into Vaila's eyes, his laughing brown face taking on a more serious expression as he voiced the question. 'Me and Maida were beginning to think you had gone off somewhere. We kept thinking you would be along to visit us at Oir na Cuan or at least have bumped into you on the beach.'

'Of course, we *have* been quite occupied ourselves,' Maida added in her rather old-fashioned way and sounding a bit huffy in the process, 'We go to Crathmor every day with Dad to help out with the ponies and we are still helping Mother get settled into the house. It's only been a few weeks after all and there's so much to do moving into a new place.'

She said the last in a mildly accusing manner and Vaila found herself answering defensively, 'I've been busy myself with one thing and another, I have to do my share of the chores and I've been helping out in the fields. We all have to take part in that and anyway, all you had to do was come to Keeper's Row to see me. I haven't been anywhere out of the usual – except . . .' She paused, coloured a little, and came to a full stop.

'Yes?' Maida probed gently.

'Oh, nothing.' Vaila felt cornered, she was about to mention the visit to Gabby's that afternoon then realised it might be wiser not to say too much about Rebecca being there in case Joshua got to hear about it, which he might anyway, though the less people knew about that the better chance there was of it escaping attention.

'Have you been seeing anything of Rebecca Bowman?'

It was as if Maida had read Vaila's mind and Vaila hesitated before answering, conscious of Maida's round blue gaze upon her, daring her to say anything other than the truth. In that instant Vaila decided it would be less complicated just to come out with it but described her adventures of the afternoon as briefly as she possibly could.

'I see.' Maida tossed back her tangled golden tresses and looked huffier than ever. 'We would have liked that too – if only we had been asked.'

'Och, it was just the way it happened.' Vaila was growing tired of the inquisition. 'We couldn't all have gone to Gabby's, and I asked Rebecca to come with me because she doesn't get out very much and has to answer to her father all the time.'

'Vaila's right,' Mark gave his sister's arm a shake. 'Snap out o' it, Maida, we'll get to go another day. Vaila doesn't have to drag us around with her everywhere and you said yourself we've been busy helping Dad, so it's not as if we would have been on the spot anyway.'

'I thought we might have seen more of Joss too,' Maida went on doggedly, unwilling to let go of the subject. 'He's nice is Joss,' she sounded wistful at this point, 'and I thought we all got on very well together that day we went to see the Henderson Hens.'

'Joss has been busy too.' Vaila was becoming exasperated with Maida. 'He goes to Croft Angus every day, bar Sunday, and never seems to have a minute to himself. Everybody's out in the fields just now and if you weren't so wrapped up in the laird's ponies you might be able to see that for yourself.'

Maida looked at Vaila for a long considering moment, as if she was trying to decide how far she could go before the other girl's temper snapped. Then her face changed, her good nature took over, and she began talking about the Henderson sisters, mimicking them as she did so, Mark joining in, till soon they were all laughing together, forgetting their differences.

Grace arrived just as Rob came back from saying his goodbyes to Charlie. Vaila introduced her father to the new tenants of Oir na Cuan. Grace put down her bundle of wood and they all shook hands. 'I've been looking forward to meeting you, Mr Sutherland,' Grace acknowledged in her pleasant friendly way.

'Call me Rob, it's the way o' things round here.'

'Alright, Rob.' Grace was having a hard job fighting off Essie who insisted on clinging to her skirts and gazing beguilingly up into her face. 'Not now, Essie, I want to talk to your father. Maida, take Essie and the others down to the shore for a minute. I'll call you over when I'm ready.'

The children went off and Grace turned back to Rob. 'It's about Essie. I've been meaning to have a word with your wife about her but I've had so much to do since moving in I haven't had a chance.'

Rob was immediately on the alert at mention of his small daughter's name. Grace laughed when she saw his face. 'Och, don't worry, Rob, it isn't anything so dreadful.

She's been coming to see me at Oir na Cuan, that's all, only I feel she's a bit young yet to visit me on her own the way she does. I love Essie, she's a darling child, a handful at times the way she wanders off when you're least expecting it but what child doesn't like a bit of freedom and she's been company for me with Mark and Maida so often away with their father. There's nothing to get alarmed about really. I know our house is well away from the road so she's safe enough in that respect but she's so little and anything could happen when she's toddling about near the water. I just thought you should know, that's all.'

'I wasn't aware of Essie doing that.' Rob shook his head. 'I'm not so long back from lighthouse duty, there's a lot to catch up on. Every time I come home the bairns have grown that wee bit more and Essie in particular seems to have a mind o' her own these days.'

He paused for a moment before going on thoughtfully. 'Mind you, I have to say this, bairns in these parts do tend to roam from an early age, I did it myself when I was knee high but if it makes you feel easier I'll have a word with Essie about it and I'm sure Hannah will too.'

'Why don't you and Hannah come to visit us at Oir na Cuan?' Grace, anxious now to impress him with her good intentions, made the invitation eagerly. 'I believe you had a lot to do with the place in the old days and Vaila tells me she used to live there with her mother when she was just a tiny wee girl.'

'Ay, she did that,' Rob sounded distant and rather cold,

and Grace, never knowing of the emotions her careless words had evoked in him, took it as a sign that she was being dismissed. 'I must be off, the rain's getting heavier.' She made to turn away but he stayed her with a touch of his hand. 'Thank you, Grace, I would like to see the old place sometime, perhaps later, when I'm more settled.'

'Ay.' She sensed something in his manner that was outwith her understanding but she was new in Kinvara after all and it would be a long time before she ever got to know the people in it, let alone appreciate their depths and their deepnesses and all the little secrets that must surely lurk beneath the surface in such a close-knit community as this.

Lifting up her bundle of driftwood she went off down the path and called on her children. Rob called on his and hurried them along through the steady drizzle, Essie's small hand held firmly in his big one as they made their way back home to Keeper's Row in silence. The children were tired after their long day, while Rob was preoccupied with his thoughts, knowing the ado Hannah would make when Essie's latest misdemeanours came to light.

The very idea of the little girl going off on her own would drive her mother crazy. Hannah wanted Essie to be there all the time, under the maternal wing, tied to the apron strings, only out of sight if it was known exactly where she was going, what she was doing, and who she was doing it with. Rob sighed. He wished he was back in Charlie's boat, looking at the land and thinking how idyllic it was without having to actually take part in all that was going on there.

Hannah was coming downstairs as Rob was ushering the children inside. Hannah clucked and fussed when she saw how wet they were and immediately began peeling off their jackets and drying their hair while Rob enclosed Breck in a towel and gave him a brisk rub. Whilst doing so he told his wife as casually as he could the things that Grace had said concerning Essie and was not at all surprised when Hannah turned an incredulous face towards him.

'On her own? At Oir na Cuan? How did that happen I'd like to know? She never goes out o' my sight, except when she's in the garden or up in her room playing – and that she does for hours and hours.'

'Not always, it would seem,' he returned drily. 'A baby Essie might be to you, Hannah, but somewhere along the way she's grown tiny wings and not of the angel variety either.'

Hannah ignored this. Crouching down beside the child she took hold of her shoulders and said urgently, 'Promise me you won't ever again go to Oir na Cuan by yourself, Essie.'

Solemnly Essie shook her head. 'No, Mamma.'

'I want you to really mean that, Essie.'

'Yes. Mamma, I mean it.'

Essie truly did look like an angel as she stood there in

front of her mother, head bowed, hands folded behind her back, a lock of fair hair tumbling over her forehead, her big blue eyes brimming with unshed tears.

'It's only because I love you, I worry so much about you, you do know that, don't you, Essie?' Hannah's voice quivered, she wanted to reach out and touch the rose-bloom of the child's cheek, feel the small body safely enclosed in her arms.

'Yes, Mamma, I know it. I'm sorry and I won't ever do it again.'

Her face reddened, she burst into tears, and without another word Hannah folded the child to her bosom, stroked her hair, murmured soothing sounds of comfort into her ear.

'She'll never learn that way,' Rob said quietly. 'Harsh words one minute, sweet nothings the next.'

'And I suppose you think you know better than me?' Hannah flung at him.

'I suppose I think I do,' he said a trifle wearily.

'Well, you know nothing, Rob Sutherland, nothing at all. Essie didn't do any o' the things she's supposed to have done. I know that for a fact, I searched her room while you were out and there was nothing to be found out o' the ordinary. When next I see Janet I'll have something to say to her as well and she might think twice about opening her mouth in future.'

'I'm going out.' Rob, his jaw working, went to the stand to retrieve his jacket. 'Clover's calving and I got

Jock to put her in the byre for me earlier. Don't wait up, it could be a long night and I don't know when I'll be back.'

Calling on Breck he let himself out. There was silence in the room for a moment. Hannah stared at the closed door, then she gave a shrug and turned her attention to the nightly ritual of making the cocoa and getting the children ready for bed.

Vaila lay on her back and thought about Rebecca, wondering if her absence from home that day had been noticed. Caleb would be good at covering up for her, he was a very capable sort of boy, one who was very much on his sister's side and who was bold and daring where Joshua was concerned.

So different from Nathan who seemed always to be afraid and who never did anything if he thought it would incur his father's wrath.

Vaila had once come upon him crying behind one of the mill buildings, crouched against the wall, sobbing quietly into his hands, so wrapped up in his misery he hadn't heard her approaching till the last minute. Only when her hand touched his shoulder did he look up, his face woebegone and tear-stained, fear invading his eyes at being caught out like this, saying nothing as he shot to his feet and scuttled away like a startled rabbit when she had asked him if he was alright.

Sad, lost, and lonely, that was Nathan, yet there was

something very likeable about him when he forgot to be afraid and talked like any other boy of his age. She remembered his face lighting up when he had described to her once the journey to Scotland, the steam train that had brought them to Achnasheen station, how he wanted one day to be an engine driver and how he would 'never ever' change his mind about it.

She hoped he would get to see old Gabby's beautiful working model of a steam engine. To her it had been just part of everything else that was enchanting in Gabby's house but to Nathan it would be something magnificent and stirring and he and Gabby would talk about it for ages and ages.

She moved restlessly in the bed. It was stuffy in the room, the open window was letting in hardly any air, the muslin curtains had trapped a bluebottle which was making some sluggish attempts to extract itself from the folds. It was the only sign of movement in the room, everything else was still with not so much as a whisper of wind to ruffle the silence. Essie was fast asleep, exhausted after a day of almost non-stop activity, her even breathing barely audible even to Vaila's keen ears.

Vaila thought about her father out there in the byre with Clover who was having her first calf. It would be nice to be there with him, just the two of them alone with the animals, no one else to interfere in what they were doing. The idea had barely formed in her mind before she threw back the covers, stuck her feet into her shoes, wrapped her shawl around her shoulders, and crept downstairs to let herself out of the house.

The rain had stopped. The sky was clearing. It was a night filled with sweet perfumes mingling with the more earthy scents filtering down from the farmlands, the moon was gliding out from a silver-lined cloud, the lights of fishing boats bobbed in the harbour. Out at sea the lighthouse flashed, aloof somehow from all it embraced, yet such a reassuring and familiar part of the landscape.

The stubble of the newly cut field scratched her bare legs as she went along, making for the squat little shed set against a corner of the boundary wall. After the wee hoosie this was one of Vaila's favourite places to be, an intimate sanctuary of privacy and peace, somewhere to go to be alone when the pressures of her small world got on top of her.

The door creaked as she pushed it open. The rich smells of ripe dung and warm straw assailed her nostrils. Breck came bounding to greet her then led her back to some hidden corner piled high with sacks of chaff and bundles of loose hay. Clover was in her stall, just patiently standing there, but Vaila didn't look over the door as she had learned from infancy that cows giving birth liked to be left alone.

Rob wasn't surprised to see his daughter. 'I thought you might come,' was all he said as she hove into view. 'I couldn't sleep, it was so warm,' she explained briefly as she sat down and leaned against him, feeling his warmth and his strength seeping into her. Breck came over and curled up beside them and for quite a while no more was said between any of them after those first few succinct words.

Chapter Twenty-three

Vaila fell asleep in the warm nest of her father's lap and he must have fallen asleep too because sometime in the early hours he came to with such a violent start she was spurred into sudden and heart stirring wakefulness. Sounds of distress were coming from Clover in her stall. The calf hadn't been born yet and Rob went in to gently rub the cow's belly and whisper soothing words into her ears. 'Will she be alright, Robbie?' Vaila asked as she sat there in the hay hugging her knees, feeling the keen air of morning seeping into her now that her father was no longer there to give her his warmth.

'It's her first, but it shouldn't be long now,' he said as he resumed his seat beside his daughter. 'Go back to sleep, I'll stay beside you to keep out the cold.'

But she was wide awake now and so was he and he got up to stretch his legs and smoke his pipe and look from the small cobwebby window to the light already beginning to break on the horizon. After a while he came back to Vaila to take off his jacket and tuck it around her before sitting down again next to her.

'Robbie,' she said quietly, 'you won't ever leave us, will you?'

'Whatever gave you that idea?'

'It's just – you and Hannah – I know you haven't been speaking since you came home.'

'Och,' he took her to him and stroked the black curling hair from her brow. 'Of course I won't leave you, as if I ever could. Sometimes it might seem as if I'm not paying you much attention but I'm a man, Vaila, and I like to be alone with my thoughts now and then. It will come alright between Hannah and me, we're just going through a sticky patch, married people don't always see eye to eye but it's nothing for you to worry your head about so weesht now and try to rest.'

Vaila didn't say anything about Essie. Her little sister was in enough trouble these days without her adding to it. She hoped there would be a simple explanation for the disappearance of Janet's trinkets and also for her own silver lighthouse pendant which hadn't been in her jewel box when she'd looked a few days ago. It could have slipped off her neck without her knowing it and that thought alone might have filled her with horror if she wasn't so sure she hadn't worn it since she had transferred it from her drawer into the box Robbie had given her.

It would be the worst thing that could happen to her if she couldn't find it again. If it didn't turn up she would have to say something to somebody – perhaps if she asked Essie about it – she had certainly been fascinated by it that time she had held it when listening to Vaila talking about her mother . . .

Her eyes were growing heavy. She cooried against her father. The thick tweed of his jacket was comforting and cosy around her. She liked the smell of it, tangy and woolly, smoky and woody, all mixing together to make a pleasing concoction. And there was something else that clung to it, the man scent of him, subtle, yet all powerful, all enduring, like the aura that surrounded him, unseen but so firmly a part of him she often sensed that he was nearby even when she couldn't see him.

The hours slipped by while she dozed and dreamed yet she seemed to be half expecting it when he came to her and shook her gently by the shoulder. 'Vaila, waken up, Clover can't seem to give birth properly and needs help. I want you to run to Butterbank House and fetch the doctor. I have to stay here in case something happens.'

Vaila, fully awake now, got readily to her feet. He made her push her arms into the sleeves of his jacket and pulled its folds closer round her body. At the last minute he sat down to remove his socks, slipped them over her feet, then somehow jammed her shoes back on while she hung onto his shoulders to balance herself. They giggled together as he was tugging and hauling at the various items of clothing but then she was off, letting herself out of the byre, flying across the fields as fast as her ungainly footwear would allow.

It was a fair distance to the doctor's house but she knew all the shortcuts, the hidden pathways through the copses, the easiest routes along the back of Calvost village. The morning air was drenched with the fragrances of bluebells and sweet clover, the tang of the sea mingled with the scent of peat smoke rising up from the chimneys, over yonder the sea was a sheet of silver lying beneath a pewter sky while the hills all around were blue and green, the peaks a rosy pink where caught by the rays of the sun spilling through a hole in a dove-grey cloud. All was new and fresh, quiet and still at this early hour.

She was still running when she reached the endrigs of Vale O' Dreip farm and she smiled to herself as she wondered what Grampa Ramsay would have had to say if he had chanced upon her in her father's jacket and socks, her nightgown tucked into her knickers to allow for easier freedom of movement, her hair awry and her face streaked with dust after a night spent in Clover's byre.

She almost stumbled over a young roe deer browsing in the thickets near the Brig O' Shee and ran full tilt into a rabbit crouched in the undergrowth nearby. The rabbit leapt up in fright, so too did Vaila, but she only gave herself a moment to brush herself down before she was off again.

The cockerel in Effie Maxwell's patch of land had awakened and was giving full rein to his vocal cords as he vied with the king cock of Butterburn Croft who had been resident there long before Effie's and was making sure everyone knew it. There was no sign of life in Purlieburn Cottage itself, Effie being out at a confinement in Balivoe, but the jewel in the nurse's life, her pig Ruby, was taking the air in her own little paddock, making rude sounds of enjoyment as she did so, poking and snuffling her snout into woody damp places in search of tasty titbits in the form of worms and slugs and anything else she could scoop into her ready jaws.

Effie's late, lamented sow, Queen Victoria, had been made into bacon some years ago, and her broken-hearted owner had vowed that she was finished with pigs as never, never, would she ever love another as she had loved her dear queen of all pigs. That was before she had seen Harriet Campbell's new litter of piglets neatly rowed against their mother's teats, one in particular catching her eye, so rosy pink was its colour, so endearingly plump its backside, its curly little tail coiled so tightly it was as if someone had taken it and wound it round hot tongs for a week.

She had immediately christened it Ruby and had fallen in love all over again, only too eager to buy the piglet from Harriet as soon as it was old enough. In those early days Ruby had been quite content just to eat and sleep but had undergone a personality change when she was older, becoming wilful and headstrong and possessed of the wanderlust.

Whenever she could she escaped from her pen in search of fresh pastures and Kinvara would never forget the day that Effie had gone charging through the village in pursuit of her pig, wielding a stout stick and bawling Ruby's name as she went. Ruby, however, had completely ignored her mistress's yells and had gone thundering on regardless, until without warning she about turned and went heading straight for Effie. Before anyone knew what was happening the nurse was swept off her feet and was somehow suddenly astride her pig's shoulders, hurtling along riding backwards, emitting ear-piercing screams that vied with Ruby's blood-curdling squeals of pure rage.

A few of the village stalwarts, eager to go to Effie's aid, took to their heels and went pell-mell after both her and her pig until soon a dozen pairs of stout boots were beating a tattoo on the road and everyone came out of their houses to see what all the commotion was about.

For several dozen yards Effie rode her pig along the main street of Calvost, both of them squealing all the way, till Ruby spied a scatter of windfall apples lying on the pavement under the spreading branches of old Mrs Leckie's apple tree. The overjoyed pig ground to a halt on all four trotters, Effie slithered over her head to land in a bristling heap among the apples, the men of the village came to a full stop also, all falling on top of one another and heaping vitriol on Ruby's floppy lugs as they did so.

Ruby wasn't listening. She had found her Shangri-La. Snorting and snuffling in ecstasy she devoured the apples in no time and was all for bulldozing her way through Bella Leckie's gate to find more when that small white-haired lady herself appeared and was quite astonished to come face to face with a very sizeable pig making its bold way into her garden.

Effie, red-faced, shaken, wondering what she had done to deserve all this, explained what had happened. In minutes she was sitting on a garden bench drinking a good strong cuppy laced with brandy, Ruby was enjoying the remainder of the apples lying on the grass, while Bella Leckie, tickled pink at such an unusual intrusion into her normal everyday life, sat with Effie in the sun and wanted to hear all about it.

'Ay, my, a real road hog if ever there was one,' the old lady chuckled. 'Some folks ride horses, others prefer pigs, it takes all sorts to make a world as I myself have found out in the years I've been in it.'

Effie knew then that she would never be allowed to forget the day she rode her pig bareback through the streets of Calvost with half Kinvara on her heels and the other half sniggering behind her back as they spoke about 'their very own nurse making such a fool o' herself in front o' the entire population'.

The feast and the excitement over and filled to the brim with apples, Ruby was now quite ready to sleep off her excesses and meekly allowed her mistress to lead her home. People came to their doors to cheer the little procession on, an embarrassed Effie fumed and fretted and swore vengeance on her pig, vowing to take her to Jake Ferguson the butcher as soon as she possibly could and see how the pig liked being strung up on hooks for the rest of her days!

Instead, Effie got Davie the Carpenter to fence in a

portion of her land to make Ruby her own little paddock. From that day forth the pig never wandered again but was perfectly happy just mucking about in her own small patch of earth and receiving all the tender loving care that her mistress had once heaped on the legendary Queen Victoria.

Leaving Purlieburn Cottage behind, Vaila climbed over a stile that took her to Butter Meadow. She was growing tired now, her feet seemed to get heavier and heavier with every step she took but she went doggedly on, swishing through golden tracts of buttercups and swathes of dew-fresh daisies that were just beginning to open up their pink-tipped petals to the rays of the rising sun.

She was at the doctor's house at last, a sturdy stone-built structure full of little nooks and crannies and quaint shadowy corners where pansies and violas grew in riotous abundance over pink and green pebbles and tubs of yellow and orange mimulus took refuge from the drying effects of the sea breezes. Most noticeable of all was the perfume rising up from the rose garden that was the absolute joy of both the doctor and his wife. Into it they put prodigious amounts of seaweed and dung and many hours of tender loving care, round it they had built a drystone wall of enormous proportions to keep in the heat of the sun and to keep out winter gales, sheep, deer and rabbits, all of which were capable of creating havoc with any sort of vegetation given half the chance.

Jeannie came to the door with her hair done up in paper curlers and wearing an ancient rust-coloured chenille dressing gown that had definitely seen better days. Her eyes widened at the sight of her small caller's unorthodox appearance but being Jeannie she soon recovered her composure and ushered the little girl hastily inside – just in case some nosy parker was lurking down at the gate and might see something they shouldn't – even at this unearthly hour.

The doctor had heard the bell also and was coming down the varnished wooden staircase in his slippers and cotton summer drawers, alternately scratching his hair and his portly belly as he advanced into the kitchen where Jeannie was putting on the kettle.

'Alistair! That's no way to be dressed in front o' a young girl,' Jeannie reprimanded as soon as she saw him. 'Go and put on your dressing gown right this very minute.'

He made no move however, but just stood there chuckling as he glanced from the homely figure of his wife to his quaintly adorned young visitor. 'I'm perfectly attired for the occasion, Jeannie, perfectly attired. No one stands on ceremony in this house at five o'clock in the morning as I'm sure Vaila will agree.'

'Please, Doctor MacAlistair,' Vaila imparted breathlessly, 'could you come to Keeper's Row at once? Clover's calving but something's wrong and my father says he needs your help.'

It was by no means unusual for the doctor to be asked to help out with an animal in this way, as there was no veterinary for miles around, and if he was at all able to do so Alistair MacAlistair gave his services without question, the resulting perks, in the form of shanks of beef, legs of lamb and pork, from grateful farmers, coming as a boost to a livelihood that was all too often meagre in the extreme.

'Right.' At Vaila's words the doctor immediately sprung into action, 'I'll hitch up Pumpkin right away and then we'll be off.'

Until recently the doctor had simply jumped on his 'big stallion brute Dandy' to get to wherever he wanted to go, now he had succumbed to Jeannie's persuasions to get himself a form of transport that better suited his age and his requirements. Jeannie had hoped for something on four wheels, a nice little motor car perhaps, picturing herself at Alistair's side, riding round the countryside in comfort.

She had got her four wheels alright, but not the sort that she had visualised, attached as they were to a smart red jaunting cart that Alistair had acquired from the laird along with a perky little pony in exchange for Dandy. The laird had always considered that Dandy was just going to waste as a beast of burden, now he would have his chance to show what he could do at stud and the deal was made to the satisfaction of both parties.

'She's a good quiet wee beast,' the doctor had said of

the pony when Jeannie first clapped eyes on it. 'You'll like her once you get used to her and her name is Pumpkin by the way.'

'Pumpkin!' Jeannie's visions of a nice comfortable motor car disappeared like a puff of smoke as she listened to the pony's spirited whinnying and watched her tossing her mane in a frisky fashion. 'She looks a fierce sort o' cratur' to me and to call her Pumpkin of all things! We'll be the talk o' the place with a name like that for a horse.'

'You can blame that on Captain Rory's bairns. Pumpkin she is and Pumpkin she stays simply because she won't answer to any other name.'

'Well, she certainly looks like nothing that ever came out o' the ground with white flesh and stripes,' Jeannie snorted.

'You seem to know a great deal about pumpkins, Jeannie,' he had parried.

'An aunt o' mine grew them in the Borders,' she answered tongue in cheek, for her aunt had done nothing of the sort and wouldn't have known one from a football. 'She made everything out o' the dreadful things, pies, jams, preserves, but never could she get me to eat any o' them.'

'In the Borders, eh.' The doctor's lips twitched. 'My knowledge of them is limited but I seem to remember from somewhere that they are large gourd-like objects that grow on vines, not borders.'

Jeannie had laughed then, they had both laughed till

the tears were running down their faces and for the time being Jeannie forgot her disappointment at having Pumpkin instead of a motor car, since the jaunting cart was something of a compensation and meant she could ride through the countryside by her husband's side after all.

Jeannie was all for plying her young visitor with warmth and sustenance but Vaila was impatient to be off and was relieved when the doctor came back to announce that Pumpkin was ready and waiting. 'Comb your hair, Alistair,' Jeannie instructed, eyeing his rumpled locks.

'It's a calf I'm delivering, not a princess,' he returned, pausing only long enough to throw his jacket over his vest and jam on his deerstalker hat.

'You can't go out dressed like that! You aren't wearing any trousers!' Jeannie cried aghast.

'Ach, who's to see me at this hour anyway? It isn't as if the tender young maids o' Kinvara are likely to throw themselves on me with the intention o' tearing off my drawers.'

'Everyone will see you on the way back!' Jeannie shouted, but it was to thin air, he and Vaila had gone and he was already driving Pumpkin at a brisk pace away from the house.

As soon as Doctor MacAlistair examined Clover he knew immediately what was wrong. 'It's a breech birth,' he announced calmly. 'Get the ropes and we'll have the calf out in no time. Don't pull until I tell you, arse in, shoulders back, she's tight so give it all you've got.'

It took a lot of sweating to get the calf out. Vaila helped her father with the ropes while the doctor did his bit at the cow's rear. But at last a heifer calf appeared, lifeless looking as it slithered out. The doctor seized it and held it upside down while Rob cleared the airways. After that they laid the new arrival on the ground and Vaila helped to rub its little body with handsful of straw. Its ribs heaved, there was a gasp, everyone laughed, and in minutes the new mother was murmuring to her baby and looking none the worse for her ordeal.

The doctor collapsed onto a sackful of chaff and wiped his brow. 'Both seem healthy beasts,' he said with satisfaction. 'Tuberculosis is rife just now, it isn't so bad in this corner o' the world, yet even so I see new cases in my surgery every other week but the farmers don't take a whit o' notice.'

'Times are hard for them,' Rob said slowly, 'all work and no play and very little profit at the end o' it. I'm lucky. I've got a job as well as my bit croft and wouldn't like to rely on the land alone to earn my living. Small farmers in particular turn a blind eye to the problems simply because they can't afford to do anything else.'

Sympathetic though his words were, he knew the truth of the doctor's words. One or two of the least advantaged Kinvara families had lost children through the illness known as 'galloping consumption', people spoke in whispers about it and prayed it wouldn't come to them. Hannah worried constantly that Essie might catch it 'with her being the youngest' though the milk the family drank came fresh in churns from Vale O' Dreip whose herds had recently been certified as free of the disease.

'Och well,' the doctor extracted a flask from his pocket, 'this is no time to be morbid, a sup o' this should buck us up and put us back on our feet.' He allowed Rob the first swig before gulping down a hearty mouthful himself. 'By God! I needed that. It isn't every morning I'm wakened from my slumbers to bring a bovine babe into the world. I'm more used to delivering the human variety but in that, thank God, I've got Effie who's more able than me to rise out of her bed in the middle o' the night to sit with an expectant mother.'

As if on cue, Malky Law came panting in, breathless and excited as he explained to the doctor how he had gone first to Butterbank House to fetch him only to be redirected here by Jeannie.

'Effie says you've to come at once,' Malky went on. 'Ma's having her baby, she's been screaming like a stuck pig all night and Da thinks she must be dying because she's never normally like that when she's birthing.'

The words he spoke would have better suited a grown man but the Law youngsters had old heads on their shoulders, having been conditioned to the hard facts of life from their early years.

'Having her baby? But it isn't due for weeks yet.'

Doctor MacAlistair was on his feet, trying to gather his wits together, stuffing his flask back into his pocket, gazing down at his unclad legs and wishing that he had taken Jeannie's advice and had stopped to dress properly after all.

'I'll get a pair.' Rob was halfway to the door as he spoke and was soon back clasping a pair of his own trousers. The doctor struggled into them. They were too long and too tight but he was in no position to worry about such trivialities in the urgency of the moment.

'No rest for the wicked,' he muttered resignedly as he went outside with Malky and down onto the road where Pumpkin was waiting. In seconds they were off, charging along as if all hell was at their heels and bringing much attention on themselves as they did so.

'There he goes!' nodded Big Bette as she watched from her window. 'What he needs is someone to wave a magic wand to turn his Pumpkin into a team o' wild horses wi' wings. I see Malky Law is with him, maybe something's wrong with Shug. Last time I saw him he was limping along and moaning about his back again.'

'When's breakfast coming, Ma?' Babs shouted and Bette unwillingly turned away from the diversions of her window to attend to the demands of her family.

Vaila felt she had achieved something pretty wonderful that morning. She had helped Clover bring her calf into the world and she wanted to run straight down to the Mill O' Cladach and tell Rebecca all about it. Instead she went back to the house with her father to get dressed and have breakfast. It had been a strange night but she had loved every minute, the bonds between herself and her father seemed stronger than ever and she knew he had really meant it when he had said he would never ever leave her.

Chapter Twenty-four

Dolly gave birth to a frail sickly mite who died a few hours afterwards. No awakening was hers from her dreamless sleep, no cry did she make as she slipped away without ever opening her eyes.

'This has never happened to me before!' Dolly wailed. 'I always carried my bairns full term and every one o' them was born healthy! It must have been that ride I took in the cart yesterday. Dancer is a lot more lively than Sorry ever was and just went flying over every pothole in the road. Oh, what is there to do. I'd like to know.' She began to rock herself backwards and forwards in an agony of grief. 'First Sorry, now this poor wee lamb!'

'You'll have to stop having them, bairns I mean,' Doctor MacAlistair stated in his forthright way. 'This had nothing to do with Dancer. You aren't a spring chicken any more, your muscles aren't as strong as they were after all the pregnancies you've had. You and Shug will have to try and exercise a bit more control over yourselves. Why don't you get him to jump off at Paisley – or you could try sleeping in separate beds.'

'In separate beds! We haven't got any separate beds,

Doctor. Every one is full to the ceiling, in case you haven't noticed. Besides all that, Shug would die altogether if he had to sleep on his own, he's aye been feart o' the dark and needs me beside him as if he was a bairn himself.'

'Get him to tie a knot in it then.' Effie, who had just finished cleaning the tiny lifeless body of Dolly's baby, spoke sarcastically. 'He's supposed to have a bad back yet there he goes, on and off like a rabbit, never a thought for the consequences and this poor wee thing is the result.'

Before Dolly had a chance to answer, Effie swaddled the baby in a layer of cotton sheet and bore it away out of the room. Dolly lay back on her pillows, weary and sad but still full of spirit. 'Hmph, what does she know, a born spinster if ever there was one wi' nothing in her life but a pig to keep her company. I'd rather die having bairns than spend the rest o' my days talking to a lump o' pink blubber who wallows in muck and farts like the bagpipes tuning up.'

Despite the sombre mood of the occasion the doctor very nearly burst out laughing at this and it was only by a great effort of will that he managed to keep a straight face. 'Effie's right.' He took Dolly's worn, thin hand in his. 'Shug will have to learn to take his responsibilities more seriously. Your house is overcrowded without adding more to it. Bunk beds might be the answer for you, one on top o' the other to save space. I've got one in my stable I use for storing my bits and pieces but I can soon knock it back into shape and I'm sure Jeannie will find a spare mattress. Send

Shug over to collect it as soon as he can and if he won't sleep in it then you'll just have to put your foot down and tie him in.'

'Doctor, you're the second person to lecture me like this,' Dolly said sternly. 'That rogue, Joshua Bowman, was the first, coming here and interfering in my private life and him too full o' nonsense to attend to his own. I sent him packing wi' a flea in his ear and a kick up the arse for luck . . . though of course I wouldn't do that to you,' she added hastily, 'you being the doctor and my good friend into the bargain.'

Alistair patted her hand. 'You'd better get some rest now. I'll come back to see you as soon as I can, I'll send Mary through with a cup of tea and I wouldn't smoke that pipe o' yours yet in case it makes you sick.'

Several members of the Law family were ensconced in the kitchen that morning. Mary had made two huge pots of tea to go round while her sister Sally was at the stove presiding over an enormous pan of porridge and another filled with eggs and sheep's brains, the latter having been acquired by Softy Law from Vale O' Dreip after Ramsay had slaughtered a few of his stock for the kitchen table.

The Law family, in common with many other families in the district, considered sheep's brains a delicacy and were always delighted when their brother came home with a sheep's head because it had so many culinary uses. Sally had already made the broth for dinner that night, meaning to keep the brains too, but there being nothing else to go with the eggs she had decided to use them for breakfast instead. Anyway, at this time of year the younger Law boys were out in the fields every day catching rabbits in the wake of the binders so there was bound to be something brought home for the dinner table.

The doctor sniffed the air, his rumbling stomach suddenly reminding him he hadn't eaten a thing that morning. Sally saw his look and dished him a big plateful of eggs and a smaller portion of brains, along with hunks of the crusty bread that was Sally's speciality, having learned to make it when she was still in school pinafores.

The doctor grabbed his knife and fork and tackled his food with gusto, Effie drank a large mug of tea, while the Law lads got on with the business of eating as usual. But the girls were too upset about the loss of their tiny sister to eat much of anything and Shug just sat with his head in his hands, heartbroken by the turn of events, because he loved all his children dearly and was truly stunned by this latest tragedy.

'I can't pay you right away,' he told the doctor when that good man was leaving. 'Two guineas is a lot o' money for a man like myself to find but I know Dolly needed you right bad and I'm grateful to you for coming so quick.'

The doctor laid his hand on Shug's bony shoulder. The head of the Law household looked woebegone and strained as he stood there in the dingy dark lobby and the doctor didn't have the heart to say anything just then regarding matters pertaining to birth control. 'Don't worry, man.

You know I'm not the sort to harass any o' my patients about money. Give me what you can when you can and no one will be any the wiser.'

'We'll all chip in, Da.' Softy was suddenly there, then Carrots, then Mary, all of them willing to part with an extra shilling or two from the meagre wages they earned from farm work and domestic service.

'You have good bairns, Shug.' The doctor nodded as he opened the door and went out into the sunlight where Pumpkin was waiting to whisk him away home to Jeannie, anxiously waiting to hear all about his morning's adventures.

Paying the doctor wasn't Shug's only worry however. There was also the business of the baby's funeral to consider. 'We can't just dig a hole and put her in like Sorry,' he said mournfully to his wife. 'She'll have to be buried right and proper and that will cost money. I'm up to my eyes in debt as it is, first the horse, then the doctor, now this as well.'

That was when the laird came to the rescue once more. He ordered Davie the Carpenter to make a tiny white coffin for Dolly's baby and arranged the funeral himself. The Law family as a whole were indebted to him and told one another no kinder man ever lived than Captain Rory MacPherson of Crathmor, even though he was often an old rogue and an opportunist to boot. On this occasion he had no ulterior motives, just a genuine desire to help out in such sad circumstances. Thanks to him, little Gloria Dawn, as Dolly had named her, was laid to rest with proper dignity and respect.

Every blind in Balivoe was drawn down as the cortège passed. Shug carried the small coffin himself, his sons beside him, Dolly and her daughters riding in the cart, neighbours and friends following behind. There was not a dry eye to be seen anywhere when the Reverend Thomas MacIntosh led prayers in the kirkyard overlooking the sea where the gulls wheeled like scraps of torn paper in the sky and the rays of the sun spilled over a land already rich with the colours of summer.

When Joshua Bowman heard the news about Dolly's baby his first instinct was to go over there and give the family spiritual sustenance. He knew, however, that his presence would not be welcome. Oh, they had been eager enough to accept his help when that old mare of theirs had collapsed on the pier and he had gone to their aid. That neighbourly act of his had not only been appreciated by the Laws but by those members of the community who had been there to witness it. Word had soon spread, exonerating him in some measure from the bad feelings that had sprung up after his run-in with the laird.

Now, however, these first good impressions were wearing thin. The Law woman, for instance, had not been enamoured when he had called in to see her one day to offer prayers and to lecture her on having too many children, when it was obvious that neither she nor her husband could give their existing family the sort of support they needed.

Dolly had not been slow to put him in his place and had been most rude in her efforts to let him know that his words of wisdom were falling on deaf ears, blowing pipe smoke all over him as she did so and opening a bottle of beer with a defiant flourish. 'Go and practise what you preach, Joshua Bowman,' she had cackled, 'you didn't get three bairns shaking your trousers at a cabbage! And if you still don't know the facts o' life after all that, then maybe you would like to sit down and I'll explain them to you over a pint and a puff.'

Joshua smarted at the remembrance of this. The Laws should feel themselves lucky to have any visitors at all in that crowded hovel of theirs. And now they had brought another life into the world only to lose it again. Serve them right too. If they took the advice of caring people like himself they would be a lot better off and might not be so smart, breeding like mice and relying on the help of others to see them through their difficulties.

Good, kind, charitable, Captain Rory MacPherson, had done it again! Gone to the rescue of the Laws, making sure the whole place knew about it too! The old goat was always popping up like a cork from a bottle, often where he was least wanted. He had been a regular caller at the mill ever since that incident over the horse, poking his nose in, prying, asking questions, going to look over Jacob as if to satisfy himself that the beast was not being mistreated in any way.

And he wasn't the only one to come snooping around. That hermit who lived rough on the shore seemed always to be near the place too, never quite showing himself, keeping well enough away so as not to be properly identified, a shadowy figure lurking about, elusive and somehow oddly disturbing.

Miriam had seen him too and had grown more nervous than ever of late. Joshua wondered why he had ever married her. She had been alright in the beginning, spirited even, believing in him, willing to go along with everything he did, aiding him without question in his mission to convert the ignorant, a true servant to him and all that he stood for.

Now, all that had changed, she was like a washed out rag. No go in her. Dragging herself about like a snail, living from day to day without hope, looking as if she would like to just cover her face and pretend that she wasn't there any more. She had brightened a bit when they had first arrived at the mill, cleaning and taking a pride in the house, showing an interest in her surroundings. Then the hermit had started to appear and she had shrunk back into her shell, as if she felt threatened by him and was afraid to go out of doors.

'It's only Johnny Lonely,' Rebecca had said somewhat loftily.

'And how come you know who he is?' Joshua had asked with jutting jaw.

'I just know, that's all,' she had answered airily and he had told himself for the umpteenth time that this daughter of his was getting far too big for her boots and something would have to be done about it.

But Joshua was too taken up with his thoughts these days to bother very much about anything else. He badly needed to make a go of it after coming to this God-forsaken spot. Business hadn't been as brisk as he had hoped, the bulk of it still going to Conrad O'Connar, the miller of Bruach.

To make anything of himself Joshua knew he had to first make inroads with his neighbours and that he had tried earnestly to do. Never mind the Laws! He had only gone there out of charity. Word had soon travelled about his visit. Whatever Dolly Law might think about him there were those who saw him in a different light. Kinvara was full of lonely women bursting for the sort of sustenance only someone like him could give. Jessie MacDonald, for example, had been very grateful, so too had many other single women and widows who needed a man's shoulder to cry on.

His visits to the sick in the area had been met with varying responses. Willie Whiskers had refused point blank to allow him over the door to see Maisie who was suffering from a sprained ankle; Bella Leckie was only too glad to let him into Appletree Cottage to pray for her speedy recovery from the arthritis that was 'giving her gyp'; Gabriel Cochrane of Clockwork Cottage had practically chased him away with a garden broom when he had suggested communing with the Higher Powers to cure a stomach ailment. 'A good dose o' cascara will soon put me to rights and that I can get from Doctor MacAlistair,' Gabby had bluntly maintained. 'I've heard all about you, Bowman. Some might be taken in by you but I know for a fact you are just a vulture looking for easy pickings, and if you don't remove yourself from my premises this very second I might feel obliged to help you on your way.'

Undeterred, Joshua had persevered with his intentions of making a good impression on the community at large and had daringly decided to swallow the taboos of a lifetime to go and see the Reverend Thomas MacIntosh whom he knew was in bed with a bronchial infection. A surprised Connie had let him over the door. From there he had progressed into the bedroom where the minister was sitting up in bed going over some papers, only to drop them to the floor in astonishment at sight of Joshua.

Joshua had picked up the papers, tidied them into a neat sheaf and laid them on the bedside cabinet. He had done everything he could to ingratiate himself with the Church of Scotland minister, finishing up by going down on his knees to pray at the bedside. The minister was too dumbfounded to utter a single word. He knew only too well this man's condemnation of any beliefs other than his own and now here he was, eyes closed, clasped hands to his lips, muttering away about sin and salvation and how everyone was alike in the eyes of the Lord and should behave accordingly.

'Bunkum!' Despite his sore chest the minister spoke loudly and clearly. 'Get up off your knees this minute, Bowman, and take yourself out of here. I am a man of flexible opinions regarding any denominations, as Father Kelvin MacNeil could very well tell you, but you, my man, are a hypocrite, coming here today and pretending concern for my well-being when all the time it is only your own ends that you serve!'

Kerry O'Shaughnessy, the minister's Irish-born wife, had come in at that opportune moment to find her sick husband red-faced and upset and not at all well-looking. Joshua had been shown the door forthwith and Connie had apologised profusely to her employers for ever having let such a man into the house, saying she had only done so because he had 'scared the breeks off her the way he had just barged in like a demented spook'.

'I don't mind telling you, I have never felt so embarrassed in all my days as a minister,' the Reverend Thomas MacIntosh had later confided to his wife. 'Him coming in here, scrabbling about on his knees, preaching like a madman. God knows I have a wider view of religion than most but Bowman is obsessed, not with the Lord but with his own sanctimonious ramblings.'

Joshua soon realised that his visit to the Manse had been a big mistake. The Reverend Thomas MacIntosh was a long-standing and much-respected figure in the community, the people of Kinvara liked and trusted him and didn't care to see him upset in any way. They were therefore not impressed when they heard about Joshua's so-called goodwill visit to the Manse. Upsetting the minister like that! Barging his way in! Storming the sickroom with nothing more on his mind than self-glory.

Joshua kept his head down after that little episode, all the while racking his brains as to how best he could handle the situation. He knew he still had some supporters left, many of them women, Jessie MacDonald in particular being very staunch in her praise of the strength and guidance he had given her during his visits to her home. Women like Jessie would soon spread the word, meantime he decided to try something nearer home. People were always concerning themselves with the welfare of children. He was aware that his strict handling of his own youngsters had come under severe scrutiny and decided that it might be to his advantage to indulge them a bit more.

'I want the children to have some time to themselves,' he intoned to Miriam. 'It is summer after all, they are new here and must be curious regards their surroundings. Be a bit more lenient with them, allow them less chores, send them on a picnic, anything to get them out of the house.'

Miriam was so dumbfounded by this she uttered not a word but just stared at her husband as if he had taken leave of his senses. 'Stop gaping at me like that!' he barked. 'Why do I put up with you, I ask myself? Hardly a word out of you! Everything about you weak and wasted. No wonder business is bad. One look at you would make anyone turn turtle and run.'

Miriam made no answer to this. She lowered her head to avoid his eyes and he never saw the glitter of hatred in hers nor the expression of disdain that flitted over her face to tighten her mouth into a hard thin line.

Kinvara

Late July 1931

[illegible]

[illegible]

Like a [illegible] running [illegible] [illegible] of [illegible] [illegible] all [illegible] [illegible] [illegible] [illegible] [illegible] [illegible]

[illegible]

She [illegible] [illegible] out of [illegible] [illegible] and [illegible]. But [illegible] enough he was allowed [illegible] me leeway and [illegible] more. So [illegible] he might change [illegible] he was [illegible] with [illegible].

Chapter Twenty-five

Like a young deer in full flight, Rebecca went running along the shores of Niven's Bay, along past the village of Calvost till she came to the banks of the River Struan. She knew all the little nooks and crannies of her surroundings now, where best to cross rivers and burns without getting her feet wet, the safest paths to go through reeds and rushes, the easiest routes through mysterious glades and shadowed woodlands.

More and more she was coming to love living in Kinvara. Despite the restrictions of her life she felt at home here such as she had never felt in any of the other places she had lived in throughout her short existence. And now her father was allowing her and her brothers a bit more freedom. He had said they could have a whole day all to themselves to go wherever they wanted for a picnic.

She knew of course that he had his reasons for doing this; it was so out of character with his usual strictness and harshness. But she didn't care. It was enough he was allowing them some leeway and she wasn't wasting a minute more for fear he might change his mind as he was wont to do if something wasn't pleasing him.

With this in mind she fairly scrambled up the steep embankment leading to Struan Bridge. Once on the road her long legs easily carried her the rest of the way to Keeper's Row where she rapped on the door of No. 6 and waited impatiently for it to be opened.

Hannah answered the knock, her face showing surprise at the sight of Joshua's daughter standing on the doorstep. She hesitated, unsure of whether to ask the girl in or not. Rebecca always made her feel uneasy somehow, that arrogant expression of hers, the impression she gave of being superior to everyone else, even her elders and betters, of assessing the world and the people around her in a mute yet strangely critical fashion. It was all there in those dark eyes of hers, blinking away behind her glasses, seeing all, saying nothing. Hannah gave herself a shake. What was she thinking about? Rebecca was only a child, after all, and she certainly had plenty to contend with having Joshua Bowman for a father.

Politely she bade the girl come inside but was thrown off course when Rebecca, with equal politeness, refused the offer, saying she would wait outside as it was Vaila she had come to see and wanted to speak to privately.

'Oh, as you wish,' Hannah said rather distantly and withdrew indoors as if she was glad to escape. A minute later Vaila appeared and was immediately seized upon by her friend. 'Walk with me for a bit,' Rebecca imparted hurriedly. Linking arms they went off down the grassy track that led away from Keeper's Row. 'I've got something to tell you,' she went on with sparkling eyes. 'Father's allowing us to go off for a day, me and Caleb and Nathan. I didn't think it would be complete without you so I came to tell you at once – also I wanted to ask you where would be the best place to go.'

'Stac Gorm is marvellous,' Vaila enthused. 'I've gone there often with my father, it's a tidal island but even if you get cut off it doesn't matter, because there's usually someone there with a boat to bring you back over. The only time it's dangerous is during storms and at the equinoxes but it's perfectly safe in the summer.'

'Sounds the ideal spot – and let's make it tomorrow before Father changes his mind and decides against it.'

'I'll get Aidan to come too,' Vaila decided. 'I don't see all that much of him and he loves it when there's a treat going. I'll see if Mark and Maida Lockhart can manage it as well. They're a bit huffed with me just now because I haven't asked them anywhere and this might make up for it. Joss too, if he can get away from the Henderson Hens, they seem to want him at Croft Angus more and more these days.'

'You can't bring them all,' Rebecca protested. 'It isn't a Sunday school outing!'

'Och, don't be so stuffy!' Vaila sounded annoyed. 'The more the merrier. Joss has always been part o' our crowd and – and if he can't come then neither will I!'

'If that's how you feel . . .' Rebecca unhooked her arm from Vaila's and positively glared at her friend, 'you needn't come anywhere with me if you don't want to. I only asked you out of manners anyway.'

Vaila glared back. 'I suppose you think you're a better bastard than me!' she cried hotly, even though the glint in her eyes belied the ferocity of her words.

'Of course I am, and I've got the marks to prove it.' Rebecca held out her arms, on the inside of each one were identical birth marks. 'I call them Sodom and Gomorrah . . .' she giggled, 'because I'm such an evil little bastard!'

Vaila clapped her hand to her mouth. The exchange of similarities that had started between them in Vale O' Dreip's wee hoosie had gone on to become one of their favourite devices for making up their differences, Rebecca in her quick way adding spicy additions to the original theme.

'I do want Joss to come,' Rebecca sighed. 'It's just that he's a Catholic and my father doesn't seem very fond of them.'

'Sounds a bit like my Grampa Ramsay,' Vaila nodded. 'He doesn't like anybody who doesn't belong to the Free Church.'

'Father doesn't like anybody who belongs to *any* church,' Rebecca said with a shrug. 'It was only for show that he went to see Mr MacIntosh. He stands on his own, spreading the gospel as he sees it, unfettered by rules and regulations – except by those he makes up himself.'

She was using her 'preaching voice' as Vaila called it, but the next minute she smiled and Vaila was struck anew by the transformation that such a simple action could make to her friend's countenance.

'Oh, to hell!' Rebecca cried, lifting up her face to the sky. 'Let everybody come tomorrow! I don't care if the whole world is there and I particularly want Joss because I do like him so awfully, awfully much!'

They joined hands and ran all the way to the Struan Bridge where Rebecca said her goodbyes until they would meet again the following day.

The morning dawned fair and sunny. Hannah had risen nobly to the occasion, making piles of sandwiches, adding some of Maudie's pies, pastries and pancakes, together with flasks of home-made lemonade and tea. Joss too came well supplied, glad to get away from the demands of the Henderson Hens for a while, delighted to be going to Stac Gorm which was one of his favourite places. Mark and Maida joined them at the harbour, swinging their bags of food and looking well pleased with themselves.

The young Bowmans were waiting at the bridge as arranged. Rebecca, impatient as always, Nathan nervous looking, Caleb big and bold and glad to see Joss whom he regarded as his equal in age and size, Aidan and Andy being too juvenile in his view to be worthy of much attention.

Essie wasn't there, much to her chagrin. Hannah having decided that she was far too young to attempt the walk to Stac Gorm, which lay a considerable distance away.

No one minded that however. They were young and strong and took their time ambling along, pausing every so often to just play about and point out various features of interest along the way. At the edge of Calvost Rebecca stopped to gaze at Clockwork Cottage nestling in its cosy setting behind all the other houses. There and then nothing would do but that she take Nathan in to see Gabby's working model of a steam engine.

Nathan hung back, reluctant to just barge in on someone without prior arrangement, but Rebecca made him go, taking his hand, telling him that Gabby had made the invitation of his own will and if Nathan didn't take the chance now he might never get to see the wonders that existed within the four walls of the clockmaker's house.

And when he finally passed over the hallowed portals the little boy was glad that his sister had persuaded him to do so. Gabby was there and he was quite willing to display his treasures to his young visitors. As soon as Nathan saw the steam engine he went into raptures and from that moment he and Gabby never stopped talking.

Caleb had come in with his sister and brother. When he saw the results of Gabby's labours he forgot to be big and bold and became the child that he was, gazing around him entranced as he touched and listened and wondered at such a life to be had without restraints or restrictions.

'I felt like that too when I first came here,' Rebecca told him, 'and one day I'm going to just up and run away and go somewhere where I can do what I want, when I want, and how I want.'

'Me too,' Caleb said solemnly as they moved back into the dazzling day where the others were waiting, anxious to be up and running. At Joss's suggestion they cut along down to the shore where more distractions awaited them. Divesting themselves of shoes and stockings they all ran into the water for a paddle, Breck, temporarily freed from his duties, going in with them, barking his appreciation, chasing after stones and sticks, clearing the gulls from the sandbanks and generally having a wonderful time.

After that they wandered barefoot along the tideline, shoes hung round their necks by the laces, plundering the rock pools for tiny crabs with which they had races before allowing them to scuttle away back into hiding.

Joss had Andy on his back, it being too difficult for Breck to pull the cart through the wet sands. The little vehicle was abandoned and left in a dry crevice among the rocks to be collected on the return journey. On passing the schoolhouse Andy was reminded of Miss Catherine and how much he missed her coming to the house and he asked that he be taken up there to say hallo, 'just for a minute'.

Rebecca grumbled at this till Joss reminded her how they had waited at Gabby's for her and so she and her brothers hung back while Joss went off with Andy, Vaila, and Aidan, Mark and Maida opting to go with them at the last moment as they were curious to see the young woman who would be their teacher when school started again.

A large chestnut mare was tethered outside the house. Joss and the young Sutherlands wondered to each other whose it was and hesitated at the door, afraid to knock in case Miss Catherine had a visitor. Not so Maida who applied her knuckles to the door and put her head inquiringly round it without waiting for it to be answered.

Inside she saw the teacher seated at the table drinking tea and laughing with a fair-haired young man of distinctive appearance and style. At the intrusion Catherine hastily arose and came to the door to just stare at Maida in amazement, sparks of annoyance flashing out of her green eyes, red spots of anger suffusing each cheekbone, opening her mouth to tell this strange girl just what she thought of her bad manners when she saw Joss with Andy on his back, Aidan and Vaila at his side.

'We just wanted to say hallo,' the latter quickly explained, afraid that her teacher was going to give all of them a good tongue lashing right there and then. 'We didn't know you had a visitor, we shouldn't have come . . .'

'Ay, we're sorry,' Joss got in quickly.

'Me too,' Maida added.

'She didn't mean it.' Mark defended his sister, despite the fact that he was gazing at her in some irritation.

'It's alright. I'm just going anyway.' Max Gilbert MacKernon appeared behind Catherine. 'I only popped in to say hallo myself so don't bother to apologise on my account.'

Briefly he took Catherine's hand and then he was

off, mounting his horse, saluting, galloping away with a thunder of hooves on the stony path leading away from the schoolhouse.

'Children,' Miss Catherine looked at all the crestfallen faces, 'I do have a private life outside the classroom you know – except . . .' A smile touched her mouth as she looked at Andy. 'I'm sorry I haven't been to see you. I promise I will when – when it's more convenient to everyone – meanwhile . . .' She turned her attention on Maida and Mark. 'The Lockhart twins, I presume. No doubt I'll be seeing you both in school when it starts. Meanwhile you must polish up your manners and learn to be a bit more considerate of others.'

'Yes, Miss Catherine,' came the subdued respectful chorus. Her lips twitched. Retreating inside she gently closed the door, leaving the children to make their deflated way back down to the beach. 'Phew!' Joss said fervently, 'that was close. I can see now why people call her a tartar. She positively bristles when she's angry.'

'I think that man's in love with her,' Maida sighed romantically. 'It was dark in the kitchen after the sunlight but I'm sure they were holding hands when I looked in and he certainly wanted to kiss her when he was going away only we were there watching.'

'Aw, shut up!' Joss said scornfully. 'It's all your fault we got into trouble in the first place!'

'Ay, Joss is right.' For once, Mark was annoyed with his sister. 'We'd better not say anything to anyone about it or we might get it in the ear for doing what we did.'

Maida looked at her brother, she looked at Joss, and before anyone knew what was happening she burst into a violent flood of tears.

'Oh no,' Joss exploded, while Mark raised his eyes heavenwards, 'I hate girls who cry for nothing. Dry up, Maida, we don't want the Bowmans to start asking questions before the day is halfway through.'

Awkwardly he put an arm round the girl's shoulders and gave her a little shake. Maida cheered up instantly. She took out her hanky, gave her nose a good blow, and told everyone how sorry she was for the bother she had caused and how she would 'never ever do anything like it again with people like Miss Catherine'.

'There's only one like her,' Joss said with a grin. 'She's beautiful and clever and I know she's really as soft as butter when she feels like it, only I'm glad I get my learning from Father MacNeil because he doesn't have green cat's eyes and hair that sends out little red sparks when he's angry.'

Maida giggled. She liked Joss, she liked him very much indeed, and she clung to his hand as he marched with Andy down through the dunes to where the others were waiting.

The tide was out when they reached Stac Gorm and they were able to pick their way over to the lumpy little island without mishap. The waters that embraced the pearly white beaches were a pale clear turquoise: the rocks a warm pink where they caught the sun; seals were lazing on the reefs; cormorants drying their wings on boulder-strewn ledges. It was a haven to be in on a day such as this and the children made the most of it, picnicking on the white sands before climbing up to the highermost hill. Caleb and Mark took turns carrying Andy on their shoulders when Joss got tired, the girls linking hands when they got to the top, running right to the edge of a sheer cliff where guillemots nested and gannets plummeted hundreds of feet down into the sea.

The clifftop was fragrant with drifts of wild thyme and the children stood there, quite carried away by the majesty and beauty of their surroundings, forgetting how swiftly the hours were passing. 'I wish I had wings!' cried Caleb. 'I would fly away and never come back – except maybe to visit Stac Gorm.'

'I'd like to be a soldier and get lots o' medals,' Joss put in, his face flushed and excited looking.

'Soldiers get killed,' Maida said quietly.

'I won't. I'll fight and win and no one will ever beat me.'

'I want never to say prayers again,' Nathan said solemnly, able to feel that his opinion mattered in such a place as this. 'Except when I'm driving a steam engine and want to get to the station on time.'

'I want to be like Joss,' Aidan said shyly, 'to be a soldier and fight.'

'I want to be like my mother.' Vaila gazed over the sea to the Kinvara Light as she spoke. 'And marry a man like my father.'

'I want to marry Vaila.' Mark sounded serious about this and everybody stared at him. 'Boys don't want things like that,' Caleb scoffed. 'And it's most likely Vaila would never want to marry you, you aren't the least like her father.'

'How do you know?' Mark growled. 'You've never even met him.'

'I've seen him, wandering about, tall and dark and strong looking and a sort of mystery about him that you'll never have.'

Joss glanced at Maida. 'What about you, Maida? What do you want when you grow up?'

'I don't know.' She sounded rather bleak. 'Except I think I do a bit only I don't want to say it here.'

'I want to roam round the world.' Rebecca spoke dreamily, hardly aware of the arguments around her. 'I want to know what it's like never to get down on my knees again. To be free, that's what I want.'

'Me too.' Andy found his voice suddenly, gruff and deep and filled with longing.

'What's the use of you wishing that?' Rebecca told him abruptly. 'You'll always be tied to that cart of yours and will never be free to do anything you feel like doing!'

She got up and went stomping away, to be followed by Joss who pulled her round roughly to face him. 'What's got into you all of a sudden? You didn't have to say that to Andy.'

'I know.' She looked shamefaced. 'It's just, all at once I felt like he must do, tied down, never able to do the things I want for years yet. I suppose I took it out on him. I'm sorry and I'll tell him so before I go home.'

Bending down, Joss plucked a tiny wildflower from the fragrant turf and handed it to her. She gazed at it thoughtfully before putting it carefully into her pocket, her face a mixture of emotions as she did so. Joss's fingers curled into hers, the expression on his face was one of boyish sympathy and affection. 'Come on. I know how hard it must be for you, but it won't always be like that, we'll get older and will do everything we want to do someday.'

She allowed her hand to dwell in his. They looked at one another for a long, long, moment, then she disentangled her fingers to go back to Andy and make her apologies.

'It's alright.' Andy readily forgave her and she turned away from him to gaze down to the swirling waters below. A defiant expression flitted across her face. With one swift movement she tore off her hat and tossed it over the cliff, watching as the air currents seized it and played with it before it went sailing away to be lost from view.

With a loud whoop of abandon Caleb followed his sister's example and everybody clapped as his hat flipped and flapped and flew for quite a considerable distance till it too disappeared from sight.

Caleb looked at Nathan as the little boy hesitated. 'Go on,' Caleb urged. 'Father can't beat you for losing your hat. It's windy up here on the cliffs, it's only natural for silly things like hats to get blown away.'

Still Nathan held back. His father had chastised him for less. Unbeknown to the others he had regularly taken his youngest son's trousers down to administer a few punishing strokes with a stick to 'keep him on his toes and stop him from getting soft'.

Nathan took a deep breath. He wanted to be strong like Rebecca, he longed to be fearless like Caleb. Several tortuous moments passed during which he fought a fierce inner battle with himself then, in a burst of decision, he removed his headcovering and followed the actions of his brother and sister, really quite delighted with himself as he did so, enjoying watching the hated hat go floating, spinning, drifting away, according to the whim of the breezes.

Nathan took a deep breath. He had loved this day, he wanted to hold onto it forever and never let go, but the sun was sinking lower in the sky, the first flush of evening was spreading across the sea. By the time they got home the shadows would be lengthening over the land and Joshua would have something to say if they didn't get in before it got dark altogether and woe betide them if they missed their bedtime prayers.

Chapter Twenty-six

Wee Fay peeped over the counter at Essie standing on the other side, eyes big and shiny, her little face, framed in its halo of golden curls, flushed and eager looking as she stood on tip-toes and tried to let Wee Fay see what she was holding in her chubby hand.

Wee Fay, not much taller than the smallest child in Balivoe school, had to stand on tiptoes herself in order to get a better look at Essie but it was no use and soon she came round to join the little girl and to find out what it was she wanted.

Slowly Essie uncurled her fingers. 'Sweeties,' she said decidedly. 'Lots and lots o' sweeties and a dolly too cos Dadda wouldn't buy me a new one.'

'Bejabers and bejasus!' gasped the proprietress of The Dunny, her Irish brogue becoming richer in her astonishment. 'A whole half-crown. Essie, wherever did you get it?'

'Old Gabby gave it to me cos I danced for him and made him laugh.'

She placed the money in Wee Fay's hand and waited, her eyes roving round the shop as she did so, dwelling on the array of colourful jars containing boilings of every description, staring at the trays of tablet and toffee and big fluffy marshmallows displayed in a stand covered over with glass.

'Essie,' Wee Fay began slowly, 'are you sure about this? Surely to goodness Gabby wouldn't part with a sum o' money like that and certainly not to a wee lassie like you.'

'Gabby gave it to me,' persisted Essie, her face beginning to redden just a little. 'He wanted me to have it cos he likes me a lot and said I could visit him any time I wanted.'

'You visit him? On your own, Essie? Without your mamma, without anybody to take you there and bring you back again?'

'I'm a big girl now.' Essie's lip was beginning to tremble. 'I can run all the way there without anybody taking my hand and treating me like a baby.'

Wee Fay looked at the money again. 'Does your mamma know about this, Essie? Gabby giving you money, you coming here to spend it as you like?'

'Yes, Mamma knows.' Essie nodded vehemently. 'She wants me to get a new dolly cos Dadda gave Vaila lots and lots o' presents for her birthday but didn't get anything for me.'

'I see.' Wee Fay scrutinised the child's face long and hard, looking for a sign of regression, but Essie stared steadily back, despite a glimmer of tears starting to drown out the luminosity of her wide blue eyes.

'Very well,' Wee Fay said slowly, 'if Mamma says it's alright then I'll have to take your word for it, but a half-crown is too much to spend on sweets so I'll give you a shilling's worth now and you can keep the change to use another day.'

'A dolly too,' Essie said quickly.

'No dollies Essie, I sold the last one yesterday. You'll just have to wait till I get more and make do with your old ones till then.'

Essie's brow furrowed. She had very badly wanted a new dolly to add to her family but soon forgot to be vexed in the excitement of having her pick from the array of jars and tempting sweetmeats.

The doorbell jingled. Kangaroo Kathy came breezing in, looking for buttons to sew on the matinée jacket she was making for a friend's expected baby, but stopping in her tracks when she saw Essie delving into the large tin containing the sugar-olly sticks that were such a favourite with the local youngsters.

'Essie,' Kathy acknowledged with a click of her tongue as she spied the child's chosen goodies piled on the counter. 'What is a wee lass like you wanting wi' all these sweet things, I'd like to know? Sugar is bad for your teeths and it's surprised I am that your mother can afford to let you buy so much stuff.'

'She says Gabby gave her the money,' Wee Fay supplied with a meaningful nod.

'Oh, ho, did he now?' Kathy was not in the least

convinced by this. 'Gabby is no' the sort to throw money like that around. A good kind soul he may be but he's got his head screwed on where sillar is concerned – though, of course, Hannah's youngest has aye been a wily wee thing and might very well have twisted him round her little finger to get what she wanted.'

Wee Fay signalled for Kathy to bend low so that she could murmur into her ear, 'She says he gave it to her for dancing for him, a whole half-crown all to herself if you please.'

'Surely not.' Kathy's round pleasant face took on a shocked expression. 'I would never have thought that o' Gabby, still . . .' She folded her hands across her ever-present lapbag and shook her head sorrowfully. 'It is a strange world that we live in, Fay, and a very wicked one betimes. I myself have aye credited Gabby wi' good manners and breeding but shocking things go on behind closed doors all the time and he has been lonely since his wife went and died on him, very lonely indeed.'

Wee Fay was beginning to feel she had divulged too much to Kangaroo Kathy whose conversation had taken on a very unsavoury twist, even if she hadn't meant it to sound that way. 'We'd best keep this to ourselves, mavourneen,' Wee Fay hastily imparted. 'You know how easily gossip gets around in a place like Kinvara and I for one will hold my tongue on the matter till I have had a chance to find out more about it.'

'Ay, you're right,' Kathy subsided with good grace, 'it

would be terrible just, to get a fine man like Gabby into trouble and him such a clever cratur' wi' his clocks and his music and all those other bits and pieces he has around him in that magical wee house o' his.'

She began rummaging in Wee Fay's collection of button boxes, the subject of Gabby forgotten in her quest to find exactly what she needed to sew onto her matinée jacket, not even looking up when a laden Essie departed the shop, highly delighted with herself as her little legs took her out into the sunlight and the winding road home.

Hannah glanced from her window and saw Essie engrossed in conversation with young Babs MacGill from No. 1 of the Row, their heads close together as they talked, Babs having got down on her knees to be on Essie's level. No easy task, Hannah thought wryly, with all that weight the girl had to carry and her not quite fifteen yet.

'What were you doing out there, Essie?' Hannah asked as soon as her daughter appeared in the kitchen.

'Just talking to Babs, Mamma.'

'I thought you were out the back giving your dollies a tea party.'

'I was, Mamma, but I got tired playing on my own. Andy has gone to see Johnny Lonely and Vaila has gone to see Mark and Maida but didn't take me with her.'

'I know.' Hannah sighed as she ruffled the child's silky head. 'It's better that you don't go back there for a while.

You know how worried I was when I found out you went there on your own. Grace Lockhart wasn't too pleased about it either so it's best to stay here where I can keep my eye on you.'

'Can I go upstairs now, Mamma? I want to play with the rest o' my dollies. They're all tired as tired can be and need to have their afternoon nap.'

She spread her hands in a quaintly old-fashioned gesture and Hannah laughed. 'Ay, away you go, my wee lamb. I'll be round the back hanging out my washing if you want me for anything, and I'll bring your other dollies upstairs when I come in for I'm sure they must be tired too after such a busy day.'

The minute Essie reached the safety of her room she lifted up her frock and pulled out the bags and bags of sweets she had hidden in her knickers. When Hannah eventually came upstairs it was to find her daughter sprawled among her dolls, to all intents and purposes as fast asleep as any child could be. Tenderly Hannah tucked a blanket round her daughter's shoulders and went out of the room to softly close the door behind her.

When Essie didn't appear at teatime Hannah went upstairs to see what was keeping the little girl amused for so long. There was Essie surrounded by paper bags, some empty, others half full, her face as white as a sheet, groaning and holding her tummy and saying she wanted to be sick. And she was. All over the bed, before her mother could do anything about it, sobbing and crying pitifully as she did so.

'That Babs!' Hannah exploded. 'Wait till I get her! Just wait till I get her for making you ill like this!' She wasted no time asking questions. Without ado she picked Essie up and bore her away downstairs to wash and soothe her. When she was certain that the child had begun to settle down and was in no danger of being sick again she told Vaila and Andy to 'bide where they were' at the tea table and went charging out of the house, straight to No. 1 of the Row to give a preliminary knock on the door before marching straight in.

The MacGill family were at their evening meal. All of them looked up in surprise as Hannah suddenly catapulted into the room, driven there by a fit of pure self-righteous rage.

'Essie's been sick,' she imparted abruptly, 'and Babs is to blame. I saw her with Essie earlier, now I know she must have been giving her sweets and this is the result! If you don't mind me saying so, Bette, I think you allow your daughter more money than is good for her. It is no wonder she's fat and can hardly run two yards without puffing like an old woman!'

Big Bette paused in the act of lifting a forkful of mince to her mouth. 'Is this true, Babs?' she asked in an ominously quiet voice.

'No, Ma.' Babs stoutly defended herself, her round face growing pink with chagrin. 'It was Essie who gave the sweets to me! She had bags and bags o' them hidden in her knickers. It's true, Ma, honest injun!'

'So.' Bette uncurled her mighty girth from the table and advanced threateningly towards her unexpected visitor. 'What have you to say for yourself now, Hannah Sutherland! Barging in here! Never so much as a by-your-leave! Accusing my Babs of things she didn't do! Insulting her and upsetting the entire household in the process. Believing everything a babe like Essie tells you!'

Hannah drew in her horns immediately and began to back towards the door. Intimidation had always been one of Big Bette's most successful tactics when it came to dealing with people. No one ever tackled her unless driven by some force outwith their control and they nearly always regretted it afterwards.

Hannah's subsiding anger left her feeling nervous and deflated. She had no intention of informing the mighty Bette that she hadn't stopped long enough to question Essie. Instead she beat a hasty retreat homewards, once inside going straight upstairs to survey her small daughter's sleeping domain. Crossing to the bed she threw back the sheets and the pillows and almost at once spotted some silver coins lying beneath one of them.

Scooping them up she took them downstairs and held them out in front of Essie's nose. The child immediately reddened. On the verge of tears she repeated the story she had told Wee Fay. When she was finished a strange sick feeling seized Hannah's heart.

'You danced for Gabby?' she reiterated in a play for time.

'Yes, Mamma,' Essie confirmed with a sob. Hannah turned to Vaila waiting patiently at the table with Andy. 'Vaila, is this true? Does Essie do this sort o' thing when she goes to that man's house?'

Vaila hesitated, a feeling of foreboding went through her. 'She does, sometimes,' she confirmed unwillingly, 'at least, she did that last time we were there – but Gabby never gave her any money. He was in a hurry to get back to his work and we all went away from his house together.'

A thought struck Hannah then, one that left her feeling more uneasy than ever. 'Do you go alone to Gabby's house, Essie? The way you went to see Grace Lockhart at Oir na Cuin?'

Essie hung her head. A few moments passed laden with tension. When finally she gave a nod of confirmation Hannah sat down suddenly on the nearest chair. 'Go upstairs, Essie,' she said in a wobbly sort of voice as if she had been running and couldn't get her breath back. 'I've taken the sheets off your bed but I'll be up in a few minutes to see to you.'

Essie did as she was bid, only too glad to vacate the room, leaving her mother to dish a belated meal to Vaila and Andy but nothing at all for herself as she had completely lost her appetite.

* * *

Hannah went to bed that night feeling lost and afraid. Oh, why was that man of hers never here when he was needed! He was out in Charlie Campbell's boat again and wouldn't be home that night, the pair of them having decided it was perfect fishing weather. Going off! Just like that! Leaving her to carry the burdens of the house alone. There was no one to turn to, no one she could confide in. She had fought with Janet, her relations with Rob were cool in the extreme. Catherine Dunbar was in the huff, and now she could add Big Bette to her growing list of antagonists.

Turning her face on the pillow she gazed at the sky outside. It had been raining earlier in the evening, now it was clearing but not sufficiently for a single star to be seen.

Getting up, she padded to the window and gazed out, hoping for a glimpse of Charlie's boat in the bay, anything that might bring her a sense of comfort in the silent loneliness of night. But no matter how hard she strained her eyes she could see nothing and with a sigh she turned back to her bed and knew she would have to face tomorrow alone and unsupported.

Gabriel Cochrane never knew what hit him when Hannah Sutherland of the Row appeared in his kitchen the following morning. He was repairing a pocket watch at the moment of her entry, and was so startled by her abrupt appearance he dropped the tiny cog he had been about to fit and just stared at her as if she were a ghost. Hannah gave him no chance to open his mouth but just stood there, the accusations dropping from her lips, telling him just what she thought of him encouraging a tot like Essie to come alone to his house, tempting her with money and her too innocent to know any better.

Gabby found his tongue then, telling Hannah just what he thought of *her*, allowing her child to wander off the way she did without proper supervision, never teaching her manners, letting her do as she pleased, when she pleased, how she pleased.

'And come to think o' it,' he added harshly, 'I *did* miss some money from the dish in the lobby where I keep it. I didn't give it to Essie, she must have taken it. Ay, and that isn't all. One o' my clockwork dolls is missing. They just sit there, on a table in the parlour, and Essie has always been fascinated by them.'

'Oh, you would say that!' Hannah was really on her mettle by now. 'Anybody could have taken it, that and your money. It could have been the Bowman bairns, Vaila told me how they all came in here only the other day to look at your things. It's easy to accuse a baby like Essie who isn't able to defend herself. I for one am not taken in by you, Gabby Cochrane, and won't stay a second longer listening to your excuses!'

With that she took herself off, leaving Gabby to stare at the door and wonder just what had happened to him in the last few minutes. He drew in a lungful of air. Those insinuations the woman had made, the innuendoes, the accusations. And here was he, trying only to do an honest day's work, never expecting a bombshell to strike him between the eyes in the privacy of his own home.

Gabby was greatly shaken by the turn of events and he sat where he was for a long, long time, just staring into space, all thoughts of work forgotten in the trauma of the moment.

Wee Fay was next to be on the receiving end of Hannah's runaway tongue. In no time at all the proprietress of The Dunny was made aware of Hannah's opinions regarding her responsibilities to the younger members of the community.

'Some people would take money from a blind man out o' greed!' Hannah raged. 'Essie was as sick as a dog last night, and I'm the one who had to clean it up. The poor wee lamb was really quite ill and you and that Gabby Cochrane between you are to blame for that.'

Wee Fay drew herself up to her full diminutive height. 'And where were you, Hannah Sutherland, when all this was going on? In cloud cuckoo land as usual, spinning rosy pictures to yourself about your little angel and how good she is. Maybe if you didn't keep her tied to your apron strings so much she wouldn't have to go sneaking about behind your back doing the things she does.'

Wee Fay paused only to take a deep breath before rushing on. 'Essie's a bonny child, I grant you that, but when all's said and done she can be as mischievous as the next bairn and surely to goodness you as her mother should be teaching her about right and wrong instead o' blaming her faults on those around you.'

'How dare you criticise my daughter!' Hannah exploded. 'A – a smout like you – little more than a— a . . .'

'A dwarf,' the little woman supplied tightly. 'Ay, well we all have our shortcomings – to put it in a nutshell – but sometimes the worst freaks o' nature are those who seem perfect on the outside, if you get my meaning, Mrs Sutherland.'

Hannah had run out of steam, all the fight knocked out of her suddenly. She could find nothing further to say on the subject of Essie, and when Wee Fay's husband, Little John, came into the shop Hannah departed, feeling as if a large hole was opening in front of her ready to swallow her up into some dark unknown pit.

Kinvara

Early August 1931

Chapter Twenty-seven

Johnny Lonely had waited a long time to confront Joshua Bowman. For years now, Johnny's heart and mind had festered with pain and unrest. He had never thought the day would come when he would have the chance to rid himself of the heavy load that had almost broken him over a vast period of time and space.

Since coming to Kinvara more than eighteen years ago, he had known quiet spells in his day-to-day existence, pools of calm when he had felt able to savour the beauty of life and to be as peaceful as he ever could be with himself. Yet no matter how hard he tried, he couldn't forget the events of his past, the memories were nearly always there, niggling away at his very marrow, disturbing his dreams, casting a blight over his waking hours.

The arrival of Joshua Bowman to the Mill O' Cladach had come to him like a bolt from the blue. It was something he had often wondered about, what his reactions would be if he ever came face to face with the man who had ruined his life. When the moment came he had been poorly prepared for it and in a state of shock he had gone home to his lonely hut under the cliffs of Cragdu to think and plan and decide how to handle the situation to the greatest effect.

In the end he had thought it best to let Joshua settle in first, to give him the opportunity to build up a sense of security, the chance to strut and postulate and show off his feathers before making the denouement that would surely bring him to his knees. In the meantime, Johnny quite enjoyed unnerving Joshua whenever he possibly could, allowing himself to be seen without actually showing himself properly, popping up when Joshua least expected it, doing everything he could to make the man uneasy whilst still imaging himself to be master of himself and all he surveyed.

For several weeks Johnny savoured the feelings of quiet power within himself, anticipated the moment of the eventual showdown, in some ways reluctant for it to happen, for then that part of it would be over and he would lose the sense of euphoria that was gradually building up in him.

He knew it had to happen sometime but he chose his moment, watching as Joshua tripped himself up in his attempts to win over the good folk of Kinvara, waiting till he had built himself up again and was feeling confident of his position in the community. After all, what went up must surely come down, and Johnny rejoiced in the fact that he would be there to witness that long-awaited event.

* * *

Joshua was feeling pleased with himself. It had been a wise move, allowing the children more freedom, letting it be seen that he could relax the rules when he wanted, that he wasn't some sort of ogre to be feared and hated, but really a kind and loving father who wanted only what was best for his family. And it had paid off too. Business was going well. After a shaky start the people of Kinvara were beginning to accept him, nodding to him in the street, passing the time of day with him, making use of the mill, fed up with the inconvenience of trundling their produce all the way to the Mill O' Bruach. Conrad o' Connar wasn't having so much of his own way now but he had plenty and enough to keep him going on his side of the fence.

Joshua knew he still had a long way to go to before winning over his neighbours completely. They were a canny bunch and he was a stranger. It would take them some time to fully accept him but they would, in the end they would, and he was really rather glad he had made the decision to come here, tired as he was of moving around, never settling in one place for any length of time, always on the go from one year to the next.

Of course, he wouldn't be here for ever, that would never do. Pastures new were a must in his way of life but for the moment there was plenty here to keep him going, lots of Jessies and Bellas and all those others who were only too ready to sing his praises to the world at large . . .

Joshua glanced around him. The weathered walls of the mill building were yellow and pink in the dimness, specks of chaff danced in the sunbeams. The wheel outside was churning around, swishing water rhythmically through its paddles, the vibrations of it reaching right up through the floor to where he was standing, enjoying the movements, the sounds of industry.

He paused for a moment to rock on his heels and puff out his chest, thinking about the headway he had made with the lost souls of Kinvara, most of them alone and lonely, eager to accept his services. Women had always fallen for him, the magnetism, the aura of strength he carried around with him, the ability he had to make them feel special and wanted and very, very much a part of some wonderful pattern that had been mapped out for them . . .

He stroked his beard and laughed . . . and was totally unprepared when a dark shadow loomed up in front of him and Johnny Lonely was suddenly there, framed in the doorway, never saying a word. There was a powerful stillness about him, surrounded by a blinding mantle of light – more a silhouette than a man of substance – controlled yet menacing, waiting, just waiting, to pounce . . .

'Johnny Armstrong!' The words were torn from Joshua in a strangled cry. 'Where the hell did you spring from?'

'It's enough that I'm here, Bowman.' Johnny's voice was taut with triumph. 'I've been watching you for weeks now, waiting for this moment, longing to see your face when you saw mine, and by God, I'm going to enjoy every second of seeing you squirm.'

Joshua seemed unable to keep his feet. Staggering

backwards he lowered himself onto a sackful of corn to fumble in his pocket for his hanky which he applied to his brow with a shaking hand.

'Stop the wheel, Bowman,' Johnny ordered in a low even tone, 'I want you to hear every word I have to say to you for I won't repeat them again.'

Joshua got up, pulled a few levers, the great wheel ground to a halt and an electrifying silence fell over the building.

Johnny gazed long and hard at the man in front of him. The years rolled back for Johnny then, so long ago it sometimes seemed, yet it might have been just yesterday that Joshua Bowman had come into his life to rob him of everything that had been good and precious in it.

Johnny had been a head teacher at a school for boys in those days. Married with one cherished daughter called Kate. She had been just nine years old when Joshua had taken both her and her mother away. Kate had never lived to see her father again and had died searching for him, in a roadside ditch, cold, frightened and alone . . .

A mist of tears blurred Johnny's vision. His lass, his bonny Kate, if she had lived she would be about twenty-eight by now . . . Abruptly Johnny dashed his hand across his eyes. It wouldn't do to show weakness in front of Bowman. He was a creature who thrived on that sort of thing, an evil being without mercy who preyed on the lonely and the ill, showing no compassion of any kind . . .

'Well, I'm waiting, Armstrong.' Joshua was beginning

to recover some of his lost equilibrium. His voice came out, harsh and cold, spurring Johnny to action. Grabbing Joshua by his collar he ground out, 'Ay, and well you may wait, just as I have waited all these years to find you! You covered your tracks well and somehow I never managed to catch up with you, but I heard about you, Bowman. I spy on people you see, find out all their little dark secrets, something I've learned to do very well over the years. In your case I kept my ear firmly to the ground and found out things about you that made me sick. Those women you preyed on, for instance, pretending concern when all the time you were robbing them of their savings and anything else you could get your hands on.'

Johnny had to stop to get his breath back at that point, so incensed was he with rage. ''Tis small wonder you had to keep moving from place to place,' he went on at last, 'never staying long enough to get caught, dragging your family with you, the wife you stole from me, the bairn I loved with my very soul.'

Miriam came in just then with a tray of tea which she almost dropped at sight of Johnny bent low over Joshua, rasping out words that fell upon her ears like ice cold spicules of rain. 'Johnny,' she whispered, rooted to the spot, everything about her growing pale and still as she gazed at the man who had been, and still was, her lawful husband.

Confused beyond belief she could only shake her head wordlessly as the years dragged her back, back to a past filled with Johnny and Kate. The delirium of emotions that had made her leave everything that had been good in her life to go off with Joshua Bowman, taking Kate with her, a little girl who had loved her own father so dearly she had run away and died attempting to find him again . . .

'Oh, God!' Miriam put her hand to her mouth to stifle her cry of pain. She had never stopped grieving for that first beloved child of hers. She could see her yet, dark haired and bonny, eager and clever, so filled with life it had shone like a lamp out of those great expressive eyes of hers.

Unable to bear her burden of guilt Miriam had deserted Joshua. Too ashamed to go back to Johnny she had left Scotland, drifting from town to town, supporting herself in whatever way she could, eventually finding a good position as a lady's maid in a big house.

Joshua had come back into her life then and had bewitched her all over again, declaring his remorse for the mistakes of the past, telling her how much he had missed her and assuring her of his continuing allegiance to her happiness if she would agree to see him again.

Soon she had fallen pregnant with Rebecca and he had persuaded her to enter into a bigamous marriage and had proceeded to rob her of every penny she had ever saved in her years of lonely exile. It hadn't taken her long to realise he had only married her to provide himself with a cloak of respectability, but by then it was too late to do anything about it. More children had started coming. Caleb, then Nathan, binding her to a man who sucked her dry in the years that followed, taking away her spirit, using her like a servant, till all that was left in the end was a woman who went through the motions of living without knowing the joy of life . . .

'Miriam.' Johnny had spun round to look at her out of eyes that were big and burning. 'Ay, Miriam,' he went on in a hushed voice, 'only you were just plain Mary when I knew you. Since then you entered into a false marriage with the man o' your dreams and changed your name on both counts, feeling maybe that a piece o' paper could make right out o' wrong. It didn't matter that your children were born without a real identity, you just went along with it and hoped for the best and now I don't suppose any of it matters to you any more.'

'Please, Johnny, don't go on, please don't go on. I can't bear it.' Miriam shook her head as if to clear it but Johnny was too carried away by now to stop even if he had wanted to. With glittering eyes he turned his attention back to Joshua to say contemptuously, 'Did you ever tell her that she wasn't the first? That there were other bigamous marriages, especially the one after she left you and before you met her again? There have been strings of them, Bowman, enough to put you in jail for the rest o' your life, that and the fact you take money from vulnerable women under false pretences and are still doing it, right here in Kinvara, under the guise of a holy man with God on your side.'

'For Christ's sake, man,' Joshua's face had turned

purple, 'I've only just got here, this could ruin me if it ever got out . . .' His mouth twisted. 'It would also ruin the children, they would never be able to hold their heads up again, and them only just begun to make a niche for themselves in the place.'

Johnny shook his head pityingly. 'That's right, Bowman, use the children, just as you've been using them as a prop ever since they were born. But don't worry, I would never do anything to harm them, it's you I'm after, Bowman, and I mean to make you pay for all the evil you've ever committed in your days as a so-called preacher. I'm going to tell you how you must lead your life, little man, how you must send your children to school when it starts, to stop bullying them and treat them with kindness, especially Nathan who is so terrified of you he cries to himself when he thinks no one is watching and dreads every minute of his waking day.'

Johnny was enjoying himself now. He went on, outlining his proposals in a cool, calm voice, while Joshua listened with ill-concealed rage and Miriam sobbed quietly to herself in a corner.

When Johnny at last finished speaking he looked at the woman who had once been the mother of his child and his wife in more than just name. 'I used to hate you, Miriam,' he told her in a flat tired voice, 'for what you did to me and Kate. Now – seeing you again – I can only find it in my heart to pity you. Yours can't be a happy life. God knows you made a mess of it and must never cease to regret it.'

'I need you to forgive me, Johnny,' she pleaded. 'Never a day passes that I don't think of you and Kate, what I did to you both, how it ended, how it has gone on . . .'

Johnny put his hand on her shoulder and squeezed it, no one noticed a stealthy figure stealing out of the shadows, nor did anyone hear as a door opened and shut as soft as soft could be down there in the dusty recesses of the big mill building.

Johnny Lonely very seldom got visitors. He was therefore alert and suspicious when a rattling came to his rickety door one morning. He didn't immediately get up to open it. He was canny and unwelcoming where callers were concerned and never let them over the door if he could at all prevent it. He hated anyone coming to 'spy' on him as he put it to himself. He disliked the pitying glances that his well-meaning neighbours were wont to throw at him when they occasionally called with offerings of a culinary nature, thinking perhaps that he had starved to death since their last sighting of him and that maybe only a heap of dry bones remained to tell the tale.

His particular aversion was to stray holidaymakers looking, perhaps, for an amusing diversion on their wanders or for shelter from the rain, others giving the impression that his hut must be there solely for their benefit and looking most pained when he stepped out to confront them, the expressions on their faces suggesting he could only be some sort of caveman straight out of the dark ages.

Johnny didn't mind children coming to see him, they rarely looked with critical eyes upon his unusual way of life but rather were fascinated by it, wanting only to know more about it and in some cases wishing they could be like him and live in liberty near the sea and the shore and the big ships sailing by.

When Johnny at last answered his door and saw Rebecca standing on the step he was not greatly perturbed by her presence. He just stood looking at her, waiting for her to speak, not asking her in because she was a stranger even if she was a child and had given him the impression of haughtiness on the few occasions their paths had crossed.

'Johnny,' she began, somewhat hesitantly for the normally forthright Rebecca. 'I'm sorry, but I heard what you said to my parents the other day. I didn't mean to snoop, it just somehow happened, and I came to find out more about the truth – especially about Kate – my sister. She never seemed real to me somehow, then I heard you talking, and it was just so sad, her running away like that, dying in her efforts to find you. Oh – I'm so sorry, so very, very sorry . . .'

To Johnny's dismay Rebecca burst out crying, throwing the skirt of her pinafore over her face as if to cover up the terrible, terrible sin of weeping, which she never dared do in front of her father because he would have called it weakness and Rebecca never wanted anybody to think that she was in any way lacking in forbearance – and Johnny himself had told her that only the weak went under. She remembered that very plainly from her first meeting with him.

Johnny glanced around quickly as if to ascertain that no one was watching, then he hustled the girl inside and made her sit down on his crumpled bed. Her face was woebegone as she gazed up at him and in a burst of compassion Johnny put his arms round her and held her close. 'Ay, Kate is indeed your sister, lass,' he said huskily. 'Even if only in spirit. She was my life, the reason I left everything behind when I discovered she had died. I wanted to die myself after that but I kept going, moving round the country, travelling further down the path of despair till finally I ended up in Kinvara and made it my home . . .'

He glanced ruefully round. 'If such a word can be applied to this mean abode that some say is only fit for animals to shelter in. But I'm used to this way o' life now. I have everything I want or need, my books, my music, my memories, I'll never be entirely happy or contented but who is in this world? We all want what we can't have, we have what we don't want, it's the way we're made and nothing will ever change that.'

Rebecca was profoundly moved by Johnny's confidences. She gazed around her, at the books piled on driftwood shelves, at the gramophone records stacked in a corner, the instrument itself taking pride of place on a table that had been washed up on the shore and carefully restored by Johnny.

Bits of marine treasure trove reposed everywhere, a wheel, a compass, a brass bell from a wrecked ship, simple ornaments like shells and polished stones, unusually shaped pieces of wood, bleached and scarred by wind and tide.

Rebecca got up to touch everything, then reaching out she took Johnny's hand and held it tight. 'What am I to do, Johnny?' she said in a small lost voice. 'Oh, what am I to do knowing all this?'

'Go on as before, lass, for the sake of your brothers and your mother.'

'What has she ever done for me?' Rebecca cried passionately. 'She acts as if she isn't all there, seeing nothing, caring less, never a thought to spare for me or my brothers, never a word to say in our defence. What kind of way is that for any mother to behave?'

Johnny sighed. 'Your mother was once a loving, caring woman, Rebecca. When your father came along she lost her head over him and paid the worst price of all for her mistake; the loss of her child. She left him after that. When they met up again I have no doubt it was loneliness that drove her into his clutches once more. She must have regretted it every day of her life since and the only way she has o' dealing with it is to shut herself off from the reality of her existence.'

'You lost a child too!' Rebecca returned hotly. 'Why

don't you hate her for what she has done to you? I would if it was me!'

'I did once, the years passed, my attitude changed, my hatred burned itself out. In its place came an emptiness perhaps even worse than my bitterness. Now I feel nothing for her – except – when I saw her again I remembered how it had once been with us and I felt only sorrow for the lost years of our youth.'

'Well, I don't like her one little bit, and I despise *him* even more. I can't think of him as my father any more . . .' Her grip on Johnny's hand tightened. 'You're still married to my mother. In that respect you are my stepfather, that is how I will think of you from now on, even if we're the only two who ever know it. You're a good man, Johnny Armstrong, you lost your Kate, now you have me, and whenever I feel I have to talk to someone I'll talk to you. We can keep one another company but don't worry. I know how much you like your freedom, and I won't become a pest or a burden to you.'

She moved towards the door. 'I really and truly am a bastard now, aren't I? It isn't a joke any more. That's what my parents have done for me and for my brothers and I'll never forgive them for it – never.'

Her voice was bleak. She was all at once the insecure young girl that she tried so hard to hide, rather than the mature sounding being who had poured out her heart in the last few minutes. She opened the door and went out, head bent as she walked slowly along the tideline.

She wouldn't tell Vaila any of this, she vowed to herself. It had been alright to laugh when she had believed that her identity was legal and binding, but it had all been a sham. Nothing was real any more, for all their squalor and poverty the Law family of Balivoe had more right to a place in society than she had, it was as plain and as simple as that.

She went home, she looked at her mother and at her father for long, long, considering moments, then she took herself off to her room to seek out her bible. But it wasn't the words that interested her, rather it was the tiny wildflower she had pressed into the pages, the one Joss had picked for her on the clifftop that sunlit wonderful day of the picnic at Stac Gorm.

The scents of wild places were locked into its petals. She breathed deeply of the fragrance, then lifting it to her lips she kissed it and felt much, much better than she had done a few moments ago.

Chapter Twenty-eight

Billy MacNulty propped his bike against the fence of Clockwork Cottage and took a parcel of groceries from his wickerwork basket. No one had seen Gabby for more than a week now. He hadn't been in the village, hadn't paid his usual visits to any of the shops. He hadn't even placed an order with Big Bette which he sometimes did when he was very busy, and Bette, growing anxious about him, had sent Billy along with some food just to make sure the clockmaker wasn't starving himself to death.

Talk had been rife in the place concerning Hannah's visits to both Gabby and Wee Fay. Word had got around about the money that Essie had come to spend in The Dunny, naming Gabby as the donor for 'services rendered' as one or two less charitable members of the community meaningfully put it. Others hastened to defend him. 'Kind, Gabby may be, but he was aye grippy wi' the pennies . . . knit one, make one, cast off five next row.' Kangaroo Kathy nodded as her needles clacked busily. 'I myself don't believe a word o' it though of course, as I said to Wee Fay at the time, some folks go queer in the head altogether when they're alone as much as he is.'

'Ay, it's in his nature to be canny,' Jessie agreed, 'but in spite o' that he has always been a gentleman and I myself have always had a soft spot for him. In my opinion, Hannah Houston from Ayr is responsible for all this. She lets that Essie do anything she likes and now poor Gabby is taking the blame – and him so good with the bairns as a rule.'

'Ay, Jessie, you're right about Miss High and Mighty Hannah,' Big Bette inserted her pennyworth into the conversation. 'You should have seen the way she barged into my house the other night, interrupting us in the middle o' a meal, blaming Babs for making Essie sick, upsetting everyone in the house. Just plain bad manners if you ask me, the Houstons are never shy when it comes to making trouble.'

'Hmph, it's their middle name,' Jessie said with feeling. 'It's been like that since the day both Hannah and her mother arrived and I've no doubt they will go on causing havoc as long as there's breath in them.'

'Hannah certainly pulled no punches the day she stormed into my shop,' Wee Fay put in. 'Sure and to goodness, she just stood there bawling her head off like a maniac, and just about tore me to ribbons when I dared to suggest she ought to exercise a bit more control over her daughter.'

'Ach, well, Gabby's reputation as a man o' great character will surely stand him in good stead,' Jessie opined firmly. 'He knows how well he is liked and will hold his head up high, in spite of all this.'

'I'm no' so sure,' Big Bette said darkly. 'One bad opinion can wipe out hundreds o' good ones – as I myself very well know,' she added, with a glower at Jessie who had once marked Bette down as a temptress and a hussy with leanings towards alcoholism thrown in for good measure.

As the days passed with still no sign of the clockmaker, one or two people began voicing their concern while others chose to make light of it, declaring that he sometimes never went over his own front door when he was busy and it was better to leave him alone anyway till the 'dust settled'.

'Get over there, Billy.' Big Bette, unable to stand the suspense any longer, gave the message boy his orders. 'Take these wee bit groceries with you and if Gabby won't let you in, break the door down or something.'

'Ay, Bette,' Billy grinned, tickled pink at the idea of actually breaking into someone's house with the law in his camp. Because to Billy, as to many of the village lads, Big Bette was the law, with far more clout on her side than even Stottin' Geordie, the village policeman.

In the event, it wasn't the door Billy had to break down, but a window, the usual access via the front entrance being jammed tight except for a mere crack when Billy had tried to force it. Slightly built and agile, the youngest MacNulty boy soon wriggled in through the window he had broken with one of Gabby's sturdy garden ornaments.

The house was airless and silent. Billy's voice echoed

through it, calling Gabby's name, feeling creepy as he did so, beginning to think that this wasn't such a big adventure after all and dreading what he might find round every corner.

But when he eventually came upon the clockmaker, lying behind his own front door, Billy's only instinct was to help out in any way he could. Gabby was inert, lifeless looking, cold and unresponsive. Billy's heart quickened. Mustering all his strength he pulled Gabby inch by inch away from the door and then he was through it, mounting his bike, haring up the road to Butterbank House as fast as his pedals would take him.

Doctor MacAlistair was in the kitchen enjoying his midday repast when a breathless Billy came galloping in with his news. No questions were asked, no more time wasted. The doctor didn't wait to harness up Pumpkin but went on Billy's bike instead, stopping only long enough to tuck his trousers into his socks, collect his hat and his bag which he threw into the wickerwork basket, Billy, on shanks's pony, galloping manfully alongside.

He was soon left behind, however, as the doctor went whizzing away in front, never stopping till he came to Clockwork Cottage where he threw the bike down, gathered up his bag, and went at once to Gabby's side.

Amazingly, a spark of life still flickered within the clockmaker's large framework and as soon as Billy came panting in through the door the doctor said curtly, 'Run for help, Billy. I must get him into bed and can't do it on my own. Get Todd Grant from next door, he's tough and wiry and it's muscle I need right now.'

Todd was soon there, helping the doctor to get Gabby through to his bedroom where the doctor swiftly examined him and gruffly pronounced, 'Heart attack. God knows how long he's been lying there and how he's managed to survive to this stage.'

'Will he live, Doctor?' Billy asked anxiously, as full of love for Gabby as any other child in the district. Doctor MacAlistair shook his head. 'It's a bad business, Billy, a very bad business indeed. Only time will tell if he's going to make it or not. He's too weak to be moved to hospital, a journey like that would kill him. Luckily he's a fine big lad and has strength in his favour to help him along. Rest is what he needs now, that and a good dollop o' tender loving care.'

'It was that business over the money that did it,' Todd Grant, the village undertaker, a chillingly accurate presence in the circumstances, spoke bluntly. 'Gabby knew everyone was talking about him, he likely just sat in his house, driving himself crazy wi' his thoughts, thinking himself into a state o' depression, never eating or sleeping or doing any o' the things he normally loves doing. I suppose, in the end, you could say he died heartbroken.'

'Ay, you could be right at that,' the doctor agreed, before adding drily, 'but hopefully it isn't the end for him yet, Todd, for while he is ill he isn't exactly ready to be nailed down. You have enough business in these parts without sniffing around after more, as I'm sure you will agree.'

Todd, a cheery individual whose unashamedly open views on 'the natural business o' dying' rubbed many a bereaved soul the wrong way, smiled at the doctor's words but couldn't refrain from rubbing his hands. 'Anything you say, Doctor, but I'll stand by just in case. Never do to get too complacent. Meanwhile, I'll get my Aggie to look in on Gabby whenever she can and I'm sure Jessie MacDonald will be only too willing to do the same.'

'Oh, I have no doubt the village ladies will do all they can to help out.' The doctor was making Gabby comfortable as he spoke, removing his shoes, loosening his collar. 'Effie will be here too, of course, and I'll never be far away from the house till he's out o' danger . . .'

He cocked an eye at Billy. 'Would it hurt you, lad, to go one more message? I need Effie here before I can go back to finish my lunch so how about jumping on that bike of yours to fetch her?'

Raking in his pocket he withdrew a threepenny bit and handed it to Billy. The boy gasped. A whole threepenny bit all to himself! Oh, wait till he showed Ma this. On the other hand he might just keep it. She would only take it off him and spend it on beer and baccy and give Dolly Law some as well. The pair were as thick as thieves and were always in each other's houses, yattering their heads off about nothing, smoking and drinking and sometimes no tea on the table for a working lad like him.

Billy slipped the money into his pocket. He grinned to himself and fairly spanked up the road to Purlieburn Cottage to deliver his message to Effie. It had been a busy day for him but it wasn't over with yet. He could hardly wait to get back to Big Bette's shop to recount all that had transpired since he had left it only an hour or so ago.

Before the day was over, half of Kinvara knew about Gabby's collapse, the other half heard only snippets, but what they didn't know they made up, as was the way of things in a place like Kinvara where the affairs of one's neighbours were far more interesting than anything going on within one's own four walls.

'Is Gabby in heaven now, Dadda?' Essie asked that night as she was getting ready to go to bed.

'No, he isn't in heaven, Essie,' Rob said drily. 'He's in bed, put there by all the talk and gossip concerning that half-crown you said he gave you.'

Rob looked pointedly at Hannah as he spoke but she wouldn't meet his eyes and he sighed to himself, wondering when all the tension was going to end. Thinking about Catherine again, her warmth, her understanding, he was tempted to go and meet her in that magical place she had spoken about, where no one else intruded and it would be only him and her, her arms waiting to hold him and soothe away his fears and troubles.

His heart beat faster at the thought. She had said she was there in that wondrous spot every evening, wandering the shores, waiting for him should he ever need her . . .

He glanced at the window. It was evening now. It had become dark and overcast early, with purple-grey clouds banking up over the sea and a strengthening wind beginning to rattle the chimney pots. Hardly a night for a romantic rendezvous on an open beach with the threat of rain hanging over the landscape.

Rob turned his thoughts away from Catherine and went out to the byre to see how Clover and her new calf were faring. It was quiet in here, quiet and warm, another world altogether and one far removed from the turmoil that seemed always to exist these days within the walls of No. 6 of the Row.

Charlie Campbell was angry, a side to him that Harriet had only glimpsed once or twice. That had been as nothing, however, to the fury he was displaying now as he stood there in the living room, the wrecked remains of a model sailing ship in his hands, staring at it as if he couldn't believe his eyes. He had spent months making it, working with it whenever he had a moment to spare, lavishing love and care into every last small detail and looking forward to the day when it could take pride of place on the mantelshelf.

'Who did this?' he demanded, in a tight, harsh voice, his hands beginning to shake with the rage coursing through him like an uncontrollable tide. 'I think I know the answer already but I want to hear it from your own two lips, Harriet!'

Harriet found herself at a dreadful disadvantage. There was nothing she could say or do that would ease the situation, only the truth would suffice now and her face was alive with apprehension when she said breathlessly, 'Essie was in earlier, she only picked the boat up to look at it and somehow it fell to the floor and – and broke.'

'Essie! Ay, Essie! Who else? She's never away from the place, poking about where she shouldn't, touching things, breaking them, and you letting her do it. Never a word o' reprimand out o' you; petting her up instead, telling her how wonderful she is, in the same way as that daughter o' yours. It isn't Essie's fault, she's a lovely wee lassie wasted, but she needs discipline and if you won't tell her about this next time she's here then I will! By God and I will! And while I'm at it I might just take down her pants and give her a good smacking. It's what she needs, something that's long overdue.'

'You wouldn't dare, Charlie Campbell!' Harriet cried, aghast. 'You would have me to reckon with if you ever lifted a finger to her. You're just jealous because I give her so much o' my attention. It's a pity you never had bairns o' your own. If you had you might be a bit more understanding towards them. As it is you hate it when Essie comes here and touches any o' your precious possessions, simply because you've been far too long on your own to ever want interference from anybody.'

Charlie's face went livid. 'It's *my* house and *I'm* the boss. It's for me to say who moves my things and who doesn't, and if you had any sense at all, Harriet Houston, you would see my point o' view for yourself, instead of taking the side of a four-year-old bairn who is too spoiled rotten for her own or anyone else's good!'

'Your house!' Harriet shouted back. 'Oh, ay, your house when I slave away all day cleaning it and looking after it, ready for you coming back from these jaunts o' yours.'

'Jaunts? Jaunts?' Charlie returned furiously. 'I'll have you know, these jaunts as you call them are part o' my livelihood! I don't go out on that buggering cold sea just for the fun o' it. I do it to keep the wolf from the door and if you were a woman of any sensitivity at all you would see that fact for yourself!'

'Oh, ay, and who sees to the other part of your livelihood? I do, in case you haven't noticed. I keep your house, I work your croft, I see to the animals. As for the buggering cold sea, you like it out there, Charlie, you like the freedom, you like the independence, you still think o' yourself as a bachelor man and now I can see I did the wrong thing marrying such a selfish person as yourself. All you want when you come home are hot meals waiting on the table and a warm bed in which to take your pleasures as you will!'

So they went at it, hammer and tongs, saying hurtful

things, casting up, taking down, until Charlie abruptly went to the stand to get his jacket and stomped away out of the house, leaving a burning faced Harriet to stare at the smashed remains of the model ship he had crafted with such loving care.

Charlie walked blindly down to the harbour, hands dug deep in his pockets, jaw clenched tight, a feeling of unrest taking the place of the anger in his belly. Thank God he was going off with the lads in the morning! He needed these spells away from home. Harriet had been right about that at least. It was in his nature to be on the move. The sea was in his blood, the one element he knew best, the one that had carried him away from the 'chattering skirts' of his mother and sisters in Argyllshire many years ago when their possessive inclinations had become too much for him.

The *Free Spirit* was tied up in the sheltered basin of the harbour, all set to go at first light. Charlie glanced up at the sky. There was a change in the weather. The clouds had rolled in, white horses were frisking beyond the bay, the threat of rain was in the air but hadn't yet descended. Nothing to worry about. He and the lads could take a drop of rain in their stride, enjoyed the challenge when the going got a bit rough.

Charlie climbed aboard the boat and made his way down to the bunkhouse. Taking off his jacket he lay down on his bed and put his hands behind his head, thinking of that scene with Harriet, how stubborn she could be, how unwilling to see his viewpoint, unmoving in her opinions regarding her handling of her granddaughter. Well, she could stew in her own juice for a while! It would do her good to let her see that he wasn't to be trifled with in matters that were important to him. He had been lenient with her since their marriage, too damned soft, perhaps, it was time she learned he too had a mind of his own and could be just as tough as herself when he wanted to be.

Turning in his bed he pulled a blanket up around his shoulders and allowed the gentle rocking of the *Free Spirit* to lull him into a state bordering on sleep. But it didn't go quite deep enough to completely rest him and he woke at dawn, cold and stiff, rising almost as soon as he awakened to go to the galley and put on the kettle. It was boiling merrily when the others came on board, six of them, including Colin Blair who worked at the Balivoe Fishery but often joined the crew of the *Free Spirit* when one of the hands had called off for any reason.

Soon they were heading out of the harbour into deeper waters, a blustering wind from the sou'west taking them beyond the bay to the open sea and the fishing grounds beyond.

Chapter Twenty-nine

The force of the storm that hit the Kinvara coastline later that day took everyone by surprise with its ferocity. By early evening the wind had reached gale force. Thunder crashed, lightning flashed, curtains of rain came hurling in over the land, while up on the hills the mist skulked in the corries and swirled over the humping grey shoulders of the higher slopes till gradually the peaks merged with the lowering black of the sky and familiar landmarks became obliterated in the squally downpours.

Rob had gone up to his bedroom to get a better view. The green-bellied sea heaved in the distance, white-crested waves were thundering to the shore, invading even the normally sheltered waters of the bay, riding up onto the land as the tide rose higher and higher.

As he gazed out at the wind-wracked landscape Rob thought about Charlie and the others out there on the sea. He knew they had gone off early that morning and hoped to God they had headed back at first hint of the storm and would be almost home by now.

Voices drifted up from below. Harriet had come to visit Hannah. The two of them were in the kitchen, commiserating with one another over some sort of row Harriet had had with Charlie the previous evening – something to do with Essie. Rob took a deep breath – Essie again, always these days Essie's name seemed to be on everyone's lips . . .

It was cold here by the window, draughts were seeping in through every crack. Rob remained where he was for a few minutes longer then moved away to go downstairs.

'Rob.' Harriet immediately turned to him, her strong, attractive face filled with an urgent enquiry. 'What do you think is happening out there? I'm worried about Charlie. He should be here by now. Surely he and the others must have decided to turn back when they saw the change in the weather.'

Rob looked at her. Once upon a time he hadn't liked his mother-in-law very much. In those days she and he had seemed always to be at loggerheads, disagreeing about many things but most of all over her interference with his and Hannah's life, trying to run it for them, browbeating her daughter to such an extent it had often seemed to him that Hannah had no will of her own but just went along with everything her mother said. All that was changed now. Hannah had learned to develop her own opinions on many issues and she no longer shrunk away from facing up to her mother. There were still times when she gave in just for the sake of peace but Harriet didn't get nearly so much of her own way any more and the atmosphere was happier all round.

Harriet had her own life to lead. She and Charlie had made a real go of it when they had married; theirs was an excellent relationship and they seemed admirably suited to one another, having their ups and downs like anybody else but on the whole remaining happy and contented.

Last night's heated quarrel had changed all that. Harriet had spent an uneasy night after her husband's departure from the house, wondering if she had said too much to him, regretting that her temper had got the better of her. She kept thinking she should have agreed with him more, going over and over the whole episode in her mind, till at one point she had seriously thought about getting up and going down to the harbour to tell him she was sorry.

But no! Why should she? He was as much to blame as she had been and shouldn't have been so hasty condemning poor little Essie like that. It was only a toy ship that had been ruined after all, nothing for a grown man to get so het up about.

Thus she had argued with herself, all through the night and into the next day, till, feeling she had to unburden herself to somebody she had hastened along to No. 6 of the Row to see her daughter, there to take comfort from that lady's ready sympathies regarding Charlie's stubbornness, ignoring the part Essie had played in the affair and 'wasn't it just like a man to be so pigheaded'.

Now, however, with the rain and wind blattering the window panes and the sea rising by the minute, Harriet was feeling too worried to care about Essie or Hannah or anybody else for that matter. All her thoughts were concentrated on Charlie, out there on the wilderness of the ocean and without waiting for Rob to speak she went on, 'Oh, I wish I hadn't been so hard on him last night! We quarrelled over nothing really but to him it was something and – and – now I wish I had seen it more from his point of view rather than my own.'

Rob was in no mood to console her. He liked Charlie. He knew the man. Felt a bond with him. Charlie and he shared many of the same interests, the same sentiments about life. He was a strong, fair character, easy to like, hard to rile, never expending energy on petty bickering unless he felt it was perfectly justified. And when Harriet went on to explain just exactly what had taken place between herself and Charlie the night before Rob felt that Charlie's reaction *had* been justified and that he might have done the same himself in Charlie's place.

'I'm sorry now I didn't side with him more,' Harriet ended bleakly. 'He's a good man, he puts up with a lot from me – and now – I don't know where he is or how he is and I wish – I wish I could learn to hold my tongue more and not allow it to get the better o' me the way it does.'

'It runs in the family,' Rob said abruptly, looking pointedly at Hannah as he spoke.' Your daughter has spent her summer arguing with half o' Kinvara, myself included, in case you don't know. I've had a hellish leave because o' it and if things don't improve soon I won't answer for the consequences – and I don't care who knows it.'

'Rob!' Hannah cried, horrified. 'How can you do this? Divulge matters that are private to us both? Mother doesn't know anything, nobody does. It's our business and nobody else's!'

'Well, she knows now,' Rob returned grimly. 'I'm sick to the back teeth of the silences, the cold tongue, the pretence of going on as if everything in my life is like a ray of sunshine.' He gave a short, bitter laugh. 'Me and Charlie are in the same boat, you might say, rocky and dangerous and never knowing when a storm is going to blow up from one minute to the next . . .'

He was rudely interrupted at that point by the door bursting open, Johnny Lonely standing there, soaked and dishevelled, holding a lantern in his hand, shouting hoarsely, 'Shipwreck! On the rocks at Camus nan Gao! Pass the word! Bring lanterns, anything that gives out a light!'

Then he was gone, leaving the door battering against the wall, letting gusts of rain through the aperture, allowing the crazed elements to come howling indoors like some tortured wild beast of the jungle.

A short, stunned silence followed Johnny's exit. Had he been real? Or had he been a ghost? Some dark phantom stalking the night hours to strike terror into the hearts of those who lived and breathed and listened . . .

Rob was the first to move. Rushing out to the lobby he stopped only long enough to struggle into his oilskins and boots and to grab the storm lantern from its place on the ledge. Breck followed, then Harriet. Hannah too, after going upstairs to tell Vaila to 'bide in bed and keep an eye on Essie and Andy till I get back'.

All along the Row doors were opening, people rushing out, to be joined by more from crofts and cottages, farms and bothies, bent double against the shrieking wind, the relentless rain, lanterns bobbing as they struggled on. It was a horrendous trek under such conditions. The tide was too high to allow access round the Point from the shore, which meant going overland above the cliffs where the gale blew louder and only the hardiest of souls persevered long enough to make it down to the bleak rocks far below.

And then they were there! Camus nan Gao, Bay of the Winds, a notorious black spot where shipwrecks were a common occurrence in days of old till the Kinvara Light had come into being.

But the lighthouse had been no help to the *Free Spirit* on her way homewards from the fishing grounds, nor had the markers beyond the reefs done anything to avert the doomed ship as the waves and the wind had taken her and smashed her to pieces on the treacherous fangs of rock piercing up through the water.

Nothing could have saved the boat, nothing, except perhaps Johnny Lonely, who had for years warned of such an event and who had faithfully lit his beacons on the Point in his efforts to avoid disaster.

But with all his recent preoccupations of mind, Johnny

had failed to light his fires or to do any of the things he normally did. Not that anyone had ever taken much notice anyway. It was just another of his eccentricities, something to keep him occupied when he had nothing better to do to fill his time. Now this had happened and more than one person there that night wished they had listened to the hermit and had perhaps done something about getting a more permanent warning fixture built on the Point.

Everyone gathered to stare horrified at the remains of the fishing boat caught up on the rocks, the womenfolk shouting in their efforts to make themselves heard above the deafening roar of the thundering surf while the menfolk surged forward to scour the waves for any signs of life.

The tide was bringing in the wreckage, and suddenly there was a raised arm, there one minute, lost the next, spurring the rescuers even further into the treacherous swell while the crowd held up their lanterns to give as much light as they could to those struggling in the waves.

The men were hauling a limp body out of the water, half carrying it up the shore to lay it gently down. 'Oh, dear God,' Harriet murmured, 'don't let it be Charlie, please don't let it be Charlie.'

But it wasn't Charlie, it was one of the other men. Two more came after that, all three of them young, married with children. Doctor MacAlistair appeared, rivers of rain running down his face, his thatch of white hair tossing in the wind that keened in over the sea. Getting down he made a swift examination of the men then slowly shook his head to signify his defeat. The women covered their faces with their hands, all hope seemed lost then, till Rob and Jock came staggering up carrying a fourth man between them.

'Charlie!' The cry was torn from Harriet. She stood there, her heart in her mouth, staring, just staring at the inert, sodden figure of her husband, lying so still on the ground, a crimson gash across his cheek but otherwise uninjured . . . unless . . .

The doctor looked up. 'He's alive! Get the blankets, make a stretcher, we'll have to get him home.' From his pocket he extracted his whisky flask and held it to Charlie's lips. There was a splutter, a cough, Charlie's eyes opened then closed, but Alistair was satisfied that he was going to be fine and told Harriet so.

Dropping on her knees beside her man she cradled his head on her lap and vowed to herself that never again would she allow him to feel that he had taken second place in her affections. She felt she had been given a second chance to let him see how dear he was to her and the hand she placed on his brow was firm but gentle. 'I love you, Charlie Campbell,' she murmured. 'And I thank God for giving you back to me.' Whether he heard her or not didn't matter, it was enough that she had said it, but when his hand came out to reach for hers she knew the words had filtered through to him and that he had understood everything she had said.

The rest of the crew hadn't been as lucky as Charlie. Of the seven men who had gone out in the *Free Spirit* only Charlie had come back whole, another was alive but badly injured, one was missing, the others dead, their bodies laid out on the beach, their womenfolk coming to identify them one by one, hushed, shocked, silent.

Catrina Blair was one of them. Her dark shawl round her head she stood gazing down at Colin. 'It's the end,' she whispered. 'The end of everything.'

'Come on, lass, you'll only catch your own death stopping here. It's time to go home now.' Mattie put a comforting arm round the girl's shoulders to lead her away but Catrina broke free and went darting back to where her dead husband lay. Falling down beside him she pressed her lips to his face. It was cold, cold and wet. His hair was plastered round his head, his arms outflung on the shingle, his eyes still open, staring; staring at that last glimpse of life before the sea had taken it from him. A dry sob broke in Catrina's throat. Remorse, raw and deep, filled her being. He hadn't deserved this, he had been so good to her, her and wee Euan. Now it was all for nothing, his efforts on her behalf had been in vain. Finished, finished . . .

Gently she drew his lids down over his eyes and then she got up and walked away, back to a life that held little meaning for her, knowing in her heart that she wouldn't rest till she could salve the wound that had eaten away inside her for more years than she cared to remember.

Hours had passed since Johnny Lonely had spread his dread tidings. And now the wind and the tide had dropped sufficiently for the exhausted menfolk of Kinvara to make their way homewards round the sandy banks of the Point, taking with them the two survivors of the shipwreck, leaving behind the bodies of those who had not made it, until more help could be mustered.

Todd Grant, the Undertaker, and his partner, Davie the Carpenter, remained on the shores of Camus nan Gao after the others had gone. But for once Todd wasn't thinking of the business he would make from the tragedies of that terrible night. His normally cheerful countenance was grim as he beheld the bodies of the young men on the beach. One of them had been a close neighbour of his and a good friend as well. They had ceilidhed in one another's houses, had played cards together, gone to the Balivoe village inn to celebrate various family events, discussed and argued, laughed and talked, with all life in front of them and never a thought about tomorrow.

Now it was over, day was done for one of them, and Todd hardly heard a word that Davie had to say as he spoke about measurements and other such talk and wondered if he had enough wood in his store to make all the coffins.

'Shut up, man! Just shut up!' Todd yelled as he stumbled away through the dark and blustery night to weep to himself in private, reflecting as he did so that 'the business o' dying' wasn't so natural after all when it had so tragically taken a young man in the midst of a full and happy existence.

* * *

A much chastened Harriet sat at the bedside of her husband, wakeful some of the time, at others half dozing, as she waited and watched and longed for him to open his eyes. When he did, the deep brilliant blue of them filled her heart with pain and love. She gave him a shaky smile and he smiled back; slowly, lazily, half asleep still, his hand moving beneath that which had held it all through the anxious moments of the long night hours.

'Good morning, Mrs Campbell,' he murmured, a flicker of a smile touching his mouth.

'Good morning, Mr Campbell,' she returned shakily, and then to her shame, she put her face in her hands and simply bawled, shoulders heaving, the tears rolling down her cheeks, behaving not at all like the Harriet Houston from Ayr that everyone knew and would surely have marked down as 'daft altogether', had they witnessed her behaviour that morning by the bedside of her husband.

'I'm sorry, I'm so sorry, Charlie,' she sobbed in a muffled voice. 'I hate myself for what I've done, and I hope you'll find it in your heart to forgive me for all the bother I've caused.'

'Harriet, Harriet,' he chided gently, 'it wasn't you who damned near drowned me on that buggering cold sea out there.' He smiled at this. 'It would have happened anyway, no matter how much or how little we'd argued. Unless you're a witch altogether you didn't blow up that storm last night, so dry your eyes for heaven's sake, before I start thinking the sea hags have carried me back to the wrong woman. If I close my eyes and open them again, promise me you'll turn back into the Harriet I know. I could never abide wailing women, one of the reasons I chose you to be my lawful wedded wife for all time to be.'

Harriet sniffed and gave a watery smile. He cocked his eye at her and said softly, 'Could my witch wife possibly get me a cup of tea? I swallowed half the ocean out there last night but despite that I'm still thirsty and could drink a potful all to myself.'

She was on her feet instantly, kissing his brow, rushing from the room, leaving him lying there on his pillows to think about many things but most of all about the twists and turns of a fate that had allowed him to live and his mates to die.

'It was meant to be, Charlie.' Harriet was standing in the doorway, a tea tray in her hands. She had known only too well what he would be thinking, the thoughts that would fill his mind for many a day to come.

'Ay, it was meant to be, lass,' he nodded and gratefully accepted the tea she poured for him out of a pot that was hot and sweet and nearly all to himself, except for the one she drank with him; the strong capable Harriet he knew and loved.

Chapter Thirty

The calm that came after the storm was breathtakingly gentle and beautiful. Dawn saw the wind completely abated, the rain clouds clearing off the hills, the turrets of Cragdu poking up through the vanishing mist like the spires of some enchanted fairy castle. The sun when it rose spread honey gold light over the sea and no casual observer could ever have guessed just how wild and dangerous the shining water had been only hours earlier.

But for the people of Kinvara the spilling sunshine did little to uplift their spirits. The dead crew of the *Free Spirit* had been brought back from Camus nan Gao to lie in the church till their families could arrange for their burial. The last body had been recovered some miles along the Kinvara coastline, taken there by the eddying currents and found by the coastguards.

People sat in one another's houses, drinking tea as they went over the events of last night, drawing together in a common bond of sympathy as they comforted those who had lost sons, brothers, husbands. Kinvara was a place of mourning, not one blind remained open to the sweetness of the day, not even the children were allowed out to play as a sign of respect for those who would return no more to the pleasures of life.

As the perfect summer's day drew to its conclusion Rob felt a restlessness growing within him. He had been to see Charlie to ascertain for himself that all was well there. He had visited his parents at Vale O' Dreip to give them a full account of what had happened at Camus nan Gao. Now, as he stood gazing down the valley to the distant shores, he knew that he didn't want to go home, not yet, not while his heart was sore within him. Not while he ached with a heaviness that didn't owe itself entirely to his exertions of the previous night.

Something was stirring inside him; a yearning, a burning need to know laughter again, the beguiling smiles of a warm responsive woman. The joy of touching and feeling and knowing he wouldn't be rejected when he reached out for emotional sustenance and love.

'Catherine.' He murmured the name softly, and then his steps were taking him down through the clover strewn fields, along by hedgerows heavy with ripening fruits and berries, over banks and verges where the perfume of meadowsweet rose into air already sweetened by wild orchids and purple vetches.

Then he was walking along by the shores of Niven's Bay, the tang of the sea in his nostrils, the call of the curlew in his ears, the deep pinks and smoky blues of the evening sky filling his vision. There was no sign of life in the schoolhouse but Rob didn't expect to find it there. This was the time of day when Catherine would be walking along those deserted coves she had spoken about; a place where lovers could meet, knowing they wouldn't be spied upon or talked about by any other living soul.

And that was where he found her. Drifting along by the water's edge, a vision of summer in her big straw hat and light floaty dress, her shoes in her hand as she wandered along in peaceful harmony with the land and sea and the sun that was sinking beneath the waves in a great fiery ball. She didn't seem surprised to see him but her eyes were aglow with a glinting green light when he came to stand beside her and speak her name in a slightly hesitant voice.

'I knew you'd come,' she said softly. 'It took you a while but I knew if I waited long enough you would come to me in the end.'

Without another word she took him by the hand and led him along the beach for a short distance before heading up past the dunes. Here, carved out in the sandy cliffs, were the caves, part of a raised beach that had once, long ago, been washed by the sea, now well above the tide line, dry, warm from the day's heat, filled with fine shell sand.

'Well, what do you think? Isn't it the perfect place? I often come here to do my corrections or to just sit and dream and wonder about life.'

In a mood of abandonment she threw off her hat and whirled round in a little dance, her bare toes digging into the sand, her dimples deepening as she spun over to him and took his face in her hands.

'Rob.' She gazed deep into his eyes and brushed her lips with his. The burning in his belly grew to a flame, her mouth was soft and sweet and ripe as he crushed it with his and drank of its nectar. It seemed only natural when they finally sunk down onto the sand and went wild with their rising passions. Her body was creamy and warm, her breasts full and firm when he undid her flimsy bodice and took them in his hands. Soft, so soft; warm, so warm. Everything about her yielding and wanting and waiting for the fulfilment he so desperately wanted to give her . . .

Then a voice seemed to be calling him . . . Robbie . . . Robbie . . . from far away, from somewhere near, a voice that had called to him long, long ago and still rang in his head to this day. An echo of the past? A memory? Or perhaps a little girl speaking his name as it had once been spoken in yonder years . . . his girls, his sweethearts . . .

Rolling away from Catherine he struggled to his feet and wiped his brow with a trembling hand. 'I can't do this, Catherine. I'm sorry, but I just can't do it!'

She sat up and stared at him in disbelief. 'Why can't you? Is it me? Don't you like me well enough?'

'No, it isn't you, you're a lovely, exciting, young woman but I'm not the one for you. Find somebody else, somebody who won't love you and leave you as I would have done had we gone through with this. Don't say anything more, just don't . . .'

He left her, sitting alone in the sand, anger on her face, a dozen questions on her lips, misery clouding the green of her eyes as she watched him walk away without a goodbye or a backward glance.

He was furious now, not with himself but with Hannah. She had brought him to this; this brink, this humiliation. She had denied him the warmth and understanding that any husband had the right to expect from his wife and she wasn't going to get away with it any longer, not if he could help it.

The house was in darkness when he got in, everyone was in bed, even Breck, who was tired out after his activities of the previous night and hardly so much as wagged his tail as Rob passed by.

Treading carefully, Rob went upstairs to throw open the door of his wife's room, determination in his heart, anger in his belly, but all of these emotions died away when he saw her in bed, curled up, sound asleep, lonely looking somehow . . .

He withdrew and quietly shut the door. Why should he go begging to her? She had conveyed to him more plainly than words that she neither wanted nor needed him and had never even questioned the fact that he had left his own bed to spend his solitary nights in the cramped confines of the boxroom.

He went to his room, sat on the bed, then in a burst of decision he retrieved his case from the top of the cupboard and began to throw clothes into it. He had to get away for a while. He needed space to think, to be alone with himself, to distance himself in order to see his life from a different angle, a better perspective. Now that he had made that decision he felt better within himself and when at last he got to bed his sleep was deeper and more restful than it had been for many a long night.

Everyone stared when he made his announcement the following morning. Andy and Vaila looked apprehensive, Essie immediately asked to go with him. Hannah shook her head and said shortly, 'That's right, run away, leave me to see to everything as usual,' before turning away to busy herself at the stove, only the droop of her shoulders giving away the anxiety she was feeling.

'It's only for a few days,' Rob said lightly. 'I'll be back before you know it. I just want to be by myself for a while – to sort myself out.'

'Where are you going?' Vaila's mouth was trembling as she asked the question.

'I don't know – anywhere, everywhere, it doesn't really matter. I'm just needing a break, that's all. Don't worry, I said I'd never leave you and I meant it.' Bending, he dropped a kiss on her cheek and squeezed her arm reassuringly. He did the same with Essie and Andy and then he went over to Hannah. His hands came up to her shoulders but she didn't look round and slowly he dropped them back down to his sides and went to the door to pick up his case. The door opened and shut and he was gone, leaving behind a silence so deep the proverbial pin could have been heard to drop for fully five minutes after his departure.

As fate would have it, Catherine too had decided to go away for a short holiday to her family in Perthshire before school resumed again. She had spent a sleepless night, thinking about her meeting with Rob, the hot tears of shame and embarrassment pricking her lids as she remembered how she had thrown herself at him. Her willingness to let him do as he would with her; the way she had given herself up to him in the abandonment of love only to have it all thrown back in her face. She felt hurt beyond belief, degraded beyond measure, cheaper than any back street hussy, someone who had let go of her pride and status and who was now paying the price for her sins.

She couldn't bear it; she had to get away from Kinvara for a while, had to have a breathing space. She couldn't take the risk of seeing him again when everything within her was raw and sore and terribly cheated. She rose at dawn and threw some things into a bag. A few hours later she was all ready to go and was most dismayed when a knock sounded on her door just as she was about to leave.

Max put his head round, his handsome face lighting at sight of her, falling quickly when she said breathlessly, 'Max, you've caught me at a bad time. I'm just going out. I feel I must visit my family while I've still got some holidays left. The bus will be leaving for the station in half an hour. I'm sorry, but I'll – I'll see you when I get back.'

'Yes, yes, of course, Catherine.' Bewildered, he stood aside as she came out with her bags and locked the door behind her. 'This is pretty sudden, Catherine,' he went on in puzzlement. 'You never said anything about leaving when I called to see you the other day.'

'Yes, I know Max, but I just realised how quickly the days are flying and my mother did say in her last letter to me how much she hoped I'd pay a visit before the end of summer.'

Reaching up she planted a hasty peck on his cheek before walking quickly away from him, not wanting to hear the questions that were trembling on his lips or see the hurt in the eyes of a young man who so obviously loved her and who had hoped for just a little bit of her love in return.

So it was that Catherine and Rob left Kinvara at the same time, albeit bound for different destinations but unable to avoid meeting on the bus that would take them to Achnasheen station. Astonished beyond measure at sight of him Catherine burst out, 'What are *you* doing here?'

'I could ask the same of you,' he returned, completely taken aback by the turn of events. They exchanged a few words, then with a toss of her red head she said off-handedly, 'Oh, well, we aren't enemies. I suppose it would do no harm to keep one another company on the journey.'

'I suppose not,' he agreed and taking her luggage he hoisted it onto the rack beside his and rather gingerly sat down next to her. At the back of the bus, Minnie MacTaggart, taking a day off from her duties as Father MacNeil's housekeeper to visit her sister in Achnasheen, tightened her lips at the sight of Rob and Catherine sitting together at the front.

So, it was true about those two after all. Here they were, travelling together to some secret rendezvous, hellbound in their lustful pursuits, no doubt lying and scheming in their endeavours to be alone with each other – and her the village schoolteacher too! The Jezebel that she was! Nothing more than a scarlet woman, unfit to associate with anyone far less teach innocent children about the rights and wrongs of life.

Here Minnie quickly crossed herself and shook her head. Small wonder Hannah Sutherland was so prickly these days, she no doubt suspected her husband of cheating, poor woman. What a burden for anyone to bear! In those moments, Minnie was very, very glad that she had never married, nor had indeed succumbed totally to the temptations of the flesh. Not that opportunity hadn't knocked at her door. She had been a bit of a girl in her day if truth be told, but had always known when to stop – not like some she could name – Kinvara was rife with that sort of thing and a bit more besides. Rob and the teacher were just another example of that.

The disgrace of it! The scandal! Minnie kept her eyes glued to the seat in front. She could hardly wait to get home again so that she could go to chapel and pray for the salvation of such sinners – she would throw one in for Hannah too, of course. If she deserved nothing else she deserved that – even if she was a Protestant who only ever went to church at her mother's coercion.

In the days following Rob's departure Hannah was too miserable to do very much of anything. She just sat, staring into space, wondering where he was, what he was doing, who he was doing it with. But she knew the answer to that already. Minnie's tongue had been busy. Before many hours had passed the whole of Kinvara knew about Catherine and Rob going off together.

So brazenly! For everyone to see! To talk and laugh about! Had he no decency left in him? No regard for her feelings? Surely she was due some respect from him at least. She hadn't been such a bad wife when all was said and done – they'd had some good times together. They had loved, they'd had children. It hadn't been all plain sailing, she knew only too well how difficult she could be, how suspicious she was of his reactions to other women. But she wasn't to blame for that! He had given her good reason to mistrust him. First Morna, now Catherine, the dozens who ogled him and bemoaned the day he had been taken from them by a woman who didn't even belong to the place.

Oh, if only she could turn the clock back to the start of his leave. She knew she had been wrong to say the things she had about Catherine, she had driven him into a corner, made a fuss over nothing. Now she had succeeded in driving him into another woman's arms because of her behaviour.

Even so, how could he throw it all away for a brief affair? But perhaps it wasn't so brief? Perhaps he had gone away forever, never to return. Never to see her or the children again – for all his fine words to Vaila about never deserting her.

So she tortured herself, day after day, night after night, until, unable to bear her thoughts any longer she threw herself into a frenzy of activity, cleaning anything she could get her hands on. Dusting, polishing, washing, scrubbing the children to such a degree they were goaded into loud and anxious protest when yet another wash cloth appeared, another fire was stoked up ready to fill the zinc tub. Not even Breck escaped a lathering to avoid the wastage of 'all that good hot water'.

'Get a bucket and go to the well,' Vaila was ordered one day when Hannah was ensconced at the sink swishing soapsuds over Essie's dolls. 'Only half fill it, mind, you'll only spill it otherwise – and be careful you don't trip yourself up on the way back.'

Vaila was glad to escape into the sunshine and took her time about getting the water, spending a few minutes sitting on the warm dyke beside the well to think about her father and wonder when he would be coming home. It was much nicer here now, like a little oasis, Rob having hacked away the bushes in advance of installing a hand pump after the scare with Kyle.

The bees droned, the butterflies flitted. Vaila enjoyed a few more moments of repose before hoisting up the bucket and taking it over to the well. The sunlight was filtering into the water as Vaila leaned over to place the bucket on its hook. It was then that something bright caught her eye on a ledge a little way down. Getting a stick she fished around with it and gave a gasp when she eventually brought up her lighthouse necklace, the one she had thought was lost forever. She had searched and searched for it but had never mentioned its loss to anyone, thinking it would only cause trouble in a household already beset by it.

She must have worn the necklace that day Aunt Maudie was here and Morven had held her brother over the well. Everyone had helped to fish him out, including Vaila, never noticing the loss of her necklace in all the fuss. If her father hadn't cut away the gorse to allow in the light she might never have found it again . . .

Forgetting the water she rushed into the house with a joyful whoop, only to stop short at the sight of Hannah, Essie's newly washed doll in one hand, a bundle of trinkets in the other, including Gabby's little clockwork doll. 'They were inside the stuffing,' Hannah said in a dazed voice, not really noticing her stepdaughter in her dismay. 'Janet's things, Gabby's doll . . .'

She straightened, and her voice was strong when she said to Vaila, 'Fetch Essie. It's time I had a little talk with her.'

When Essie came and saw what her mother was holding in her hands she hung her head, put her thumb into her mouth, and burst into a flood of guilty tears. Hannah knew then how wrong she had been about her perfect little daughter. She also saw that a lot of the blame lay at her door and realised how much she had to do and how many people she had to see in order to atone for the mistakes she had made in treating Essie like a goddess – when all the time she was just like any other child and needed to be treated the same – despite having the looks of an angel.

Chapter Thirty-one

Ramsay wasn't in a very good mood. He had just been to River House to see his daughter-in-law and had found his son there as well, both of them in a very compromising position. Maudie's skirts were around her head, Finlay's trousers at his ankles, passions having erupted between them when the latter had come in for a cup of tea and had stayed for a bit more while he had 'a minute or two to spare'.

'You can't do that with children in the house!' Ramsay had raged, unable to keep his eyes from Maudie's naked bosoms in spite of his astonishment.

'But Father, everybody does it,' Finlay had protested as he strove to recover both his trousers and his equilibrium. 'You must have done it when Rob and me were just bairns; in fact many's the night I heard you with Mother in your room. Rob and me used to listen and wonder what all the noise was about before we grew old enough to realise what you were doing.'

'That's as may be,' Ramsay blustered, 'but at least I was decent enough to wait for the privacy o' my room, not in broad daylight for everyone to see.'

'Och, come on, now, Ramsay,' Maudie said a trifle breathlessly, doing up her buttons as she spoke, 'it's only us three who are here, and it was only me and Finlay till you came in without knocking. We weren't doing anyone any harm and we are married, after all. Besides, the bairns aren't here, they're upstairs having their nap, and wi' Finlay having time only for a quick one we would have been finished long before they ever woke up.'

The frankness of his daughter-in-law's tongue had always taken Ramsay's breath away and never more than now, when the sight of her nakedness had started up the old familiar ache in his belly, something that had always tormented him when provoked by the sight of naked young flesh.

'You should be out there working,' he curtly told his son. 'I don't pay you good sillar to fritter your time away in lustful pursuits and I'm warning you not to let it happen again or you'll have me to reckon with – and that, my lad, is a promise!'

With that he had turned on his heel to make his way down to his own house, struggling to compose himself as he walked along, sweat breaking on his brow at the remembrance of Maudie in all her naked glory. Those breasts! Big and bouncy and bonny! Those thighs! Just made for a man to bury himself in! No wonder Finlay was into her at any chance he got. She was just wasted on him. Too bad she had never known the experience of a real man in her bed, she wouldn't have looked at Finlay if she had . . .

He shook himself angrily, annoyed at having allowed the incident to get under his skin. Women! Nothing but trouble all of them . . . The sight of Catrina standing at his door with Euan on one hand, a suitcase in the other, made him stop short in his tracks. What did she want? Surely she wasn't going to start pestering him again. More money perhaps, as if she hadn't soaked him enough for the upkeep of her son.

That would be it, her little runt of a husband was dead and buried by now and she would be looking for someone else to support her. Well, she wouldn't get anything more from him! He had enough to do with his money, he had paid through the nose for Catrina and her mistakes and he was damned if he was about to give her any more handouts.

Rita was letting the girl in, smiling a welcome as she did so. Always glad to see Catrina, giving him the impression that she enjoyed watching him squirm, never letting him forget the one act of weakness that had cost him dearly in more ways than one.

'I've brought your son, Ramsay,' was Catrina's greeting the minute he appeared. 'When I saw Colin lying there dead on the beach at Camus nan Gao I knew what I had to do, what I've wanted to do ever since you raped me all those years ago.'

'Whatever do you mean by that!' he said harshly. 'What you do with the boy is your affair. I've played my part, I have my life, you have yours, and that's the end o' the matter.'

'Oh, is it, now?' she said tightly, her face white and weary in the bright frame of her hair. 'My life, ay, the life o' drudgery you carved out for me when you took what you could from me and left me to rot! Well, it's finished now, Ramsay Sutherland. I've worked hard all these years. I scrimped and scraped and put away what I could. Now it's your turn to take your share o' responsibility.'

Rita shoved a cup of tea into the girl's hand and bade her sit down but she remained where she was, standing in the middle of the room, facing up to Ramsay. 'I'm going away, Ramsay Sutherland, and I'm leaving Euan here with you till I can come back for him. It won't harm you to get someone in to look after both him and Aidan. You've got the money, you can afford it. Euan will have a far better life here than I could ever give him. He doesn't mind, in fact, he's quite happy about it, not in the least sentimental about anything – a bit like his father in that respect.'

'You'll leave him here over my dead body!' Ramsay bawled, so consumed with rage his face had gone purple. 'I've given you all I'm going to give and I'll thank you to get out o' my house this minute, you and your boy!'

For answer, Catrina turned to Rita and took her hand. 'You were always good to me, Rita, and I'll never forget your kindness. I know this is unfair on you but I have to do it. Get away from Kinvara, from everything that holds unhappy memories for me. I haven't said goodbye to my sisters or to Granny Margaret, they would only try and persuade me to stay. It isn't easy, it isn't easy at all. I love each one o' them dearly and thought we'd be together for always.'

Rita shook her head. 'In my bones I felt a day like this would come. You go, Catrina, I'll look after Euan. What's one more mouth to feed anyway? He'll be company for Aidan and I know Maudie will help in any way she can. He'll be more at River House than he will be here, she's that kind o' lass, great with bairns and they love her in return.'

A sob escaped Catrina. She gathered Rita to her heart and remained in her motherly embrace for several moments. Then she turned to her son to take him in her arms and stroke his hair. 'You be a good boy till I come back for you – and I will, Euan, someday I will.'

'Yes, Mam,' Euan said obediently but already his eyes were on the landscape beyond the window, the animals grazing in the fields, the cats and dogs in the yard, the farm machinery in the shed.

Blindly Catrina turned away. She was free, free of the shackles that had bound her for so long, but that didn't make it any easier to just walk away from everything that had once been so dear to her. She took a deep breath. She had to do this, even if it killed her she had to do it . . . the door opened and shut and she was gone, leaving Ramsay staring after her with his mouth gaping and his eyes bulging.

'The chickens have indeed come home to roost, Ramsay,' Rita said softly.

'Whatever are we going to tell people?' he stuttered.

'The boy here, his mother gone, just upped and left without a thought for anybody but herself.'

'That's your problem, Ramsay,' Rita said calmly. 'Life is full of them, ins and outs, ups and downs. I've had my share and now it's your turn – and hell mend you!'

She picked up Euan's suitcase and took the little boy by the hand. He smiled up at her and she led him away upstairs to show him the room he would be sharing with Aidan till she could get his own sorted out.

It wasn't long before Catrina's granny and sisters presented themselves at Vale O' Dreip, shocked at the turn of events, a million questions on their lips.

'How could she do this to us?' Granny Margaret cried, holding her hanky to her eyes. 'That lassie was devoted to me and her sisters. She couldn't just have run away, leaving her laddie behind, leaving us to worry and wonder about her.'

'Ay, it is strange, very strange indeed,' Cora nodded. 'She was in visiting me and Ryan Du only the other day and while she was naturally upset about Colin she was otherwise sane and normal.'

'Ach, she's never really been the same since she married herself to Colin,' Granny Margaret said thoughtfully. 'Something's been eating away at her for years. I asked her once or twice about it but she would never say . . .'

Glancing up at Ramsay she barked out suddenly, 'And

why bring the bairn to you? It isn't as if you're part o' the family – in fact, I got the distinct impression from Catrina that she wasn't all that struck on you, Ramsay Sutherland. And I mind fine, her coming home from your place in a terrible state one night years ago. I have often wondered about that.'

Rita opened her mouth to speak but Ramsay got in there first. 'Now, now, Mrs Simpson,' he said smoothly, 'you mustn't upset yourself any more. I myself told Catrina that she could rely on the help o' Rita and me if she ever needed it. We had a special affection for the girl when she worked here and made her feel just like one o' the family, so I suppose it was only natural she should turn to us in her distress over Colin, her desperation to get away and start a new life.'

Connie said nothing. She had guessed Euan's true identity long ago, had sensed her sister's turmoil of mind, her unhappiness at having to live a life that had been forced on her by events beyond her control. And this was the result. She was making Ramsay pay for what he had done to her, giving him a taste of his own medicine, though to Connie's way of thinking it wasn't enough, not nearly enough.

Yet, even while she thought these things she knew she had to go on with the pretence, for Rita's sake and for Euan's. Turning to Cora she said softly, 'Catrina knew how unfair it would be to ask you to take care o' Euan now that you're expecting your own baby. She didn't ask me because I've got Granny Margaret and my mother-in-law to look after, as well as my husband and my job at the Manse . . .'

'Here, what do you mean, look after me?' Granny Margaret hooted. 'I'm more than able to take care o' myself in case you don't know. I need to keep myself alert living wi' the likes o' Prudence Taylor-Young wi' a hyphen! She and me get on well enough but she's getting dottery and is worth the watching. I've got to keep an eye on her every minute o' the day, like a bairn she is, wi' her wants and demands and all the wee annoying habits she has about her. Only the other day she forgot to put salt in the soup and burned the porridge, yet she keeps on insisting on doing her share o' the cooking – as if she had ever known what she was about, even when she was the full shilling!'

'That says it all,' Connie sighed. 'We all have our own lives to lead. Catrina knew that and took the only way out in the circumstances.'

Getting up she went into the scullery where Rita had gone to escape her husband's affable lies. If she had stayed in that room a minute longer, listening to his tales of sympathy and understanding, she knew she would have given the game away, and despite everything she knew within herself she had to keep up the pretence of respectability, if only for her own sake and those of the family she loved and would have done anything to protect.

'It's alright, Rita,' Connie told her kindly, 'I know all

about the sacrifices you have made. I will never ever say anything to anybody, you can trust me on that, but I want you to promise, if any of it gets too much, you will tell me and we can sort out something between us. I know Euan can be a handful at times, bad enough for a younger woman, but you . . .'

Rita put her hand on Connie's arm and smiled. 'I'm not in my dotage yet, Connie, my lass. I've had boys o' my own. I know what they're like. So far Euan has settled in well. He's got Aidan, the pair o' them are getting on a treat, I've hardly seen either o' them since Euan came. There's always plenty to do on a farm. I'm keeping Ramsay on his toes in that respect, and Maudie is always there to ease the burdens so stop worrying.'

Connie squeezed Rita's hand. They made the tea together and carried it through to where Granny Margaret was waiting to pounce on it, Catrina temporarily forgotten in all the talk of village affairs that followed. The forthcoming fête at Cragdu Castle was much discussed, a date on the calendar of prime importance to Kinvara as a whole.

'I've been hearing all about it from Polly,' Granny Margaret stated with satisfaction, referring to one of her cronies who worked at Cragdu Castle and was always able to provide first-hand information about anything that went on there. 'There's a whole pile o' gentry coming for the event and poor Polly is working her fingers to the bone to get everything ready. All the laundry to wash and just four silly wee lassies to help her, the rooms to get ready, never a minute to herself, only a pittance for all the effort she puts in and that American wife o' The MacKernon swanning about as if she owned the place.'

'But, Granny,' Cora protested, 'she does own the place; at least she and The MacKernon own it between them ever since she poured a fortune into it.'

'Ay, she bought her way in, right enough, and got herself a title into the bargain,' Granny Margaret said smugly. 'But that doesn't mean to say she has the right to pretend she's a lady. Only breeding does that and the Scottish blood she doesn't have and never will.'

Ramsay had had enough; he had work to do and wasn't prepared to listen to any more tittle tattle. 'Don't forget, Euan and Aidan want to see the farm implements,' Rita reminded him as he went to the door. 'They'll be waiting for you now.'

He snorted and went stamping away. Connie and Rita winked at one another in complete understanding, while Granny Margaret demanded a third cup of tea and settled back in her chair to drink it and enjoy the rare treat of 'getting away from Prudence for a while with all her wants and wiles and never knowing if she was coming or going from one minute to the next'.

Shetland

Late August 1931

Chapter Thirty-two

Despite his words to the contrary, Rob had known in his heart where his footsteps would lead him when he left Kinvara behind. The place that he wandered in his dreams, the land that beckoned to him in his awakenings. A country where memories became reality and all that filled his mind grew fresh and alive as if someone had taken a magic wand and opened his eyes to love and beauty once more.

He and Catherine had gone their separate ways at Inverness Station. On the way they had thrashed out their feelings, ending up by understanding one another better and parting amicably, though not before he had told her how much he admired her and how he hoped she would continue to visit No. 6 of the Row.

'Andy misses you, Catherine. Hannah too, if truth be told. She said things she didn't mean. It's just her way and I suppose I gave her good reason to suspect that something was going on between us.'

'Chance would be a fine thing,' she had said ruefully. 'I was – am – infatuated with you, Rob Sutherland. I would have gobbled you up if you had let me. If Hannah knew that, she would never speak to me again, so it's better that

I stay away for a while. I need a chance to recover from all this, I'll come back when I'm ready. We all need time to settle down before the summer is over and life goes back to normal – if mine ever will again.'

'It will, Catherine.' He had taken her hand then and held it tight. 'You will find someone wonderful, someone who will appreciate you and everything you stand for. It would never have worked between us, you deserve something better than just a quick fling with a married man, so . . .'

He had smiled into her eyes then, melting her heart all over again . . . 'Go into the future with an open mind and you'll find that someone special waiting for you – it's there for us all, that once in a lifetime opportunity – and I know it's bound to happen to you if only you let it.'

He had been glad when they had reached Inverness, drained as he was with his own emotions as well as trying to cope with those of Catherine.

He had to find quietness for a while, to be alone with his thoughts, a place where no demands were made on him, where life moved at a more even pace than that left behind in Kinvara, with all its doubts and fears and unanswered questions.

Mirren hadn't been all that amazed when he had knocked on the door of Burravoe House. She had taken him in and made him feel welcome and had asked no awkward questions, just being Mirren. No nonsense about her, self-possessed, self-contained, her cool blue eyes gazing directly into his in that honest way she had about her. He knew then that he had come to the right place. Mirren would let him go his own way, do his own thing, would feed him and tend to his comforts and then go about her own business, feeling no obligation to entertain him or be polite.

She was Mirren and she didn't fuss. Take her or leave her, the words could have been written for her personally, so different in every way from Morna with her warm eager impulsive nature and the delight of life that had so infected everyone around her.

He was free to do what he had come to do. Wander the vast spaces of Shetland, all day and every day, feeling the wind in his face, the spirit of the land in his soul, savouring his solitude, feeling the peace of empty places soothing his troubled heart.

He went to the cliffs and looked down from impossible heights; he wandered the moors and marvelled at vast carpets of purple heather stretching on into forever; he gazed out to the island from which Morna had drawn the inspiration for their daughter's name – Vaila – a green and blue paradise where smoky blue clouds hung suspended over the landscape and curtains of rain drifted and fell and passed on over the sea in slow unhurried motion. A timeless yet ever-changing scene, one he had shared with Morna when they had stood here together on this headland in another time, so many, many years ago.

It was alright to cry out here where no one could see him. No one to tell him he should stop crying now for a love that was gone, never to return. He wanted to weep, he felt it was his right to do so. He needed to properly mourn that lost love of his as he had never truly done when surrounded by people wary of such emotions, especially those that were forbidden and better kept hidden from the eyes of a critical world.

And then he went to the little graveyard where Morna was buried. The wind ruffled his dark hair as he stood there looking at the headstone. It was the first time he had seen it. He had been too dazed with grief to attend her burial, had wanted to think of her as she had been, vibrant and beautiful, alive and warm.

More than five years had passed since then. Five years! How could time pass like that yet stand still long enough for him to feel that it had been just yesterday that they had walked and talked and loved together. His Morna. His love. No one could take those memories away from him. They were locked in his heart for all time to be. He would always see her as she had been, eternally young, eternally alive.

The old stone was moss covered now but the words on it seemed to leap out at him.

> Morna Jean Sommero. 1902–1926. Beloved wife of Finlay Sutherland, sister of Mirren, mother of Vaila and Aidan. Sleep till the morning breaks and the dawn lights the day with its silvery beams.

He felt shut out. He who had loved her most had no claim on her in the end. He had been denied the right to have his name on her stone. People would look and see that Finlay had been her husband and they would think that it was he who had fathered both children. It didn't seem right somehow, didn't seem fair . . .

He retraced his steps to Burravoe House with a leaden heart, seeing nothing, hearing nothing, thinking only of Morna and how she had once roamed these windswept places as a child, young and carefree, with all her life in front of her.

That night, sitting by the fire with Mirren, he had very little to say for himself. 'A penny for them,' Mirren said as she leaned forward to put another lump of coal on the fire. Then all at once her hand was reaching out to enclose his and her voice was soft when she went on. 'You didn't just come here for a change of scenery, Rob. I knew as soon as you stepped over the door that something was troubling you and it won't go away until you get it out of your system.'

He found himself pouring it all out then. His row with Hannah, his worries about Essie, Hannah's indulgences concerning the child, even confiding the part Catherine had played in his emotions that summer and how tempted he'd been to turn to her for the comforts that were so sadly lacking in his marriage.

'Smothering!' Mirren said promptly when he had finished speaking. 'History repeating itself. Hannah's doing to Essie what I did to Morna. She was all I had after our parents died and I desperately needed someone to hold on to. As it happened, I only succeeded in chasing her away and ended up with nobody. At the time I didn't think of that, I suppose I was insecure. I was only fifteen after all when I was left with a young sister to look after and she became all the world to me. I saw the error of my ways too late. I lost Morna as surely as if she had died and then she *did* die and ever since I have felt that I was in some way to blame. Hannah's worship of her daughter is much like mine was with my sister. Essie is too young to understand the pressures placed upon her and so she has reacted in the only way she knows how; by disobedience, by rebellion, by trying to prove that she is a separate individual with thoughts and feelings of her own. By trying to free herself from the apron strings, being tugged this way and that, divided by anger and loyalty and all the emotions that are brimming over in her little heart.'

They were both silent then, thinking their individual thoughts, before Mirren went on slowly, 'I have to admit I resented Hannah for denying me the chance to raise Vaila here in Shetland. I see now I was wrong. It was a big gesture for her to make. She's doing a marvellous job bringing Vaila up and – from what you've told me – you haven't made it very easy for her. You have allowed Morna's memory to come between you. As long as you feel like that Hannah will always be just second best. You'll have to throw yourself more wholeheartedly into your marriage, Rob, before it's too late. Hannah's alive, Morna is dead. Let go of the past, it's as simple as that.'

'But I can't forget Morna so easily!' he cried passionately. 'She meant too much to me. I love her still, I always will!'

'Nobody's asking you to forget, just to let go a little bit. How would you feel in Hannah's place, knowing that she pined for someone else, someone who isn't of this earth any more but who yet manages to come between you every waking day of your life together.'

'You've missed your vocation, Mirren,' he said a little sourly, 'you should have been a counsellor in some field or other.'

'God, no!' She shuddered. 'I'm quite happy with my farmwork and my animals. Anything more complicated would turn my world upside down.'

'You never married, I've often wondered why.'

'I told you once before, I haven't found the right man yet,' she said off-handedly and he was struck all at once by her likeness to Morna, not physically, but in her gestures. The way she inclined her head, her smile, an expression that crept into her eyes when she was searching for words, a pensiveness that belied her level-headed demeanour.

'You would have made a good wife for somebody,' he said, bending to kiss her cheek before making his way up to bed, his heart lighter than it had been for many a long day, now that he saw the road ahead in a clearer perspective.

* * *

When he was leaving he took Mirren's hands in his and held them firmly. 'Thanks for everything, Mirren. I came here bewildered. Now, thanks to you, I've managed to straighten myself out a good deal. Promise me one thing though, I want my name on Morna's headstone. Just Goodnight Morna, from Robbie. That's all, she'll know what it means.'

'I'll do that, Rob, but I want you to promise me one thing also. Bring Vaila and Aidan here to visit Shetland, to see me, to go and look at their mother's grave and know where she lies. It seems terrible, all these years passing by and never a visit from me to you and vice versa. I'd like Hannah to come too, she's very much part of the family and I think it's time we got to know one another.'

He nodded, 'Ay, Mirren, you're right on all counts, we should all get together. Vaila often talks about you. She remembers you from away back and I know one of her wishes is to come here and see her mother's birthplace.'

His lips brushed her fair cheek, then he was gone, striding along the harbour to the waiting boat, leaving Mirren to go slowly back to her pony and cart and drive home to a strangely empty Burravoe House where only the clocks ticked and the sparks from the fire crackled loudly up the chimneys.

Kinvara

Early September 1931

Chapter Thirty-three

It was time to forgive and forget in Kinvara. Rob was very aware of this as he let himself into the house and found Hannah sitting alone in the kitchen, not doing anything, very still in her repose, but starting up in great surprise when her husband strode in. He took her immediately into his arms to hold her close and press his warm face against hers.

'I'm so sorry, Hannah,' he whispered, 'for all the hurt I've ever caused you. It was wrong o' me to shut you out of my life but all that is over with and I hope you'll give me the chance to prove it to you.'

'Rob.' She pulled back to look at him dazedly. 'Why are you here? I – I thought you had gone away and were never coming back.'

'Away? Of course I've been away. I told you I wanted to be by myself for a few days.'

'But – Catherine – you went away with her, you were seen on the bus by Minnie MacTaggart, she told everyone the minute she got home.'

'That nosy old parker! One o' these days someone is going to cut her head off and boil it in oil! Catherine and me parted company at Inverness, she bound for Perthshire, me for Shetland. I saw Mirren, we talked, she listened, she made me see everything in a different light.'

'You talked to Mirren. Oh, Rob, I hope you didn't tell her about – about us and our differences. It's our business and no one else's.'

'Hannah, there are times when it does nothing but good to confide in someone. Mirren's a fine woman, she isn't the ogre we imagined her to be. She's on your side, Hannah, and wants you to visit whenever you can.'

'We'll see,' Hannah said with typical reserve. Then her face changed. It lit up, years seemed to roll off her shoulders. 'It's so good to see you, Rob. I thought I'd lost you forever. I didn't know what to do, where to turn . . . Oh, why can't we talk about Morna together? I loved her too, you know, and think about her a lot. We should bring her more out in the open instead o' keeping her buried the way we do. In that way we'll lay the ghosts o' the past to rest and get it out of our system.'

Rob didn't know whether to laugh or cry at this but had no chance to do either. Hannah's emotions got the better of her at that point. Her fears, her doubts, her loneliness, erupted out of her in a flood of tears and she cried as if she would never stop while he held her and soothed her and murmured reassuring sweet nothings into her ears, words that were like healing drops of balm to her aching heart, taking away all her troubles in those first few precious moments of their reunion.

* * *

Her confidence bolstered by Rob's homecoming it was now Hannah's turn to make her peace with her neighbours, going first to see Big Bette, her heart in her mouth at the very idea of facing up to the formidable lioness in her den, single-handed and alone.

'Forget about it,' Bette boomed, whittling feverishly away at a bit of wood she was carving for a stall at the forthcoming fête. 'It's old hat now anyway and I've got no desire to dwell on matters that are past. If it's atonement you're after you can grab that brush and sweep up those shavings. I must get these damt carvings done for the weekend or I'll never hear the end o' it from Wee Fay. I promised I'd do some things for her handicrafts stall and I've got no spare time left to harbour grudges – and while you're at it you might make a cup o' tea for us both before I choke to death wi' all this wood dust in my lungs.'

A most relieved Hannah had partaken of a hasty cup of tea before heading for The Dunny where Wee Fay was also busy for the fête, hardly looking up from the furry toy she was making as she listened to Hannah's apologies.

'Sure and to goodness,' the little woman shook her head impatiently before Hannah was halfway through, 'you didn't come all the way from Keeper's Row to tell me that. The fête's on Saturday, woman! I'm trying to get all this done for then, and if you had anything better to do with yourself you would be home doing your bit also instead o' standing there wasting your breath on nothing!'

After that, Hannah didn't feel nearly so bad about facing Gabby, only on this occasion she took Essie with her, and that little lady made her peace with the clockmaker most prettily, her angelic face solemn and contrite as she said in a small voice, 'I'm sorry, Gabby, I'll never be bad to you again, honest injun I won't. Mamma says I've to save up the money I owe you and haven't to buy a thing for myself till it's all paid back . . .'

At this point she handed him the little clockwork doll she had taken, a tremble of tears hovering in her big blue eyes as she did so.

'Keep it.' Gabby gave it back to her. 'It was meant for you anyway, only you didn't give me a chance to give it to you. I can make more, it's only a toy, after all . . .' His hand came up to touch her golden curls then, thinking better of it, he snatched it away again.

'Can I come and visit you sometime, Gabby?' Essie's thumb was in her mouth, she was gazing at him with pleading in her eyes.

'No,' Gabby shook his head vehemently. 'I don't think that would be a good idea . . .' Then he relented. 'But I tell you what, why don't you bring Vaila and Andy with you? I'm sure you could manage that now that you're such a good, big girl.'

'Me, bring Vaila and Andy?' Essie was very taken with this, the idea of actually being in charge of her big sister and brother appealing to her enormously. 'Alright, I'll bring them, and I'll make sure they behave themselves when I do.'

He chuckled. Hannah smiled at him gratefully. She and her daughter departed, and it was hard to tell who was the most relieved by the visit as all three participants had shed many an anguished tear since the day Gabby had been accused of a wrongdoing that had all but broken his spirit and his health as well. It would be a long time before he recovered both, but his heart was a lot lighter than it had been, and when Jessie came in to make his tea he was able to tell her with alacrity that he liked his eggs sunny side up and 'no' too much fat in the pan in case they swam away before he had a chance to eat the damt things'.

Hannah left Janet to the last, feeling that the amends she had to make to her friend and neighbour would take more than just a few minutes of her time. Janet received her somewhat coolly, her young attractive face showing the hurt she had suffered during these last difficult weeks of huffy silences on Hannah's part and the absence of Essie from her home.

But she was Janet, good-natured and forgiving, and it wasn't long before the tea was made and the ginger snaps and spicy buns set out on plates. The two women sat by the fire talking as if nothing untoward had ever happened between them, thoroughly enjoying the exchange of news and gossip. There came a lull, filled by Hannah after a moment or two when she said, 'I hate to admit this, and I've never told it to another living soul, but when I was carrying Essie I was worried in case she might be born defective – and – and I took something.'

'Really?' Janet looked surprised. 'And what might that have been?'

'Poison. At least it tasted like poison, only a mixture of beer and soda really but it was so bad I poured it down the drain after only a few mouthfuls.'

'Well, it obviously didn't work. You had Essie and she's perfect.'

Hannah shook her head. 'That's just it. When she started all her naughtiness I began to think it must be due to that stuff I'd taken. Because it *did* work, Janet, for days I was never away from the wee hoosie, and while at the time it was only me that suffered I was always worried it might go on to have some effects on Essie after she was born.'

Janet tried to look serious at these revelations but failed completely. Throwing herself back in her chair she gave vent to helpless laughter, soon to be joined by Hannah, each letting go of the tensions that had beset them in the complete and utter abandonment of the moment.

Life had been full of surprises for Hannah in the last few days. Now, just as she had thought they were done with, Rob came bursting in one afternoon to say breathlessly, 'I've made a decision, Hannah. I'm not going to accept the post as head keeper of the light. I need to be here more with you and the children. I've just been talking to Charlie, we think it might be a good idea to buy a fishing boat between us. I've got some money saved, it would pay for itself after a while. I would be home more often and you wouldn't have to worry so much about being here on your own.'

'A fishing boat!' Hannah cried aghast. 'But, Rob, look what happened to Colin and the other lads! It would be far too dangerous a life for you. I would worry about you all the time, far more than I do now. Besides . . .' She looked at him askance. 'Me and Janet have been talking too. We thought it would be a good idea to start up a bakery shop in Calvost. Nothing too grand, me and Janet could do the plain stuff, Maudie and my mother the fancy things. I've talked to them, they've agreed to give it a try. Essie can be with me till she starts school in the spring, Catherine has said Andy can sit in the classroom with the rest o' the bairns. In that way he'll get a bit more learning and I'll be free to do my bit in the shop. You would just get under my feet if you were here all day, Rob, and as well as all that, you know you've wanted to be head of a lighthouse ever since you were a lad. What a pity to spoil your chances now.'

Rob stared at her and shook his head. 'Well, you've certainly thought of everything. I would never have believed all this if I hadn't heard it for myself. Janet, your mother, Maudie, Catherine!'

'Ay, Catherine. I told her I was sorry for driving her

out o' the house as I did. We got talking, she had already thought about having Andy in the classroom before I mentioned it. So, it's all arranged, and I thought you'd be pleased having a wife who can look after herself instead o' one who goes moping about all day thinking the worst of everything.'

'Hannah! I'm delighted!' He picked her up and swung her round to kiss and hug her just as Andy appeared in the doorway. 'Dad,' he said and his voice was loud and clear, 'can I come with you to the lighthouse sometime? Now that I can sit by myself in a boat?'

'Why not?' Rob laughed. 'But first I want you to come with me. I need your advice about something, so just you hold on and we'll get started.' He hoisted the boy onto his shoulders and bore him away to the shed at the back of the house. Very soon the sound of his saw could be heard as he got to work on the desk he had promised his son. Hannah smiled to herself.

Who would have thought this time last week it would all have turned out so well? She hoped Minnie MacTaggart's ears were burning, not to mention those of her cronies. If that was the case they would be getting off lightly. Witches like that deserved to be boiled in oil, as Rob himself had said when he had heard about the rumours that had been spread concerning himself and Catherine and all the talk and misery that had followed.

* * *

Rebecca walked pensively along the shores of Mary's Bay, thinking about many things but mostly about the changes that had taken place in her life since Johnny Lonely had come into it. Her father had noticeably quietened down since the day Johnny had confronted him in the mill building. Life for the young Bowmans had brightened considerably since then. They had been allowed to spread their wings a bit more and were enjoying what remained of the summer. Joshua had learned a few lessons, though he had many still to learn. He was improving, there was no doubt about that, but Rebecca knew that if it wasn't for Johnny's vigilance he would quite easily just slip back to his old ways.

She smiled to herself when she thought about an incident that had taken place only a few nights ago, Joshua, sick to the back teeth of the laird's poking and prying and Johnny's continued watchfulness, had decided to load up the cart with the most necessary of household possessions and take his family back on the road once more.

Johnny hadn't give him the opportunity. Up he had popped, into the cart he had hopped, to sit on the seat with folded arms and declare, 'Doing a moonlight, eh, Bowman? Well think again, whither thou goest I will go also – I'll spread the word alright, by God and I will! Only it wouldn't be the sort o' things you would want other folks to hear.'

A furious Joshua had been forced to hump his goods and chattels back into the house, presided over by Johnny till every last item had been restored to its original position. Johnny had then issued instructions to Caleb to watch his father like a hawk and to report back to him should there be a reoccurrence of the night's happenings. Caleb had loved that. They had all loved it, including Miriam who had stood silently by, marvelling at Johnny's composure, his authority, his ability to make her husband squirm like a naughty schoolboy caught in the act.

Rebecca felt an affinity with Johnny that she had never felt with her own father. She went to visit him whenever she could and now went scrambling up the beach to his hut, where he was repairing the damage left by the storm. At sight of her he threw down his hammer to greet her warmly. They sat together on a bench in the sun, drinking tea and eating the scones she had brought, talking as if they would never stop, about Katie; he revelling in the chance to reminisce about his beloved daughter, she to listen entranced to the stories he told about the sister she had never known but felt close to during those precious hours spent with Johnny Lonely under the lowering cliffs of Cragdu.

Chapter Thirty-four

Gabby watched the procession of people going past his window. Many on foot, others on bicycles, some riding horses, a good majority in ponies and carts. One very sedate car crawled along – a recent acquisition of John Taylor-Young with a hyphen – whose passengers included his wife, his mother, and his granny-in-law, all of them urging him to take it easy as they didn't want to be killed in the rush and them with a reputation to consider.

The Law family went sailing past Gabby's vision, their cart hung with streamers and bells, Dancer in her traces, all dressed up in feathers and bows, her tail wrapped round with fancy cords and ribbons, stepping out proudly in all her livery.

It was the day of the fête in the grounds of Cragdu Castle and it seemed as if the whole of Kinvara was making its way to that turreted abode high on the cliffs with its thousands of acres stretching away to the faraway hills and beyond.

The sun was shining, the sea was like glass, the festive spirit pervaded the air, and there Gabby sat, watching it all from his window, while Jessie bustled about, cleaning every piece of brasswork she could find and looking very purposeful and useful as she did so.

Without a word Gabby arose, went to his wardrobe and withdrew his kilt. He retrieved his sporran from a shelf, a white shirt and a tartan tie from a drawer. In half an hour he was ready, his magnificent beard washed and brushed and flowing down his sark in silvery splendour. His belt buçkle was gleaming, his Skian Dhu nestling in one cream-coloured stocking, the Cairngorm stone in the handle flashing when he whirled round to admire himself in the mirror.

Gabriel Cochrane was going to the fête, an occasion that merited only the best of effort from any man of good taste and he was out to prove that he had more and enough of that kind of quality.

Into the parlour he strode to make his entrance. Jessie looked up and gasped. 'Gabby Cochrane! Just where do you think you're going? It's almost time for your nap. The doctor said you must rest.'

'If I stay any longer in that bed I'll die in it,' Gabby asserted firmly. 'I'm going out, Jessie. I'm going to the fête, every last bugger in Kinvara will be there today and I'm damned if I'm going to be left out.'

Jessie's chin trembled. She had been enjoying herself looking after Gabby. She missed her little sojourns to Charlie's house and this had somehow made up for it. She liked taking care of helpless bachelors and widowers, and it had been lovely, him lying in bed like that, dependent and reliant, but now . . .

'Are you decent under your apron, Jessie MacDonald?' he inquired in his deep voice.

'Of course, I'm decent, Gabby Cochrane! Whatever makes you ask a respectable woman a question like that?'

'Take it off then, and I shall personally escort you to the castle. We're bound to get a lift along the way though I myself will not object to the walk after all the time I've spent in that damt bed.'

Thrilled beyond measure Jessie made not a peep of protest. She peeled off her apron, jammed her straw hat on her head and at the last moment remembered to remove a duster from her cardigan pocket. Then they were off. She with one of the finest looking men in Kinvara at her side, he with one very sparkling member of the clan MacDonald on his arm, who was hoping everyone in the place would see her which was not beyond the bounds of possibility on a day such as this.

The grounds of Cragdu Castle were alive with bustle and noise. The laird had brought along some of his pedigree animals for the event. The horns of the Highland cattle were sleek and polished, their shaggy coats the colour of red bracken; the tails and manes of the ponies braided through with little ribbons and furbelows. Captain Rory was holding his own little gymkhana in one corner of a field. Many of the local children were participating in the equestrian events, Mark and Maida Lockhart among them, used to ponies and horses all their lives and not averse to showing off their skills on this occasion.

The Henderson Hens had been persuaded to set up a stall and were now loudly proclaiming their wares: apples, plums, pears, carrots, leeks, potatoes, all home-grown and hand-picked, rows of fresh chickens hanging on hooks, sides of cured pork, legs of lamb. The sisters rhymed it all off and did their bit, all striped butcher's aprons and clumpy big shoes, their eyes gleaming behind their specs as they bawled through a megaphone and made folks part with their coppers if only for the sake of peace.

Wee Fay and Big Bette were also there with their stall, selling cakes and biscuits, carved toys, soft goods. Kangaroo Kathy's knitted scarves and hats, woolly jumpers and gloves, many other items donated locally, the proceeds from the entire fête going to the nearby Fountainwell Orphanage. Lord and Lady MacKernon were strolling among the crowd, the latter revelling in her role as lady of the manor, being very gracious and charming to everyone she encountered, her cultured New England accent drawling through the mellow air of the September day Their elder son, Max Gilbert MacKernon, was strolling too, by the side of Catherine Dunbar, the schoolteacher, their heads close together as they walked and talked and seemed not to have eyes for anyone but each other.

'She'll be giving up her job now,' Jessie said meaningfully. 'I always did say it was just a stopgap till something better came along, now it looks as if it has – and with a MacKernon too.'

'Oil and water,' Mattie nodded. 'You can't mix them, but knowing Miss Catherine she'll have the cheek to try.'

'Och, well, they're young and foolish but they'll learn,' Jessie hastened to amend her unthinking words. After all, she was in the company of the best-looking widower in Kinvara, and had no reason to be envious of anyone.

'She's a good lass and he's a nice lad – in spite of thon awful murdering motor car o' his.'

The MacKernons' guests were arriving, a colourful gaggle of big hats and fashionable clothes, coming up from the private little jetty in Mary's Bay where they had anchored their steam yacht. All eyes were turned on them. The comments began and the ladies of Kinvara were in their element as they watched and discussed, praised and criticised.

Rebecca and Vaila, heads close, were walking arm in arm in a quiet corner of the garden. 'If I tell you something, promise you won't let on to another living soul,' Rebecca said solemnly.

'I swear on it,' Vaila agreed.

Rebecca told her friend all about Johnny, the part he had played in bringing her father to heel, the complicated twists and turns of fate that had brought the two together again in a showdown that was as tragic as it was spectacular.

'It's the most beautiful story I ever heard,' Vaila said with swimming eyes when it was finished.

'Only thing is,' Rebecca pulled up abruptly, 'I really and truly am illegitimate. It isn't a joke any more. Perhaps you won't think I'm good enough to be your friend now.'

Vaila's eyes gleamed. 'Earth sisters,' she said with a catch of her breath.

Rebecca's smile transformed her face, taking away its maturity, making her suddenly the young impressionable girl that she was instead of the little adult she often appeared to be.

'Earth sisters,' she verified. They hugged one another and laughed, remembering the uncertainties of that summer, the joys, the adventures, the confidences shared, the burgeoning of a friendship that was stronger now than it had ever been.

Joss came running. Rebecca smiled at him and held out her hand. His boyish face turned pink and he hesitated. But she wasn't standing any nonsense from him, her fingers were warm and soft as they slipped into his. Something passed between them that day; a new awareness of one another, an excitement, an anticipation of that yet to be, of a future they didn't know about yet, but would some time. They were young and all of life was before them.

A few moments later they were joined by Mark and Maida. Linking arms they all went on through the gardens and along by a little stream that was gurgling and splashing its way over the stones.

Essie was there, sitting in the long grasses, a vision of innocence in her white pinafore and blue ribbons. In her hands she held a butterfly, only this time she meant it no harm, instead she was staring at it with wonder in her big blue eyes. 'Essie's butterfly,' she whispered. The butterfly fluttered its wings, she held it up, and watched with just a small regret as it went flitting away to freedom. Off, off into the great wide yonder till it became just a tiny dot against the misted purple of the slumbering Kinvara hills.